D1018338

In a world in ru...
only passion su...

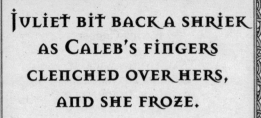

JULIET BIT BACK A SHRIEK
AS CALEB'S FINGERS
CLENCHED OVER HERS,
AND SHE FROZE.

For a long moment, only his labored breathing filled the silence. Then, pain wrapped through his tightly restrained voice, he said thickly, "Knife in my boot. They didn't check."

She stared into the endless wall of black and weighed her options.

Could she leave him behind? *Yes*.

Could she make it far without him? *Maybe*.

Would she ever sleep again, knowing what Alicia planned to do? Imagining the uniquely creative ways the witch could get what she wanted without ever putting him out of his misery?

She set her jaw. "Which leg?"

By Karina Cooper

ALL THINGS WICKED
LURE OF THE WICKED
BLOOD OF THE WICKED
BEFORE THE WITCHES

KARINA COOPER

ALL THINGS WICKED

A DARK MISSION NOVEL

AVON

An Imprint of HarperCollinsPublishers

AVON BOOKS
An Imprint of HarperCollins*Publishers*
10 East 53rd Street
New York, New York 10022-5299

Copyright © 2012 by Karina Cooper
ISBN 978-0-06-204693-2
www.avonromance.com

First Avon Books mass market printing: February 2012

Avon Trademark Reg. U.S. Pat. Off. and in Other Countries, Marca Registrada, Hecho en U.S.A.
HarperCollins® is a registered trademark of HarperCollins Publishers.

Printed in the U.S.A.

10 9 8 7 6 5 4 3 2 1

This one is for Alex,
who has been impatiently waiting
for a story about a little brother.

And for Esi and Laura,
who make up one of the most fabulous teams
I could ever hope to work with.
I wouldn't be so awesome without you.

CHAPTER ONE

No such thing as rest for the wicked.

Caleb Leigh opened gritty, burning eyes, giving up on the fitful doze that was all his pain-wracked body could manage for sleep. The filthy motel room came into focus as the neon lights outside the grimy, patchy curtains popped and fizzled, thrusting red and orange knives into his retinas.

How long had he managed to sleep this time? Two hours? Three? Hellfire sparklers of pain spasmed in his muscles. His skin twitched as if it wanted to crawl off his abused body and slink away for painkillers and a shower.

God. He'd kill for a shower.

Muffling a groan, he reached down for the shirt

he'd left on the floor, caught the edge with his fingers, and froze as a whisper of a breeze ghosted across the sensitive scars on his back.

Off. The room felt off. Unbalanced.

He inhaled, smelled New Seattle's own peculiar brand of acid-tinged summer rain, acrid smog, rotting garbage and . . . something else.

Get up!

A floorboard creaked behind him.

Caleb threw himself off the bed as a black silhouette loomed out of the neon-spattered darkness. Beads and rock clicked as his charmed necklaces clattered together; rusted springs screeched, a high-pitched shriek rising in a crescendo as his assailant landed lightly on the mattress. Caleb's grunt of pain as his feet hit the floor drowned in the raw fury clamping around his head.

He'd had no warning. Not even a *whisper* of magic.

He should have been less surprised.

The shadow pushed off the bed as Caleb leaped to his feet. Silver winked a deadly promise in the orange-red glow spilling through the single broken window; serrated steel, wicked edge gleaming. Knife gripped in a black-gloved hand, the figure pointed at him.

"Why aren't you dead, you bastard?"

The already cramped motel room walls slammed in tight around him. That voice. Feminine. Breathy with exertion, with fear, but so fucking familiar that it sucked out his breath on a raw sound.

Memory. Affection. Worry.

Love.

It rose like a dream, a sigh of lazy summer days and laughing secrets, and Caleb fought the slick, blissful whisper back behind gritted teeth. It wasn't *his* love. It wasn't his affection, his worry, his goddamned memory that fisted in his heart.

And Juliet Carpenter had no fucking business being anywhere near him.

A year wasn't nearly long enough.

The neon lights snapped and crackled in rhythmic chaos outside the window. It slanted lurid color over her black hair, cut shorter than he remembered and in a fashion that suggested she was aiming for edgy and tough. The dark, choppy fringe framed her face, her faintly square jaw, and the ghostly green eyes that he'd last seen half closed and luminous as he sank balls-deep inside her warm, straining body.

Promise me. His fists clenched at the echo of his own words, so long ago. He'd done his part, damn it. "Get out," he said flatly.

"You son of a *bitch*." Deftly, the sawlike blade in her hand rotated as Juliet jumped onto the thin mattress and launched herself at him.

His body locked. Every goddamned nerve in his left side detonated as he plucked her from the air. Her legs swung to the side, knees ramming into his ribs and jarring a painful grunt from between his clenched teeth as he fisted both hands into her jacket collar and used her own momentum to slam her against the wall behind him. Plaster cracked.

The breath left her on a hard, wordless snarl.

His chest squeezed, his own breath banding tightly under the fiery protest of unhealed wounds on his weakened left side. "You still can't listen worth a damn," he growled, glaring through the sizzling edges of his vision. "I said get out."

The knife glinted. He shackled her slender wrist with one hand and slammed it back against the wall. White dust floated to her dark hair in a gritty cloud.

Sweat gleamed on her face, an echo of the perspiration drying across his shoulders. It wasn't all courtesy of the unusually muggy summer heat that had settled into the deepest crevasses of the city. Holding her in place shouldn't have been as hard as it was, but his body still wasn't recovered from the burns that had nearly killed him a year ago.

Every day was a lesson in pain. Pinning a witch against a wall as her feet thrashed a foot above the floor wasn't helping.

Pinning *this* witch wasn't something he'd ever expected to do again.

She'd lost weight.

Her jacket was a little too loose, her black shirt baggy where he'd tangled his fingers into the collar of both. The warmth of her full breasts against the back of his scarred hand wasn't a reminder he needed, but he couldn't afford to let her go for his own comfort.

He wasn't a fool. Or some teenage virgin who had never gotten a handful of a woman before. Especially *this* woman.

The dark circles under her eyes couldn't take

away from the visual impact she'd always had on him. Her mouth, top-heavy and so damned expressive it made him crazy for it, twisted as she struggled in his grip. She managed to gain an inch of momentum as she jerked her hand out from under his, but Caleb locked his teeth and shoved it back. Fragile bones grated under his grip.

Pain flickered. Hers. His.

You promised.

Oh, Jesus. That voice. It made itself heard at the worst fucking moments.

Caleb sucked in a breath that seemed harder than it should have to get and drowned out the feminine presence echoing through his head. "What the hell are you doing here?"

He didn't have to ask. The venom spewing at him from a look filled with revulsion was all the answer he needed.

His grip tightened on her collar, beaded bracelets around his wrist clacking softly. "Let me rephrase that. The coven doesn't operate alone. Where's your backup?"

Her teeth clicked together. Her gaze slid away, flicked back as she raised her chin.

She'd never been a good liar.

Narrow-eyed, Caleb stared at her as fury throbbed between his temples. "You don't have backup," he said softly. Then, much less quiet, he snarled, "You came alone? You came after me *by yourself*? Jesus Christ, Jules!"

With monumental effort, Juliet raised both feet and planted them against Caleb's thigh. Instinctively he braced, swore as her move raised her out of his grip and threw him off balance. She reached up with her right hand, grabbed the knife out of her left, and swung it back around. Caleb swore again, jerking away, but not before the jagged teeth of the blade snagged the puckered flesh of his left arm. *Damn it!*

Raw, red static shorted his vision as he backpedaled into the mattress. His knees collided with the edge, buckled, and sprawled him backward onto the springs.

Sensing her intent, he rolled, blood smearing the stained sheets, and grunted as her weight barreled into his back. Her knees rammed into the vulnerable hollow beneath his shoulder blades, dug into his barely healed scars hard enough that he threw his head back, teeth locked against a brittle surge of pain.

"Don't move!" Her fingers twisted in his too-long hair.

Caleb froze.

Her thighs clenched around his waist. They were warm, even through her pants. Warm and familiar. And the press of her soft breasts against his shoulders shouldn't have mattered more than the knife she held at his throat.

Muscles shaking, taut with the effort to stay still, Caleb waited. It hurt. God, it hurt, but it had nothing on the clash of memory, fantasy, hell, *wanting* that roiled in his blood now.

They'd never made it to a bed. He remembered that. There weren't that many beds in Old Seattle.

Behind him, on him, Juliet panted for breath. "I just," she managed, "want to know one thing."

"Then what?" His voice grated harshly. "You'll cut my throat?"

He knew it wasn't true the instant he said it, but that wasn't the point. Juliet had always been too soft. Everyone had known it.

Her sister had known it.

The same sister who'd occupied a dark corner of his mind since she'd died in his arms over a year ago.

The knife at his throat jerked. A thin, slick line of fire told him how sharp the damned blade was. It'd make a bloody mess of his flesh faster than he could get it away from her.

"You could only be so lucky," she spat. "I want to know why, you bastard. Why?"

She wasn't asking why he wasn't dead. He didn't have that answer, anyway. No, he knew what she asked in the single, strained syllable, and closed his eyes.

Why had he betrayed the coven?

Not precisely.

More like, why the hell had he wrapped her body around him like silk and rain? Lost himself in her, pulled her apart with anger and need and mind-scorching heat and then betrayed everything she'd ever believed in?

The fact that he'd murdered her sister was something she didn't know to ask. Fuck.

And you promised!

God, he wished he hadn't. "Why what?" he asked, and because he already knew the answer, added, "Why didn't I say no when you threw yourself at me or—"

The fingers in his hair tightened, wrenching his head back at an angle that threatened to pop his neck. She leaned over him, body pushed forward to thrust her face over his. Her eyes were wide, too wide, shimmering with tears that crawled deep inside his chest and twisted. Bloodier than the knife at his throat.

Darker than the rage that beat at the iron chains of his self-control.

"You know!" The words broke on a ragged sound. "Why did you kill them? Why? When we—"

"We," he said flatly, cutting her off with barely leashed scorn. "There never was a *we*."

She blanched. Recovered so quickly that he wasn't sure he'd seen the blood his verbal dagger had drawn. "We," she repeated through gritted teeth, "as in the Coven of the Unbinding. We as in your friends!"

"Liar." Her knee dug into the hollow beneath his left shoulder blade. Neon flashed, and only part of it was the monotonous color outside the seedy motel. The rest popped and sparkled behind his eyes, accompaniment to the ruined skin she pushed on.

"They were your family—"

"Bullshit," he rasped, all but a growl under the pressure. "They were users. Curio only kept you for your magic." And, rumor had it, for her body.

He didn't ask. Even as the words leaped to his lips, he didn't want to know.

He'd had that body, too. One of many things he'd shared with the late coven leader.

The knife lowered, a fraction. "You killed them.

All of them," she accused, a sharp whisper. "They gathered because they trusted you—"

Fuck. They'd gathered because they had intended to sacrifice Caleb and his sister for their power-hungry cause.

"—and you just . . . killed them." Her voice trembled.

"Most of them," he agreed. Some, like her, he'd managed to distract. Some he'd gotten free.

Her eyes flickered, her face upside down but still so fragile, it stole the breath from his body. Black hair dye wouldn't make her tough. "Why?"

His jaw locked. Ticked hard. "Because I could."

He hated himself for doing it. He hated that it had to be done. But Caleb was a lot of things, and gentle wasn't one. Reversing her flimsy position of power was simple. Reaching up, he seized the back of her jacket and hauled her bodily over his head.

His scars stretched, felt as if they split from the root to the skin, and the angry buzzing in his ears almost drowned out her howl of rage and surprise as she hit the ground on her back. The knife went flying, and Caleb rolled off the mattress seconds before it embedded itself into the wall beside them.

Plaster drifted lazily on the air as Caleb knocked her fist away, seized both hands, and pinned them above her head. The motion barked his knuckles on the rusted bed frame, and he grunted a curse as her knee found his gut. Twisting, he pinned her legs, clamped his thighs around hers, and locked her down.

She strained, but succeeded only in turning herself red with the effort. Dust puffed languidly around them. Sweat dripped from his nose as he stared down at the face he'd hoped to hell to never see again.

Love. God damn it, it had never been *his* to *feel*.

"Stop it," he ordered roughly as she twisted her hips.

"You traitorous son of—!"

"Son of a bitch. Yes, I know." He transferred her wrists to one hand, dropping his forearm to her throat. He shoved hard, forcing her head to lie still against the dirty green carpet, and met her eyes precisely because he didn't want to.

The accusation in them didn't quite hide the helplessness she struggled to bury. The grief.

Guilt had a punch like a prizefighter.

What the hell could he say? He'd done so much more to her than even she knew.

He knew, though. It was enough. His mouth thinned. "Let's get this straight, girl. Yes, I turned on your coven. Yes, I killed Curio—" He pushed hard as her back arched, fury snapping through her like a conduit. The beads on his bracelet scored her pale skin, and he set his jaw. "I killed Curio," he repeated curtly, "and probably about two dozen other witches who didn't know when to get out. If I had to do it all over again, I'd make the same choices."

But he wouldn't, he thought as tears shimmered in her narrowed glare, choose to touch her again. He wouldn't commit his body and soul in a single moment of mind-blowing weakness, and he sure as hell wouldn't promise the impossible to Cordelia Carpenter before he killed her.

But life gave only one chance. His bed was made; he was damn well going to lie in it.

Alone.

"We can play this all day, Jules," he said, thrusting his face so close to hers that she flinched. "You're on your own, and I'm stronger than you."

Her lips twisted, teeth baring as if she would try to bite him. Under the strained pressure of his forearm, her skin flushed nearly purple. It colored her cheeks, her lips. Her eyes flashed, hatred and fear.

Protect her. He'd promised. Shit. Just *shit*.

Caleb relented. Loosened enough so she could breathe.

She coughed, choking. "I hate—I hate you," she managed between rough spasms. "I'm going to kill you!"

He stared at her. Then, his smile a grim slash, he reached over her head and drew the serrated knife out of the wall. She flinched as plaster crumbled around them. "Fine," he said, and put the metal hilt in her hands.

Her lashes widened, and he noticed the smudge of mascara that made them thicker. Darker.

He didn't know what color her hair was naturally, but it sure as hell had never been black.

Caleb forced her fingers to close on the knife and rolled off her and to his feet, a fluid motion that belied the torturous effort it took to make it. His left side was rapidly going numb. Blood slid down his arm from the flesh wound she'd already inflicted, and he watched her eyes trace the wet gleam as she, too, clambered to her feet.

He spread his arms. "Do it."

Juliet's full upper lip curled under her teeth, her tongue sliding along it in that way she did when she was nervous.

Just thinking it made him clench his fists. Not his to know, damn it. But the unfamiliar memories wouldn't fade. Not for as long as he lived.

Not for as long as Cordelia's lifeblood mingled with his.

"Come on," he said flatly, his voice rough. Impatient. "You want to kill me so badly, do it."

Conflict. Determination. Uncertainty. He read it all in the trembling of her hands, her white-knuckled grip around the hilt. The way she studied the livid scars on his chest.

And the flash of empathy she couldn't hide. Not from him.

Exactly the point.

He took a step forward, seizing her shoulder, relief and fury entangling together to grate across his nerves. "Then for Christ's sake," he began roughly, and she moved. Sudden. Erratic. The knife flashed once in red neon, sketched an upward arc.

Agony snagged on four inches of sawlike steel.

Juliet shuddered as she clung to the metal handle, her hair hanging forward in a black curtain. Sweat turned her skin clammy.

In front of her, his fingers tight on her upper arms, Caleb stared at the blade half buried in his shoulder. Blood welled over the puckered wound, trickled like a crimson tear down the sculpted planes of his pectoral. It slid past his nipple, and for a wildly crazy moment, Juliet wanted to lick it away.

The world froze around her.

"Oh, God," she whispered, jerking her hand from the hilt as if it had burned her.

Caleb fell to his knees, expression transfixed: shock, anger, and pain. Lips white with strain, he reached up and wrenched the knife out, swearing as flesh and muscle shredded beneath the jagged edge. It made a sound like wet paper, like gristle parting. Blood splattered the peeling wall.

Juliet slapped her hands over her mouth as his eyes, shockingly blue, met hers. Stunned. Accusing. "You . . . missed," he managed, and slumped over.

She sobbed out a laugh. It cracked. Her knees folded, dumped her gracelessly on the floor, and the unforgiving surface jarred every aching bone in her body. Raising a hand to her face, she saw the blood—*Caleb's* blood—gleaming wetly on her fingers and squeezed her eyes shut.

She swallowed down a violent surge of bile.

Blood. His blood. Wasn't that what she'd wanted? To kill him for everything he'd done to her friends? To make him suffer?

Yes!

Not like this.

Oh, God. She wasn't a killer. But it was too late now.

Or was it? She opened her eyes, very cautiously

forced herself to check. His chest rose and fell. He was breathing. White-faced and clammy, but breathing. The shoulder wasn't a vital organ, after all.

And yet he'd pitched over as if she'd gotten him through the heart.

She scrubbed her hands along her thighs. Had she really taken down the soothsayer? The man who could read the future like it was a book? He hadn't seen *her* coming, had he?

Now what?

She couldn't kill him. The queasy knot in her stomach told her that; the screaming denial in her head told her she couldn't just . . . just *murder* a man. Okay. She got it.

But she *could* give him to the people he'd hurt the most.

Now, she needed her comm line. She needed to contact whatever was left of the coven. Would they be glad to hear from her?

She'd be bringing them the betrayer. Of course they would.

Maybe they'd take her back, forgive her for not being there when everything had fallen apart.

She could be part of them again.

That meant something. Didn't it?

But only if the comm frequencies she remembered actually worked. It had been over a year. She'd returned to find the coven in ruins, most scattered or hiding or captured or dead.

She took a shaking breath, and the metallic smell of Caleb's blood drilled into her nose. She pressed shaking fingers into her eyes, gouged deeply until she could see through the panic forging chaotic lines through her brain.

No. She had to be honest.

She hadn't tried to reach them. Hadn't bothered to do anything but look for her sister. In the empty, desperate months that followed, with her world turned upside down and everyone she'd known dead or gone, Juliet had focused only on her sister. She'd traced every lead, every rumor, every damned ghost, but it was as if Cordelia had just . . . disappeared into thin air. Leaving no trace of her passage.

There was no reason. Delia wasn't a witch like Juliet, she was a prostitute—one of the amazingly pampered women who worked at Waxed. She'd enjoyed her life. Loved Juliet.

Then she'd vanished.

Despair had set in. Ridden Juliet hard until she'd found that the lower street bathtub gin was the best medicine she could find. It cured everything. Sorrow. Anger.

Guilt.

"Oh, God, get a grip," she whispered, hand to her throat where a manic beat threatened to choke her. There wasn't time for this. The soothsayer was out cold, but for how long? Could she tie him with anything? She hadn't brought any rope, no cuffs, nothing.

She'd thought no further than killing him. Hell, it was *all* she'd thought about in her alcohol-fueled anger. She didn't have a *plan* for this!

Maybe she should have borrowed some of the fake fur sex cuffs off the girls at the bar. Hysterical laughter threatened to bubble out of her throat. It wouldn't be the first bondage play this filthy place had seen, she was sure.

The motel room wasn't any different from the thousands of rooms just like it in the streets below the civilized edges of New Seattle. It was the kind of place that charged by the hour, loved and loathed by prostitutes and the johns they serviced.

The faded carpet was threadbare and stained beneath her boots, and the neon glow of the omnipresent electrical net of city lights couldn't hide the water stains eating at the plaster, the slimy mold gathering under the single curtained window or the dingy pile of blankets flung into the far corner.

It smelled like dirty laundry and old vomit; like sweat and rot and the lingering aroma of hours upon hours of cheap sex soaked into every available surface. It was a scent as familiar to her as her own name, branded into her brain from too many years surviving in a city that didn't care. Juliet resisted the urge to cover her nose, but her stomach clenched, roiled.

Later, she promised herself. Later, she'd curl around a toilet and puke until her stomach didn't remember the quantity of gin she'd cleaned out the night before.

Then she'd start on a new bottle until Caleb Leigh's face was a distant memory.

It'd have to be a really, *really* large bottle.

He wasn't moving. Sprawled out in the flickering light, his skin gleamed white and red and sallow yellow, and the wound at his shoulder bled sluggishly in a steady rivulet.

The months hadn't been good to him.

Caleb had always been lean, but the past year had scraped the last vestiges of excess weight from his body and hardened him into something rangier. Wiry. Her fingers trembled, and she shoved them against the floor by his inert form before she did something stupid. Like touch him.

Instead, under the sparking wash of red and orange neon, she surveyed the sinewy muscle defining his pale skin.

His shoulders weren't overly broad, but they were strong. She wasn't made of feathers, and he'd practically pinned her to the wall with one arm. His chest tapered to a narrow waist framed by the unbuttoned vee of his jeans. Shadows gathered in the well-defined edges of a physique that put most of the men she'd ever known to shame. He'd changed.

And it had hurt.

Before she could catch herself, before she realized what she meant to do, the very tips of her fingers skimmed the morass of scars carved into his body. Rough ridges rippled across his left shoulder, twisted the flesh and muscle of his arm into a grotesque pattern of hardened tissue and shiny, melted skin.

She flinched as his muscles leaped under her touch. And the wildly knocking pulse low in her belly warned her that whatever her mind was telling her, her body remembered a whole different side of Caleb Leigh.

The man who'd stripped away every defense she'd ever had. Who had filled her mind and body and tapped into something she never knew she'd wanted, and then. . .

And then betrayed her.

"You sorry son of a—" She bit her lip.

Son of a bitch. Yeah, I know.

He'd always been cold.

She traced the nodules of tight, healed rivulets across his left pectoral. They rasped against the sensitive nerve endings at her fingertip. The wounds climbed up his shoulder, up the left side of his throat to splay like twisted claws over the hard line of his jaw.

Any boyishness the high cheekbones and sculpted planes of his face might have maintained was stripped forever, marred by monstrous furrows of bone-white skin at his cheek. It touched the corner of his mouth, giving his lips a permanently flippant quirk.

The tip of her finger settled there, tracing the line where smooth skin met rough. Her throat closed on an unwanted wash of sympathy.

She swallowed it down. Hard.

He deserved a hell of a lot more than a few ugly wounds.

The amount of charms he wore said he knew it. Colored threads knotted around both wrists, thick with beads and bits of unpolished rock. A rough cord wrapped around his neck, braided twine that she knew without having to look would have threads of hair woven in. White flint hung from a wire catch, effective at breaking bonds.

Amber, jade, and labradorite shared strings with stone beads rudimentarily carved. He used every trick in the book to stay hidden. With warding charms like those, it was no wonder it had taken her a year to track him. Never great at rituals and charms herself, she'd had to settle for plain sleuthing, and even that hadn't worked until now.

Finally, he was out of tricks.

Jerking her hand back, she got to her feet, stepped over his inert body, and pulled the blood-stained sheets off the dingy mattress. Using the knife, she cut strips and bound his arms behind him. Her fingers hovered over the puckered, oozing wound at his shoulder, and her stomach pitched again.

She'd done that.

Before she could talk herself out of it, she wadded more material against the seeping hole and wrapped strips of the dingy sheet over it. He muttered something in his sleep, and Juliet jerked back quickly.

This had been easy. Not as easy as she would have liked it, but a hell of a lot easier than she'd ever expected.

Was it paranoia that made her wonder when the other shoe would drop?

Shaking her head, she fished out her battered comm unit and flipped the lid. The hinges popped threateningly; the old thing would break soon. Getting another would be hard, but she'd deal with that when the time came. She dialed an old frequency, typed out a message, and sent it with the press of a worn, disintegrating button. Hopefully, someone still monitored the feed.

What would she do if no one came? Kill him herself?

Could she?

She snapped the lid closed.

"How soon until they get here?"

Surprise spun her around. She met intense blue eyes across the dim floor and fought the urge to raise her chin in challenge. To make excuses.

His gaze was speculative, and filled with pain.

But his mouth thinned into a hard, white line. "You called them," he prompted, voice impatient. It wasn't a question. "Did they know you were coming here? Did you tell them you found me?"

Juliet very carefully pushed the unit into her jacket pocket instead of answering. Why, damn it? Why now?

Why had he only reappeared now?

She picked up the discarded knife, dropped to her knees in front of him again, and this time, his blond-tipped lashes narrowed as she seized a handful of the rope around his neck.

"Don't touch that," he warned, leaning back.

Ignoring him, she set the blade to the twine and jerked, hard enough that he flinched. The edge tore through the weakened material like it was nothing. Beads clattered to the threadbare carpet, a rain of pebbles and wood.

She didn't have to be a good witch to sense the magic spill free around her; a whisper of something intangible turning to vapor, to nothing, even as she recognized it.

"Or what?" she asked, every syllable clipped to a venomous barb.

Caleb wrenched his shoulders, but she grabbed his bound arms and slid the knife under the handmade bracelets wrapped around his wrists. More rock bounced and clattered, and she watched a muscle tic in his jaw. "You have no idea what you're doing."

"Don't I?"

"No," he said tightly. His eyes met hers. Blazed. "You never did."

Her fingers flexed against the knife handle. "But you always did, didn't you? Caleb Leigh," she spat, "the almighty prophet."

The skin around his eyes tightened. Pinched.

"You just crooked your fingers and we all danced for you, didn't we?" Juliet couldn't stop the words once they formed in her head. Couldn't beat them back as she jammed a finger under his nose. "Now it's your turn. *Murderer.*"

He looked down at her finger, then at the bandage she'd wound around his shoulder. His smile lacked anything even remotely close to humor. "You can't give me over, Jules."

She jerked. "Don't call me that."

"You're too soft." His eyes flicked back to hers, gaze filled with something she didn't know how to label. Something raw. Something angry. "You always were. Even Cordelia—"

She didn't recall raising her hand. The crack of her palm against his stubbled cheek echoed like a gunshot, shooting aching little bursts of pain through her forearm to the elbow.

In the oppressive silence that followed, Caleb slowly turned his head back, a lock of honey gold hair curled over one eye. His cheek glowed red, contrast to the ice in his gaze as he finished, dangerously soft, "Even your sister knew it."

"My sister is gone," she said through clenched, aching teeth.

A flicker. Pain? Anger? She didn't know, but he didn't apologize. Why would he? He'd screwed Juliet up against a wall and then betrayed them all.

"Not," she added, so quietly that she marveled at her own brittle calm, "that you were there for me to ask for help. Not that you cared."

"You're absolutely right," he told her, and Juliet wasn't sure what she'd intended to do. The world flashed red, her skin itched with the pressure of it as anger crawled through her veins. It burned, throbbed behind her eyeballs. Like fire and ice and—

The door swung open behind her, cracked into the wall.

Juliet lurched away, spun in surprise and relief that faded as a tall, thin man barreled at her. Caleb threw himself toward her as Juliet yelped, but the man grabbed her jacket, yanked hard even as one booted foot slammed into Caleb's chest.

She hit the ground on her knees. The rough hand transferred to her head, shoved her down, kicked out her knee as she struggled. Pain twanged through her legs. Rage subsided to confusion. Fear.

"Get them both!" a raspy voice yelled over her head.

In her peripheral vision, Caleb strained at his bonds as a thin man dressed in stained brown corduroy struggled to subdue him.

"I got the girl." The voice was like a rusted razor blade, completely unfamiliar. "Damn it, Louie, just kick him in the head!"

Juliet wrenched free. A fragrance both sharp and sweet filled the muggy air, and she launched herself at the discarded knife, closed her fingers on the cold edge of the blade.

It skittered out of reach as something hard and unyielding slammed into the back of her head. She sprawled, crying out, earning a taste of grimy carpet. Yellow fireworks slid behind her eyes, joining the pop and crackle of orange neon.

Adrenaline flooded her veins, gave her the strength to push herself to her hands and knees, but the room spun wildly. Sickeningly.

"We have to have her alive, man, watch the dosage!"

Someone grabbed the back of her coat and hauled. Her back arched, knees aching. In the wobbling field of her vision, a tattooed face leered at her.

"Motherfucking Christ, little girl," he grunted, shaking her hard enough that her head snapped back on her neck. "Where the hell have you been hiding?"

He didn't give her time to answer, shoving a dirty blue rag over her mouth and nose. He clasped the back of her head with his free hand, forcing the cloth harder against her face.

More figures pushed into the motel room, hazy

silhouettes that ignored her as she clawed at the callused hand at her mouth. She gasped for air around the soaking material, gagging as something chemical and acrid seared through her nostrils. Stung her eyes.

Across the room, Caleb lurched to his knees, fighting off the hands that struggled to hold him. She watched his lips move, eyes flashing blue fire and muscles bulging as he fought the ropes she'd tied herself, but she couldn't hear him. What was he saying?

Was he yelling? At her?

A hand slid over her jaw. The tattooed face was back, dimming now. So muddled. Ink smearing. Running, oozing across his teeth.

He said something, shaped something with a smile that sent ice sliding down her spine, but her limbs dragged. Refused to move. The rag tasted bitter as she opened her mouth—had she intended to ask something?

It didn't matter. Her muscles gave up, gave in with a fluidity that sent her sliding bonelessly to the dirty floor. Sleep closed in.

And with it, peace.

CHAPTER TWO

Maybe the Coven of the Unbinding had been more than killers and thieves in the past. Maybe years ago, it had struggled for equality and peace and whatever noble bullshit principles the oppressed spouted, but Caleb had never known it to be anything more than what it was: a gang, worse than guerrillas in an urban jungle.

Thugs. With *magic*. How had everyone else been blind? Were freedom and power so seductive? They must be. There wasn't any other excuse for Juliet's willful ignorance.

He'd known that Curio sheltered her. Known, also, that he'd used her single magical ability for himself. Her inherent gift to fuel others' magic became Curio's own personal battery.

He'd suspected that Curio kept her as a mistress, a lover.

The man was old enough to be her grandfather.

Killing him had been cathartic in so many ways.

But Caleb didn't know why. Why did Juliet Carpenter stay with a coven that only used her? Why did she let herself be sucked dry, again and again, as Curio reached for more and more power?

Why did she play with the younger witches the coven sheltered, why hadn't she taken her dying older sister and gone somewhere? Anywhere?

Anywhere but near him.

Yet here she was again. Near him. Tied up, yes, and unconscious; lashed to a chair in a dark basement deep below the bowels of the city, but too. Fucking. Close.

His fingers flexed, already aching from the loss of blood flow, but it was a small pain in the scheme of it all.

He'd promised Cordelia Carpenter anything she asked for, and had been fool enough to be relieved when she'd demanded only two things: get her sister out of the Coven of the Unbinding, protect her from Curio's madness. And never, ever tell Juliet what she'd done. What she'd asked him to do.

It seemed easy. After he destroyed the coven, he never expected to see Juliet again.

So he'd sworn it. He'd repeated it as Delia lay bleeding out in front of him, reassured her as he'd taken the worn gold promise ring from her finger, and said it again as he drew the last vestiges of her life from her dying lips. It was part of the bargain, the deal she'd offered him. Her heart's blood in exchange for her sister's safety.

What an idiot he was.

He'd done his part. Killed Delia, arranged to have Juliet sent on a wild-goose chase guaranteed to keep her the hell out of the way, and wrecked the coven while she was gone.

It should have been enough. Should have, and wasn't. The coven was obviously rebuilding, and they hadn't forgotten him. Juliet wasn't out of his life at all, and that damned meddling sister of hers still lived on in his mind. His memories, his every waking moment. He could have happily gone his whole life without knowing she'd called Juliet her little rose.

Fragile. Sweet. Beautiful.

Fuck it. Over a year had passed, but as Caleb listened to Juliet's even breathing, he couldn't help but think about all the ways he'd failed.

Spectacularly.

The room they'd been unceremoniously dumped in had nothing going for it. The witches had dragged them inside, tightened his ropes to make sure he couldn't so much as wiggle a finger, and left, shutting a heavy door behind them. Silence reigned, broken only by the faint *drip, drip, drip* of water echoing from somewhere in the dark around them and the soft, even breathing of his fellow captive.

It was cold, dank like all subterranean basements seemed to be, and tomblike. It stank, wet mildew and stale air, and he shivered, goose bumps rippling across his naked chest.

To make matters worse, they'd left him facing Juliet Carpenter—the one bright spot in a sea of black shit memory—across the expanse of a dirt-crusted cement floor.

His own personal brand of hell.

They were in Old Seattle. He knew that much— the tomb of the ruined city had a smell that infected the brain. Like time fallen apart, all moldy and decrepit.

That meant that this was one of many abandoned basements under New Seattle. One of countless structures that hadn't collapsed when the earthquakes hit decades ago. He'd made use of his fair share of dilapidated buildings and tunnels when he could, and the coven had maintained a handful as a base of operations. So did squatters, or at least those too stupid to go anywhere else.

This cellar was nothing to boast about: cement walls, cement floor, cement ceiling. All of it lined with decades of dirt and the silt remains of old flooding.

In the circle of light provided by an old camping lantern, Juliet sat slumped against her bonds. His fists clenched behind him. They'd traveled through the black expanse of the underground city for an hour; it worried the hell out of him that she hadn't surfaced from the chemical cocktail they'd served her.

Caleb shifted, gingerly testing the knots cutting off the circulation in his arms. His body hurt, but it always did. Some days were worse than others.

This one was going to be a winner.

If he managed to survive it.

He didn't have the strength to tear through the constraints Juliet had so kindly tied for him, and he wasn't sure he'd be able to carry her out if he did.

Leaving her wasn't an option.

He'd already done that once.

Look at her.

He didn't want to. But the insistent echo in his head, in what he would have once upon a time called his soul, couldn't be ignored.

You promised.

Against his will, his gaze flicked back to the woman who haunted his every waking dream. She was slumped back in the metal chair, her arms pulled behind the metal frame and secured in place. The position arched her back, thrust the shape of her full breasts out from her open jacket in ways that suggested it hadn't been on accident.

Caleb knew a grade-A fuckwad when he met one, and the tattooed witch qualified.

He shook his head hard enough to jerk the ends of his hair out of his eyes. He didn't know the witches of the coven anymore. They hadn't re-built, not really—he'd have known if they'd managed anything more than campfire troupes in the dark—but there were enough new faces to make him worry.

A year was a long time. Things were bound to be different.

Who led them?

He closed his eyes, caught himself straining

to see something—*anything*—in the darkness behind his eyelids. It wouldn't work. He already knew there was nothing to *see*.

Hadn't been since he'd woken, his body nothing more than a smoldering mess of ash and carnage, deliriously wandering the lowest streets of New Seattle. Stripped of magic. Stripped of everything that had made him who he was.

Hounded by the too-strong vestiges of his final victim.

That was the price he'd paid for his betrayal.

"Fuck," he seethed between clenched teeth, sweat gathering over his shoulders as he wrenched at the ropes. How the hell was he supposed to protect her—protect *anyone*—without his magic?

What would his sister do?

What she'd taught him to do. Run.

Impossible.

He glanced at Juliet. Her chest rose as if she could shift from the position that strained her shoulders, but she didn't open her eyes. He wished she would.

He was going to need help. And he didn't need the visual reminder of her open jacket to remember what her generous curves had felt like in his hands, warm and soft and—

"Give me a break," he muttered. The faintest echoes rebounded from the shadows, hollow and ghostly. He shook his head harder, wincing as it pulled at the scarred tissue at his jaw.

He would never get used to that feeling, as if bits of him had been peeled off, rolled like dough and super-glued back onto the rest.

He wondered what Juliet had thought when she'd seen the scars.

Then remembered the knife and let his head rest against the chair back in grim humor. He didn't have to wonder, did he? She wanted him dead.

Even if she couldn't do it herself.

Too damned soft.

Metal creaked, and he raised his head again as her lips parted on a sigh. Ear-length black hair framed her pale skin like a velvet curtain, hanging awkwardly over her closed eyes. Her mouth curved downward in sleep, fuller top lip slanted in a deep line of sadness that scored a brand through Caleb's conscience and set it on fire. Great. It matched the excruciating pain in his shoulder where she'd plunged the knife.

This wasn't going to be easy. But then, when had it ever been?

The dark fan of her lashes fluttered open. Her gaze, as light green as the rare jade she'd cut from his wrists, was hazy, shadowed. Uncertain. It glittered in the dim light as she searched the dark corners of the room.

He watched awareness slowly fill the vacant uncertainty of her expression. Watched her lips twist as those pale, soul-wrenching eyes settled on him.

He opened his mouth. Hesitated.

What the hell could he say?

Nothing.

Slowly, firmly, he shut his mouth on the words that filled his head. They weren't his.

Taking Delia's life had left him with far too many of her fringe memories. The others he'd killed were in there somewhere, he could sense them sometimes, but Delia was by far the strongest. It surprised him at the time, but there was always a price for power.

The side effect to the transfer ritual was something he'd damn well learn to live with.

By himself.

Juliet stiffened, jerked on her ropes, and bared her teeth as the metal legs of her chair scraped against the cement floor.

"Son of a bitch!" Her voice shattered the near silence, bounced back in a flurry of sibilant whispers.

They scraped at his nerves, tightened his already edgy voice to something rougher. "Shut up. We don't have much time." He forced himself not to look away as her gaze once more tangled with his. Narrowed.

"Where the hell are we?" Her shoulders shifted. The open zipper of her coat slid away, baring more of the thin material of her tank top.

The pale line where her skin met black fabric.

Caleb's eyes drifted lower, to the shadowed juncture of her thighs wrapped in black denim. Something uncoiled deep in his veins.

Something deeply buried hummed in approval.

Not on his life. *Or hers.*

"Cellar in the Seattle ruins," he said shortly. "Old coven ground."

"How long was I out?"

"An hour and change." He wrenched a shoulder, growling as tightened loops bit into his flesh. "Jesus Christ, Jules, what the hell were you thinking?"

Her head snapped back as if he'd slapped her. Her eyes glittered, and he watched the skin around her mouth go white with strain.

Suddenly, his head throbbed.

"Not really sure," she bit out, every word as precise as if she'd carved it with a razor. "I think it had something to do with seeing you dead."

Amusement cut a bloody swath through the buzzing pressure in his skull. "Then you should have killed me yourself."

"I'll keep that in mind for next time."

"If you're lucky."

Escape looked downright unlikely. No tools. No excess anything. They'd left him with two chairs, a battery-operated light, and a lot of empty space. He knew this kind of space.

Sweat trickled down his temple. It was too cool beneath the city foundation for the summer heat to travel far, but it wasn't heat that caused him to break out in a cold sweat now.

"Shit," he muttered.

Juliet sighed, frustration clear as a candle in the dark. "Don't you have any rituals stored up?"

Not for a year.

He'd be damned if he told her that now. Without bothering to open his eyes, he said wearily, "Neither one of us can cast anything while tied up."

"Oh. Right."

"If you didn't want to die here," he pointed out, finally opening his eyes, "you shouldn't have called them. Haven't you learned *anything* about coven solidarity?"

She stiffened, cheeks turning red. Damn, but she heated up fast. "Are you even *human*?" she demanded. The word broke, and she jerked hard enough at her ropes that the chair rocked. "Do you even think about the crap that comes out of your—"

Muffled voices filtered through the dusty air, a murmur that gathered intensity and cut her off. Caleb jerked his head around, craning to look back over his shoulder.

"Whatever happens," he told her, "you keep your mouth shut."

"But I—"

His head snapped back. *"No,"* he cut in. Her eyes narrowed. "Shut up, be silent, don't even breathe."

Juliet tipped her head back to look at the ceiling, hidden somewhere out of reach of the light. Her throat worked silently to swallow the verbal dagger he was sure she'd meant to fling at his heart, and he cast a fervent prayer to whatever the hell kind of demon watched over people like him that she would obey.

The door scraped open behind him. His pulse spiked a staccato tempo in his ears.

Keep her safe.

"Oh, finally."

Two words. Breathlessly spoken. And even at a near-whisper, more than enough volume to set off every alarm he had and send them howling with dread.

Across from him, Juliet's eyes narrowed, her jaw tight. This was going to take some serious verbal footwork, and Caleb wasn't sure he had it in him to try.

He didn't have a choice.

He looked away. "There's a voice I haven't heard in a while," he said, tilting his face until he could just barely see the outline of the door in the corner of his eyes. "Alicia. I'm surprised you aren't dead."

"One whole year." Alicia's voice was the same as it had ever been, sharp and effortlessly seductive.

"Fourteen months," he corrected with deliberate calm, "but who's counting?"

She moved silently, suddenly behind him, her warm, bare thighs bracketing his twisted hands. Her palms slid up his arms. "Oh, I've been counting." Her left hand dragged over his scars, and he flinched. "I've been counting every. Single. Day."

Curio had always favored Alicia for her raven-haired beauty and wicked mind. She'd hated Caleb for the attention his visions had given him, schemed and plotted to unseat him from her master's esteem, but Caleb had been more than secure in his power.

Back then, he could see the future.

But he hadn't *seen* this. Even when the dreams had woke him, sweaty and gasping. When they clawed at his eye sockets and spilled like acid from his head, he never once *saw* himself here.

Powerless. Angry.

With Juliet's life at stake.

God damn it. How the hell had Curio's pet witch escaped the trap?

In his peripheral, Juliet's face drained of color as Alicia's fingers slid back up his sweat-slick chest. His neck. He could feel them, warm and somehow strange. Clumsy. Her hands framed his face, and Caleb fought back the urge to twist his head away.

Alicia lowered her mouth to his ear and purred, "I am so *very* glad to see you." Her breath stirred the ends of his hair.

He gritted his teeth. "I can't say the same," he said from between them, then grunted when she gripped his hair, wrenching his head back. Pain locked in on his vertebrae. "Jesus, Alicia." He forced a smile, toothy and flat. "You look like hell."

Alicia's grin didn't slip even a fraction. It couldn't. Half of it had already been twisted by the oozing remains of flesh gone shiny from extreme heat, leaving her teeth bared in a permanent grimace. Her right nostril had melted, dripped across her cheek and healed over in a gleaming ridge, and one of her sky blue eyes stared from the confines of a keloid growth that had been sliced open to allow her to see through it.

So she hadn't escaped his trap at all.

Like him, she'd only survived it.

Her eyes glittered from behind a curtain of raven black hair, or what was left of it. A full half of her scalp shone in the same rippled scars that oozed over most of her face. A grotesque mask.

She touched a thumb to Caleb's eye, so close that his lashes fluttered under the pressure. "Aren't. You. Cute?" Every word cracked; a whispered staccato.

"Alicia!"

Watery eyes jerked to Juliet. The witch's grip tightened in his hair.

Damn it! "This is tedious," he said, but the twang of pain in his voice was clear even to him. Overriding whatever idiotic thing Juliet intended to say, he added, "Get to whatever it is you want and let's get this over with."

Her gaze returned to him. "Tedious. You are unshakable, aren't you? Nothing ever surprised you." Her teeth flashed in the lantern light. "Except for that day Curio sacrificed you."

"Tried to," he corrected. "Failed. So what's it to be? Are you after revenge? Predictable."

If she was coping with even a fraction of the daily agony that threaded through his own bone-deep damage, then she was going to be dangerous as hell. A mind had a lot of time to think while pain lanced a rusty nail into every synapse and held sleep at bay.

She let him go so suddenly that his head snapped forward. "We've been looking for you for a very long time, *soothsayer*." She spat the word like a curse, but didn't wait for a response before she straddled his lap.

One long leg curved over his hip, the center of her body settling too damned familiarly across his thighs, and he gritted his teeth as the point of her elbow dug into his wounded shoulder.

The wound parted, edges splitting open beneath the pressure. Perspiration broke out on his forehead. "Not," he gritted out, "long enough. But who's—" The pressure increased, and he gasped as pain stole his voice.

Across the faint circle of light, her face pale over the pink curve of Alicia's T-shirted shoulder, Juliet flinched. "Alicia, don't."

On his lap, the witch's shoulders went rigid. Her head came down like a dog sensing a challenge, and Caleb wrenched at his ropes with a low growl. "Get to the point. You're pissing me off."

"What's wrong, pet?" she crooned, but she stared at Juliet over her shoulder. "Going to vision your way to safety?"

"I never needed visions to handle you, Alicia. You've never been anything but a third-rate witch."

Alicia's head snapped around. Suddenly, Caleb found himself eye to deformed eye with sheer, naked rage.

He heard Juliet gasp as the witch's hand curled around his throat. He jerked his chin up; fingers like sharpened vises tightened, brutally digging into the flesh around his windpipe.

She thrust her free hand in front of his face, splayed wide.

Three digits waggled in front of his face. A twisted thumb, keloid scarring overgrowing the nail bed. A forefinger, miraculously untouched and capped by a single long nail. Her last three fingers had fused together, seared into each other until only an enlarged, grotesque flipper remained, mottled by scarred, ulcerated growths. The scars climbed all the way to her elbow, bared in her faded T-shirt with the sleeves cut off.

"Look at this," she hissed, somehow worse for it being no louder than a whisper. "Look at what you did to me. Look at what's left!"

Caleb struggled for breath. His fingers pulsed in time with the flow of blood trapped beneath the ropes, his head buzzed as if filled with angry hornets, but he didn't dare move.

He was desperately, acutely aware of Juliet watching him. Watching them both. Within reach.

Alicia's thighs tightened around his bare waist, and he grunted as she slammed that grotesquely malformed hand into his scarred shoulder. "Give me what I want, soothsayer." Another punch, this time with her closed fist. His stomach jerked as pain radiated from the punctured, scarred tissue, and his lungs clamored for oxygen. "Give me the transfer ritual."

Juliet's chair scraped. "Leave him alone!"

Caleb choked out a laugh, drowning out Juliet's wild cry. *Shut up, damn you.* "And what," he rasped, "would you do with it if I did? Take my magic?"

Her smile curved upward, so angelic on the one side. So monstrous on the other. "You think you're so clever," she purred. "You think you can get off pretending it's just about living magic? Oh, baby." Her other hand stroked his face. "She doesn't know yet, does she?"

Despite his efforts not to, his eyes slid to Juliet. She stared at them both, her mouth set into a thin line. Spots of angry color turned her otherwise pale cheeks blotchy.

Alicia followed his gaze, and her smile widened. She slid off his lap with a hell of a lot more skin against skin than it required. He sucked in air, gasping. Grateful for it.

"She doesn't," she said breathlessly. Almost

eagerly. "Oh, heaven. You'll know soon enough, won't you, pretty Juliet?"

Juliet's shoulder moved. Her expression settled into carefully blank lines. "What are you babbling about?"

Caleb cut in before Alicia could say anything. Reveal anything. "Remember the harvest ritual?" He carefully tested the ropes that hadn't stretched even a millimeter, despite his efforts. "She wants that. And she's going to use it on you." His muscles ached, wrists burning, but he didn't stop working his bindings.

Damn the fool that had taught Juliet Carpenter about knots.

Alicia spun in a circle, her feet filthy to the ankle. She ran her hands over the bare half of her shiny, rippled scalp as she laughed. "Oh, yes. How long do you think Curio tapped that power?" Her voice dropped as she sank to her knees in front of the bound Juliet. "How long did he have to fuck you before you let him use your magic, pretty Juliet? Did he make you beg for it?"

She reached up and traced the side of Juliet's face with her unscarred hand. "Did he make you choke on it?"

Juliet stared at the ground. Caleb's muscles locked as black rage slammed home inside his skull. "Juliet," he grated out, his voice taut with the effort to speak through the drums throbbing a ragged beat in his head. "Explain your magic."

Her jaw shifted, but she didn't raise her gaze above Alicia's dirt-smeared toes. "You already—"

"Just do it."

"It . . ." Her lips flattened. "I enhance other witches' power."

Alicia studied the top of her head, her half grimace carved by shadow and lantern light. "Yes, lovely," she said patiently, "we know that."

"It means," he explained, "that she doesn't *have* anything else. Her power doesn't help her. If you take it, you'll never get to use it on yourself, just everyone else. She's more useful alive."

"Maybe you're right." A beat, and Alicia bent to thrust her misshapen smile into Juliet's trembling stare. "And maybe she just doesn't tap into the best of it *because* she lacks anything else. Maybe if someone like, say, *me* had that power, I'd be able to use it better. We'll find out."

"Damn it, Alicia—"

Alicia turned on him, and her blue eyes widened dramatically. "Will you kill me again, Caleb? Will you set fire to my skin? Maim me? Put me through hell? Oh, wait," she amended, laying her disfigured hand against her scarred cheek. "You already have. But our pretty Juliet wasn't there, was she? She never got to feel that burn." Her twisted grimace of a smile lengthened. "And neither did her sist—"

"Come on then," Caleb snarled, cutting her off. "Let's see what kind of crazy you are."

She laughed. "Last chance," she singsonged gaily. "I can play fair. We can start with you, if it'll make you feel better." She beckoned to the door behind him. "You want to be the hero, don't you? Sailing in to sacrifice yourself in penance for all your terrible misdeeds? I'll let you."

Footsteps crunched on the floor.

"Banner." Alicia pouted as a giant of a man stepped into the circle of the light. She leaned against his side, disfigured hand braced against a chest that put cinder-block walls to shame. "The soothsayer isn't being nice to me."

His heart pounded. Adrenaline slammed through him. Alicia always had a way with the big, mean, stupid ones. The man towering over them was all three. A face rearranged by too many meetings with back-alley brawlers leered down at Caleb. Then at Juliet.

She shrank away.

Caleb jerked at his ropes and bit back a curse as the knots dug into his flesh. The small pain was just another sensory fuck-you in a litany of them, and he squared his shoulders. Forced himself to look directly into the big man's fleshy features.

Alicia smiled. "I want that ritual, Banner. If he won't talk, I want you to beat it out of him," she directed, withdrawing from the circle. Her bare feet made no sound in the muck coating the cement floor. She paused. "Oh, and don't break his jaw, just in case. We need him to form words."

"Yes, ma'am," the giant rumbled.

Caleb risked a glance at Juliet. She watched him steadily, her face carefully blank again. He couldn't keep the corner of his lips from twitching.

Show no fear.

That's my girl.

"You going to tell her what she wants to hear?" Banner asked slowly. "So that you can maybe hurt less?"

Caleb's gut jerked, stomach churning with nervous anticipation. His eyes narrowed until he realized the man meant Alicia.

He'd never be able to tell Juliet anything. Not his girl, God damn it. *Not his.*

"No," he said flatly.

The first blow took forever to land. The giant raised a punch-scarred, hairy fist and drew back as if winding up a difficult toy. There was a palpable sound of effort, a hard exhale as it pushed through the air, and Caleb's head snapped around. The skin over his cheekbone split, almost audible in the sudden silence. It throbbed through his head, sloshed around in his brain until his ears rang with it.

When another didn't come straight away, he cracked open an eye.

Juliet's light green stare met his. Too shiny in her white face. Tears?

Little rose.

"God damn it," he said tightly, staring at her as blood dribbled into the corner of his mouth. It tasted bright and thick, warm salt and liquid copper. *"Toughen up."*

She bared her teeth.

"Now?" Banner's voice thundered like a freight train.

Caleb sucked in a slow breath, and signed his death warrant with a grim smile. "Let me make this easy on you," he said, stretching out every word as if talking to a particularly dim child. "Go. To. Hell."

Banner took a moment to mull this over. Then,

nodding, he stepped around the chair on boots built out of scrap rubber and knelt to peer into Caleb's face. "She says not to break your mouth," he rumbled.

He braced himself. It didn't do him any good. The next fist caught him in the gut, cutting off his breath with spectacular precision. Then the sternum. Caleb gritted his teeth as wave after wave of pain spiraled from each point of impact.

The next fist to drive into his flesh set off a torturous chain reaction that sparked through every fried nerve he had left. Blood oozed through the bandage around his shoulder, and he bit his tongue. The small pain wasn't enough to mask the agony tearing through his body.

As if finding a particularly pleasing button, Banner hit him again in the same spot. Harder.

Flesh stretched, popped, and tore. Like an obscenely red flower, blood blossomed around the makeshift bandage, splattered over his shoulder. Caleb threw back his head, clenched his jaw so hard that the joint cracked. More punches, more savage blows that didn't leave him time to breathe.

Time to think or brace.

New blood splattered, almost black in the flickering light.

It overwhelmed him. Filled his skin like acid and fire. Desperately aware of Juliet's horrified stare, he locked his teeth on a rough scream.

CHAPTER THREE

S he didn't know how long the giant worked him over. Too long. Long enough that each groan, each crack of bone on flesh and muffled howl of defiance tore through her head like rusted knives.

Juliet watched Caleb in wretched silence. Her heart pounded against the cage of her ribs and queasiness kept her teeth clenched firmly together, but she did watch.

Wasn't this what she wanted?

His hoarse screaming stopped, as abruptly as if he'd flicked a switch. He slumped over, his battered body slack. The bloody-fisted giant grabbed his hair and wrenched his face to the light.

Blood dribbled out of Caleb's lips. His lashes

clung to his sweat- and blood-damp cheeks, and she sucked in a horrified breath as the man wiggled Caleb's head side to side. Then he dropped it, leaving Caleb's chin to thunk against his own chest, and shuffled out of the room.

The lantern had gotten dimmer and dimmer, and now it flickered threateningly. Shadows skimmed over the gleaming, pale muscles of Caleb's chest, made the runny, blotted splashes of blood look foul. Intrusive.

Was he alive? For now, maybe. But he didn't move, not even when the door slammed shut.

She'd made a terrible mistake.

Juliet closed her eyes as the batteries finally guttered out. Darkness settled into place, as heavy and thick and stifling as a blanket over her head.

Fear. Oh, God. It slid down her spine, infused her nerves with ice. The silence smothered her. Choked her, a dreadful miasma broken by her uneven breathing and the creak of her jacket as she moved.

She had to get out.

Twisting her arms, she writhed and worked her wrists until sweat or blood made them slick. She didn't know which. Her fingers had long since gone numb.

Get free. That's all she needed to focus on now. Get free, and she wouldn't be alone.

But in the hollow space behind her eyelids, the scene replayed over and over. Fists like cinder blocks drawing back, colliding with flesh and muscle. Caleb's features, wracked with pain and drawn so tight that she could see each individual angle of his face. His scars white with it. His eyes radiating anger and desperate resolve as he thrashed against the chair.

The idiot. What the hell was he trying to prove?

Did she care?

She caught her upper lip between her teeth as she tried to see through the dark. Felt the fine hairs on her skin prickle and shiver beneath sweat that turned her skin sticky and cold.

She cared. Cared enough to hate the treatment he'd gotten. Cared enough to flinch with every blow, every grunt and smothered gasp.

But hadn't her intent been to kill him? Now it was to *save* him?

What was *wrong* with her?

"Caleb," she whispered. Her voice skittered back at her, sibilant whispers tossed a thousand directions.

There was no answer. She hadn't expected one. Hoped, but not expected.

Biting her lip harder, she twisted her left hand until her fingers curled up in an angle. It burned, probably sloughing off skin with it, but she couldn't let that stop her.

Calling the remnants of the coven was, she admitted to herself, a really, really stupid idea. She'd barely been part of it when it was whole. Without Curio to protect her, she was just fodder for the rest.

So Caleb had been right. Of course he'd been right.

It galled. "Hate him," she muttered. "Hate him so— Ouch!"

Gasping with the effort, she jimmied her wrist back and forth, pulling and twisting as she did. She clenched her teeth, locking her jaw as pain ripped through her arms. Just as it reached a crescendo, felt as if she were scraping off her own skin with jagged razors, her hand slipped free with a wet, tearing sound.

Relief outweighed the agony. Tears of pain slid down her cheeks, but she didn't have time to sit and nurse it. She was getting out of here.

And yes, she was going to rescue Caleb Leigh while she was at it.

No one deserved to be tortured to death.

Hurriedly shaking off the loose rope from her other hand, she bent and fumbled with the knots by her ankles. As the ropes hit the dirt, she pushed herself to her feet and thrust her hands out blindly in front of her. Six steps, maybe seven. She took them cautiously. Her fingers slid through air warmer than the ambient temperature, and she sighed shakily in mixed relief and anger as they collided with muscle.

"Caleb," she hissed. "Wake up."

No response, not even as she pressed forward and found her palms full of wet, warm skin. Muscle flattened. Rose and fell beneath her touch and as heat climbed her cheeks, she realized she'd found his chest. His lean, beautifully defined chest.

He breathed, slow and even. Thank God, he was alive.

And she was an idiot.

Muttering under her breath, she blindly

mapped the contours of his torso, skimmed the taut, round shape of his shoulder and slid her fingers over smooth flesh. No ridges scraped under her fingertips. She'd found his right side, then.

Slowly, holding her breath, Juliet traced the very tips of her fingers across his chest. They glided across smooth skin and dipped into the valleys of muscle; a warm flush slid to her belly. Pooled lower. Without anything for her eyes to adjust to, her sense of touch seemed somehow stronger. Infinitely more sensitive. She found herself leaning forward, outlining tendons and sinew.

Smelling the warm, musky fragrance of his body.

Oh, Jesus, she had it bad.

Corrugated skin rasped under her shaking touch, and she blew out a hard, surprised breath. In the dark, the nodules of his scars felt monstrous. Terrifyingly thick and oh, how much pain he must have suffered.

A muscle tensed under her probing stroke, and she jerked upright, appalled. An arm. No time to be stupid, it was just an arm. Harmless and exactly what she needed. At the end of this arm, there would be ropes.

She sank to her haunches, sternly setting her jaw, but her palms glided over his elbow in slow exploration. Her fingers dug into the overwhelming contradiction of his body—soft and hard, smooth and ridged. Warm and alive and damp. She traced his unscarred forearm. The wiry hair tickled the pads of her hands, and she stifled a groan.

She knew exactly how strong those arms were. Remembered the feel of them tight around her, iron and silk and so secure. Like they'd hold her forever.

"Lies," she hissed, shaking her head hard enough to catch a tiny breeze from her swinging hair. She bent forward, running her fingertips over the binding with effort. The ropes were tighter than her own had been. The ridges where it puckered into his wrists would hurt later.

Every nerve thrummed, high alert, her ears straining to hear even the smallest change in sound around her as she concentrated. She found the knots by luck. Cursed silently as they evaded her damp grasp. Grimacing with the effort, her temples throbbing, she sat back on her heels and worked her fingers between his limp hands.

The ropes twanged. Juliet bit back a shriek as hard fingers clenched over hers, and she froze.

For a long moment, only his labored breathing filled the silence. It echoed her pounding heart. His hands were damp, hot around hers. Hard enough to hurt.

Then, pain wrapped through his tightly restrained voice, he said thickly, "Knife in my boot. They didn't check."

She stared into the endless wall of black and weighed her options.

Could she leave him behind? Yes.

Could she make it far without him? Maybe.

Would she ever sleep again, knowing what Alicia planned to do? Imagining the uniquely creative ways the witch could get what she wanted without ever putting him out of his misery?

She set her jaw. "Which leg?"

"Left." He let her go.

Moving as quickly as she dared in the black void, she located his leg by touch and slid both hands down his calf. His muscle jumped under her palms, tightened, but he said nothing as she hiked up the frayed hem of his jeans and found the knife tucked into his boot.

She withdrew it, clenched it tightly in one hand, and blindly groped for his arm again. Her fingers clanged against the metal chair, and she yelped.

"Careful," he murmured. "It's dark."

No shit danced on the end of her tongue, but simmered to bruised pride instead. She almost stuck her stinging fingers into her mouth, smelled the nose-curling fragrance of drying blood and whatever filth infested the rough ground, and thought better of it.

"Don't move," she snapped instead, opening the folded blade by feel. "I'd *hate* to accidentally cut off a finger."

He chuckled, but there was no heat to it. Only something dark, something grimly reserved and hurting.

Juliet found the edge of the rope and very carefully placed the blade underneath it. The bindings unraveled with ease.

The metal chair creaked. Air wafted across her face, and the solid heat of him was suddenly gone. She fumbled the blade closed and shoved it into a pocket, shutting her eyes before they widened any farther and strained out of her sockets.

Sweat clung to her back. Her chest. Nerves. "Now what?"

"Over here." The voice came from her right, not where she'd imagined him standing. "Follow my voice. I'm not that far."

She thrust out her hands and took three steps before something grazed her arm. Fingers curled around her wrist, pulled her flush against a wall, and she gasped as a broad hand flattened over her chest.

She stared down at it, seeing nothing, feeling, oh, God, everything. The warmth of his palm. His body heat pressed against her shoulder, so contrary to the cool, dank slab of concrete at her back. He smelled like sweat and blood and something indefinably him, and even as she thought it, she realized that the hand plastered against her sternum was shaking.

How badly was he hurt?

"Caleb—"

"Be quiet," he whispered. Wood grated. A seam of light speared through the absolute dark, and Juliet flinched. "Follow me."

He slipped through the open door and Juliet wordlessly obeyed, stumbling over the uneven stairs. His hand shot back again, gripped her upper arm as her eyes struggled to adjust.

"Okay?"

"Fine," she muttered, shaking his grip off with—she could admit it, if only to herself— childish pride. His smile flashed in her spotty vision as he turned away. He crept up the stairs with more grace than she would have given his battered body credit for, ducked low and peered around the open corner.

Nothing moved. She didn't so much as breathe.

Where were they? The walls flickered, painted in orange light and dull brown shadows. That meant fire, real fire. The underground was the only safe place to light anything short of a cigarette, and they made special tools for those.

New Seattle cops wrecked anyone caught lighting fires, even for warmth. Down in the bowels of the city, the police didn't care all that much if a family froze to death in the winter. But God forbid the wealthy upper city burned.

Her fists clenched, and she tucked them hard against the wall as Caleb watched whatever claimed his attention around the corner.

He was a pale blur in her watering vision, and she still couldn't ignore how badly her guts twisted up at the sight of him.

How long had she nursed a crush?

At least two years. Since the day he'd shown up at Curio's side, a serious-faced witch with cool blue eyes. Juliet had been twenty-three and high on the coven master's promises of family. Of commitment and safety and home.

Caleb had been quiet and cold, even then.

Two long, bloody years later, and nothing had changed. Except, she reflected, throat aching around a sudden stricken knot, all the family she'd ever known was gone. Dead, disappeared, or worse. And it was all Caleb Leigh's fault.

Alicia's words floated through her mind. *She doesn't know?*

Of course she did. Everyone knew how Caleb Leigh had turned against them.

"Move it," he whispered, then vanished around the corner. His shadow danced across the walls, a wicked flicker in gray and black as she hurried up the stairs, wincing with every creak and groan of rotting wood.

The room was empty of all but Caleb, crouched by a fire pit hastily dug in the center of the eroded floor and circled by broken slabs of mortar and concrete. He rose, features expressionless as he studied the gaping hole that was all that remained of one wall. His fingers glistened, damp from the drink he'd dipped them in, and he gestured at the abandoned mug by his feet. "He'll be back," he said brusquely. "Drink's still warm. Grab that light and let's go."

"Can you—" She swallowed as he tipped his head toward her, his mouth tight with impatience. The firelight painted everything over in radiant orange, colored the lurid bruises marring his face into vivid welts. Purple and red and angry and so raw, it hurt to look at. She squared her shoulders. "Are you okay?"

"You're concerned?" His eyes narrowed. "Don't be. Let's go."

It wasn't as if they had much of a choice. Still, his casual dismissal stung, and she turned away before he noticed her disappointment. And her exhaustion.

She found the flashlight he indicated, discarded

on an end table whose finish had long since peeled away to a cracked, gray shell. She palmed it neatly, watched him pick up a rough denim jacket discarded on the floor. He slid it on, and if she hadn't been watching, she would have missed his flinch.

So he did actually feel pain. Only human, huh?

Yeah, right.

He strode out through the jagged hole, buttoning the jacket as he went. Shadows lapping at his heels, the devastated tomb swallowed him as completely as if he'd walked off the face of the world.

With a last frown at the yawning black void that had been their prison, she hurried after him.

Shapes rose alien and menacing in the shadows cast by the campfire's orange flicker. It seemed that her footsteps clattered in the pressing silence, that every inhale and exhale rasped and echoed back at her until it became a rickety hiss of sound and motion. She caught herself holding her breath as she stepped over the slimy, moss-ridden stones of what had probably been some kind of street or sidewalk. It was impossible to tell now.

Fifty and some odd years of neglect had only aggravated what a world-changing earthquake and massive flooding had started.

To look at it now, it was hard to imagine the chaos, the sheer hell that had overwhelmed a once-thriving city. Five decades had worn the worst of the cavity to a dull edge, helped along by industrious rich people who had built a new city right on top of the half-eaten ruins of the old.

They'd planted a few thousand columns, paved over the whole damned thing. It was a solution, of sorts.

A Band-Aid.

The lucky ones got to live within the walls of the new metropolis. Rumors and stories whispered of the unlucky ones, the people trapped outside the new city's walls to be hunted down, torn apart by the things that existed between the remaining cities of the world.

She didn't know what was true, she'd never been outside the guarded walls. She'd never met anyone who had. She knew there *were* other cities, and that heavy transports moved between them—how else could goods be imported in?—but that was all she knew.

As far as she could tell, it was all anyone down in the layered city was allowed to know.

Old Seattle existed somewhere in between the real world and the old. It was a cesspit of forgotten legacies, secure behind the city walls and all but alive with history and, she'd always felt, malicious hunger—dying to feed on the corpses of the unwary.

The coven lost witches every year to the ruins. Carelessness, sheer rotten luck; it didn't take much.

Juliet looked back again, dragging her free hand through her sweat-damp hair and out of her face. The fire left untended behind them shone like a beacon, practically a comet in the vast emptiness. If they were true to old habits, the witches wouldn't risk the light if they were anywhere even close to the roads that led up to the city proper.

They were deep, then. Deep enough that they could light fires and set up shop, sloppy though it was.

The light dogged their footsteps until Caleb jerked to a halt, seized her arm, and yanked her into a side alley. She stumbled over chunks of loose rubble and found her back pressed against cold cement, her palms splayed over hard, denim-clad muscle. It was a thin barrier. The heat of his body worked its way through his stolen jacket, and for a shuddering moment, she couldn't think of anything but how cold her hands and feet were. How cold her extremities had been since she'd woken up in a grimy basement.

How cold all of her had been for too many long, empty months.

His body was warm and hard and strong against hers, and as she opened her mouth, he slid one hand over it, murmuring a wordless warning.

Her breath caught in her chest. She couldn't see anything but the faintest impression of his silhouette, his angled jaw tilted to the side as he studied something, listened for something somewhere out in the black and barren ruin.

His elbows hemmed in her shoulders, caging her between them. His long legs braced hers, his chest rose and fell against her own in slow, rhythmic breaths that only pushed a slow, rhythmic— oh, God, an all too familiar burn to the juncture of her thighs.

She swallowed, opening her mouth again to complain. To protest. Her lips rasped against his callused palm and he froze.

She forgot how to breathe as Caleb turned his head. Forgot how to think as his breath warmed over her cheek. She didn't have to hear it to know his breathing hitched; she felt it in the startled catch of his chest against hers. Felt it in the sudden slam of his heart.

Echoed in her own.

Her lips moved again. Shuddering, her lower lip brushed his palm on words she couldn't form, and the hand splayed against the wall beside her head shifted. Slowly, so lightly that she wasn't sure if she imagined it, the side of his fingers skimmed the curve of her cheek. Ghosted over her jaw.

His gaze gleamed in the faint light, chips of diamond. Unreachable. Unreadable.

Had she ever seen them warm?

Once, breathed a traitorous sigh deep in her body. Once, they'd caught fire. Just for her.

She shoved at his chest with a low, raw sound. He let her go, released her as easily as if she hadn't just shivered under his touch. His weight shifted, drew away even as he lowered his head to whisper, "The guard came back. Keep the flashlight close, but not on. Can you keep up?"

She'd die before she admitted to anything else. "You're the handicap," she muttered, struggling to sound as calm and unaffected as he was.

The bastard.

In the diminishing light, his teeth flashed. A smile? A scowl? She didn't know. She gripped the flashlight in her fist as he turned and whispered, "Hold on to my coat. We're moving fast."

Juliet grabbed a handful of the jacket. "How will you see?"

"Better than average night vision," he said matter-of-factly, and eased into a jog.

Before they'd taken twenty steps, she realized that concentrating on not tripping over rotting city would take more energy than she was sure she had. After only five minutes, Caleb was running in a smooth, easy cadence and she was struggling to breathe.

Within ten long, interminably slow minutes, she was ready to beg for mercy. She clenched her teeth and kept up.

She didn't know how long they ran. At some point, Caleb slowed, asked her for the flashlight, and took off again, the thin light paving his way. Her breath rasped through her dry throat, rough as chalk, and her lungs seized as every breath tore through her right side. The cramp locked barbed hooks under her rib and made every step a new-found riot of torture.

She jumped, climbed, sidled, and jogged until she thought she was caught in a nightmare, an endless stream of rocky, slimy, treacherous, rubble-strewn road. It was all she could do to focus on putting one foot in front of the other until he finally stopped.

Her numbed fingers fell from his stolen jacket. Juliet sank to her knees and bent over nearly double, gasping for air. The ends of her damp hair clung to her lashes, her face, and she wheezed as she scraped it back with shaking, sweaty fingers.

"Never," she panted, "again . . . Ever. Would rather . . . die."

Caleb said nothing.

The light skated over piles of fallen, decomposing timber and jagged edges of rusted metal. A fetid smell punctuated the air, like things left too long in the rain and musty air. Flesh and bone; wood and decay.

Dragging the sleeve of her jacket over her forehead, she staggered to her feet as Caleb braced himself against a moldering wall. He was flushed, at least. Sweaty and as breathless as she was.

Small favors.

"Where are we?" she finally asked when she could manage it.

He hesitated, swinging the flashlight back the way they'd come. "Somewhere near the trench."

"How can you tell?"

"Listen. You can just barely hear the water."

Juliet stared at him. At his outline, just a glimmer behind the light. True to his word, the faintest whisper hovered just out of auditory reach; a trace of sound that felt like pressure. Like depth and motion and— "Oh. Oh, *Jesus*. That means we're . . . We're going to die."

"Relax."

"Don't you tell me—!" Juliet caught herself, clipping off hysteria before the world around her got any more sharp and shiny at the edges. "Being lost this far into the ruins is as good as a death sentence," she said tightly, fingers curling into aching fists. "You know this."

After the fault had opened up under the city,

the Old Sea-Trench had eaten away at the abandoned carcass long after the aftershocks stopped. The place was a death trap then. Fifty years later, it was suicide. Pitfalls, loose ledges, nature's own booby traps had claimed more than one explorer over the years.

Every so often, the occasional tremor still rumbled through the fault. Sometimes, more shifted, fell over, or crumbled. The trench bottom was a rushing river of glacier-fed water, and she didn't want to be just another body washed down the fault line.

"Relax," he repeated. "We're not dead yet."

Exhaustion knocked on her skull. She dragged her hands through her hair. "Okay," she said after a deep breath. Much, much calmer. She could do this. "How do we get back?"

"Not sure."

"What can we do?"

"I'm working on it." He straightened as she closed the distance, his expression shadowed and wary. Forcing her brain to override her feet, Juliet spun before she could do whatever it was her body had intended. Slap him. Push him.

Throw herself at him and beg to be comforted.

He didn't touch her. God help him if he tried. Anger warred with fatigue and left her feeling that the dark glittered hungrily around her, like some kind of starving crevasse.

"Fine," she managed. There. Civil.

He clicked off the light. "Sit. Rest. We'll set off again soon."

"I don't want to rest," she said, squeezing her

eyes shut as the thick web of shadow threatened to smother her. Her voice tightened. "I want to get back to civilization."

"Rest anyway. If you collapse—"

"If I collapse," she cut in, aware that she was talking through her teeth, that she was being unreasonable and whiny and so beyond caring, "you'll have one less worry, won't you?"

Silence met her accusation, flung with wild, angry precision. She couldn't see him. Couldn't hear him, *damn it, she couldn't see him.*

And in the suffocating dark, Juliet felt abandoned. Isolated. Completely and terribly alone.

Fear.

"Look." Caleb hesitated, barely a fraction of a second, then said crisply, "You're going to have to get it together. If you panic, I'm going to leave you behind."

"You wouldn't."

His voice thinned. "Wouldn't I?"

It was as if he'd pushed her off some indefinable edge. Everything in Juliet's body, her mind, spilled free. The fury—*terror!*—battering at her control cracked, and it seemed as if she watched someone else wearing her skin turn and launch herself in the direction of that so calm voice.

As if it wasn't her body that collided with his, her voice that strangled on a sound shredded from a throat gone tight and raw.

Caleb caught her, but not easily. He deflected her, struggled to grab her shoulders, her arms, cursing in surprise and warning and staggering as she battered at him. As she twisted her fingers into claws and sobbed something that didn't make it into real words, his back flattened against the wall. His boots scrabbled for purchase amid the rocks that crumbled at their feet.

Something cracked. Juliet hoped it was bone—she would have settled for his thick head. Then the world tilted on its axis. Vertigo slammed home as Caleb's arms tightened around her, and the weak cement crumbled into nothing behind them.

They toppled as she screamed.

CHAPTER FOUR

Air rushed past her ears, air and darkness and screams that echoed from all sides. It seemed as if she hung forever, trapped and falling all at the same time, her fingers somehow twisted in his jacket.

Juliet didn't have time to think. Didn't have time to watch her life play through the projector of her mind. One wide hand wrapped around the back of her head and Caleb's voice roared by her ear, "Inhale!"

She managed to open her mouth, to reverse the flow of air from an endless scream to a breath sucked into her burning lungs as the rushing sound grew louder and louder.

Between one second and the next, air turned to

ice and she gasped as they plunged into the frozen river at the bottom of the trench. Caleb's jacket wrenched out of her grip.

Bubbles streamed around her face, mind spinning wildly as the cold sucked every ounce of warmth from her body. It stole her breath, her thought, her ability to move. Her memory. The current wrapped liquid fingers around her limbs and dragged her tumbling downriver.

Was this how she'd die? Sucked into the icy currents and thrown against some desolate shore miles away?

Juliet flailed. She forced her eyes open as her lungs burned for air, thrashed and fought through water that seemed thick and viscous from cold. Water filled her ears, her mouth and nose, her skin, and she struggled to kick her booted feet. To climb through layers upon layers of freezing currents until finally, thank God, her head broke through the surface.

Lungs burning, she sucked in air, choked on a mouthful of water and thrashed as a cresting swell sloshed over her head. The flow moved too fast to see anything in the near dark, and she didn't tread water so much as force herself to float on the top, to not fight as she relearned how to breathe.

"Caleb!" The white-capped rush of icy water swallowed the sound, threw it back at her in taunting, muffled echoes. She caught a mouthful of water, choked again, sobbing.

It was as if she floated in freezing, weightless nothing; a void of sensory deprivation so intense that it took her breath away. She fought the current—didn't she? She could feel herself thinking about it, but she couldn't shape the words in her head.

Swim. Stay afloat.

Rest.

Something closed around her ankle. She barely managed a breath before her head slid beneath the surface, hands grasping at nothing. The river pulled at her, fought to keep her, and the grip tightened to near pain.

Then another anchor, an iron band laced around her upper arm, and she gasped as it yanked her back to the surface. Panting, she couldn't fight it as she was bodily hauled through the vigorous tide. She slammed against something hard, garbled a protest as jagged rock grated against her chest, her cheek. Maybe it hurt. How could she tell?

Sobbing with every breath, all she could do was cling to the cliff face, heaving up what bits of the river she managed to inhale.

"Don't fight me, I've got you."

Caleb's voice, soothing at her ear. He curled one arm around her ribs, under her breasts, as secure a hold as she'd ever known in her life. It didn't squeeze. He only held her, solid support against the current.

Juliet sobbed in relief. The river pulled at her, swirled around her waist, but he wedged her tightly between his braced legs and let her tremble. Let her cling to the cliff wall and pull herself together.

It was harder than it should have been.

When her panting sobs had eased to hiccups, and then to forced calm, she realized that his left hand hooked into a crevice, fingers twisted just so to provide an organic clasp. His arm extended, a mottled line in the dark and so taut that she knew it had to hurt. The other still splayed at her ribs, fingers tight. His hips braced hers against the wall, his chest warmed her back even in the cold water.

She couldn't help herself. Adrenaline and fear drained out of her like a sigh, leaving her empty and exhausted and so cold that it hurt to think, much less move. She let her head fall back against his shoulder. Weary to the bone, her eyes drifted closed.

His heartbeat slammed near her ear. She timed her breathing to it. Four beats in. Four out.

Water slid down her face. Dripped from the end of her nose. Slowly, saying nothing, he settled his chin against her wet hair. The arm at her waist tightened, and she trembled.

They were trapped in the bottom of the Old Sea-Trench, barely hanging on to a cliff face with witches intent on killing them somewhere beyond. It was dark, freezing cold, and hopeless.

And yet. . .

Juliet had never felt so protected in her life.

And that was his strength, wasn't it? Making people trust him. She clenched her teeth as a full-body shiver set them chattering.

The reassuring weight of his chin lifted. "Can you climb?" The question was even. Matter-of-fact.

Juliet almost laughed, but her heart wasn't in it. It was only hysteria, anyway. She tightened her grip on the rock. "I don't know."

"We're going to try. Give me your jacket."

"Wh-what? Why?"

"I didn't think to bring the rope you cut." He pulled at her collar, and she sighed. It clattered with cold. With too much effort and his help, she somehow managed to wriggle out of the synth-leather jacket and let him take it.

He fumbled behind her, his muscles sliding against her back. Cold was rapidly replacing any sense of feeling she had left, not that the sodden coat had helped at all.

"We're tied together," he said, his voice strained. She could feel the shudders he desperately tried to suppress, a constant vibrating line down her back. "Just do as I say. Left hand first."

Slowly, so slowly she was sure she'd die of hypothermia long before they got out, Juliet followed his directions. He lifted his left hand to search for a cranny to use, found one, and guided her hand to it. "Put your fingertips together, like you had a puppet. Good."

She wedged her fingers inside, teeth clattering so badly that the sound peppered his every word.

Then he found his own niche. Followed it with his right hand. Left foot. Right toes. His body strained behind hers, and she realized how much of her weight he took as he pulled himself up behind her. Knew and couldn't do anything about it as her numbed fingers slipped.

He caught her, the synthetic leather coat snapping taut between them. His breath wheezed out on a gasp that might have been a curse. For a moment, all she could do was catch her breath, muscles screaming.

"All right?" he asked.

"S-sorry," she whispered.

"It's okay," he said, keeping his voice low and calm. "You're doing fine. Let's go." Little by little. Aggravatingly, mind-bendingly slowly, the water eased from her waist to her knees. Another bout of directions. His voice became a steady rasp of sound, a constant stream of encouragement and direction that she couldn't decipher as she struggled not to picture the yawning crevasse below them.

One misstep and they'd fall right back into the current. She knew she wouldn't have the strength to fight it this time.

She must have made a sound because his arm curled around her ribs again, and his breath warmed her ear as he said, "Take a rest."

She clung to the rock, shuddering. "Can't," she muttered thickly. "Won't go again. K-keep going."

He hesitated. Then, as if he understood her desperation, he let her go and instructed, "Right hand, reach up."

She could barely feel the sharp rock anymore. She was only vaguely aware of his weight behind her; he supported her more than she was herself. Inch by inch, the icy currents below them dropped away. It was something she felt more than saw. Or did she imagine it?

Were they only a foot up? Only a few inches out of the water?

Juliet squeezed her eyes shut, moaning.

"Nearly there," he said behind her, and she almost believed it. Almost.

"H-how do you st-st-stay so c-calm?" she managed, teeth chattering together. It felt as if her whole body vibrated, graceless as a puppet.

"The alternative sucks."

She laughed. It shuddered. "C-can imagine. Aren't y-you cold?"

"Freezing."

"Can't tell," she said on a sigh that frosted the air in front of her.

"I just think about better times." A smile touched his voice. Or did she imagine that, too?

"Like warm fires, r-right?"

His hips braced her weight, holding her for a moment as if he knew that her arms screamed in mutiny. "Like warm skin," he said roughly, almost too low to hear. "Like sweat and spring green eyes and all that other crap I don't need to be thinking about."

Tears gathered behind her eyes. Exhaustion. That's all. Her head ached incessantly; just another note in a symphony of misery.

"Left foot," he added, and if there had been even a glimmer of lightness there, it was gone now.

"C-Caleb."

"Now right hand, where mine is. Wedge your fingers in. What?"

Juliet jammed her twisted fingers into the crevice he guided her to and rested her forehead against the cliff face. "Did y-you know . . . this would happen?"

There was a pause as he found his own niche. A grunt as the muscles in his shoulders and chest contracted, supporting his weight and most of hers. The fluidity of motion behind her, the flex and tightening of his body, fascinated her.

She'd seen how badly scarred he was. He had to be in excruciating pain.

When they were tight against the wall again, he finally said, "I don't see everything. I don't even see things I think I should. It's not a feed I can just dial into, it doesn't work like that."

"Why not?"

Another beat of silence, filled with the whispering current below them and the sound of her own hard breathing. Then, so quietly she almost missed it over the roar of the water, he replied, "I don't know."

"Are we g-going to die here?"

"Right hand," he directed, and Juliet didn't have the energy to do anything but obey. She let him dodge the question, let it hang beside them as they crawled up the cliff wall for what seemed like an eternity. They paused only long enough to shake out stinging fingers and talked only as much as directions required.

And every step of the vertical climb, he held her. Supported her weight, caught her as she fumbled and slid. Pain ratcheted through his voice as the climb wore on, and she struggled to maintain her own momentum. Carry more of her own weight so he wouldn't have to.

When her fingers closed over nothing, her heart plunged into her stomach, then bounced up into her throat as Caleb gritted out, "We're up. Wait." The jacket pulled taut around her, then suddenly went slack.

Energy surged through her, strong enough to allow her fingers to get a grip as he helped her over the edge. She clambered over it, grabbing fistfuls of rock and dirt and God knew what else for leverage, until her feet cleared the shelf and Juliet sprawled, pressing her cheek to the ground in relief. "Oh, thank God," she breathed. "Thank you, thank you."

She heard him scrabbling behind her. Quickly, she turned and wrapped both hands around his wrist, dug her heels in and strained every muscle she had left. Fatigue welled through her aching limbs. She groaned.

Caleb's muscles tightened, bunched suddenly in her hands and he surged over the lip, an explosion of raw strength and adrenaline. She bit off a surprised yell as he slammed into her, taking them both down in a tangle of exhaustion and fear and relief.

Panting, Juliet found her arms wrapped around his chest as he braced his elbows on the ground on either side of her shoulders. His chest heaved against hers; his breath just as harsh. Without warning, he muttered something hard and edged, and unerringly in the dark, his mouth closed over hers.

Shock warred with exultation; fear with anger. As his lips pushed hers apart, as he ignored her dazed stillness and slid his hot tongue into her mouth, something deep inside her stretched. Snapped.

Her fingers tightened over wet denim.

His tangled in her soaking hair, forced her head still between his clenched fists, his mouth hot and demanding as he thrust his tongue between her lips without any pretense of gentility. She fought it, fought him.

But not to escape.

Her tongue slid over his, tangled and pushed. He groaned incoherently, kissed her breathless.

Kissed her stupid.

She forgot the cold, the rocky ground; there was only the heat of his mouth, the hard, muscled weight of his body covering hers. She arched into him, gasping, and he swallowed the sound with another low, shuddering groan. Her pulse sky-rocketed. Her temples throbbed where his fingers locked into her hair, and it slammed a bolt of heat to the suddenly too sensitive ache between her legs.

He had always been cold. Right up until he burned.

She wanted that heat now.

Her legs fell open, jeans rasping against the ground, and his hips settled more firmly into the cradle of her thighs. Lust slammed through her body, her head. Need.

She whimpered.

On a rough sound, he tore his lips away, leaving her gasping for breath. For sense. His forehead rested at the curve of her neck, his shoulders heaving with every breath.

Shocked into silence, mouth wet and tingling, Juliet let him.

For this single moment in the dark, as memory and need and regret tangled together low in her body, she struggled to find an even keel and said nothing. Did nothing.

Didn't know what else to do.

She was alive. Desperate to be touched by a man she thought she hated and God only knew where they were now, but alive. The bulge settled into the vee of her shamelessly open legs wasn't a product of her imagination.

It was, she admitted through the melting fragments of her own thoughts, much better than the alternative.

The tension at her scalp eased. Caleb forced himself upright, fumbling in the dark, and cool air slid into the vacuum left by his body heat. She shivered.

Something clicked, and a thin beam of light seared through her vision. She flinched, throwing up a hand.

"Jesus, Juliet."

She thought he'd meant the kiss. She opened her mouth to protest hotly when he caught her wrist, and Juliet cracked open her eyes to find him peering at the abrasions decorating her knuckles. Ruined flaps of flesh puckered in a bloody mess, gleaming wetly in the light.

His own weren't any prettier.

She didn't fight as he tugged her upright, forcing her to sit up, but she couldn't summon the energy to pull her hands away. "They don't hurt," she said wearily. "Not more than yours do, I bet."

"They hurt like hell," Caleb replied evenly, and she couldn't help her crooked smile. Even her humor was tired. "Are you hurt anywhere else? Is anything broken?"

"I don't know. It's all numb."

The light slid up her legs, picked out her soaked jeans and glossed over her arms.

Juliet tipped her head back, closing her eyes again. "Well? Am I alive?"

Could she be any less alive? Her body all but hummed under his perusal, and she clenched her knees tightly together.

Get. A. Grip.

This was memory talking, that was all. She'd already screwed up by sleeping with him once; she just needed to break that habit of easy freaking arousal.

No problem.

He said nothing. Some sense, an inner warning caused her to raise her eyelids. She practically had to peel them apart. God, she was tired.

He stared at her, his gaze glittering in the faint light afforded by the thin beam centered squarely on her chest. Her breath caught in her throat. Slowly, dreading what she knew she'd find, she looked down.

A flap from her black tank top hung over her chest, its ragged edges clearly visible against the pale, dirt-speckled curve of one breast. In some calm, objective part of her frozen mind, she realized that the rock wall must have torn it free when she'd wriggled against it. Her simple black shelf bra was askew, and the edge of one dark nipple was clearly visible.

Calm slammed into mortification. Heat seared her cheeks as she made a grab for the torn material, but Caleb caught her wrist, his grip rigid.

She pulled at it. "Let me—"

"What is this?" His voice bit, sharp as a whip crack and colder than the water below.

Her laugh cracked. "I'm pretty sure you've seen boobs before." He knocked her other hand away and hooked a finger in the edge of the gaping fabric, peeling it away from her ribs. It revealed more of her bra. More of her flesh, half freed from the constraining band.

She jerked.

Caleb splayed his hand against her chest to keep her from twisting away, his mouth a thin line. The warmth of his palm drilled into her skin, swelled to a burning ache, but he didn't seem to notice.

She did. Damn him.

He let go of her wrist and instead stroked a finger over the three-inch-long bar code stamped just under the heavy swell of her left breast. Her skin prickled under his touch. Her stomach clenched.

Confusion sizzled to stunned disbelief. "What, my tattoo?"

"Where did you get it?"

This time, he let her push him away, and she scrambled backward as he stood. "I can't believe— You act like you've never seen it before," she said with a scornful laugh.

His jaw hardened. "We didn't exactly get naked, Jules."

Heat climbed her cheeks. Blazed away the cold under a fierce pulse of humiliation.

The memory hit her all at once, of her discarded jeans cast in shadow. Of her bare legs wrapped tightly around his waist as he braced her against the wall, muscles rigid as he thrust himself so deep inside her that he'd been forced to muffle her shameless cries with one hand. And then his own mouth. Her shirt had never made it off. Neither had his.

She jerked the fabric back up to cover herself. "It's always been there," she snapped, mortified that he had to remind her. The memories of that night, of the raw, fervent sex that had left parts of her psyche permanently embedded into that wall were too much to handle now.

Maybe ever.

"What do you mean, always been there?" he demanded, and her shoulders rounded.

"I mean," she threw back, "Delia said I was already branded when she found me."

His eyebrows winged upward.

Juliet sliced a dirty hand through the air. "Save your pity." Her voice cracked. "Delia found me when I was a baby, okay? She took me home, God knows why, but there you are."

The rectangle of black ink had never meant anything to her. Why should it? All her life, Juliet had never seen anything else like it. Speculation was all well and good, but it didn't pay for food.

Now she studied Caleb's taut expression, tying the ends of the torn fabric together, and remembered why she never spoke of it.

Pity. It always came on the heels of her parentless confession. Well, screw that for a laugh. She didn't need his pity. "Fine, now you know, can we move on?

His shoulders moved, twisted faintly. "You're an orphan?"

"Like I'm the only witch who is," she scoffed. Grief knotted her throat; she fought it back even as fatigue beat at the edges of her thoughts. She slumped. "Look," she said wearily, "Delia found me when she was six years old. She lived with a couple of strippers, okay? So I did, too."

"How old were you?"

"Don't know." Juliet plucked at the knot holding her tank top together. "Young enough to still need milk."

"Jesus—"

She cut him off with a sudden, sharp shake of her head. Droplets of water scattered across the pitted ground. "Don't even. So we were raised by prostitutes and strippers, so what? It wasn't the worst life ever."

"And the tattoo?"

"Will you listen to me?" she said sharply. "I already had it when Delia found me."

"She never said—"

"No," Juliet cut in, and she pressed two fingers into one throbbing temple. "She didn't know what it meant, and neither did anyone else. What's the big deal?"

Caleb centered the beam on her chest again, and Juliet resisted the urge to check the knot. "What did Cordelia—"

"God damn it, Caleb!"

The words exploded from her lips, bitter. Sharper than she meant, more ragged. So much more emotional than she ever wanted to reveal, especially to him.

Juliet surged to her feet with renewed vigor, adrenaline slamming through her body. Her head. The ache between her ears intensified.

The light in Caleb's hands jerked.

"Stop it," Juliet pleaded, almost a sob. She dragged her forearm across her lips, as if it would wipe away the grief. The regret; the not knowing. "Just stop it. My sister—fuck you," she cut in brokenly as he opened his mouth. "My sister is missing, okay? She's been missing since that day you killed everyone else I knew, Caleb. What do you *want* from me?"

His eyes narrowed. The light shifted, pointed down to the ground at her feet.

"I looked everywhere," she continued, leashing it down to a low, tense pitch. It hurt. It slammed through her chest like a howl demanding to get out, but she forced herself to be quiet. Contained. Like him. "I asked everyone I could find, everyone left. She knew about the coven, so I even went back to the park. I thought maybe she'd gone looking for me that day. I sifted— Jesus." She dragged her forearm over her eyes. "I even sifted through the rubble once the missionaries were gone, but they took all the bodies."

Caleb didn't blink. Didn't look away. "Are you blaming me for your sister?"

Juliet opened her mouth to say yes, to skewer him with all the rage and hatred and . . . and *loneliness* that she'd drowned in for the past year, but her breath snagged. Twisted. Something in her chest popped, pressurized, and Caleb flinched.

Features tightening, he splayed out a hand as if it could ward off a blow. "Jules. Stop it."

She seized her head between her palms. As if untwisting, uncoiling like a spring, the power rushed through her veins, thicker than blood and more intoxicating than any gin. It hammered at her temples, beat against the fragile cage of her ribs, and Juliet groaned from behind her clenched teeth.

"Juliet." Caleb's voice was much closer than only a moment ago. Warm hands fell on her shoulders. Callused fingers dug into her bare skin and shook. "Jules, get a grip on it."

Was that pain in his voice?

She sucked in a breath. Magic clawed at every lock, every restraint. Sweat gathered between her shoulder blades as she pushed her fingers into her temples. Hard enough to hurt. Hard enough to clear a space behind her eyes for thoughts to form.

"S-sorry," she gasped, her eyes squeezed shut. "Sorry. I can't—it comes like this. It . . . Oh, God, it always hurts."

The fingers left her shoulders. Cupped her face, framing her cheeks. Caleb tipped her face up. "Brace yourself," he said, so quietly that she wasn't sure she heard it. Or if her fevered, magic-high mind simply made it sound like that was his voice, suddenly gentle and tender.

Then a sharp pain, jarring and sudden across her cheek. Juliet gasped, eyes flying open.

Caleb's face was only inches from hers. His eyes, shrouded and intense, glittered into her own. Her cheek stung.

The pain helped. Pain always helped. She sucked in a gasp, mortified to find herself shaking from head to toe. "Str-stressed," she said, somehow managing to inject wry humor into it.

The thin press of his mouth softened. Just enough. "How long has this been happening?"

"I don't know. A while." Because she couldn't help herself, she slipped her fingers around his wrist. He stiffened. Juliet tightened her grip. "Please, I—"

She what?

Needed too much.

The magic slid from her, drained out from her skin like so much air and nothing. Slowly, unable to find the escape it needed, it flowed out through her feet and back to whatever grounded source her magic came from, leaving her feeling tapped. Drained.

Caleb disentangled himself. Gently.

Resolute.

"You just tried to get inside my skin," he said, matter-of-fact. Face impassive, he stood and offered her a hand. "Your power looked for magic to attach to. That's going to be a problem later."

"Later," she repeated, her chuckle catching. She cleared her throat. "When I . . . when I'm stressed, or tired. Sometimes it's stronger. It's one reason I . . ." She hesitated.

"Why you didn't rejoin the remainder of the coven," he supplied, as if he wasn't the reason the coven only *had* a remainder left.

"Yeah."

His hand hadn't moved. She took it, flinching as his fingers curled over hers. Warm. Warmer than she was, anyway. Steady.

"They used you," he said.

She flinched. "I know." It was barely a whisper.

His fingers tightened around hers, and smoothly, he lifted her easily to her feet. "Try to keep it under wraps," he said, suddenly brisk again. Cool. "I can't have you falling behind."

Juliet extricated her hand quickly, folding her arms over her chest as if that would help make up for the torn remains of her shirt.

As if it could keep her heart from picking up speed.

Anger curled into the base of her spine.

"You're intolerable," she said quietly.

He turned away. "I know," he said, but as if to himself. He palmed the light, swept the beam over the rocky ground. "Are you ready to walk?"

Ready, oh, yeah. And eager. She stamped her sodden feet. "Fine, absolutely. Let's."

He pushed off into the dark without another word and she followed, telling herself that she wasn't disappointed that he hadn't cared more to argue. She was ready to drop. He couldn't be feeling any better.

But if she stopped, she thought as she jammed

her hands into her jeans pockets and shivered, she'd only try to push him into the damned trench again.

Or dwell on the heat swirling inside her body. It wasn't all anger. It wasn't all fear and exhaustion and the lingering whisper of magic she wasn't sure how to control anymore.

Damn it. Why was she so thickheaded? Why did just the touch of his hands make her crazy?

She had been down that road and paid that toll until she'd bled. He was right. She was too soft to cut it. She even failed at revenge.

Juliet had nothing more to give.

CHAPTER FIVE

The man seated at the scarred bar table was the type Alicia ordinarily thought of as her kind of candy.

His hair was a gold-streaked brown, long enough to lead a girl to twine her fingers through it and short enough that he could style it away from his face. His features were precisely defined by edges, giving his expression a severity only softened by fine lips quirked up into an ever-present smirk.

His body beneath a blue flannel shirt and faded jeans was fit, the kind of hard body that wouldn't get tired easily. Muscled, broad without overwhelming, and relaxed in his own skin.

Alicia adjusted her hood with a quick tug of

two fingers, her eyes devouring every last inch of the latest man the Church had sent to yank her leash.

He liked to play. She'd put money on it. All the signs pointed to a smug sense of self-confidence, which was par for the course when it came to the Holy Order of St. Dominic. As far as she could tell, there were two kinds of Church operatives: zealots, and assholes.

This one had asshole written all over him.

She straightened, prepared to push through the small knot of rowdy barflies between her post at the back door and the table he'd so cleverly chosen in the middle of the dive. He shifted.

Alicia stilled.

She couldn't tell what color his eyes were, not in this horrific miasma of neon and smoke, but she couldn't possibly miss the intensity of it as he looked her way. As if reading her mind, the man smiled, and her brain power plummeted to a hard knock between her legs.

Oh. He was *good*.

No wonder men like Curio came to lead the coven. A witch had to be twice as sharp to keep up with the clever Church boys.

Giving up any pretense of subtlety, Alicia made no attempt to hide as she slipped through the noisy crowd. The few people who bothered to look away from the press of drinks served up at the bar would see only a slender woman in shiny black vinyl, with legs up to her chin and a hood shadowing most of her face.

They wouldn't know anything about the witchcraft simmering under her skin, and she relished the thought. One word, one gesture of her black-gloved fingers, and she could have them all begging for her.

Her power was more than sex.

The man didn't bother to get up. He kicked out a chair, and in the weak bar light, his eyes looked brown. "Have a seat."

She didn't. "Make this quick, pet," she said breezily, resting her hands on the back of the chair. "I've got things to do."

His smile edged into a crooked slant. Amusement sparkled in his gaze, all but leaked out every pore as he hooked an elbow over the back of his own chair. Not a care in the world. "What, no flex of witchy muscle? No attempts to seduce me with your sex-kitten wiles?"

Impatience flickered. What was this, a game? Well, to her, sure. She didn't like it when they thought so, too.

It was tempting, of course. But as her gaze slid over the corded muscle of his neck, traveled the vee of exposed skin at the collar of his shirt, she picked out the discolored edge of a tattoo.

Fuck the seal of St. Andrew. So this wasn't just any Church dog sent on an errand. He was a missionary, one of the witch hunters in the Order.

She wasn't stupid enough to flex magical muscle at a man protected by so-called holy magic.

Alicia leaned forward, just enough that he could see beneath the shiny black folds. Enough to see the gleam of her teeth, bared between strings of ropy scars. "Don't," she warned softly, "waste my time."

His eyes crinkled. "As you wish." He pulled a thin nylon envelope from his lap, tossed it artlessly to the table, which rocked on its single unsteady column.

Alicia eyed it. "What the fuck is this?"

"Language," the man chastised, laughter lacing his expression as her gaze flicked back to him.

"Look around, choirboy," she replied, stung despite herself. "Who the hell do you think will care?"

He laced his hands behind his head, leaning back precariously on a tall chair that creaked with the effort. Even under the thin flannel, muscles shifted. "Job for you, ma'am," he continued, as if she hadn't said anything at all. "And let me continue this novel idea of not wasting time. No, you have no choice. No, I don't think you'd survive refusing. And yes, they want it done now."

Her grip tightened on the chair back, vinyl gloves squeaking as her fingers rubbed against roughened wood. An icy claw of rage curved subtly, neatly into place behind her eyes.

Conceited asshole.

"What, then, is the job?" she asked sweetly.

"I bring you blood."

"Whose?"

"Not going to open it?" His eyes watched her face, steady and dark, and Alicia resisted the urge to pluck the edge of the hood forward. She knew damn well he couldn't see much more than the gleam of her eyes in the smoke-filled bar, and it pissed her off that uncertainty made her fingers twitch.

The unscarred side of her lips twisted. "Just tell me, pet, before I—"

"Fail to make it ten steps toward the door," he pointed out, his smile widening to something edged, with lots of gleaming white teeth. This time, the table rocked as he propped one brown work boot against the single center leg.

Another finger of fury snapped neatly into place. "Is that a threat?"

"I'm unarmed." And utterly unconcerned. Annoyed, she reached for the folder, stilled as he pinned one edge down with two fingers. "But I'll humor you . . . pet," he drawled. "You've been busy tonight, haven't you?"

"Not all of us sleep," she replied, smirking even as she forced herself not to tug on the trapped sachet. Instead, she braced her palms against the table, knowing how the shiny black pants she wore hugged her ass for the men at the far table to admire.

She loved that effect. Shame that current company was ruining her fun.

"Uh-huh." Unimpressed, the man whose name she refused to have to ask for let go of the folder. His fingers curled loosely around an unlabeled glass bottle; some bathtub swill dives like this hole-in-the-wall brewed in the back.

She didn't care. She hated beer. Classless stuff.

Wordlessly, she unzipped the envelope, straightening to tip its contents to the light. Plastic tubes glinted, banded neatly into place and filled with a dark fluid. Each tube sported a plain white label. *J. Carpenter*.

Well, well, well.

She plucked out a thin sheet of paper, pristine and probably expensive. She took her time reading its brief directions, and her eyes narrowed as she studied the letterhead at the top.

What the fuck was GeneCorp?

She turned her head back to him, raising an eyebrow he couldn't see as he tipped the contents of the bottle into his mouth. He swiped at his lips with the back of one hand. "Word has it that you caught Juliet Carpenter."

Dents formed in the padded neoprene. Alicia's knuckles ached with the sudden force of her grip. "So what?"

"Word follows," he continued with lazy good cheer, "that you lost her."

"*I* didn't—" she snarled, only to cut herself off. She hadn't lost anything. Banner had, the moron.

It was the last mistake he ever made.

She tucked the paper back inside, then set the binder down gently. Once more bracing her palms on the table, she framed the contained tubes of blood and asked icily, "What the *fuck* does the Holy Order want with Juliet Carpenter?"

"You just use that blood to get her back," he said, and tipped the bottle to his mouth again.

Alicia refrained from smacking it out of his hands. Just barely. Her palms itched with it. "How do you know about that ritual?"

He took his time swallowing. Finally, after he'd

swooshed the foul-smelling brew around in his mouth for a while, he swallowed and said with a shit-eating grin, "We're the Church, ma'am. We know everything."

"Fuck—"

"Language."

One word. It wasn't as if his expression changed. His smile remained. His eyes steady. His grip loose around the bottle, fingers leaving smudges on the brown glass.

But suddenly, Alicia felt as if every fine hair on her body was standing straight up. Sweat gathered under her arms, her palms, and she straightened with slow, deliberate calm.

Fury hammered at her skull. "Fine. We'll use the blood. We'll even deliver her to your precious GeneCorp."

"Yes. You will." The man raised his bottle once more, a salute that screamed dismissal. "Good luck. The Church will be in touch."

Alicia turned, tucking the nylon folder under her arm. Across the pitted, splintering floor, the three men huddled around the nearest tottering table smiled, nodded. If they only knew what kind of face topped an ass like hers, she thought, and forcibly relaxed.

"One more thing," she said, pausing just long enough to toss the sultry words over her shoulder.

The man leaned back in his chair, watching her. Her face, she realized, or where her face would be without the hood. Not her body.

Goddamned religious boys. What a waste.

"What's that?"

"If I ever catch you alone, pet," she said huskily, tightening her grip on the case, "I'm going to gut you."

His teeth flashed in her peripheral as she sauntered across the beer-stained floor. "My name's Simon," he called. "And you have yourself a deal, sweet cheeks."

The heavy, dented metal door swung closed behind her, and Alicia stepped over the filthy, prostrate figure of a drunk. The fumes practically seared her nose as she strode out into the alley.

The rain pounded the mottled pavement, splashed from the streets built in layers above and leaving everything in the lower streets slick and treacherous. Her heels clicked, counter to the rhythmic chaos of the city streets. Cars rattled by in irregular intervals, beaters and junkers too far gone to do anything but nurse along until they died.

She bypassed the streets for the back alleys, leading any Church operatives following her on a merry goddamned chase.

Fuck the Church. Fuck the smirking operative with his shitty taste in beer swill.

She might have inherited one hell of a partnership from Curio—and wasn't that the surprise of a lifetime?—but she wasn't going to marry the Church for it. Curio had milked the Holy Order for everything it was worth, and in exchange, they demanded the occasional errand.

It was, for the moment, a partnership she had no choice but to keep. The coven was all but shattered. The best and most powerful of them had been killed in Caleb's trap—God fucking *hate* him.

Even a year later, they were weak. They needed an infusion of power.

The pretty whore was going to make them strong again. No, Alicia would make them strong again. That was her job, now. Her goal.

Her calling.

Coven mistress.

Her smile stretched as she hugged the folder to her chest. Scar tissue twanged, stiff and corded. Pain mingled with pleasure; amusement and the lingering tendrils of bitter rage.

The Holy Order could send all the dogs it wanted to sniff her crotch. She'd use them all.

And flay the skin from every last one.

CHAPTER SIX

Caleb had always thought it fitting that the Coven of the Unbinding made its home down amid the unmarked graves of the forgotten. He knew that corpses seeded the ruins, many buried under tons of rock and plaster and cement. Most were victim to the earthquakes, and many more casualties of the fires and flooding that followed.

But some were more recent. Some he'd put there himself.

Like Cordelia Carpenter. The only family Juliet had ever known. An orphan.

Like I'm the only witch who is.

Damn.

It was raining, as only Old Seattle could know

it, and misery simmered into a dull, throbbing ache from his forehead to feet. Water streamed from the twisted nest of tangled pipes embedded into the cement ceiling far above. They helped drain the lower dregs of New Seattle into the empty ruins.

Helped keep the underground moist and rotting.

They walked in silence, step by bloody step. Every minute became a struggle, and he found himself focused on Juliet in front of him.

Pretty Juliet, Alicia called her. Lovely Juliet.

Snide. It was supposed to be. Few could have held a candle to Alicia's striking raven-haired beauty back in the day. And of the sisters, he had to admit, Delia had been prettier with her long blond hair and emerald-bright eyes.

But it was Juliet who had haunted him all those months ago. Whose wide, green eyes watched him from the fringes.

And who he had watched back, despite every fucking voice of reason in his head telling him not to.

What was he supposed to do?

Leave her the hell alone.

Especially knowing that her sister, a powerless prostitute dying from some unknown disease, had volunteered to be his final sacrifice in a bid to destroy a coven he had *seen* reaching for the stars.

A sacrifice that had cost Juliet so much more than it ever did him.

But he'd promised.

And she was a goddamned orphan. Why the hell

hadn't he known? In hindsight, he supposed it was obvious. Aside from shades of green eyes, she and Delia hadn't looked that much alike, but for Christ's sake, he and his own sister weren't exactly identical, either.

How was he to know?

And would it have mattered? Even knowing he wrenched away the only family Juliet had ever known, would he have stopped?

No.

The Coven of the Unbinding was bigger than his feelings. His needs.

Bigger than a sister.

That's what he'd told himself.

He dropped his head, blinking away the water as it dripped into his eyes, but that only put his gaze in line with her ass. The damned flashlight she held outlined her body in a halo of gold, knocking sense out of his skull with every feminine swing.

He knew that body.

Knew the feel of those legs around him, the heat of her skin beneath his palms, the sound of her voice as she climaxed— *For God's sake.*

He'd killed her sister and still lied about it. Destroyed the coven she had relied on. Screwed her and left her and dropped out of sight for over a year. Sacrifice and failure.

And then to find out that something about her, something in her magic, called to his?

Fuck. Shit. "Asshole," he muttered under his breath. Caleb was exactly that. An asshole. He had to be.

Because in order to find out exactly what Alicia and her remaining witches were up to, he was going to have to wrench open whatever vault sealed his power away.

Juliet Carpenter just might be the only key he had.

The pain in his head, the angry sound of hornets droning in his ears, had started with her. Her magic had reached out, feeling, extending. He could sense it. Something in him had responded, hammered at the invisible barrier that walled his magic off. Struggling to meet hers, merge with it.

Use it.

How, why? That, he didn't know.

Why did she share the same bar code tattoo as his own sister? That, he also didn't know, and he didn't like not knowing.

He'd find out. He had to. Everything depended on his visions; everything always had. Juliet, Jessie. The city.

The future.

Caleb tore his eyes from the tempting insanity of Juliet's hips and gritted his teeth, focusing his burning, watering gaze on the patch of ground separating them.

Fate was a bitch.

Trapped in a red mist of concentration and pain, he misjudged a step.

He stumbled, toe snagging on the ragged edge of a protruding metal cylinder. The next step barely made it off the rubble-strewn path, caught against something his blurring eyes couldn't see anymore and he pitched.

The ground was a hell of a lot closer than he'd thought. Grunting, joints cracking loudly in the endless, stifling quiet, he fell to his hands and knees. Sharp gravel gouged into his palms; excruciating pain lanced through his spine, his brain, out of his mouth on a four-lettered objection, and his sight crackled to white.

Splattered by flecks of red where drops of his own blood blurred into rivulets of water.

Weakness battered at his defenses. Exhaustion plucked at his resolve. He couldn't go on like this.

He couldn't stop, either.

Juliet sank to her knees beside him. "You're bleeding," she said sharply. "How long have you been— Damn it, Caleb!"

God, her voice, all sweet and breathless. Even when angry, even while poking at him in the middle of hell.

Caleb's laugh stuck in his throat. He shook off her restraining hand, forcing himself to sit back on his heels. He immediately regretted it as the world spun wildly around him, a thousand shades of black outside the tiny path of light the flashlight gave them.

He shook his head, swiping his forearm over his eyes. His vision cleared on her face. Concerned. Tired, hell, exhausted, but she'd always been a fighter.

Never tough enough, but determined as hell.

His fingers dug into the grit. "We can't stop," he said, but the words came out thick. Wrapped in fog.

"Yes, we can." She caught his unwounded shoulder, digging her fingers into the jacket to pull him back down as he struggled to stand. "And we're going to before you pass out. Take your jacket off."

"No."

Frustration etched grooves into her mask of concern. "There's no reason to be a hero here. We'll rest."

Caleb reached up, shackled his fingers around her wrist and tugged her hand away. "We keep moving," he said, and summoned every last ounce of willpower he had left to surge to his feet. The ground yawed wildly under him. He staggered, swore.

And found five feet and five inches of warm woman tucked against his side.

Juliet's fierce green eyes crackled a warning as she wrapped her arm around his waist. The other hand curled around his wrist, securing his arm over her shoulders and pinning him neatly to her side. "If you're going to be an idiot," she huffed, bracing against his weight, "I may as well help."

Warmth collected somewhere behind his breastbone, insidious and sweet.

He swallowed it down. "Can do it myself."

"Just shut up, please."

"It's not—"

"Caleb, I swear to God, if you don't shut up—"

He straightened so fast, she stumbled over her own feet. Without pausing to work it out, to think it through, he grabbed her shoulders. He told himself it was to steady her. To keep her from falling, to keep *him* from falling. Her eyes widened, her lips parted.

Caleb reminded himself that he was a liar.

He pulled her close enough to fit her body to his, to mold her curves from chest to thigh and invade every last inch of her space. She sucked in a breath.

He tightened his grip on her shoulders and dragged her up on her toes. The semihard ache between his legs strengthened to blinding lust as he rasped, "Just once more," and covered her mouth with his.

Short circuits shifted to fireworks. Sparklers of heat and need and fear and frustration shot through his veins and lit every nerve he had left. Her mouth opened helplessly beneath the onslaught of his kiss, her soft lips clung to his, rubbed until static became fire became savage need. He devoured her breath, her sweetness, swallowed her gasp and skimmed his fingers up the curve of her shoulder as she shuddered.

His thumbs slid along her jaw, tightened as she pushed herself harder against him. Angling her head, he swept in for a deeper kiss, tongue thrusting between her teeth to taste the dark heat of a craving he damn well didn't want to acknowledge.

Pain simmered into longing, satisfaction with the raw edge of a bone-deep anger. He growled deep in his chest, slid his tongue along hers. Her arms twined around his neck, her nails skimming his nape and forcing another rough sound from his throat as she bit at his lower lip.

The small pain, rough and surprising, slammed straight to his dick and squeezed.

He'd done this before. He knew how easy it would be to sweep her off her feet, haul her into his arms, and plaster her body against some wall somewhere; spread her out on the wet ground and sink into her until he didn't have to remember anything but his own name as she whispered it in the dark.

You'll break her if you try.

Guilt sliced through his conscience, leaving bloody furrows that tore his mouth from hers and left him reeling.

With a low sound of impatience, Juliet twisted his shirt in her hands and slid the hem up. Logic and desire clashed. Burned. "Not again," she whispered, but her eyes were heavy-lidded, veiled by the lacy fan of her smudged lashes. "Heaven help me, but something about you—"

Groaning, he threw back his head as her fingers slid over the clenched muscles of his stomach. Her touch left a trail of fire in its wake, shimmers of wanting and impatience and, hell, raw lust that shot straight to the pulsing erection trapped beneath the confining rasp of his jeans.

"God." Her voice caught as her hand curved over the ragged tissue at his left side.

The scars he bore. The scars he'd created himself.

He wrenched back from that touch, jerked away before her single syllable could turn to revulsion. Moved too fast, too eager to put distance between them; his body fought him, and he sank to a knee as pain swamped his synapses. It overwhelmed everything in a flurry of craving and agony and fatigue.

The buzzing in his head was back, like rusty nails on glass. He panted for breath.

Juliet staggered, her cheeks flushed in the dim light, eyes hazy as she struggled to help him and keep herself from pitching over at the same time.

The world turned orange and white. A column of flame arced overhead, lighting the ruins like a comet, and she jerked, startled. As effective as a bucket of ice water.

Caleb lurched back to his feet with more intensity than he had the energy for. "Coven," he hissed, as if it wasn't obvious. He tried to push her behind him, but Juliet caught his arm, draping it around her shoulders.

He couldn't argue. It beat falling on his face in front of the enemy.

They slipped out of the shadows around them. Caleb fought to keep from swaying as one of the figures stepped into the light. He managed to put together a face covered with tattoos and grimaced.

A faint gleam of blue winked out as the witch tucked something small and glassy into his pocket. He raised a silver revolver in his other hand, pointing it at them with steady ease. "Well, damn. It worked," he said, and grinned. "How about that?"

Caleb's chin drooped. "How many are there?" he murmured. "I might be seeing double."

Juliet shifted under his weight. "Two."

"That's all?"

"So far," she told him dourly. "Give them time."

No kidding. "Get ready," he murmured, tensing as the tattooed witch stepped closer.

"So this is how it goes," the tattooed witch began, only to swear as Caleb snapped out a hand and flung the flashlight at him. The light spun, end over end, and Caleb shoved Juliet to the ground just as a gunshot cracked through the false night.

She yelped, pained sound cut short as he landed on her, barking his elbows and one knee. The breath knocked out of her, she gasped as the gunshot echoes slammed back from every direction.

Real guns, real bullets, real magic. They had to be out to kill.

Or were they?

Maybe not.

Juliet shifted beneath him, and he closed his eyes.

Gentle. He didn't have the luxury.

Firelight flickered into sudden, vivid life. It threw shadows across the wicked orange panels of light dancing over every ruin, every crumbling wall and twisted remnant of structures gone to rot. Fire outlined them all in stark radiance.

He didn't have any other options.

Rolling off her, Caleb jumped to his feet, seized Juliet by the arms, and yanked her up. Wordlessly, ignoring the shocked flare of her eyes, he spun her around, pinned one arm behind her back, and locked his forearm at her throat.

Juliet froze in his arms, every muscle clenched. "Caleb?"

He didn't look at her. He stared at the two witches, each outlined by the fire witch's flame. "The way I hear it," he said, almost conversationally, "you're not supposed to kill her."

The tall, lanky man with a shock of bleached hair over one eye took a step forward. Fire pooled over his palm like water. It dripped to the ground, liquid flame that sizzled out as it hit wet rock and dirt.

One wrong move, and that magic could engulf them both. Just the thought of it made the skin between his shoulder blades itch in memory.

Caleb wrenched Juliet's arm higher, forcing her to cry out.

The fire witch stopped mid-step, but the tattooed witch watched him calmly. "Where will you go?" he asked, the black line of his lower lip set into a smirk. "You can't run, soothsayer." He patted his pocket. "Not from us."

"You think," he lied, forcing Juliet to take a step back with him, "that I haven't *seen* this? Go ahead, gentlemen. Ask me how you die."

The younger witch glanced at the tattooed one.

"I can't believe I trusted you," Juliet hissed. Her voice cracked on the arm he lodged against her esophagus. She clung to his forearm with her free hand and spat, "I hate you."

Let her.

Caleb shook his head as the pressure in his temples mounted. Pulsing in his ears, the droning hum thickened; he fought back the pain.

The knocking onslaught of Juliet's magic.

Focus. He had to focus.

The tattooed man sighted down the length of his extended arm. The gun winked, catching the light and reflecting it back to his wild grin. "You think I can't make this shot?"

"I think you're not stupid enough to try," Caleb replied. *Please, God, don't be stupid enough to try.*

Juliet shuddered, her skin suddenly clammy under his grip. "Oh, no," she whispered. The pain in her voice was worse than any bullet could ever be.

Caleb locked his jaw.

"Alive doesn't mean unhurt," the witch said simply.

"I hate you," she said brokenly, voice scratchy and raw. "I'm so stupid. I let you do it again, I can't . . . I can't—"

Sweat pooled at the base of his spine as Caleb met the leader's eyes over the glinting weapon. "You hurt her—" he began, so softly, so dangerously that even he didn't recognize his own voice, but the man winked.

Bang, he mouthed silently.

Shit.

Caleb was already moving as the witch pulled the trigger. Juliet shrieked as he whipped her around, locking his ankle between hers, and sent her sprawling to the broken ground. Pain detonated through his left side; too-tight skin and ligaments shrieked as they stretched and popped and tore.

A new pain sliced through his right, meeting somewhere in the middle and culminating in a rough, ragged breath as Caleb completed his spin. He lowered his head to charge, but the buzzing noise in his head turned to something white-hot and frenetic.

His feet scraped over rubble. His legs gave out, sent him sprawling.

Juliet sobbed something behind him, and he struggled to push himself to his feet. His elbows folded, dumping him face-first to the ground and earning him a mouthful of grit. Swearing, gasping, he struggled to push through the feverish pressure.

His limbs weren't working.

Somewhere to his right, a column of fire erupted into a geyser of flame. A thousand shards glittered back as it licked the ceiling pipes, rusted stars in his pulsating vision. A man shrieked; was it him?

No, Caleb couldn't breathe deeply enough to scream. Agony shredded his head, lanced through his nerves and filled every reduced breath with something thick and wet and torturous. The ruins turned orange, flickered violently to an eerie, demonic blue as Juliet screamed behind him.

Another voice rose. Long and loud and excruciating. Caleb scrabbled at the rock, his fingers too thick, his body slipping and sliding as he half crawled, half dragged himself toward her.

Pale skin, wild hair, lunatic eyes; her features branded themselves into his mind as the fire guttered out. Juliet screamed. Screamed and screamed until her voice became claws piercing into his brain, digging and scrabbling and wrenching until something tore.

Corpses. Twisted limbs and no faces; numbers. Only numbers, burning to ash.

Caleb collapsed. As the world went black around him, as something warm and wet pooled beneath him, the droning died to blissful nothing.

CHAPTER SEVEN

Juliet was dreaming. She had to be. Nothing else could explain the blissful comfort soaking through her weary muscles, or the softness she buried her head into.

Warmth. It settled over her skin like a blanket, sweet and all but alien, while her body drifted aimlessly through nothing.

She didn't hurt.

Of course it was a dream.

She opened her eyes.

The sweet intensity of summer sunshine speared through her head like a diamond spike. Juliet sat up, yelped as her forehead scraped against blue canvas, and rolled over so quickly her head spun.

She stared at the downy pillow trapped under her braced hands while the world settled back into place. Beneath her face, the patchwork pillowcase was soft, worn from repeated washing.

Wholly unfamiliar.

She turned her head. A few feet from her covered bed, giant swaths of green fronds fanned out in a lacy frame. She inhaled, smelled a fragrance that was all at once thick, oddly suffocating, and spicy at the same time, and shook her head hard.

This wasn't a dream, but where the hell was she?

Where was Caleb?

And why, she thought as she pulled herself gingerly to her knees, didn't she hurt?

She stared down at the worn brown skirt wrapped around her hips, plucked at the snug, short-sleeved yellow T-shirt now doing its best to contain her braless chest.

Who had undressed her?

"Where the hell is my underwear?" she asked aloud, cupping her breasts in each miraculously clean hand. It felt odd to be without a bra. She'd always worn at least a sports bra, even when she slept. The street didn't usually give her enough peace to strip down for anything longer than a quick shower in a stolen room, so she'd gotten used to the support.

Of course, now someone had seen her naked. Someone unknown.

And taken all her clothes!

Heat singed her cheeks as she gathered the skirt in one hand and eased out from under the canvas.

The sunlight struck her full in the face, blinding her. She let go of the skirt to shade her eyes with both hands, then stared down at it as the material floated to her calves. How long had it been since she'd worn a skirt?

She had been twelve, she remembered suddenly. A baby to Delia's eighteen. Her hair had still been light brown and soft, pinned up by garish ribbons and bows while she'd strutted around in drooping layers of fake silk and worn lace. Delia and the other women at the club had thought it adorable.

Now it seemed like a lifetime ago.

She shook her head. The streets of New Seattle didn't leave room for adorable. So, what? Pushing aside the wistful thought, she studied the patch of open dirt surrounded by towering plants that looked like pronged, flat fans.

There was the tent—little more than blue canvas strung taut between thick stakes and a waterproof tarp beneath it—and a path behind it. The plants, the smell, the humid air all made her feel as if she'd stepped into a tropical paradise.

And somewhere in the distance, she heard voices. They were indistinguishable, but it meant she wasn't alone.

And if she wasn't dead. . .

Juliet crossed her fingers and followed the path.

Carved stepping stones had been placed at regular intervals, worn smooth and gleaming against the dark earth. They were warm against her bare feet—where the hell were her shoes?—and oddly glassy. Each had been carved, and she bent to run her fingers over one with speculative interest.

The ritual symbol for home decorated it. The one after revealed a character for protection. So . . . she was among witches?

It might work out in her favor. Then again, if they were aware of her power, it might not. It was a rare witch who refused the opportunity to become so much more powerful than their inherent magic allowed.

Like Caleb.

He'd never wanted her power.

Just her body.

She squashed that inner voice before it hit her heart, focusing instead on the stepping stone in front of her. Juliet hated her ability. Useless on its own, but she could be used. A perfect word. *Used.* Like a dishrag, or a puppet.

Right, then. As usual, she'd have to stay on her toes and keep her mouth shut. And find Caleb.

She didn't have to travel far before the giant fronds opened into a clearing that took her breath away. Cliff walls rose high into the brilliant blue sky, surrounding a cove carved into the shape of an uneven crescent. To her left, a dock jutted out from the rocky ledge of the shore.

Sunshine sparkled on water the color of cut green glass, so vivid and still that she was seized with an urge to see if she could walk on it. Not a ripple marred its surface, though a faint gray haze lingered over it.

The smell of sulfur was stronger here, curling into her nose with its acrid afterburn.

Juliet sidled out of the concealing foliage, tracing the same glassy path stones leading to a small house set at the point of one end of the semicircular bay. It was painted a darker green than the water, with a handful of mismatched windows set into its walls.

They caught the sunshine, threw it back in a diamond sparkle and sent fingers of light dancing through a twisted mass of violet flowers hanging high over the house's roof.

Juliet scraped her hair back from her face with both hands and stared at the fairy-tale house with its fairy-tale purple bower. Had she gone crazy? Was she still somewhere in the depths of Old Seattle, aimlessly wandering around while her mind languished in this made-up haven?

Had Caleb bled to death in her wake?

The voices, muffled and indistinct, came from the house. People were arguing. She couldn't make out the words, but she knew the cadence. Someone was angry.

She hurried away from the concealing foliage, toward the house with its reinforced front stoop. One bare foot settled on the first step as one of the voices rose. Feminine. Furious.

"That's *twice*. We're going on two times that you pulled this same bullshit on me—"

"It wasn't by choice." The sound of Caleb's voice rumbled through the barrier of plaster and wood and whatever else lay concealed by the paint. Juliet found herself splaying her fingers against the sun-warmed surface, as if she could feel him there.

He wasn't angry like the woman was. Her voice shook with it; his was quieter, calmer. As it usually was, she thought, grimacing.

The woman laughed. It lashed. "You're so full of it. How many times are you going to go sailing off into the dark?"

"I told you—"

"You've told me nothing." Juliet flinched at the raw emotion in the single sentence, hesitated as it continued bitterly, "You go out of your way to tell me nothing. How many charms did you have to wear this time, huh? Did you find some flint? Is that why I couldn't find you?"

White flint, to sever bonds. Juliet flashed to the memory of the sharpened white stone as it fell to the carpet at Caleb's feet. Who was this woman that she knew so much?

What was she to Caleb?

"It was better for you to think I was dead," Caleb said.

She snorted. "I knew you weren't dead. You idiot, I *always* know. Were you ever planning to come back? Don't lie to me," she said, so quickly that Juliet knew she'd cut him off. "I taught you how to do that, remember? I'm not stupid, Caleb."

She rested her cheek against the wall. Their voices became rhythm and sound, muffled through paint and plaster.

"Look, it was necessary," Caleb said curtly. "Trust me, I didn't have a whole hell of a lot of choices."

"If you say that one more time," seethed the woman, "I swear to God, I'm going to hogtie you to a goddamned heater. It didn't work for me, but maybe, just *maybe* it'll work for you. And who the crap is the girl?"

Juliet held her breath.

"No, don't," she added bitterly. "I can already see the lie forming."

He said something too low for her to hear, but the woman made a sound halfway between a groan and a laugh. Footsteps thudded somewhere inside.

"Visions," the woman spat. "It's always the same with you. You forced me out of the game *again*, and all you can do is sit there and tell me you had to. *Had* to. You stupid, moronic, holier-than-thou, *macho*— Don't!" she snapped, so suddenly that Juliet jerked away from the wall.

"What's wrong?" Caleb asked, and his voice seemed nearer. Louder. "You're hiding something from me."

"Oh, can I join the fucking club, then?"

"What's going on?"

"What," the woman said, amusement sharp in her tone, "you can't *see* it?"

Juliet looked up at the violet flowers and held her breath.

"That's not my gift, and you know it." Caleb's reply was much calmer than Juliet felt, with her heart pounding in her chest. Should she be here? Should she be listening to this?

What if they were lovers?

The thought caused a knot in her throat that ached to swallow. It coiled an answering throb through her temples. Slowly, cautiously, she eased her foot off the stoop.

Somewhere inside, ceramic clattered.

"Damn. She's awake," the woman said. "Go get her before she runs."

Juliet jerked back, turned. She made it two steps toward the side of the house before the door slammed open behind her, and she froze with her hand braced against the wall.

"Juliet."

Her name. One word. It fisted in her gut like a curse.

A bloody benediction.

She turned slowly, but no amount of fortification could shield her from the shock of seeing him. Caleb's eyes pinned hers, trapped her in a field of blue, but it wasn't his gaze that made her gasp. "Your face!"

He took the two steps to the ground with ease. There wasn't a hint of pain, not a wince or whisper of discomfort. His features were stern, but unmarred save for the scars. No bruises. No cuts. Just the healed fissures climbing his jaw.

His faintly twisted lip quirked. Self-deprecation. "We were lucky enough to find a healer. Can you travel?"

Behind him, a blond woman braced her arms on either side of the doorframe and glared. Her brown eyes glittered in her fine, pixie face, though her skin seemed too pale. Faintly clammy. "Oh, no, you don't," she said firmly. "You're not going anywhere."

"I can," Juliet said, her gaze darting between them both. "Where—"

"Get your things. Let's go." Caleb ignored the

woman. "We aren't safe here." The woman stepped onto the porch. "We're leaving," he added over his shoulder.

"Over my dead body."

Juliet shook her head, amused and bewildered and feeling too much like she'd just stepped into a minefield. "I don't know where my things are."

"Jess," Caleb warned.

"Cale," the woman mimicked in the same tone, her grip white-knuckled on the frame. "You want to throw down? I'll kick your ass. I've been getting lessons."

Juliet's gaze snapped to the woman, took in the tumbled waves of her golden hair. The high cheekbones and her fine, straight nose, almost identical to Caleb's. Her features were daintier, with a delicate definition that Caleb lacked, and the eye color was different, but there could be no mistake.

She'd never met Jessica Leigh. But coming face-to-face with the witch Curio had wanted to sacrifice was a kick to her already bruised conscience.

She covered her mouth with both hands. "You're the seer," she groaned through her fingers. "Oh, my God."

The woman flipped her a crooked smile, ignoring her brother. "Don't call me that," she said. "My name's Jessie. And don't worry about it. Caleb tells me you weren't among the party trying to kill us."

She wasn't, no. The day the Coven of the Unbinding had gone up in flames, the day they'd captured the seer, Juliet had been gone. Afterward she'd thought Jessica Leigh—the witch who could see the present—was dead.

Then again, she'd thought the same of Caleb, the witch who could see the future.

Had the seer worked with her brother to destroy her coven?

Who else had lived that she now thought dead? Curio?

Delia?

Juliet straightened, her shoulders going rigid as Caleb reached for her arm. "Don't touch me," she hissed, and he froze. His palm hovered for a half second before he shook his head, fingers locking around her forearm.

Juliet wrenched at it, but his grip was implacable. "Who else is alive, Caleb?" she demanded, rounding on him.

He took a step back, surprise flickering through his eyes. "What?"

"Who else is alive that I thought dead? Curio?" Her fist jerked, trapped in his hold. "My sister?"

His gaze flicked over her shoulder, then back. "I killed Curio myself," he said flatly. "He's dead."

She couldn't deal with this. "Where am I?" she demanded. Her head pounded.

On the porch, Jessie leaned against the back of a worn wooden rocking chair. "You're safe," she said. Despite her pallor, she smiled reassuringly as she added, "Naomi healed you both, for what good that'll do." The look she shot Caleb crackled.

He ignored her, staring at Juliet with fixed intensity. "Trust me," he said, so seriously that she had to laugh.

Laughter would only have choked her. "What happened?" she demanded instead. "Why am I here?"

A muscle ticked in his jaw. "I don't know."

"Bull," she shot back.

Jessie snorted. "He was out cold when we found you guys," she offered, resting her chin on her folded arms. "You both were. There was a charred body about ten feet away and a whole lot of blood. Some of it my little brother's."

Despite herself, Juliet's eyes trailed over Caleb's shoulders. His chest, covered in a threadbare T-shirt.

"He's fine," Jessie added, more astutely that Juliet was comfortable with. "He'd been shot in the back, though." She arched a fine eyebrow. "Your doing?"

"No," Caleb answered flatly, his grip tight on Juliet's arm. She tugged at it, but her attention wasn't on him, or the byplay between the siblings. She wracked her memory, frowning.

All she could recollect was pain. Pressure.

The certainty that Caleb would die.

"Did you save us?" she asked.

"Oh, yeah. As much as my brother pisses me off," Jessie answered, her smile tired, "I love him. As soon as I got the message"—the word held a depth of meaning that Juliet found puzzling—"Naomi and I went looking."

"Message?"

Caleb pointed at his sister as she hesitated. "Okay, that's it. Why the hell are you so pale?" he demanded.

"Staying up all night worrying is hell on a girl's complexion. You were practically dead on your—" Jessie straightened abruptly, shading her eyes as she stared at something beyond them. Her smile faded. "Oh, shit."

They all turned as a splash echoed out in the lagoon. A boat glided over the green water, manned by a woman with magenta-streaked hair and a face full of silver piercings that caught the light, returning it in a flurry of bright color. The line of her too-full mouth was tense.

She guided the canoe to the dock, but it was the man forging through knee-deep water that seized Juliet's attention. He was big, broad-shouldered, and heavily muscled. His close-cropped dark hair matched the thick eyebrows furrowed over eyes narrowed into slits as he pushed toward the house at a pace that promised violence.

Caleb's grip tightened over her forearm. Juliet winced. "You're hurting—" It broke on a gasp as he jerked her behind him, so suddenly that she stumbled, forced to grab the back of his shirt for balance. His muscles bunched under her touch, rock hard and leashed in rigid anticipation.

The action placed him squarely between her and the man with murder in his scowl.

"What's going on?" she demanded.

Caleb said nothing.

Jessie leaned over the rocking chair. "Silas, don't you dare!"

The big man ignored her. Ignored Juliet, who could only stare, frozen in place, as he seized Caleb by the collar and landed a punch that cracked like a gunshot across the crescent canyon.

His shirt ripped out of her hands as Caleb slammed into the side of the house. Windowpanes rattled, something crashed to the floor inside, and Jessie swore fiercely as she tripped over the stairs. She hit the ground so fast that Juliet spun, torn.

The woman's fingers dug into the packed earth. As she shuddered, Juliet knelt, wrapping a supportive arm around her shoulders. "Are you all right?"

Jessie grabbed her shirt, fingers digging into Juliet's ribs. Her face was paler, almost yellow, but her mouth twisted into a hard, angry line. "Naomi!"

"On it." The extraordinarily tall woman with Asian features breezed past them to hook an arm around Silas's raised fist. She locked her legs as the momentum of the trapped punch wrenched her shoulder. "Smith! Come on, I just fixed him."

Caleb watched dispassionately, blood and mucus streaming from his nose. It edged his mouth, set in a fine line that mirrored his sister's.

Silas tried to shake Naomi off. "You can fix him again," he growled, his gaze locked on Caleb.

Naomi grunted, twisting the larger man's arm behind him with effort. She hooked his other arm at the elbow and hauled him awkwardly backward.

The man wrenched at her grip, his face red, teeth bared. "You murdering bastard," he said, his voice like thunder. "Let me go, I'll beat his fucking—"

Naomi kicked at his knee as he jerked one arm

free. The man grunted, face going white. "Don't say I never do nothing for your princess," she told the top of his head.

He cursed.

Juliet's confusion flipped to sudden alarm as Jessie's eyes fluttered. "Not," the woman murmured, "good."

"Caleb!" Juliet cried.

The seer turned to deadweight in her arms, and Jessie buckled, pitching to the ground in a tangle of gold hair and flailing limbs.

In the space of a single second, chaos flattened to frozen, brutal silence. Then it exploded. Naomi let Silas go, locked an ankle around his legs, and swept his feet out from under him.

The man hit the ground swearing. Juliet cradled Jessie's head, stared helplessly as Caleb blotted at the blood streaming from his nose and yelled something lost in the fury of Silas's angry orders.

He surged away from the wall, tripped as Silas grabbed his ankle and wrenched him off-balance. He sprawled on his ass, furious.

In the disorder, Naomi calmly knelt by Jessie and laid two fingers against the woman's throat. She flicked Juliet a glance, her eyes impossibly trapped between blue and purple in color.

"Who're you again?"

"Juliet," she replied, taken aback.

"Can you help me get her inside, Juliet?"

"What about—"

"Let 'em kill each other." She heaved the unconscious blond into her arms. "Right now, I need a little common fucking sense."

CHAPTER EIGHT

Parker Adams, New Seattle Mission director, slowly laid her fingertips against the scarred surface of her borrowed desk and struggled to keep her features impassive. "With all due respect," she began, then forced herself to bite her tongue as the woman in front of her raised one imperious hand.

"As you know, the Holy Order of St. Dominic requires a certain level of competency from each of its core foundations," the woman said. Her tone oozed disdain. "The latest audits are beginning to show a disturbing pattern. Turnover, betrayal, and neglect."

The director's spine straightened. "With," she repeated, icy precision, "all due respect, Mrs."—

she glanced at the digital readout in front of her—
"Parrish, I think that if you take the time to look
over the New Seattle Mission's docket, you'll find
that our percentile of success meets or exceeds
every minimum requirement laid out by Mission
protocol."

The woman smiled.

A headache threatened. Earlier this morning,
Parker had been foolish enough to think that today might actually have turned into a good day.
One team was out in the field on a mission that
had every probability of ending in success, and
the typical office emergencies had been kept to a
minimum.

To be fair, she realized that her own office was
run too smoothly to have many emergencies, and
the lower city offices still didn't trust her enough
to risk bothering her with their own.

But for now, she'd take it. The betrayal of their
last Mission director had hit them all where it
hurt. A year's worth of hard work and longer
hours hadn't quite smoothed over the chasm David Peterson had caused.

Still, there was some small success.

Which had been shredded the instant she had
received a summons and arrived at the mid-low
headquarters to find this pale, diminutive woman
tearing into her missionaries.

They'd all stood to attention, staring at a spot
just over the woman's head, but Parker could only
imagine how many verbal daggers the woman
had flung with authority.

No one spoke to her missionaries that way.

Except her.

Parker had icily ordered the missionaries back to their desks, hoping to spare them any more venom from the sharp-tongued Mrs. Parrish. Now, she found herself fighting a headache as she went toe to toe with a woman whose authority, as far as the digital readout could tell her, went as high as Sector Three. Exactly two clearance levels higher than her own.

Damn and blast.

"As I was saying," the woman said through thin, colorless lips. Her voice was like gravel, grating even in quiet tones. "There is a certain amount of accuracy required in every foundation, and although the Mission's record has been fairly reliable, there are some small matters that require a . . . more precise touch."

Political code for internal affairs.

Parker studied her quietly.

The woman was short, rail-thin, and pushing sixty. The kind of woman whose brown hair was probably chemically maintained, and whose neatly pressed brown skirt suit likely had never seen a department store rack. Her cheeks were thin and hollow, her brown eyes nondescript behind frameless glasses.

Her hair was pulled back into a neat bun at the nape of her neck, glossy and unforgiving, and Parker didn't miss the speculative glances the other missionaries kept sending through the slatted window of the office.

Parker's own hair, though a detested copper red, was also pulled into a severe knot at the back of her head. It was the easiest way to keep it out of her face. She resisted the urge to pat it into place, disliking her own silent comparison between them.

"I'm afraid," she said with careful calm, "that I'm not sure what you're trying to convey, Mrs. Parrish."

The woman's fingers folded around a readout of her own, and she flipped it open. Its knitted cover boasted flowers, like something a grandmother would make. "Missionary Silas Smith," the woman said.

Parker's face remained impassive.

"Missionary Naomi West," Mrs. Parrish continued, peering through the bifocals carved into the bottom lenses of her glasses. "Mission Director David Peterson."

Blast. "Silas Smith and David Peterson both turned rogue," Parker replied evenly, "before my tenure. You *have* read the reports, yes?"

No matter what angle it came from, Mrs. Parrish's smile was disturbing. Thin, precise, and pinched. "Refresh me."

Politics. She could play them. "Of course," she said. "Agent Silas Smith was trained here in the New Seattle Mission. After a particularly difficult operation, he was released from city service to work abroad. Fourteen years later, he was brought back during David Peterson's occupancy as director. Agent Naomi West detailed in her report the events that led to Smith's betrayal and subsequent death. In the interim, Peterson was ousted as a coven infiltrator."

Not even a flicker of an eyelash.

The Church knew all this. Maybe more. What Director Adams wanted to know was *how*. How did a witch make it to Mission director without anyone knowing? How had he passed the tests?

Parker braced her legs behind the cover of the desk and continued coolly, "Agent Naomi West went missing after completing a mission that was ordered, of course, by the Church itself."

"Missing."

"She had already been flagged for surveillance," she explained with brusque efficiency. "Director Peterson had been less than apt at keeping an eye on the ongoing health of his teams. I've rectified that."

"Of course you have," Mrs. Parrish said, reassurance served with a twist of condescension.

"The bounty on Naomi West is currently at fifty thousand dollars dead, twice that if brought in alive. She's an apt candidate for processing," Parker told her. "*If* she's still alive, we'll find her."

"I'm sure you will," the woman said, again in a smooth tone that didn't match the words. "Unfortunately, these stains are not something that can be simply . . . talked away."

Parker's unwavering gaze had been known to make the biggest men of her units resist the urge to sidle behind the nearest heavy object. "Is this a disciplinary action, Mrs. Parrish?"

"Not yet." Mrs. Parrish had a gaze of her own, and Parker forced herself to meet it head-on. "In that readout," the woman continued, "you'll note a new priority."

She hadn't yet, but then, the woman hadn't given her any time.

Mrs. Parrish continued blithely, "I don't care what you choose to name it, but this will be placed at the top of your to-do. Now, the Church has inferred that you'll need extra hands, given your . . ." She paused tactfully. "Shall we call it, *loss* of experienced agents?" With the same disturbing little smile, she turned and picked her way across the clean but threadbare carpet. Her sensible, one-inch heels rasped across the floor, making Parker's jaw ache as she set her teeth.

This wasn't going well.

Regardless of what Parker said aloud, the Church had every right to investigate her teams. Two rogues—one a witch, even, straight from the greatest coven threat known to the Mission—and a missing agent who had long since been flagged for processing were a black spot on everybody's record.

The woman opened the door. Parker's fingers spasmed against the desk. She very carefully placed them on her hips, resisting the need to smooth down the tailored cream-colored suit she'd worn.

Two men stepped into the frame behind Mrs. Parrish. They split, one flanking each side. "Director Adams, these men are missionaries. As of this conference, they are assigned to your offices."

Parker's eyes narrowed. A fraction.

"This is Agent Tobias Nelson," Mrs. Parrish continued, gesturing to a tall, very broad man at her left. He nodded, a faint, more than slightly pa-

tronizing gesture. His eyes were a brown so dark
that they were almost black. His hair shadowed
his scalp, thick black fuzz buzzed short. He was
large, wide, meaty, and probably good to have in
a fight.

Parker didn't fight, but her street-level teams
did.

Their casual, loose clothing and well-developed
builds suggested they did, too. Nelson's T-shirt
did nothing to conceal the thick bulge of his arms.

The other man didn't wait for an introduction.
He slid into one of two chairs arrayed in front of
Parker's borrowed desk, kicking one ankle up over
his knee in easy comfort. "I'm Simon Wells," he
offered, tipping an imaginary hat. His brown hair
was longer, the same shade as the coffee-colored
desk between them. His eyes twinkled at her, an
odd mix of green and brown, and his lips curved
into an engaging smile that she didn't return.

Flirt. She knew the type.

Parker offered them both a nod. "Gentlemen,"
she said coolly. Then, to the woman who waited
expectantly between them, she arched one icy
eyebrow. "Explain to me why the Church is plac-
ing their men in my Mission."

The woman's expression hardened. "Your Mission, Director Adams, is the Church's Mission. Ef-
fectively *my* Mission. Your job is to oversee and
maintain the Church's interests—*my* interests—in
this field, at the whim of the Order that you serve.
These interests include, but are not limited to, the
investigation and execution of witches, the ongoing protection of the innocents of this city, and

whatever else I say." Her eyes glinted behind the cut glass edge of her spectacles. "Shall I presume that there is no confusion on the subject?"

Parker's lips compressed into a thin line. "None."

"Excellent. Then I trust you'll see that my new missionaries are welcomed and made comfortable. They will, of course, be assigned to the docket spoken of earlier."

Parker didn't look at either man, certain that if she did, she'd snap. Instead, she inclined her head in a frosty nod. "Thank you, Mrs. Parrish. And in turn, I trust that with their acclimation, the Church will see that the New Seattle Mission continues to thrive."

"Of course," the thin woman said, poker-faced. "Missionaries. Director." With that, she turned and left the office. Her padded shoes didn't click once the carpet turned into scuffed, bare tile. Parker watched her round the corner, then pass the glass walls that separated this office from the open desks filling the main room.

More eyes than hers watched the older woman go. Parker didn't relax.

The one called Tobias Nelson turned for the door.

Parker snapped her gaze back to him. "Hold it."

He halted, but only just. His head turned enough that she could see the set of his jaw, and Wells tipped back in his chair with an inquisitive smile.

"Have you both been sealed?" she asked.

Nelson grunted. "Yes."

"I want to see them."

In front of her, Wells's smile edged into something wicked. He rubbed two fingers along the shadow of his stubbled jaw. "Why, Miss Adams, I hardly know y—"

She cut him off with a look carved from ice. "That's *Director* Adams, and I reserve the right to inspect my team anytime, anywhere I so choose." Her voice hardened. "Your loyalties can fall to whomever you want outside this office, but while you're in my unit, you follow *my* orders. If there is *any* doubt, there's the door."

She didn't have to say aloud what fell between her and the men arrayed in front of her. It was as crystal as if she'd carved it on the desk.

Your choice.

Damn, but she hoped they made the wrong one.

That easy smile reached Wells's eyes, and from a frame of dark lashes, something glinted. "Yes, ma'am," he said solemnly.

Her fingers twitched. She forced herself to keep them from curling into fists. Her glance flicked to Nelson, who had only half turned. He watched her.

Her stare drilled into his.

The seconds ticked by.

"Just do it," Wells said quietly, and the big man's scowl bit hard. Wordlessly, he yanked up the right sleeve of his plain cotton T-shirt.

To her left, Wells slid two of his shirt buttons free, baring more of a chest defined by muscles that were thick, but hardly as meaty as his partner's.

Parker circled the desk, her four-inch spike heels snagging on the carpet with every step. She ignored it. She didn't touch Nelson's skin, only bent enough to study the black circle seal engraved into the curve of his shoulder. The symbols etched through the sigil seemed legitimate, though only magic could serve as a real test.

What she didn't understand was the inked rectangle comprised of thin black lines beneath it.

Maybe the man liked tattoos. That wasn't her problem, or her concern. God knew she had her share of walking ink canvases in her teams.

"Thank you," she said. It took effort to keep from jumping as he jerked his sleeve back down and all but pushed past her for the door.

Setting her jaw, Parker turned to the other missionary.

Then choked on her own tongue as she found him standing shirtless behind her, the worn button-down hanging from his back pocket. He had a chest designed to make women drool. His abs were rock-hard, chiseled beyond anything she'd ever seen, tapering in to the waistband of his jeans, and Parker swallowed hard as her gaze took in the expanse of swarthy muscle.

"*Director* Adams?"

She jerked her attention back to his face, and fought back a flush as she realized he was smiling. That half-crooked twist of lips sat so close to a smirk, it only made her angry.

She wasn't a kid. She was the lead director in a citywide organization whose function was to protect; a woman who had seen more than her fair

share of hard-bodied men. The Mission was full
of them. Women, too, for that matter.

He raised a broad finger and tapped the dark
circle of ink imprinted on the front of his left
shoulder, just under his collarbone. "As you re-
quested."

Parker crossed the room with short, sharp
strides. She studied his tattoo, nodded even as she
eyed the same black bar code embedded beneath
the traditional seal.

Two men with the same set of tattoos?

A brotherhood? A unit tattoo?

She glanced up to his face, frowning as he
smiled into her eyes. The question died on her
tongue. Instinctively, she knew he wouldn't answer.

Probably just to jerk her chain.

"Thank you," she said dispassionately. "You
can dress yourself."

"So I'm good to go?"

"Agent Eckhart will show you and Mr. Nelson
through the training," she said, turning her back
on him. Deliberate dismissal.

He drew his shirt over his shoulders. Parker
watched his reflection in the wide bank of glass
windows. "Training?" he asked.

"I have no knowledge of you. Consequently,
I don't know what kind of training Mrs. Parrish
thought would qualify you for this team," she
said as he redid the buttons over his washboard
abdominal muscles. "You'll be put through the
paces just like all of my other agents."

His jaw tightened in the glass. Then, as if it

was only a flicker in her imagination, he grinned. "Ah, well. She did say make us welcome. Hey, *Director*."

Imperceptibly stiffening, she turned.

Then studied the hand he held out to her as if it were some strange bug to be scrutinized. It was a large hand, callused like so many of the street-level missionaries' hands were, with nails torn down to the quick.

And it *was* a challenge. His eyebrow quirked. The same side as the apparently permanent smirk tugging at the right side of his mouth.

Silently, she clasped her palm to his. Her skin was inordinately white against his darker color, as if he'd spent a lot of time in the sun. How could that be? Was he a topsider?

Was he from somewhere beyond the city?

"Thanks for having us," he said.

"This isn't a guest stay. I fully expect you both to carry your weight."

His eyes lit with amusement. "And then some, right?" He squeezed her hand, calluses scraping her softer palm, then let go. "See you around . . . *Director* Adams."

Parker watched him saunter out of her office, making no effort to hide the lazy way he finished buttoning up his shirt. Something about the way he'd said it had made his farewell seem like a . . . promise. An invitation.

Damn.

A new operation. New missionaries she knew nothing about.

She sat and scrolled through the readout, skimming the material swiftly. Halfway through the cover letter, surprise flickered.

Who was Juliet Carpenter? And why did some woman off the street suddenly jump known ritual murderers on the priority list?

Not that it mattered. Her orders were clear. She gathered the digital readout and what few operational dockets had collected in her in-box and left the office.

A flurry of activity preceded her.

Like she knew it would, a fully fledged headache blossomed behind her forehead. She didn't dare wince. "Agent Eckhart."

A bald man industriously bent over a computer turned, annoyance twisting his round face. It only slightly eased as he recognized her. "Ma'am."

She handed him one of the dockets. "Give this to Mr. Stone. I want all the information he can find in two hours. Then deepen the search and feed me whatever he finds in relative intervals."

Alan Eckhart took the docket and scrolled through it quickly. His free hand rubbed at the shiny bare scalp Parker had assumed early on came from shaving every day. "Will you be needing the whole team? I can call Neely in."

"Not yet." Possibly not at all, depending on Jonas Stone's findings. The man was the best information gatherer this side of the divide. Possibly even the best the Mission had ever had, anywhere, ever. Parker knew she was lucky to have him.

Luckier still that Stone didn't mind her. Possibly even liked her. Then again, the guy seemed to like everyone.

"All right," Eckhart replied, "I'll put it in his queue."

She studied him levelly. "Jump his queue, Mr. Eckhart."

He whistled, a faint three-note tune as he glanced at her. "This takes priority over Operation Ghostwatch?"

She didn't hesitate, well aware of how many ears were straining to hear her response. Juggling priorities. That was part of her job. "Yes," she said, bracing one hand on her hip. "Only for the first two hours. Then keep him on the dragnet. He's a bright boy, I believe he can multitask. I rather assume most of my agents can."

Somewhere in the background, someone snickered.

Eckhart snapped the folder closed. "Yes, ma'am."

"Be ready to call Agent Silo in from R&R, I'll need the library manned immediately."

"It's already—"

She cut him off neatly. "Agent Silo is the only one who knows that library inside and out. I'll let you know when to send out the call."

"Yes, ma'am," he repeated, but couldn't quite hide the doubt in the slow acquiescence.

Fine. As long as he did what she ordered, she'd take it.

"Oh," she added before she turned away. "There are two new agents in the roster. Get them on training." She paused, tucking the stack of readouts more firmly under her arm. "Advance to level four immediately."

His eyes widened. "Right out of the gate?"

"Yes, Agent Eckhart," she said, every word crisp. "Level four, right out of the gate. Is there a problem?"

His cheeks flushed. "No, ma'am," he said, but Parker didn't give him the opportunity to say anything else. She strode through the suddenly bustling office, her chin up.

As the elevator doors closed behind her, someone's voice carried through the narrowing gap.

"Total ice bitch."

The elevator rocked into motion. She touched a button on the panel. "Bring the car around," she said calmly.

The speaker crackled. "Right away, Director."

Parker smiled.

CHAPTER NINE

Thunder grumbled in the distance. Outside the windows of the small green house, the sunshine faded to muted gray. Clouds edged in black rolled in, and someone had lit candles for light.

Caleb didn't know who.

He sat on the only available surface—a heavy wooden trunk surrounded by stacks upon stacks of junk. Old junk, prequake junk, he didn't know.

He didn't care.

Elbows braced on his thighs, he hunched over, rotating a small gold ring over and over between his fingers. He stared at it, watched it catch the light in tiny glints. He'd been staring at Delia's ring for what felt like hours. It didn't have any answers for him.

She didn't have any answers for him.

And still Jessie didn't wake up.

She seemed so frail in the bed. The quilt tucked in around her looked obscenely bright against her sallow skin, and her eyelids flickered repeatedly as if she dreamed. Or was *seeing* something.

Caleb wanted to do something.

Christ, *anything*.

Instead, he was forced to sit quietly, staring at the ring as the witch who introduced herself as Naomi West sat on the mattress beside his sister, hand to hand.

His sister's lover hadn't moved, either. Silas Smith filled a chair by the bed, his pose similar to Caleb's in every way save for the direction of his stare.

He hadn't taken his eyes off Jessie since Caleb had come in. Even then, Caleb had gotten only a flick of attention, a tightening of his mouth, and then a jerk of a thumb to the wooden chest.

So they continued. Silent. Waiting.

And a terrible, nameless fear gripped Caleb's heart.

This was worse than even the most awful of his visionary fits. *Seeing* took effort, it took energy and concentration and a release of magic usually kept bottled up beneath the skin. Caleb knew as intimately as anyone how much effort the magic required.

Sometimes *seeing* came without warning. Most of Caleb's visions were like that. Jessie had always been able to control it.

But this looked like he felt.

What would she tell them when she woke up?

If she woke up. This wasn't right. The hollow space behind his heart, the rhythmic ache that tunneled deeper than just his head wasn't right.

He squeezed his eyes shut. Thunder trembled through the aching silence.

Finally, Naomi stirred. Caleb raised his head, watching her as she stretched, working out the kinks in her back from hunching for so long. She opened her eyes on a puzzled frown.

Silas leaped to his feet. "Is she all right?" he demanded. His voice, deeper than most, rumbled on his version of a whisper.

The witch tucked Jessie's pale, unresponsive hand back against the blanket. "I don't know."

Caleb's gaze flicked to Jessie. Her wide mouth, mirror to their mother's, was pinched. As if in pain. Or struggling. But she didn't make any sound, and her breath remained jerky. Uneven.

His hands clenched together over the ring, fingers tangled until the pain forced him to ease off.

"What's wrong with her?" Silas demanded.

She put a hand on his broad shoulder and pushed him to the side of the bed. "Stay with her. She's going to need help."

"Help? Help, how?" He looked helplessly between Jessie and Naomi. "Is this a witch thing?"

Caleb studied Naomi's face, the sudden flare of

her thickly lashed eyes. His shoulders slumped. "She's dying," he said.

Naomi's glance flicked to the ceiling.

Silas surged off the side of the bed, sending the springs into a cacophony of protest. "You shut the fuck up," he growled, but Naomi gripped his shoulder again.

The single action, wordless and infinitely poignant, confirmed what Caleb had only suspected.

He'd always had a bond with his sister. That's why he'd worn the flint. To save her from his pain.

A pain he no longer carried. Had it moved to her? Could it?

Silas sank back to the bed, and it was as if the strength simply leeched from his big frame. Suddenly ashen, he looked up at the woman with the blue-violet eyes.

She shook her head. A fraction.

Claws sank into Caleb's heart. Venom slid through his veins; guilt, rage. A maelstrom of it locked in his throat, and he stared at his clasped hands as they trembled. The ring pressed into his palms, ridged and unbending.

In his peripheral, Silas reached for Jessie's hand. His own dwarfed hers, but even Caleb could see the gentleness, the sheer tenderness of the gesture.

Caleb gritted his teeth. "What's the cause?"

"I don't know." Naomi shrugged, as if to emphasize her bewilderment. "I'm still pretty new to this stuff, but for all I can tell, she's not hurt. I can't find any physical damage. She's not bleeding anywhere, she hasn't suffered any falls lately. Aside from a few bruises, she's in perfect health. She's just . . . fading."

Caleb stared at his fingers. At the scars that turned his left hand into a patchwork tangle of rough and shiny skin.

"Her magic's going haywire," Naomi continued quietly. "I got fringes of it while I was poking around." She scrubbed her hands over her face. "I need to refuel. I'll be back to try again as soon as I've got enough juice."

Caleb said nothing.

She paused, hand on the door, and slid him a thoughtful, speculative stare. "I just about gave myself an aneurysm healing your wounds, Leigh."

Well, that explained his general lack of pain. Caleb glanced at her. "Thanks."

Her eyes narrowed. Flicked to Silas. Then, saying nothing else, she left. The door closed quietly behind her, leaving Caleb trapped in the stifling one-room house with the man who wanted him dead.

And the sister Caleb had already risked everything to save.

Power going haywire? As much energy as it took to fuel the visions, if it were just going and going, it could explain the fading.

Loss of control. Caleb braced his chin on his fists, staring blankly at the floor. Magic going haywire.

Like Juliet.

And like Juliet, his sister had been tattooed with a bar code. Like Juliet, she'd simply always had it.

What was the connection?

Silas's thumb stroked back a lock of golden hair from Jessie's eyes. It shook.

Fury carved another notch into Caleb's restraint. "Look—"

"She never gave up on you." The rumbled voice slammed through his uncertain words; quiet, but with an impact that plowed into Caleb's head like an avalanche.

He jerked his head up.

Silas didn't look at him. He laced his fingers through Jessie's and stared somewhere past the bed.

Caleb closed his eyes.

"Nothing to say to that?" Silas chuckled, the sound filled with knives. "Guess I'm not surprised. You're the one who left her to die."

Caleb's shoulders went rigid. Every muscle in his body locked. What could he say?

The man was right.

He'd turned her over to a coven who wanted to kill her—her own brother—while a missionary obligated to destroy her ended up saving her life.

Sacrifice. Wasn't that what Lydia Leigh had taught her children? Sacrifice to survive. Sacrifice for love.

He'd done that.

He'd done it all for her. Murdered and lied and schemed and manipulated, atrocious things he'd sold his soul to do. He'd done *everything* for her. For her and the city Jessie loved so much.

The city he hated. Magicians and fools.

His fingers tightened over the ring. Wasn't it all supposed to *mean* something?

Then Silas had saved her. He owed the man everything for that; he'd wanted nothing more than for Jessie to be happy. To live her life.

Wasn't it *supposed* to be happily ever after for her? Not . . . this.

"She never gave up on you, though," Silas repeated, and Caleb exhaled hard, an angry sound. Silas didn't look back. "Even after she learned about all those people you killed. And after you tied her to that fucking altar—" His voice broke. With inhuman effort, he gathered himself again. "She made me promise. If you ever showed up again—"

"I don't want to—"

"Too bad." Silas's gaze dropped to Jessie's pale, pixie features. "Your sister made me promise to give you a chance. A fucking chance to prove yourself again."

A chance. God *damn* him.

"Now," Silas said hoarsely, "I wish I never did."

Caleb shot to his feet as something black and nameless seized hold of his head. Across the small room, Silas stiffened.

Wordless, echoing with a rage he didn't know how to channel, Caleb strode for the door. It slammed shut behind him, shut on the pathetic image of the big ex-missionary hunched over the frail figure of his lover.

Of Caleb's sister.

For a long moment, fists shaking at his sides, Caleb stared over the green bay and saw nothing but Jessie. The girl who had raised him after their mother had been murdered. The girl who had taught him to lie to survive, to stay low and out of sight.

The woman he had once *seen* burning in a fire set by the coven he'd then set out to destroy.

For what? For her to die anyway?

"Shit," he said through a throat gone tight and ragged. "Shit. Shit, fuck, no." It wouldn't end like this.

It would not—*could not* end like this.

Jessie hadn't given up on him. He'd be damned if he gave up on her.

He leaped off the porch, pushed the ring into his pocket and sprinted across the flagstones. In the ravaged depths of his mind, he knew what he needed to do, and his body acted on instinct while his thoughts raged on.

He knew the game. He knew the pieces and would force the hand of fate, even if it killed him. He'd *see* what he had to do and take care of it. Back in the ruins, Juliet had peeled him open with a wild flare of her magic. Sharper than he'd ever known. For a moment, a split second, he'd *seen*.

He'd see those visions again. The answers were there.

But he needed *her* to do it.

Promise me.

Not this time.

He found Juliet on a black sand beach at the opposite end of the crescent bay, her bare feet mired in the wet sand and the warm, green water lapping the shore. Sulfurous vapors danced around her, licked at her skin. Touched everything he wished so fucking badly he didn't know the feel of already.

He surged out of the hedge of fronds like a man possessed.

She jerked in surprise, tried to jump to her feet, but the sand she'd buried her toes in sucked at her balance. She flailed, staggered, and fell to her knees as he loomed over her.

Her eyes flashed at him. The hot spring water soaked into her borrowed skirt. "What—"

Caleb grabbed her upper arms and yanked her upright. The sand gave way with a soft, wet, sucking noise. "How much do you hate me?" he demanded.

Her lashes, tinged by a faint golden sheen without her mascara to mask it, widened. "What?"

Don't do this.

"How much," he repeated between gritted teeth, dragging her face close to his, "do you hate me?"

"I don't—"

He shook her, hard enough to snap her head back in shock. Hard enough to clack her teeth together, to see a flush of red climb her cheeks. "I gathered your coven together," he said tightly, every word rasping with the effort as the darkness filled him. Swallowed him. "I brought them together knowing that I'd already set bombs across the field."

The color in her cheeks heightened.

Please. . .

"I watched them as they burned, Juliet. Your friends. I set them on fire. Have you ever smelled burning flesh? *Have you?*"

Her eyes glistened, and something in Caleb's chest twisted. Hard. "I hate that," she said softly, her lips trembling. "I hate that you throw it in my face. I hate that you used me for a shield when those witches came after us—"

Caleb set her down, hard enough to jar her words loose, but she jerked her chin up. Shoved at his chest.

He staggered back a step.

"I hate that you had to do it," she continued, even as a tear slid from her pale green eyes. "But you took the bullet for me, Caleb. You think I didn't notice?" She shook her head, the black fringe of her hair sliding over one eye. "I don't know what you're trying to do, but you won't get it from me."

Rage battered at him. Clawed into his throat, his lungs, forced itself through his lips in a wordless, helpless, inhuman sound.

Juliet took a step back, flinching.

He matched it, forcing a step forward. "Tell me you hate me," he ordered. He needed to trigger that spill of power that tried to get into his head. Needed to crack her open, to force the visions that would tell him what to do. How to do it.

No matter what it did to him, to her, he had to know. To help.

She backed away and he crowded her, step for step. Foot for foot. The black sand clung to her bare feet, her hands and skirt. "Tell me you hate me for pushing you against that wall and taking you that night," he growled.

Her lips parted, eyes wide. A breath shuddered from her chest, but she shook her head even as her back came up hard against the cliff wall. He flattened both hands by her shoulders, caged her with his body.

A whisper of warning ghosted through his head; a murmur of raw lust speared through his gut. His temples twinged.

"I—" She licked her upper lip. "I always—"

She's just a rose. . .

No. She was the key. She could tear him open. Without his sight, Jessie would die in that bed. Everything he knew, everything he loved would go up in smoke. *Again.*

Not if he could help it. So he pushed her. Pinned her. "You hate me," he said fiercely, leaning in until her breasts curved into his chest, soft and warm and like a punch to his nerves. Crowding her until she couldn't possibly miss the telltale signs of his arousal against her thigh. "Tell me you hate me for fucking you. For leaving you."

Her eyes squeezed shut. She tried to turn her face away, but he caught her chin in one rough hand and forced it back. "Tell me to fuck you again," he told her, so softly that she gasped. "That you want it."

Color swept up from her throat, over her cheeks. It flooded her fair skin, and her eyes opened. Glassy with need. With confusion.

Anguished.

She had to give him what he needed.

But as he watched her emotions clash inside her dazed eyes, it infuriated him to know he needed *her.* Visions be damned.

He trapped her jaw in his hand and crushed his

mouth to hers. The instant their lips touched, the moment the contact sizzled across his body like a live wire, the needling whisper in his head simmered to a faint buzz. Pressure so mild that his own damned lust nearly drowned it out.

She gasped, and Caleb forcefully tilted her head to fit his lips more firmly against her own. He deepened the kiss without gentleness or permission, stabbing his tongue into the dark heat of her mouth to taste her. To devour her; damn him to hell, he wanted to crawl inside her head and possess everything she was.

She whimpered, and everything in his body thrilled to life. To sudden, electric attention. She raised her hands to twine them around his neck but he wrenched them away, captured her wrists in one hand and jerked them high above her head. He pinned her there, shackled to the cliff wall as she panted beneath him.

Her eyes were glazed, but snapping. Crackling with raw emotion. With lust?

With anger?

With magic.

The pressure in his head intensified as she sucked in a hard breath. "Don't do this," she said raggedly. "I can . . . I can just give you—"

Inside his own head, Caleb staggered under the crushing weight of guilt. Of condemnation. But her body strained against his grip, giving lie to her words. She wanted him.

She needed to hate him. It would be so much safer for her if she just hated him.

She doesn't know how.

He found the hem of her skirt and hiked it up with one hand. Juliet pulled at the grip around her wrists. Gasped as his palms found the warm flesh of her upper thigh.

His fingers skimmed the soft curls between her legs. Her head fell back against the cliff wall, and something in him bent. Cracked.

She closed her eyes. "Caleb, please— Oh!"

And with her cry, shuddering and sweet, the presence—that sensation of *other* in his head—was gone.

And he was lost.

He stroked across the cleft of her warm, soft flesh. Traced the delicate folds of her body as she shuddered in his grip. Her legs opened and hunger swamped him. Filled him with a need so bright and sharp and ravenous that he groaned.

Without warning, he slid two fingers into her.

She cried out. Her hips jerked.

He cursed as he found her already wet, her warm channel so tight that her muscles clenched around his fingers. Her eyes slammed open, wicked bright and half gone already, and he struggled not to throw her skirt up and take her right here, right now. Hard and fast against this cliff wall.

He knew what it could be like.

He knew how badly he craved it. Wasn't this what he'd wanted all along?

Caleb coaxed her legs wider, stroked her slowly. "Tell me you want me," he whispered again, a refrain that hammered at his conscious mind. *Tell me what I need to hear.*

She sucked in a breath, but it arced out on a

sound that curled into his cock and pulsed. Sexy, so feminine. Wanton as hell, and oh, God, he was in trouble.

"Tell me you want me to do this."

"Why?" she cried, even as her hips thrust against his fingers. Rode his hand, all but stroking herself against him. "Oh, please. Please."

Keeping his other hand firmly around her wrists, he dropped his mouth to her breasts, breathing out against the thin yellow fabric. She arched into him, sobbing out a sound between a gasp and a laugh as he touched her clit with his thumb. Just a graze.

A tease.

"Say it, Juliet," he said against her soft curve. She shook her head, writhing. He took her nipple into his mouth, laving it through the fabric of her shirt, sucking it deeply until she shuddered.

His thumb came down hard on the swollen bead of nerves, stroking it, over and over as he transferred his attention to her other nipple. She was sobbing, flushed and so ripe that his fingers slid in and out without any resistance.

With inhuman effort, Juliet wrenched at her arms. His grip broke, and she tunneled her fingers into his hair to yank his face up.

Her eyes were wild, mouth parted, breath heaving.

And she kissed him.

Against everything he expected, everything he'd craved and desperately hoped he never got, she fit her lips to his, voracious and wild and demanding, and kissed him.

Intentions snapped.

Control shattered.

He forgot the need to *see*. Forgot the coven, the conflict. Her mouth opened under his and something wild in him flared. Away from anger and violence. Away from fear.

So much trouble.

Groaning, Caleb withdrew his fingers from her warm body and fumbled at the snap of the borrowed, too-large jeans sitting low on his waist. Wrenched at the button fly as she whimpered against his mouth and tried to help. Somehow, God, somehow, he got them pushed past his hips. Somehow, he pulled her skirt out of the way.

When the very tip of his erection nudged her swollen flesh, he thought he'd go up in an inferno that would claim his soul.

She braced her hands against the cliff wall behind her, eyes closed. Cheeks flushed. Sweat gleamed on her skin, and she breathed in spiky knots that whimpered and begged.

Caleb framed her face in his hands. "Tell me," he demanded.

She shook her head.

"Tell me you want this." God, was that his voice? So angry and harsh. So . . . needy.

She caught her upper lip between her teeth and said nothing.

His hips jerked as she tilted hers, forcing her sex to rub against his flesh. Slick. So hot he could feel it saturating the head of his cock. His gut clenched. Muscles locked.

He growled, seized her hips in his hands. "Juliet, God damn it!"

Her eyes flew open, met his. Linked. He could drown in spring green. Drown in her tremors as she held her breath. Drown in her.

He could be the bastard she needed him to be.

"Lie to me," he rasped, and plunged deep.

The ragged sound she made echoed in his wild groan. The slick folds of her sex parted for him, too fast to be painless, but oh, God, so wet that he threw his head back, clenching his teeth.

She hooked a leg over his hip; he held it in one splayed hand, her skin warm, her body hot and tight as he withdrew, braced himself against the cliff, and thrust again. Balls deep, coated in her, surrounded by her as she wrapped her arms around his neck and held on.

Her breath spiked with every thrust, shook as he gritted out a curse. Heat gathered at the base of his cock, slid into his body like liquid flame. Harder, faster, angrier, more and more desperate, she rose to meet him, matched him thrust for thrust, until she was gasping for breath and crying out his name.

Her muscles clenched around him, tighter than anything he'd ever known before her. There was no before. There was only Juliet, riding him, milking him, shuddering in his arms and draining his strength with every sobbing cry.

His orgasm detonated without warning or care, uncoiling like a spring wound too tight and leaving him gasping for breath as he shuddered, his hips pinned to hers and her body wrapped like silk around him.

As his vision slowly cleared, as the fragments of

his mind and body pulled together, Caleb found himself cradling her, his arms curved around her back, her legs around his hips. Found his nose buried in her hair as he panted, sucking in oxygen as pinpricks of light detonated around him.

She smelled like warm wind and rain; like raw woman, like—*fuck*, what he'd always thought flowers should smell like. The T-shirt she still wore bunched in his fingers.

Gradually, her shudders eased.

Bit by bit, his heartbeat mellowed. The buzzing pressure in his head hadn't gone away, and with it came the memory.

The anger.

She uncurled her leg from his hips, pulled away so fast that he staggered, sucking in a breath as his flesh slid out of her warm body at last.

Juliet sidled away, shaking out her skirt, and Caleb quickly pulled his pants back up. "I can't—" Her voice cracked.

The ache between his temples intensified.

Do it. He closed his eyes, fingers halting over the buttons of his jeans.

He couldn't be gentle. He needed to *see*. No matter what the cost.

Quietly, he said, "You can't be surprised."

Her gasp forced him to look at her. Her back was to him, now, her shoulders rigid. "You *really* don't think about this stuff before it comes out of your mouth, do you?" she demanded.

Of course he did.

His smile humorless, Caleb leaned back against the cliff wall, arms folded over his chest. "What did you expect? We'd done this once, it was only a matter of time before we needed it again."

She was so still, he wasn't sure that she'd even heard him.

But the pressure in his skull told him she had.

Good girl.

"*Needed it* is a poor choice in words," he went on conversationally. "You can't say no to me. I think I made that clear."

Now she turned, spots of color high on her cheeks as her eyes flashed echoes of the fury peeling her lips back from her teeth. "You conceited son of a bitch."

He shrugged, forcing himself to respond like the asshole he needed her to understand he was. "You didn't say no."

"I didn't say yes!" she shouted, fists clenched by her sides.

"You think that matters?" he told her, inwardly flinching at how much of a dick that made him.

She stepped back as if he'd slapped her. Guilt twisted, sharp as a knife.

Pain lanced through his head.

She took a step forward. Then another. Her fists unclenched. Curled up again. Caleb watched her.

I'm so sorry.

"I hate you," she bit out.

"No, you don't," he replied. "You just want to fuck me. There's a diff—"

Her fist was a hell of a lot bonier than her open-handed slap had been. Caleb's head snapped around with the impact, collided with the cliff wall behind him and he saw stars.

The angry buzz of her magic slammed into his skull, and he dropped like a stone. He didn't even feel the rocks jab into his flesh as the universe stretched, humming, and turned white.

It tore free of its moorings and howled from her skin, as physical as a hurricane. Painful as a scream.

She felt the magic explode from her, spread out like a wild net and slam into Caleb. She experienced it as the power filled his skin the way it filled hers; as it tunneled and burrowed and overflowed from nerve to throbbing nerve.

Something more than sexual.

Worse than torture.

Draining.

Juliet sank to the sand in boneless exhaustion, her own consciousness flickering. He'd wanted this.

She didn't know how she suddenly knew, but she did.

He'd wanted this, right here, and that's why he'd done all those things. Why he'd goaded her, and then pushed her against a wall—the bastard, what *was* it about walls?—and said what he'd said. Done what he'd done.

Now she could only stare, hands over her mouth, as he fell still.

Deathly still.

"Caleb?"

His eyes flickered, hands twitching as they scrabbled at the rock and sand. Blood trickled from his temple.

She reached out.

Caleb's hand lashed, fingers snapping viselike around her wrist. "I see a mountain of flesh," he said hoarsely.

Juliet stared at his hand. Slowly, her gaze traced the trembling line of his arm. Slid across his chest, panting with effort.

Ice filled her spine.

Caleb's eyes had opened, fixed on her, but it wasn't her they saw. They blazed a shade of blue she'd never seen, something made of the bluest sky and the deepest ocean and every shade in between. Lightning crackled deep inside that unseeing stare, wicked and wild and unrestrained.

Primordial fear.

This is why they hunt witches.

The thought made her shiver.

His grip tightened, bruising. "They're nothing but tangled limbs and putrid flesh and dead, staring eyes, but I see the tattoos. Branded like ownership, marked into the skin of each carcass like a name, but they don't have names. They're lines and numbers; no faces. There aren't any faces."

She sank back to the sand, silent with fear.

"She sits at the top like a queen, rotting bones and tattooed flesh her throne."

Juliet gasped as he let her go. Fingers digging into the sand, she swallowed back a surge of nausea.

These? These were the visions of the future? Vivid scenes of symbolism and carnage? Oh, God. No wonder he was so cold.

These weren't things for people to see. To *handle*.

"She is marked, too, and her face is empty, but she *has* a face. She's the only one, so they gather. Movement in the shadows. I see silhouettes of humans, but they aren't," he continued quietly. "One holds the leash. The leash that fastens to the queen's own flesh. It sags between her legs, dripping already, filled by them. Filled by all of them, one after another. There is no rest for the wicked. She is the key."

Juliet held her breath as a sudden, vicious tremor rippled through Caleb's body. Black sand clung to his shirt, his hands as they fisted.

"Mine," he growled. "You can't have her. She's mine to protect, damn you all." A ragged sound forced free from behind his bared teeth, Caleb surged to his feet, every muscle locked and ready, eyes wild.

Juliet flung herself against his chest, unthinking and desperate. She wrapped her arms around his waist, pressed her head to his heart and held on for dear life as he strained against enemies she couldn't see. "Caleb, wake up!"

"I swore I would protect her," he whispered hoarsely, and his arms banded around her. Tighter than steel, unyielding. "Mine."

She clenched her eyes shut, burying her face against his chest. "Just fight it off," she begged. "We can settle everything else later, just—just, please." Her words snagged. Broke. "Please don't leave me alone."

The sulfurous haze slipped across the emerald water, ghostly fingers extending across the bay. Juliet clung to him, praying silently, desperate as she mentally rifled through the small number of rituals she had ever bothered to learn. None would help.

She had none prepared.

Oh, God, she was a worthless witch. A tool, only fit to be used.

Slowly, the hard edge of fists at her back relaxed. His hands opened, splayed over the grimy T-shirt and stroked from her nape to her waist. "It'll be okay," he whispered against her hair.

She'd meant to say something reassuring. Something flippant and wise. Something tough.

Instead, her words caught on a sob.

"I'm sorry, little rose."

Shock sliced through her. Slid like ice water into her veins. She stiffened, fingers clenching in his shirt as she raised her head. "Wh-what?"

Caleb stared blankly beyond her. Confusion filled his eyes as she searched them, now the blue she remembered. Normal blue. He blinked hard, turned one hand palm-up to study it over her shoulder. "What," he rasped, and cleared his throat to try again. "What happened?"

I'm sorry, little rose.

Cordelia. How had he known? How did he know that her sister had called her that? He was a witch. She wasn't. There was no way they'd ever met.

She jammed a shaking hand against his chest, desperate for space.

Caleb's gaze locked on her. Studied the line where her body pressed against his. It trailed up her throat, over her mouth. Flickered.

When he met her eyes, his own softened.

Juliet raised her chin.

Slowly, cautiously, he slid his scarred fingers over her throat. Her chin, along her jaw. The ridges rasped against her skin, rough and oddly warm.

Helpless before the wonder filling his face, the uncertainty, she turned her cheek into his palm. "Caleb, I don't—I mean, I can't . . ." She shook her head. "I just can't."

His mouth quirked. "I give up," he whispered, leaning in.

"Give up?"

Without answering, without giving her the time to gather the shrapnel of her thoughts, he seized her mouth in a kiss so gentle that frissons of confusion, of sweetness and breathtaking temptation whispered through her.

His hand flattened at the small of her back, held her in place as his lips rubbed, nuzzled against hers. Not taking. Seeking.

Asking permission.

Her eyes fluttered closed, body melting in his hands. Against him. Surrender.

So right.

Then he pushed her away. Backed up, raising his hands as if he could ward her off. "Go back to the house," he ordered, voice hoarse. Curt.

She took a step closer. "But you—"

"Go!"

He turned his back, shoulders set in unforgiving lines, jammed his hands into the pockets of his too-big jeans and strode down the sandy shore. Bits of black sand kicked up under his shoes.

Juliet watched him walk away.

Little rose.

She rubbed two fingers over the sudden, yawning ache under her breastbone. Damn it. She didn't have the energy for this. She didn't want to keep up with his moods, volatile and rough on her already bruised heart.

She didn't want to try and understand the secrets he seemed so determined to keep.

What she desperately wanted was a drink.

CHAPTER TEN

A faint orange glow shimmered from behind the little house, casting a warm radiance as the cloudy sky rapidly darkened beneath a summer storm. The local weather patterns had never been anything but seasonal with an eighty percent chance of acidic rain, and as Juliet trudged around the side of the house, the first fat drops splattered around her.

Just great.

Juliet hurried around the corner, darting under a beige canvas pavilion just as the skies unleashed soaking fury. Rain pounded the treated cloth like a drum, canvas thunder echoed by a clash of the real thing rolling overhead. She ran her fingers through her damp hair, grimacing.

Warmth and firelight seeped from the open face of an old-fashioned iron stove at the edge of the patio. Beneath her feet, the rock gleamed with the same smoky facets as the flagstones by the bay. Plastic furniture served as seating, arrayed near pots of giant flowers with petals as large as both of her hands together. The wood inside the stove crackled and popped.

It was, for the moment, bliss.

"Gets old real quick, doesn't it?"

Juliet jumped as the husky voice floated out of the dark. She surveyed the shadow-rimmed patio until she spotted a pair of black, heavy-duty street boots crossed at the ankle in the corner.

"Sorry?" she asked blankly.

The figure leaned forward. Firelight painted the healer's exquisite features with shadows and reflected glints from her jewelry, but her teeth gleamed in a smile not entirely friendly. "The rain," she explained, gesturing to the sheets of gray veiling the air. "Always with the rain. Have a seat, kiddo."

Pride eyed exhaustion. It was no contest. Knees giving out, Juliet sat.

Naomi blinked at her. Then pointed to one of the white plastic chairs. "I meant in an actual seat."

"I'm fine."

The witch shrugged. "Suit yourself. Juliet, right?"

"Yes." Tucking her knees under the skirt, she wrapped her arms around them. It helped keep her warm while the snapping heat of the fire built strength. "You're Naomi."

"Yeah."

"Were you the one who took care of me?"

"That's me."

She hesitated. "Thanks." For a long moment, only the thunderous echo of the rain and crackling wood peppered the silence. Juliet stared into the heart of the stove, acutely aware of the strange violet eyes fixed on her.

The healing witch didn't move much. She didn't fidget. She stared, still as a feline on the prowl. It made Juliet's skin itch. She flicked the woman a glance, eyes narrowed. "What?"

"Once upon a time," Naomi replied in a slow, husky drawl, "I would have hunted you."

"What?" she asked again, straightening. "Hunted me?"

Heedless of decency or reserve, Naomi stretched out her legs and hooked a thumb at the waistband of her low-riding jeans. It didn't take much to shove the band down, revealing a scrap of electric blue nylon, taut, sleek muscles Juliet would have killed for, and a dark circle of black ink tattooed low on her abdomen.

Juliet's gaze snapped back to hers. "But you're a witch!"

"Go figure." The woman let go of her waistband, resettling into a lazy, comfortable sprawl. Her piercings glittered, points of reflected fire at her eyebrow, nose, lip, and ears. "Used to be a missionary."

"Used to?"

The look she slanted Juliet was wry. "Clearly not anymore. Last fucker who tried to be both got his ass scalped."

She couldn't imagine it. "How can someone be a missionary and a witch at the same time?" she asked, perplexed. How could the holy tattoo that so terrified witches like her allow it? Then, because she couldn't help it, she added, "And what crazy witch would join the Order that murders them for fun?"

"For a living."

"Whatever," Juliet replied, in a tone that made clear how little she thought the difference was. Dead was dead.

Naomi searched her face, pierced eyebrow arching. "So no one told you?"

"What?"

"Peterson." Her lip curled. "You all called him Curio."

Juliet's hands jerked, and she drew them to her chest, fisted tightly. "That's a lie."

"Hooked you as bad as he got us, huh?" The witch's sneer only deepened; disappointment, anger. Her gaze flicked to the fire as she said flatly, "His name, far as we know, was David Peterson. For about nine years, he was the Mission director. The boss."

Juliet shook her head, ears ringing with the words she didn't want to hear. But even as she did, even as her lips shaped the words, doubt filled her. "But he was . . ."

"A friend? Took care of you?" Her eyes gleamed. "A lover? Just about any lie'll do, take your pick."

Damn it. Juliet looked away, back toward the gray mist settling beyond the canvas roof. "How do you know?"

"On that day down at the Waterline," Naomi told her, and didn't even pause as Juliet winced, "Silas and Jessie saw him as Curio. *We* knew him as Peterson." Her boots scraped as she adjusted her feet. "*Mission Director* Peterson, 'scuse me. The shitfucker."

"I don't understand."

"Join the club, kiddo." Naomi laced her hands behind her head, tipping her head back against the chair and once more into shadow. The light painted wicked patterns across her chest, saturated the synth-leather jacket she wore like a second skin, but only the faintest gleam from the dark suggested she still watched Juliet closely.

Juliet's mouth twisted. "I thought witches and missionaries just killed each other."

"Yeah, so did I. That's the mission statement." Her tone flattened, bone dry. "Somehow, Peterson didn't have to sign the same dotted line."

"How?"

"Told you," Naomi said, only somewhat patiently. "We don't know. He was killed before Silas and Jessie could expose him. *I* didn't even know 'til I joined this merry band of outlaws, and I worked with the fucker."

Juliet's fingers knotted under her chin, twisted so tight it barely registered as pain in the turmoil of her mind. Curio, the coven master. The man who had taken her in, laughed with her, been stern and firm and kind.

A missionary?

And a witch. . .

Curio only used you for magic.

And she'd let him. Every time. Even when it left her feeling empty and aching and cold, she came to his hand like a puppy starving for love and he—

A shudder slid down her spine. "He was right," she whispered, mostly to herself. Even she could hear the revulsion, the tears, thick in her voice.

Naomi watched her uneasily from the dark. "You aren't going to cry, are you?"

She almost laughed. "You expect me to, don't you?" The woman said nothing as Juliet wiped at her still-dry eyes with her bare arm. "Poor little orphan witch, taken in by a witch hunter."

"Wasn't a hunter," Naomi replied, her voice so even that Juliet almost missed the way it edged. Like a razor. "And I've got news for you, kiddo. Every missionary out there is an orphan."

That one gave her pause. "Really?"

"We're *cultivated*," Naomi told her, drawing the word out scornfully. "At an orphanage. Yeah, even me," she added before Juliet could ask. "Whether we lose our parents young or are one of hundreds of kids abandoned in some gutter, all missionaries come from the same pool."

"That's . . ." Horrible? Efficient? Juliet shook her head, uncertain if the witch wanted her sympathy or just her attention.

Naomi shrugged. "That's the way they do it. Then a funny thing happened, and I ended up a witch."

"Ended up? You weren't born with it?"

"Not even a glimmer of a genetic anomaly." Naomi sighed, a deep gust of something that could have been annoyance. Or relief. "About a year ago, I inherited some abracadabra and that was that." She dropped her hands, fingers tapping an uneven rhythm against her stomach. "So, witchcraft and the seal of St. Andrew live harmoniously together, blah, blah, blah."

"Without . . ." That brought them back to how a witch could be a missionary, didn't it? Juliet's brow furrowed. "I don't know, doesn't your magic set off the seal?"

"Mine? Nah. Other witchcraft does."

It was unheard of, as far as Juliet knew. She fidgeted, digging her toes into the hard stones of the patio. It was easier to concentrate on the subject at hand and the heat slowly warming her skin than the ache behind her heart.

Caleb was right. Caleb was *always* right.

Used.

Juliet shook her head, hard enough to swing the damp ends of her hair out of her eyes. "You were a witch hunter, and now you're a healer?"

"Doesn't matter how often I hear it," Naomi said, snorting. "That word sounds wrong. Doctor, fine. Nurse? Whatever. Healer? I feel like I should have long white hair, flowing robes, and be chanting something."

"With bells?"

The woman chuckled. "Yeah. With bells." She sighed. "Then there's the Leigh witches."

Juliet hesitated.

"Relax, I've been working with Jessie for a while, now. I get that she sees the present, or whatever."

"What about Caleb?"

"The other funny thing." Naomi shifted, grabbing the edges of the plastic chair and hauling it closer. It scraped, like nails across glass. She kicked her feet out again, casually crossing them at the ankle as she sat back, this time fully bathed in the furnace's warm glow. "Was a time I actually *was* hunting Caleb Leigh." Her eyebrow arched again, silver winking wildly. "He was top of the list."

"The list?"

"The Mission has a list. Most-wanted witches, usually the type that get executed on sight. Sometimes, though, they want 'em alive."

Juliet hugged her knees as a shudder rippled through her. "Why?"

"Questioning, maybe. Usually, witches like that aren't working alone. Don't know, we just bring them in. Or kill them." She tipped her head. "Caleb Leigh once topped that list, and so we hunted him. Mostly Silas."

"By himself?"

Sparks leaped from the stove, showering the gleaming stone underneath with embers. It cast Naomi's features into devilish angles as she grinned. "More or less. Always had a loner streak."

Juliet thought back to the way he'd forged through that water, all brick-house muscle and savage strength. Remembered, too, how stern he'd been as he entered the house. How careful as he'd sat beside Jessie's unresponsive body.

"He loves her," she blurted, and Naomi's overly full mouth quirked.

"Went rogue for her." She sighed again, even as her tongue flicked out to trace the silver hoop pierced through the center of her lower lip. "He turned his back on all of us . . ." She paused. "Them. Anyway, point is, both of them have nearly died more'n once for each other. This is something he can't do anything about."

To know that kind of love, unconditional and more powerful than any magic. . .

She couldn't imagine it. Juliet stretched her legs out toward the stove, leaning back on her hands as she studied the tips of her toes. "So," she said slowly, "what's wrong with her?"

"Same thing that's wrong with you."

Juliet's head jerked up, gaze snagging on a steady blue-violet scrutiny.

"Not," Naomi drawled, "that I know what *that* is, either. But you're both showing the same signs."

"What signs?"

"Breakdown." Lightning cracked overhead, coloring the canvas a bright white for a breath. Naomi glanced up, lips moving, and then nodded with a faint smile as thunder rumbled a few seconds behind. "Acts like a disease, looks like nothing. Can't pin it."

"I'm . . ." Juliet stared at her, her mind struggling to make sense of the words. She heard them. She knew what they meant. But it may as well have been another language. "I'm what?"

"Dying, probably."

Juliet shot to her feet so fast, the canvas rippled overhead. "What?"

"Relax," Naomi said, shaking her head. "You've

got some time. More than Jessie's got. She's . . . worse, you could say. If it were a disease, I'd say hers has progressed farther."

Fear gripped her throat. Locked into her knees and made them tremble, but Juliet clenched her hands into tight, white-knuckled fists. "Why? What is it?"

"Don't know," Naomi said on a long, tired exhale. "I can't fix it. But I'll tell you a secret."

"What?"

"You and Jessie have something else in common."

Juliet stared at her, uncomprehending.

"Your tattoo," Naomi clarified. "Jessie has one like it, on her back."

"No way."

"Yup. Too bad you can't ask her about it, right? Where's Leigh?" She paused, fine black eyebrows working together, and amended, "Caleb, I mean."

And she thought Caleb was cold. This witch watched her like someone would watch a bug; with lazy interest, some amusement, and the kind of wariness that suggested she was ready in case Juliet did anything rash.

Like what? Cry?

She shook her head. "Out there," she said, somehow managing a calm that she didn't feel.

"He sees the future, right?"

Juliet nodded, jerkily.

"Go ask him what's in store. Maybe he'll have something for you." She hooked one leg over the plastic arm of her chair, propping her chin up in her palm. "I spent a lot of energy healing him," she added. "That man . . ." She hesitated, as if searching for the right words. Finally, she shrugged one shoulder wordlessly.

"You sound impressed," Juliet said, glancing over her shoulder at the rain-dark vista. He was out there, somewhere. Sitting by the water, maybe.

"It takes a fuck ton of grit and guts to stay upright, as much pain as he was in," Naomi replied simply. "Yeah. I'm impressed. I think anyone else would have long since keeled over."

"Anyone else?" She frowned. "What's so special about him?"

Besides the fact that his presence made her heart beat double-time. And the fact that one look from his impenetrable blue eyes was enough to make her forget every shred of common sense she claimed to have.

"I don't know," Naomi was saying slowly, but her gaze rested on the furnace, thank God. Juliet jerked her attention firmly back to her.

And not on the clever, manipulative fingers that he'd eased between her legs not half an hour before.

"But something is special. Different. Something," Naomi mused, "was keeping him upright long after he should have been put down. I'd be curious to find out what."

"He's stubborn," Juliet told her matter-of-factly.

The woman's lips curved into a crooked smile. "We all are, kiddo."

"Yeah, well." Juliet got to her feet, shaking out clinging bits of grit from her skirt. "He wins."

Naomi's laughter followed her as Juliet turned

and stepped off the patio. Her bare feet splashed in a puddle forming between stepping-stones.

"Hey. Before you go."

Rain dripped into her eyes. She flicked it away, glancing back at the witch. Something fluttered through the air, glinting. Juliet caught it out of reflex, fingers closing around hard plastic edges.

"There's no good time for mistakes," Naomi told her.

Flipping the small square around, Juliet's eyes widened in horror at the words imprinted on the packet. Her grip clenched on the condom foil, embarrassment and shock and—God help her—lust tightening her throat.

"I don't—I mean, we aren't . . ."

"Oh-kay." The word drawled out on a slow, obvious tide of disbelief. Naomi leaned back in her chair and closed her eyes. "Keep it anyway. Busty thing like you'll find a use, I'm sure."

The witch's husky, knowing chuckle followed her as Juliet turned and hurried into the darkness.

The rain soaked her through before she'd managed ten steps out of the light. She held the packet in one tight fist, its stiff edges cutting into her palm, but that small, insignificant pain wasn't what dogged her steps now.

The first time she'd had sex with Caleb Leigh, she'd used protection. Delia had always insisted that she get physicals with the rest of the girls at Waxed. Because of her job, she had easy access to the birth control her employers provided for the girls. She'd set Juliet up.

"Only one of us gets paid for it," she'd said, "but both of us can enjoy sex."

And how. Sex with Caleb Leigh had blown everything that came before out of the running.

But it'd been a year since her sister disappeared, and Juliet hadn't even considered sex in the interim.

Until today. With Caleb. *Again.*

And she hadn't been protected.

Juliet's footsteps faltered at the edge of the large frond barricade. Rain streamed into her eyes, slid through her T-shirt and plastered the brown skirt to her legs, and she dragged her forearm across her face to clear her vision.

Could she be . . . pregnant now?

Unbidden, the hand holding the condom packet pressed against her abdomen.

Dying, probably.

No. No possible way. Rapidly, Juliet counted back until her last period. Sighed in relief. The odds were in her favor. Not without some margin of error, but. . .

Without warning, her knees gave out. She sank to the compressed ground, clutching the little plastic square with its little black words to her chest, and suddenly couldn't breathe.

A child.

Family.

Her throat closed on the word.

Overhead, the thick bank of gray clouds turned into a purple-white sheet, and thunder swallowed her sudden, wild sob. Shoulders shaking with the effort, Juliet bent her head over her fisted hands and swallowed back a sudden, painful press of tears.

She couldn't think about it. How selfish would that be? To bring a child into a world bound and determined to hate him? To persecute him because of his parents' witchcraft.

Or worse, because he actually inherited magic.

She'd never be able to survive it if her child died at the hands of a mob, or a missionary.

Fear clutched at her throat. Fear and grief and a yearning so poignant, it hurt to breathe.

The rain battered at her head, her skin, the ground around her. The fronds rustled, waving back and forth as the fat drops of water pushed them this way and that. Her heart hammered in her chest. In her ears. Too long, too loud.

"Jules." *His* voice. Quiet. Steady.

She squeezed her eyes shut.

"Juliet?" Long fingers closed over her shoulders. "Juliet, what's wrong? Are you hurt?"

Her eyes snapped open. Sudden and furious, she wrenched away from Caleb's grip, pushing hard against his chest and sending him sprawling on his ass. His eyes flashed, wet features settled into surprised, angry lines.

"You knew," she seethed, somehow getting to her knees. The rocky soil dug into her skin, the condom wrapper bit into her fisted fingers, but she didn't care. Didn't feel it, didn't feel anything but anger, white-hot and brilliantly edged.

He didn't move, staring at her as if she were crazy. His hands braced against the ground, heels dug in.

She pointed at him. "Did you know about my tattoo? Do you know what it is?"

"Is that what this is about?"

"Do you know?"

"No, I don't know what it is," he replied quietly. "All I know is that my sister has one like it."

She shook her head, hard enough to drown out the thoughts roiling in her own head. Sharp enough to make him reach out a hand, words ready on his lips. "Do you want me?" she demanded.

His eyes widened. Narrowed just as fast. "What are you—"

"Do you?" she cut in fiercely, voice taut. Trembling. "Do you want me, Caleb? Or do you want my magic? Are you just like Alicia? Like—" She flung it out like a curse. "Like *Curio*?"

Fury banked behind his suddenly tight features. He lunged to his feet, knocked her hand away as she held it out in warning, and seized her T-shirt in his scarred fist. Wordlessly, savagely, he yanked her upright. Fabric stretched, popped as seams gave way.

She gasped as his hand slid around the back of her head. Tangled through her dripping hair and gripped it tight, hard enough, strong enough that she couldn't move. Couldn't look away as his eyes blazed blue and white and wild in the searing display of light piercing the sky.

"I'm not doing this," he growled, each furious word a hot fan of breath across her cheek. "My sister is in that house, *dying*, and you—you . . ." He made a rough sound. "I never wanted you."

The bottom fell from her stomach. Heat swept through her cheeks; shock, mortification. Anger.

She tried to turn away, to hide her face, but his fingers tightened painfully in her hair. His scarred hand gripped her wrist as she tried to push him away. Tucked it hard and fast at the small of her back, forcing her body against his. Her back arched under the pressure, her breasts pushed against his chest, and she realized then that he was shaking.

Every muscle vibrated with an effort she couldn't define.

"Every time I turned around and you were there," he gritted out, "with your spring green eyes and unguarded smile. I never wanted you, God damn it."

His eyes traced the downward line of her lower lip. Her throat, and lower. Anger gave way to something Juliet didn't know how to read; something hotter than fury, sharper, even more visceral.

Like desire, but starved.

She swallowed. His eyes flicked to the motion of the fragile bones of her throat.

"Then let me go," she said, marveling at how calm it seemed in the fury of the rain. Of him. "If you don't want me, let me walk away. Go back to Jessie, and I'll go—go anywhere you want. Away from here."

His eyes flicked to hers. Breath rasping in his chest, Caleb inhaled deeply. Touched his tongue to his lower lip, gleaming with rainwater, and said huskily, "I can't do that."

Juliet shook her head, sobbing out, "Why?"

"I don't want you," he replied, his intensity folded into a hoarse whisper. "I can't." His blond hair dripped into his eyes, tangling in his spiky lashes.

Juliet raised herself on the balls of her feet, forcing him to jerk back in surprise as more of her weight settled onto him. Against him. The hand in her hair loosened suddenly, fingers sliding around the curve of her neck. Palm at her cheek.

He groaned, a sound filled with the agony of indecision. With an emotion that wrenched at her heart, her soul.

Who was this man?

Was this the reality that hid beneath the rigid mask?

"You make it hurt less," he said roughly. "God help me, I don't know what else to do. I—*I need you.*"

Juliet grabbed the back of his head, threw everything she'd ever known to the wind, and pulled his mouth to hers. His lips were wet and cool to the touch, but his mouth—God have mercy, his warm, greedy mouth opened under her assault and reversed the control so quickly, so thoroughly that she was left reeling.

Suddenly, she was on the defensive, his arms banding around her waist and lifting her off the ground. She tunneled her fingers into his hair, seizing wet handfuls for balance as she matched his probing tongue with her own. Darted into his mouth, rasping against his tongue, tasting him.

Craving him.

His breath wrenched in his chest, sharp, short pants that only served to drive her higher, hotter; need coiled from her lips to her womb in a savage spring that begged release, and she moaned against his lips. Gasped as he caught her lower lip between his teeth and bit down, then swept the small ache away with his tongue.

The rain fell over them both, bounced from the wide fronds around them as he carried her through the minuscule jungle.

She didn't know how, when, but Juliet found herself laid out on the pallet beneath the makeshift blue tent. The blankets were soft beneath her, clinging to her wet skin.

Caleb knelt between her upraised knees, hair dripping into his eyes. With the jagged scars curving over his jaw, he looked dangerous. Wild and untamed. His eyes blazed in blue fire.

His lips settled into a tight, faintly crooked line.

She sat up, reaching for the hem of her shirt as he opened his mouth. A thrill rippled through her when whatever he'd intended to say caught somewhere between mind and desire as she whipped the wet fabric over her head. Water splattered the canvas roof, but he didn't notice.

He stared at her, at her full breasts and tattooed bar code. At her dusky nipples, puckered and standing proudly to attention.

His hands seemed frozen in mid-air. Cords stood out in his neck; visible signs of a faltering control.

His eyes devoured her. Feasted as if she were the most beautiful thing he'd ever seen.

"Juliet," he rasped.

Trembling, aching, she touched her own nipple with a finger, jolting as the sensitive nub lanced an arrow of liquid need straight to her loins. He threw back his head, groaning.

"Don't," he said sharply, all pretense of restraint fading. "Juliet, you need—"

Anger slid through veins already molten with wanting. Juliet pinched her nipple between two fingers. "I need you," she said, and moaned as the sweet sensation filled her skin. Her mind. "You asked me to tell you."

"God help me."

She reached for her skirt. He stopped her, grabbing her wrist in his scarred hand and staring down at that small connection as if he'd never seen anything like it. His eyes narrowed. His throat worked; air or words or regrets, she didn't know.

Then, slowly, he let her go. Finger by finger. "More," he whispered.

Juliet smiled. She reached for the end of her skirt, pulling up the hem bit by bit and reveling in the way his eyes followed the motion. They burned an unholy blue, like fire at its very heart. Searing. All but tangible.

As the fabric cleared her thighs, he locked his jaw.

The skirt pooled between her legs, rough against her sensitive flesh, and Juliet couldn't help it. She pressed the material against herself. The sound she made evoked an answering sound from him, rough and wanting; a warning, a four-letter plea.

She looked down at her hand, pale against the dark skirt, and her hips jerked. Once.

It was enough.

Caleb curled his fingers into the end of the skirt and pulled hard enough that the waistband stretched. The material slid from her legs, tore out of her grasp, and left her naked to the night air.

Naked to his voracious study.

For a moment, uncertainty flashed through her. She raised her hands, but he grabbed her wrists, once more tugging them above her head. She leaned back as he guided her, her back cradled by the blankets, her wrists locked above her head.

"So beautiful," he murmured, dropping his face to nuzzle one tender breast. His lips rasped across her skin and she shuddered. "I never imagined—" He caught himself with a harsh chuckle. "Hell, I imagined. Every. Fucking. Night." His lips closed over her nipple with the last word, and she arched off the blankets, crying out.

She didn't know what it was about him. About them together. Need, surprise, elation; she felt it all in his arms.

He laved at the sensitive peak, little jolts of electricity shooting through her nerves with every flick of his tongue. Every graze of his teeth.

Not to be forgotten, Caleb moved to her other nipple and bit down. Hard enough that she jolted out of her skin. Thunder stole her wild sound, but he murmured approval, even as the rest of her writhed beneath him. Ignored.

"Pl-please," she gasped.

"Are you lying to me?"

Her eyes squeezed shut. His hot breath warmed the underside of her left breast. "No," she managed. "I'm—oh, God." His tongue slid over the faintly raised lines of her tattoo, sending another jolt through her.

Suddenly, his weight was gone, and Juliet was able to move her arms. She elbowed herself up, shaking back her wet hair, and watched as he shrugged out of his shirt. He tossed it over his shoulder. Muscles gleamed in the sporadic light, edged in hard lines and jagged furrows.

The shirt splatted against the wet ground, ruined and forgotten, but Caleb hesitated. Her stare fixed on his scars.

His expression hardened.

Juliet reached out a shaking hand. The skin around his eyes flinched as the tip of her index finger traced the most lurid of the ropy ridges at his side. His hands closed painfully over hers. "This is what I am," he said, his voice taut with effort. Masked. "It's what I've become."

A traitor. Branded for life. The knowledge sizzled between them. Unspoken. Unable to be ignored.

Cautiously, using his grip on her hand for leverage, Juliet eased closer. Her free hand splayed over the old wounds. Covered them, her soft palm to his rough skin.

He shuddered.

Slowly, shivering as droplets of water dripped from her hair and rolled down her skin, she traced the scarred nodules over his ribs. Down his side, across his hip.

Wordlessly, she twisted her trapped hand free and slid it up his other side. Rough in one palm and slick, smooth in the other. Muscles bunched. The mouthwatering wall of his abdominal muscles rippled.

Could she accept this?

Accept him?

"Jules—"

"Yes," she said fiercely, looking up. His gaze met hers, and in it, she saw everything he had never let her see. Caution. Uncertainty. That guardedness he held so close, and deeply buried, mired in shades of blue, something fierce.

Something desperate.

His expression softened. "God help us both," he whispered, and bent an arm around the small of her back.

CHAPTER ELEVEN

Caleb's hand flattened over her chest, pressed her down, pushed her until she lay back against the blankets, naked and damp and shivering.

Only part was from cold. Raw lust clung to every nerve, dragged reckless nails over her skin. He bent over her, powerful arms braced, and searched her face.

Juliet bit her upper lip. Rain and thunder and the slam of her heartbeat filled the wordless tension between them, stretched thin and fragile.

She held her breath.

The scarred corner of his mouth twitched, and he lowered his lips to her chin. Nipped, hard enough to make her exhale on a gasp, before tracing a warm, wet line down her throat.

She tilted her head back. Stretched languorously beneath his slow, thorough exploration. He kissed each breast, tongue flicking over her nipples with quick, maddening precision, and trailed across her navel. She squirmed as that heat coiled tighter in her belly. As if her blood had been replaced by raw need, by fire and something smooth and silken.

His breath fanned the brown curls between her legs, and she twined her fingers through her own hair, eyes squeezed shut.

Caleb chuckled.

Before she could do anything, say anything—put him in his place, beg for more—he buried his mouth between her legs and sent her reeling for the stars. His slick tongue parted the folds of her swollen flesh, swept over the hardened, nerve-shattering nub of her clit. She gasped, arching, knees falling farther apart and he grabbed her thighs, holding her open. Exposed.

She didn't dare open her eyes. Thunder rocked the sky, but all she could hear was her own heartbeat, fast and loud, and her own cries. They got faster and tighter, mimicking the gathering pressure between her legs, jarred loose by every flick of his tongue. His lips closed over her, sucked hard, and her hips jerked so fast that she slapped her hands over her mouth.

The lightest touch made her tremble, legs locked tightly and her head thrashing. Caleb dragged the wet, flat side of his tongue across the cleft of her body and slid a finger inside her.

Her hips shot off the makeshift bed, forcing Caleb to flatten his free hand against her abdomen to keep her still. Juliet shook her head, all but sobbing with the mounting pressure, hips twisting, but he didn't let her up. Over and over he licked her, clever tongue and wicked fingers working her, plunging in and out of her body until she shuddered.

"Please," she begged, "please, Caleb, please!"

He raised his eyes, eyes glinting. Two broad fingers penetrated her sensitive flesh, sliding into her. Sliding out. "Do you want me?"

"Yes!"

"Now?"

Her own hands slid down her body. Seized her breasts in each palm and squeezed. Wild sensations shot through her. His eyes narrowed. Glittered dangerously.

"Yes," she whispered.

"Beautiful," he managed, and shucked his jeans with a few deft pulls. He crawled up her body, warm skin to the throbbing mass of sensitized nerves that was all she had left. Every touch, every press, every brush of his body left her that much closer. That much hungrier.

Caleb positioned himself at the entrance to her body and paused.

Alarms flickered.

"Wait!" she cried, and he froze.

His expression closed, shuttered as neatly as if she'd pulled a switch, but she grabbed his arm in one hand and wildly patted the blankets with the other. "Don't you dare," she managed, grit-

ting her teeth with the effort to focus. "I have a—
Somewhere, damn it."

"Jules—"

"Here!" Crowing with triumph, she found the
discarded foil and held it up between two fingers.
Her gaze met his over the corrugated edge.

His filled with laughter.

Despite the need curling through her, singing
in her blood, her body relaxed. Her lips twitched.
"Well, it's just . . . You know."

He took the packet from her fingers, cupped
her hand, and pressed a kiss to her palm. Need
slammed hard and fast and bone-rattlingly deep.

Need, and something else that curled into her
heart and ached.

Caleb tore the packet open, unrolled the rubber over the erection thrust thick and hard from a
thatch of golden hair, and grinned at her expression.

"You look like you're going to eat me," he said,
raw approval in his eyes.

"Give me the chance," Juliet replied. She sat up,
breasts heavy and swollen and so sensitive that
even the air whispering across them made her
gasp in wonder.

His eyebrows climbed as she crawled across the
small space. Knitted with intense concentration as
she braced her hands on his shoulders. The deluge
continued over their heads, wave upon wave of
thunder and rain, but she didn't care.

There was only him. Caleb Leigh.

Soothsayer.

Hers. For now.

Straddling his waist, she thrilled as his hands settled on her hips. His breath caught in his throat as the center of her body slid over his erection. She was wet, pulsing with her arousal, and he shuddered.

Taking him in hand, she positioned his cock just right, slid closer until just the very tip of him nudged at her swollen flesh.

It was going to drive her mad.

But not before he broke.

He growled something rough and low, fingers digging into her hips, and pulled her tight, flush against him, impaling her with a sudden thrust.

She threw her head back on a savage, exultant cry.

"Yes," he sighed, muscles standing out from neck to thigh. His arms bulged as he raised her again, tightened as he guided her back to him; each time filling her more and more, deeper and thicker and so tight, she gasped with each thrust.

She didn't have control here. She hadn't thought she would. Instead, he guided her, pushed and pulled her body, eyes feasting as she arched her back in overwhelming delight. Her breasts glistened with sweat, and he dropped his mouth to taste them.

Harder, faster, he let her ride him but set the pace, his jaw tense. The pressure built slowly this time, circling out from the point where their bodies joined into a rippling, pulsing tide of pleasure and greed and desperate desire.

His hands swept up her back, but she didn't need his help anymore as their hips rocked in tandem, bodies slamming together. It swept up through her knees, planted on the rain-dampened blankets, filled her belly. Her chest, her mind. Over and over he stroked himself with her, thrust against her, into her, fingers curling into her hair and holding her still as he stared up into her face.

Love me, she thought, and came apart in his hands. It exploded through her, a detonation of nerves and feeling and raw emotion, leaving her skin tingling and blood singing as her breath left her body on a long, desperate moan.

His muscles surged under her hands, shoulders rising, and he shoved her back to the blankets so fast that her body had no time to register the change. Harder, faster he pumped into her, eyes glittering, face drawn taut. Without warning, while she still clenched and pulsed around him, his hips jerked, lost rhythm, and pinned hers. He groaned her name, gasping on it, muscles jerking hard as he struggled to keep his own weight while his features hardened, reddened with effort.

With release.

For a long moment, only the slam of her heart filled the rush of rain hitting the greenery outside the open tent.

Juliet's eyes drifted closed. Her breath evened with effort.

Then caught again as Caleb's weight shifted away. He withdrew from her gently. She bit her upper lip.

Was this where the apologies started?

Suddenly, his weight settled beside her again, naked shoulder to legs, and he curled an arm around her tightly.

Tears pricked at her eyes.

She kept them tightly closed. His head settled on the pillow beside her, his cheek nestled into her hair, and Juliet didn't dare breathe. What if he realized what it was he was doing?

What if he reverted back to ice?

Caleb's breath fanned her cheek, and she shifted. His arm tightened, and the silence between them grew. Stretched until it seemed as tense as a rubber band on the verge of breaking.

Juliet stared blankly into the dark. The rain beat down on the wide leaves, sprinkling water everywhere as the slender stalks snapped back with every heavy raindrop.

She took a slow, deep breath. "I'm sorry."

Against her back, the line of Caleb's body went rigid.

She forged on hurriedly, getting it out, forcing the words from her aching chest before he could leave, make her look at him, hell, *anything*. "I blamed you for the coven and I'm sorry. I know they used me—Curio used me," she amended bitterly. "I know I wasn't anything more than a . . . an energy boost for them. I'm sorry I tried to kill you, I'm sorry I— Oh, God." Her voice shook. "I'm so sorry I stabbed you."

Caleb rose over her on one elbow, his features a hard silhouette in the dark. But his fingers were gentle as he traced the shape of her lower lip.

"Don't apologize," he said. Rough, low, it all but vibrated with an intensity she didn't understand. "Don't ever apologize to me. I don't— *Damn it.*"

As if pushed, as if touching her burned, he rolled away. Reached for his jeans, every motion sharp and angry.

She squeezed her eyes shut before the tears could start.

Fabric rustled. For a long moment, only the whisper of clothing donned and the steady pitter-patter of rain filled the empty, aching silence.

Then, Caleb's voice. "Juliet." Quiet, again, that damned calm she loathed so much.

Juliet's mouth twisted. The lingering surge of ecstasy, the endorphins released from the orgasm that had rocked her down to her soul, faded under a sweeping veil of . . . anger? Disappointment?

Exhaustion.

She was too tired for anything else.

Like she hadn't seen this coming.

"Go, then," she said, rolling over as if she could wipe away his presence by not looking at him. She crossed her arm over her chest, fighting back a raw, shameful surge of tears.

"Jules," he said, insistent. His hand curved over her bare hip.

She sat up, knocking his hand away, and opened her mouth to lash out, to hurt him; hell, anything that didn't involve hating herself for making another bad choice.

His scarred hand slipped over her mouth.

His eyes traced the dark foliage around them,

narrowed. Only then did she realize that his body was locked down, leashed taut.

Ready.

Fear slipped in behind anger. Squeezed her heart with icy fingers. She reached for her discarded clothes, then jumped when he shook his head. "There," he whispered, pointing to the corner of her pillow.

Her jeans and sports bra were folded beside it, rumpled during their lovemaking, but clean. A sweatshirt lay nearby. Not hers, but in better condition than anything else she had.

"Get dressed," he whispered, tense and barely a sound. He did the same, not a single motion wasted. "Something's wrong."

"How can you tell?"

He shook his head again, finger to his lips, and slid out from under the canvas tent.

She was just pulling down the dark purple sweatshirt when she heard it. Voices. Muffled and trying to be quiet, but clear. He got dressed quickly.

When Caleb reached under the canvas, beckoning, she slid her hand into his.

He helped her out, tugging her into a crouch. "I want you to wait for my signal, then run to the house."

Juliet blanched. "What if they're already there?"

The look in Caleb's eye promised more than murder. "Stay with me, then. Stay close, and do what I say."

As if she ever got the chance to do anything else.

Juliet nodded, her eyes wide in the dark.

The voices didn't come again, or maybe she couldn't hear it over the steady drum of rain and thunder and her own frightened heartbeat. Caleb remained crouched, making his way down the small path, her hand tight in his.

She was grateful for it. Whatever lingering remnants of the satisfaction she'd felt at his hands had flipped to fear. And to anger.

How dare they? How dare they continue to harass her? To interrupt what had been a moment of pure . . . pure. . .

Pure stupidity.

She winced as she stubbed her booted toe against the raised edge of a stone. His grip tightened, made sure she was standing, then let go. In the gloomy light that was all the storm provided of what had to be late afternoon, Caleb's expression was grim. He raised a finger to his lips.

She nodded. Not a word. She could do that.

Slowly, he eased out of the fronds, bending back the foliage so she could climb out. The rain battered the volcanic sand to black mud, which squelched as she stepped into it.

Skin crawling, she studied the small beach. Nothing moved. Only the rain, sharp and steady, and the plants that bent and swayed beneath the pressure. The steam rolled like a living thing, a specter of gray pushed and scattered by the rain pouring into the hot springs.

"I don't see anything," she whispered.

He stood. "Keep down, keep low. Stay on my tail no matter what."

"Got it." She hesitated. "Caleb?"

He cupped the back of her head with one broad palm, his eyes meeting hers. "We'll get you through this, Jules." He let her go and strode toward the far bank of giant fronds.

Juliet shook her head. "It's not me I'm worried about," she muttered at his back, and sprinted after him.

She managed to close half the distance when the rapport of gunfire echoed from the house across the valley.

Caleb broke into a run. She lengthened her stride, only to flounder when he stopped abruptly. Mud speckled her legs as he whirled, face white and set in wild edges, and tackled her at the waist.

She hit the ground, every muscle and bone jarred, but the back of her head rebounded off his palm instead of the rock she expected. "Roll!" he roared.

She did. The world tilted, end over end as she rolled over and over, until the foliage slammed into her back and she was left staring at splotches of mud leaping into the air where they'd been only moments before.

Caleb covered her body with his, wrapping his arms around her head and holding her tightly to his chest. His heart thudded in her ear.

Thunder boomed directly overhead, a crack of sound that covered his curse. "Crawl!"

Blindly obeying his orders, her own heart hammering a staccato beat of terror between thunderous surges of electricity, Juliet pushed to her hands and knees and crawled along the foliage line.

More gunfire peppered through the steady thrum of rain. Her chest squeezed. What was happening at the house?

Were the others dead? Fighting?

Oh, Jesus, Caleb's sister was vulnerable.

Caleb grabbed her ankle. When she looked back over her shoulder, he pointed at a rocky outcropping tucked into the side of the crescent point. The bay's volcanic water licked against the edge of a shelf, just big enough to hide one.

She shook her head vehemently.

"It's either you or me," Caleb said tightly, his eyes narrowed beneath the fringe of his dripping air. The rain traced his features, saturating both of them to the skin, and she shivered. "Can you shoot someone?"

"If I have to."

"Have you before?"

Juliet hesitated. He read it as clear as day on her face, and mouth twisting, he surged past her on the narrow path. Without saying anything, he reached back, grabbed her arm, and yanked her to her feet.

Her skin crawled, as if it would peel back from the bull's-eye she felt sure was painted between her shoulder blades. She stared at the empty black maw of the nearly hidden cleft and balked. "I can't—"

He spun her around, gaze fierce as he grabbed both shoulders and pulled her to him. "Don't make me watch you die, too," he said savagely, and kissed her. Hard. Angry.

Desperate.

Before she could do anything, say anything, kiss him back and beg him not to leave her, he pushed her into the narrow opening and melded away into the storm.

She staggered, slammed against the back of the small crack, and clenched her teeth. Pain shredded through her elbows, her shoulders, as they hit the rock.

Terror speared through her mind.

Her chest.

Stole her breath.

Alone. He'd left her alone. He'd left her.

No. He'd be back. He wouldn't leave her for long. He'd come back for her.

He had to.

Her fists tightened against the stony cliff face, fingernails digging hard enough into her palms to draw blood, but it didn't help.

He wouldn't leave her.

Wouldn't I? he'd asked her. It seemed like ages ago.

"Oh, God," she whispered, shuddering. Lightning shimmered across the sky, little more than a narrow line above her head, and she wrapped her arms around her chest.

He'd already left her once. He'd do it again.

They all left.

Juliet pushed away from the wall, tears thick in her eyes, her throat, and stumbled across the uneven ground. The tiny chasm walls clung to her, scraped across her arms, her hands as she felt for the opening.

The rain slapped against her face as she staggered back into the open. A glint of blue shimmered in the dark, and strong arms folded around her.

Fear slammed into raw, angry relief. "Caleb," she sobbed, clinging to his sodden coat.

Lightning flashed. In the nanosecond of light, everything sheened with purple and white. Dark eyes narrowed. Rain slicked over a face both broad and hard, set in edged lines that shifted as those arms tightened around her. Wet metal glinted in her peripheral.

Relief flipped back into terror.

Juliet shoved at the man's broad chest with all her might, screaming. Pain rocked through her temple. Detonated through her skull. Her vision flashed, purple and white and raw, bloody red, and she sagged.

The world shifted. Suddenly, Juliet found herself folded in half, a shoulder digging into her soft middle. Lethargy sucked at her, clung to her as she tried to shape the words. "Cale—Caleb . . ."

The breath slammed out of her as the shoulder rammed into her stomach. She choked, struggled to scream and couldn't shape the thick cobwebs of her thoughts around it. Her head throbbed.

Help . . . me. . .

The world faded.

CHAPTER TWELVE

Rain sluiced over the cracked glass windows. Director Adams reached over without looking up, turning up the lamp on her borrowed desk until the bright light washed away the storm-shrouded gloom infiltrating every inch of the city.

Summer storms were the worst. Sudden and violent.

And about as familiar as anything else in New Seattle.

Parker rested her chin in her hand, poring over the new Mission docket the bloody old bat had left her. Operation Wayward Rose. The call sign suited the woman's name, Parker thought. Juliet.

She doubted anyone below topside education would get the reference, but that didn't bother her.

Old books didn't see much play in this world.

Parker tapped the end of her pen against the readout frame as thunder rattled the glass. No matter how many times she read the file, it didn't change.

As director, she controlled every case that crossed her desk. Many at the same time. At least three main offices served as headquarters where Mission teams came and went, and there were at least eighty-six sanctioned safe houses at any given time. The men and women and monsters on the list were mass murderers, ritualists, and even worse.

Some unknown girl had single-handedly jumped the most dangerous witches known to the Mission, and Parker wanted to know why.

Juliet Carpenter.

It meant nothing. But because she didn't like not knowing, Parker ran the name through the Mission database again.

Like the five different attempts before it, the search came up blank.

"And that," she murmured, studying the error message on the computer monitor, "is the problem."

Any name on the list should have had *something*.

She took a deep breath, checked her watch, and gave up all pretense of patience. Clipping the tiny comm earpiece to the shell of her ear, she punched in Jonas Stone's comm number by memory.

Parker memorized everything. It was her thing.

The earpiece vibrated faintly as the signal searched for the frequency.

The line clicked over. "Yes, ma'am."

Parker blinked at the clear, almost perfect tenor voice. "How did you know it was me?" she asked, curiosity getting the best of her. "I've never contacted you directly."

Pleasant amusement filled his voice as he replied, "I've got nearly every frequency on the Mission database keyed in, ma'am. Including yours."

"I assume that information is kept secure, Mr. Stone?"

"Unbreakable, ma'am."

"Good." She pulled the digital readout closer to her. "Operation Wayward Rose. What's your status?"

Stone hesitated. Keys clattered in the background, wrapped in white noise. Electricity, maybe. Machines. "I realize that you gave me two hours, but . . ."

"But?"

"I'm looking for a very, very tiny needle in a really large city," he said slowly. "The crawl is still compiling."

"How long?"

"Soon, ma'am. It'd be sooner if I could dedicate every resource to the search. If you need me to drop everything else—"

"Unnecessary," Parker cut in evenly. "Get me what you can when it's time, but I've got something else I want you to look for in the interim."

"Above Ghostwatch?"

Parker checked the delicate gold watch at her wrist. The filigree face ticked faithfully. "What's the status of Ghostwatch?"

"Miles is in position and keeping tabs on the supposed mark, but I have to tell you, ma'am, I don't think we've got the right one."

"Why is that?"

"The MO goes against everything this woman is doing. Either she's the best actress in the universe, or it's not her."

Momentarily sidetracked, Parker studied the dark glass window beside her, sheets of rain picked out by the flickering streetlights beyond. Natural light didn't make it down this far on average, but the pitch-black quality suggested that topside wasn't seeing much daylight through the storm clouds.

She shook her head. "Stay on her."

"Banking on acting school, ma'am?"

She tipped her head, once more checking her watch. "Are there any other leads?"

"Two. Eckhart's tracking one from his desk."

"And the other?"

"Compiling over here."

"Fine. Don't pull Miles until you either catch her, or clear her. No guesswork. Am I understood?"

"Yes, ma'am," he replied good-naturedly. "About the extra work on Wayward Rose?"

Parker snapped her fingers. "Juliet Carpenter. I want you to run her through every system you can get access to."

Another hesitation on the line. Parker stood,

smoothing down her pantsuit, her smile a grim line as he said slowly, "I don't mean to be rude, ma'am, but I'm already doing that."

"Maybe I didn't make myself clear," she replied in level tones. "*Every* system you can *get access to*. And I want you to begin on the Church's mainframe."

A whistle punctuated the line. "I don't have access to that one."

"Let's not play games, Mr. Stone."

Another pause. Then, "So, you want me to . . . uh, crawl all the databases. Right. Yes, ma'am." Every word was cautiously even. "I'll be giving you this information directly, then. Anything else?"

"You have your orders, Agent Stone. Be in touch."

Parker pulled the mic off her ear, pinching the tiny metal bit between thumb and forefinger as the unit on her desk went dark.

She would be damned, she thought, if the Church pulled her teams into something less than aboveboard. Not without informing her *every* step of the way.

She was responsible for the safety of her missionaries. *She* would make the decision to put them in jeopardy, or get them out.

And if Mrs. Parrish was playing politics, Parker wanted the dirt.

The lights in the office flickered, quick enough that she paused to rub at her eyes. The lower level electricity grids were slipshod at best, but Parker knew the Mission offices maintained private generators just for this sort of problem.

Muttering, she swiped the comm unit from her desk and inserted the earpiece into its designated holder, crossing to the door as she did. She swung it open, mind already on her mental to-do list, and froze.

Her tongue stuck to the roof of her mouth as six feet and five inches of raw man filled the space behind the door.

Simon Wells lounged in the frame, fingertips caught loosely on the upper ledge and muscles idly bulging. His blue tank top sported a vee of sweat, his hair damp against his forehead. Workout pants slung low on his hips, button-down legs open at the bottom to fall over trashed sneakers.

The pose showed off every mouthwatering muscle in his arms and shoulders, and the smile shaping his mouth could only be called easy. Indolent.

Parker stiffened as his hazel eyes mirrored her own study, from the crown of her neat copper hair to the tips of her pristine, four-hundred-dollar shoes.

"What?" she snapped, and caught herself as his mouth lifted at the corner of his damned smirk. She forced calm. "What do you need, Mr. Wells?"

"I caught the lights flickering."

His voice was easy, too. Everything he did was easy, she thought crossly. Easy smile, easy way of speaking, easy appraisal.

Easy flex of muscle as he lowered his arms, hands fisting at his hips.

"So," he drawled, amusement slipping into his

tone, "I figured I'd come see if you all had some sort of generator."

Parker shook her head.

"You should look into it," he offered, misreading her attempt for clarity as denial. "Days like this don't—"

She flicked her fingers at him, as if by the action he would only just vanish. She couldn't be so lucky. "We do," she interrupted. "I was just on my way to see to it."

"You, Director?" One of his dark eyebrows arched, and he made no attempt to get out of her way. His body blocked the hallway beyond—her jaw set as she thought it—with ease.

"Yes," she said, every word arctic. "Me, Mr. Wells. Is there a problem with that?"

"Certainly not, ma'am." He straightened, but he didn't step aside. His eyes glinted over that telltale smirk. "But you're busy. Why don't you tell me where it is and I'll—"

"If you'll get out of my way, I'd already intended to handle it."

Wells's arms rose, forearms bracing against the doorjamb. The sheer arrogance of the idle lean set Parker's teeth on edge. "I don't mind doing it," he told her. "It's a nice break from training."

"Then you need more training," she replied coolly. "I think you can handle two more hours."

The amusement left his face so quickly, it was as if shutters slammed shut. His eyes glittered, harder. Edgier. "You think so?"

A cold snap gathered in the pit of her stomach.

Parker's chin lifted. "Tell Mr. Eckhart to ramp it up to level five. Your spirits are too high. Clearly, we're not testing you at your optimal level."

Slowly, his muscled arms lowered. He leaned aside, but he didn't give her a wholly clear path. "Yes, ma'am," he drawled.

It was a choice. A test. Remain trapped in her office, or push by a man who could break her in two if he felt so inclined.

Parker refused to be trapped by a Church mole.

She angled her shoulders to ease by him, trying to touch him as little as possible, then froze as one sweaty arm braced against the wall in front of her face.

Heart pounding, she looked up into eyes that met hers without reserve. They still glittered, that odd intensity that seemed to define his every move.

He was good.

Hell, he was probably as good as her top agents.

Parker didn't want to know that.

"Yes, Mr. Wells?" she said calmly.

His nostrils flared as he inhaled. "Whatever perfume you're wearing," he told her, "I like it. Wear it again."

Reeling under the casual arrogance of the command, Parker didn't move when he dropped his arm, staring at him for a long, silent moment. Then, eyes narrowing, she said, "Four hours, Mr. Wells. Level five. I expect nothing short of stellar scores."

His lips were already twitching into a smile as she turned and strode down the hallway, heels clicking on the scarred linoleum.

"Yes," he said to her back, "*Director* Adams."

She paused as a thought occurred to her. Turning, hands on her hips, she asked, "Where is Mr. Nelson?"

Wells hadn't moved, watching her. Watching her rear, more like. Men like him were all the same. But his gaze shifted to hers. "Tobias is on a mission."

Her eyebrows snapped together. "I approved no such mission. Whose?"

His eyes crinkled. Laughter. He was *laughing* at her, blast it. "Let me know if you need help with the generator." A beat. "Director."

Parker turned away before she lost the temper roiling behind her teeth. She picked her way across the open floor, for once grateful that the mid-low teams weren't the type to stop her to chitchat.

She didn't want chitchat.

She wanted answers.

If she'd even had an iota of doubt, Wells blew it away. The so-called missionaries weren't hers to use. They were nothing more than rats, pawns in some greater game, and they weren't answering to her.

To whom, then? Mrs. Parrish?

A sour-faced queen if there was one. But who was playing the game?

Once she located the maintenance doors, she pushed inside and reaffixed the earpiece to her ear. Stone's frequency clicked over to his voice. "Yes—"

She cut him off. "One more thing, Agent Stone.

Two new agents have been placed in this Mission. Church agents, let me be clear."

"That's . . . odd," he said. "Did you send for them?"

"Absolutely not," she told him. "I want you to comb everything you can and get me information on Tobias Nelson and Simon Wells."

"Are we sure that's their real names?" he asked as a keyboard clicked rapidly in the background. "I mean, most of us got new ones."

She thought about it. "Right. Search for any information regarding a particular tattoo."

"Hit me with it."

"It's a bar code."

"Do you know what it says?"

Parker glanced over her shoulder at the maintenance door. It remained closed. The hum of machinery around her would keep the rest of her conversation covert. "I am fluent in several languages, Mr. Stone, but computer is not one. Just see what you can find about bar codes on missionaries. In fact, search up anything regarding bar codes within the Holy Order mainframe. Dig as deep as you have to."

The agent coughed politely. "Director, am I to assume this is off the books?"

"Indubitably."

"Man, I love that word," he said happily, and clicked off the channel.

Parker stared at her comm unit for a long moment. Then, shaking her head, she went in search of the generator.

CHAPTER THIRTEEN

A corpse thudded to the ground in a graceless tangle of limbs. Blood gushed across the muddy earth, forced out by the impact of the man's own dead weight.

Lifeless limbs and ashen skin. A pile of faceless corpses—Jesus Christ, what did it mean?

Why had he *seen* Juliet at the top of it all?

Who was she to them? Who the fuck were *them*?

Caleb's boot crunched against ribs that felt nothing. His curse echoed savagely in the tomb-like silence that followed in the wake of the transient storm.

Clapping the clinging grit from her hands, Naomi slanted him a wary look from beneath the fringe of her magenta bangs. Wordlessly, she rolled the body he'd kicked back toward herself.

"Settle down," Silas ordered, stepping over the corpse he'd dropped. "We'll get rid of the bodies and begin a search pattern."

"She's gone," Caleb snarled, as if Silas hadn't been there when Caleb had gone tearing back toward the water. As if he hadn't witnessed Caleb's fury and panic.

I blamed you for the coven and I'm sorry.

Rage clamored inside his skull, vicious claws tearing at the thinning confines of his own restraint. His fingers curled and uncurled, fists clenching as he struggled to breathe deeply. In and out. Slow and steady— *"Fuck!"*

Naomi stepped over the only female corpse and knelt by the ruins of her face. Dispassionately, she tipped the remains of the jaw up. Her purple eyes flicked to Silas. "Nice shot."

The man nodded, but his gaze remained on Caleb. "See what you can find out, Nai. Leigh, if you don't settle down—"

Caleb whirled on him, watched as Silas's shoulders squared. As his massive chest broadened, feet braced, legs steady.

He was almost stupid enough to go for it. A fight. A brawl—*fuck it*, a murder. He didn't know. He didn't care.

Juliet was gone.

"You need to calm down," Silas was saying, his rumbling tone just this side of reassuring. Just *that* side of a threat. "You aren't going to be useful to anyone if you don't stick a lid on it." His eyes narrowed. "Now."

Caleb closed the distance between them, fists balled. Silas towered over him, but he was beyond seeing. Beyond fucking caring.

Juliet was gone.

And the visions he'd had suggested she was so much more to them—them, Christ, whoever *they* were—than just . . . just. . .

What the hell was she? A mascot? A tool?

A battery?

He hated that he could glimpse the future. Hated it. "Where's Jessie?" he demanded.

"Not going to help."

"Bullshit, she can *see* where they are!"

The ex-missionary was bulky, but he wasn't slow. A big hand shot out and twisted in Caleb's collar. "You listen to me," he growled. "Jessie's still out. I'll be damned if—Fuck me, kid, knock it off!"

Caleb pulled back a fist and grunted when the momentum of his swing snagged. Bone to bone, pain snapped a warning through a black tide of rage and he jerked his head around to find Naomi's arm hooked through his.

It was the same catch she'd pulled on her partner.

His eyes narrowed.

"Can it," she said flatly. "Or I swear to God, I'll kick both your asses."

Silas's grip tightened on Caleb's collar.

Her lip curled. "This isn't helping Jessie." Caleb jerked at her arm. She let him go so fast, it sent him staggering, saved only by Silas's grip on his shirt. "And it sure as shit isn't helping your girlfriend. Man up, the both of you."

Abruptly, Silas let him go, and Caleb wrenched backward with a savage, snarling curse.

"I know what you're feeling," Silas said. "Believe me, I know. Whatever happened, we'll get her, okay? But we can't go running in blind."

Caleb forced himself to breathe. In. His fists clenched. Out. He closed his eyes.

Why the hell had he left her?

Silas turned his back. "Are they missionaries?"

"Nope." Naomi nudged the girl with the toe of her boot. "If I had to call it, I'd say witches."

Caleb dug his fingers into his eyes. "Alicia. Son of a bitch."

"Friend of yours?" Silas knelt to rifle through pockets.

"No. Hell, no. She's the current leader, took over after I killed Curio."

"For which I owe you one," Silas told him. With one tug, he flipped the girl's body over, checking the back pockets of her filthy cargo pants. Blood dribbled into the sand, lightened to pink with brain fluid. "You know these guys?"

Caleb studied a thin, whiskered face. Hook nose, fleshy lips slackened in death.

Nothing. Not even a ghost of a memory. If he'd ever met the witch, he didn't stand out.

A cursory inspection of all three corpses yielded nothing but equal parts frustration and impatience. "None of them look familiar." He scraped stiff fingers through his hair. "I've been out of that coven for a year. Damn it, Silas! What do they want with her?"

Naomi glanced at him. "Ever consider that this goes beyond your girlfriend?"

Finding nothing, Silas rose, his gaze straying to the house behind her. "I was thinking the same thing."

Caleb frowned at the bodies, already turning waxen in the faded light. Two men, one woman. Witches. Not missionaries. Forcing himself to be still, to *think* through the anger ricocheting across every nerve, he followed Silas's gaze to the house.

His eyes narrowed. "What do you mean?"

The look Naomi slanted him was barely this side of pitying. "Seriously?"

"Nai," Silas warned, then nodded to Caleb. "Jessie and Juliet both have the same tattoo."

"You know?"

Silas sighed. "Leigh, I've been living with Jessie for a year," he said flatly.

Caleb took the hint.

"I'll take care of these," Naomi said, bending to haul the girl into her arms. The ruins of her face dribbled, blood and fleshy gibbets spattering Naomi's shoulder, but the pretty witch didn't even flinch.

Tough. Caleb locked his jaw. Everyone was tough.

Except Juliet.

"Fuck," he hissed out. "Jess has had it all her life. Until I saw it on Juliet just yesterday, I didn't think anything about it. For all I knew, it had something to do with before I was born."

"Your mother never said?" Silas clasped his hands behind his back, an idle readiness that only helped remind Caleb of what the man had used to be. Still, in a way, was. A soldier.

On Caleb's side, if barely, but a soldier nevertheless.

His smile thinned. "Witches get shit for lives. For all I knew, she and Jessie had escaped some kind of human trafficking ring before I was born. God only knows, okay? Our mother taught us how to run and hide and survive. Then she died."

Silas said nothing, his gray-green eyes steady.

Caleb jammed his hands into the pockets of his too-large jeans and stared at the cloudy sky, instead. "Looking back, I can't help but think that she had a reason. Maybe that tattoo ties in to something our mom did, or used to do. Maybe it's the reason we always had to run, I don't know."

"I asked Jessie about it once."

"And?"

Silas hesitated. "She said the same thing you did, that she's had it for as long as she could remember. That you both only ever knew your mother."

"That's true," Caleb conceded.

"That much, anyway?"

His smile twisted. "Jess is the best liar you'll ever meet."

"Next to you?" Silas's tone wasn't gracious.

Caleb shook his head, exhaustion eating away the last of his reserves. "Better than me," he corrected wearily. He turned, walking to the edge of the green bay. Behind him, Silas's footsteps crunched.

"So, what?" he prodded. "What happened?"

Frowning into the green water, Caleb said, "I asked Mom once." Slowly, he dredged through the soup of memory and adrenaline and sheer exhaustion. "I wanted to know why Jess had a tattoo and I didn't."

"And?"

"She said she hoped to God we never found out. Three months later, she was dead."

Silas grunted. His version of comfort, maybe. "How?"

"Murdered. I was ten or so."

"Missionary?"

Caleb shrugged. "Does it matter?"

"It might," Silas said, easing into Caleb's peripheral with his hands in his own pockets.

A wary sort of truce. It was almost worth a laugh.

"Maybe, but if it was, he didn't stop long enough to do anything official," Caleb said. "No words, no orders, no nothing. Just killed her. Imagine my surprise when my mom's magic shunted into me."

Silas's jaw shifted. "Did you see her die?" When Caleb only nodded, he muttered, "Jesus Christ."

"Jess found me later, hiding in the engine block of the car," Caleb said, and though the emerald water spread out like a jewel in front of him, all he saw was darkness. All he felt was edges and metal, smelled oil and sweat and fear.

He'd been a small kid. It was all that saved his life that night. That and the voice of his mother, warning him away.

"We went on the run that night and never stopped."

"So you came here," Silas said. "Why?"

Her magic had bored through his skull. Twisted him from the inside. Branded. It had been so surprising, so sudden, that he'd only been able to lie there as it filled him. Like molten metal.

"Caleb?"

He glanced over, blinking hard. "What?" he asked. "With the where?"

Silas stared at him, astonishment clear on his features.

Caleb frowned. "What?"

"You . . . sounded exactly like Jessie for a minute," he said quietly, and pinched the bridge of his nose between a thick thumb and forefinger. "Never mind. Why did you come to New Seattle?"

"Our mother grew up here," Caleb replied, but slowly. Why *had* they come? "Jess thought it a safer bet. Hundreds of thousands of people live in that shithole, so what's a couple more?"

The sound Silas made was noncommittal. "And the tattoo? Jessie's and Juliet's?"

"I already told you," Caleb growled, and caught himself. His eyebrows snapped together. "Why would both of them have the same tattoo?"

"Are they . . ." Silas hesitated, rocking back on his heels. "Are they related?"

"Oh, Jesus, fuck, I hope not," Caleb replied fervently. The mere thought sent cold chills down his spine. If Juliet was related to his sister— "No way. Mom would have said. Something. *Christ*, Silas."

"Just a thought."

Behind them, Naomi returned for a second corpse. Caleb half turned, watching as the long-legged woman yanked one of the remaining dead men up onto her shoulder. He didn't appear to be bleeding, but his head lolled awkwardly on a neck that Caleb suspected had one too many kinks to be healthy.

Silas followed his gaze. "Caught him walking into the house," he said, matter-of-fact. Caleb recognized the ragged black edges underneath the so-calm words.

He didn't have to say anything else.

"What bothers me," Silas continued, "is how they found us. This place is supposed to be hidden."

"Warded?"

"Probably," Silas replied, shaking his head. "I don't know the terms. Up until recently, the place had some kind of witchcraft in place to keep even the smallest lies from going unnoticed."

Caleb's features locked before he could flinch.

Silas's mouth hiked into a thin smile. "It's no longer the case. We decided to put more effort into going undetected. This sanctuary's supposed to be all but invisible to most detection. How did they find us?"

"Blood," called a feminine, surreally familiar voice.

His heart slammed.

He knew that voice. Knew the cadence, the roughened, imperious authority of it. Knew it, and recognized the woman who rounded the corner of the painted house.

Her long red hair had a lot more gray in it than it used to, but she still twined it into a braid that hung nearly to her hips. Her features, even at a distance, were aristocratic, thin and shaped by an age that was partly years and mostly a knowledge that went deeper than any normal stretch of life.

Matilda.

The woman who had taught him how to kill.

She raised a whip-thin hand. "Blood's the tool and the key. Caleb, my dear."

His fists clenched. "You!" Conflict waged a brutal war inside his head. Anger. Confusion.

Fuck it all, fear.

"How do you know her?" Silas demanded.

"I can answer that," Matilda said as she approached the rocky shore. Brushing off her overalls, she added briskly, "Hello, Silas, I came as soon as I could. Have you taken good care of my home?"

"Up until tonight," Silas replied flatly. "Matilda, what is going on?"

"Hey, stranger!" Naomi called.

The woman raised dark brown eyes to the last corpse, lips thinning. "Just in time to miss the starter event, it seems. Naomi, love, you've got blood on your cheek."

Caleb's teeth bared. "What the hell is going on here?"

Matilda frowned. "Young man, as delighted as I am to see that you still live, there are much bigger fish to fry. What visions have made it through that blinding curtain of yours?"

Shock slugged him in the gut.

Silas grabbed his shoulder. "What in God's name—"

"It's all right," Matilda said calmly. "I once taught Caleb a bit of magic." She strode past them both, peeling off her oversized rain coat. The end of her graying braid swayed as she took the porch steps lightly.

"A bit of magic," Caleb repeated. His tone flattened. "Yeah, sure. Let's go with that." He shrugged out of Silas's grip.

"Gentlemen, I'm sorry," Matilda said, draping her coat over the back of the rocking chair. "We've very little time, and even that is running out faster than I'd like. Silas, dear, I love you dearly, but I need your focus."

Caleb glanced at Silas. Who looked back at him.

Silas jerked his head toward the porch. "After you."

"Visions," Matilda repeated. "I need to know what you've seen, and quickly."

"What makes you think I've had any?"

Silas muttered a hard word, but Matilda only sank into the old rocking chair, eyes narrowed. "The warding magic against lies is gone," she said archly, "but I am not senile. Shall we get this out of the way? I'm still a witch, child, and there's tricks up these old sleeves that you haven't seen yet. I know a great deal."

Caleb didn't step onto the porch. "Great. Fine. Now *I* want to know—"

"Everything," she cut in quietly, "will be explained in time. You want to know who I am, and why I taught you the harvesting ritual. You want to know why it matters, and what's wrong with your sister, and why Juliet Carpenter bears the same mark as she does." Caleb flinched. "I will tell you, but things are dire. We have to be faster than explanations will allow."

Silas sat on the porch steps, elbows on his knees, and stared at Caleb, his expression hooded. "Jessie is dying, man." His mouth worked for a moment, and then, even quieter, he added, "Please."

Fuck. Caleb scowled. "Just tell me one thing."

She cocked her head, inquisitive and birdlike.

"Are—" He swallowed, forcing the words out through the tightened rasp of his throat. "Are they related? Is Juliet my . . ."

Sudden amusement lit the old woman's expression, vivacious and brilliant beneath her paper-thin skin. Her eyes crackled with laughter. "That's your one question? No," she said quickly, seeing his face. She sobered just as fast. "Rest assured, no blood ties them. I can promise you that."

"Thank God," Silas muttered, and Caleb locked his knees as relief turned them weak. He didn't say anything.

He wasn't sure he could. What was there to say? So he banged a girl who wasn't his sister. Simple as that.

His fists clenched.

Matilda rifled in a small wooden box beside the chair, withdrawing a worn pipe and old-fashioned matches. "To answer the deeper question, both of them are teacups. Very, very old teacups."

Caleb blinked at her. Then glanced sidelong at Silas, who shrugged.

Matilda smiled faintly. "I did say I wasn't senile, didn't I? Picture a teacup, gentlemen, filled with tea. Most people sip from their teacup; not them. They can't. They must break to get the tea, and now all the tea is pouring out. You can clean the mess, but you can't stop the leak."

"She's . . . leaking?" Silas asked, brow furrowed deeply. "Something cracked her . . . what, her control, and now she can't stop it?"

"More or less," the old woman allowed, and settled her dark, serious eyes on Caleb. "Visions. Tell me."

Caleb pushed his fists into his pockets. "I've had one."

"Just one?"

"The same one twice, but only a glimpse the first time. It starts in darkness," he said. "I see a pile of bodies, twisted and broken."

"Like them?" Silas asked, gesturing to the night that swallowed each of Naomi's hauled corpses. "Did you see this fight?"

Caleb jerked his head in denial. "It's a mountain of them, hundreds . . . maybe thousands of bodies, all tangled. They don't have faces. I see a smear of ink, bar codes stamped on legs and arms and shoulders and God knows." Matilda's eyes remained trained on him, unblinking and steady. "They're putrefying into the ground. I can't smell, but I know it's awful. Worse than anything I've ever smelled before. Worse than anything I've seen."

Silas grimaced. "That's . . . disheartening."

The man had been to at least one of Caleb's ritual scenes. Caleb knew that of them all, the ex-missionary understood exactly what it was Caleb meant.

He nodded. "At the very top," he continued, "there's a woman."

A match head hissed, sparked and flickered to life. Matilda cupped the flame in one weathered hand and touched it to the bowl of the pipe. "Does she have a face?" she asked, teeth clamped on the wooden stem.

Caleb's fists tightened in his pockets. "She's the only one that does. It's Juliet. She's naked and spread out, chained in place." The images overwhelmed the darkness behind his eyes. Juliet's pearly skin, grotesque against the waxen, rotting flesh of her throne. She sat locked at the top of that fleshy mountain, rings piercing the flesh of her vagina, spreading it wide. Chains hooked into each ring, vanished into the dark.

"I can only see one hand holding one of the chains in the shadow, but I can't see who it belongs to. There's a lot of people," Caleb said hoarsely. "Silhouettes."

Silas stirred, but froze when the old witch raised a silencing hand.

"I see one at the forefront, just a shadow. He's the one holding the chain. Or maybe it's a woman. Hell if I know, but the voice is too rough to tell."

"What does it say?" Matilda asked, her eyes dark pools as the last cloudy light of day finally slipped into shadow.

Caleb looked up at her. His mouth thinned. "Eve."

"Right." The witch drew on the end of her pipe, and the smell of tobacco floated through the night air. When she spoke again, it was on a stream of smoke. "We need to move fast."

"Eve?" Silas shook his head. "What does that mean?"

"Whoever it is," Caleb said, "they've been waiting for a long time."

"Exactly," Matilda said, nodding. "Silas, my dear, can you operate?"

The man scowled. "What the hell is that supposed to mean?"

"It means," Naomi said as she rounded the porch, "that your woman is dying inside that house and she needs to know if you can function knowing that."

Silas's shoulders went rigid. "Jesus Christ, Nai!"

"He can," Caleb said, not looking at the man he wished his big sister hadn't fallen in love with.

And was so fucking *glad* she had.

"He'll work harder than anyone else," he added firmly.

The man's foggy eyes shifted to Caleb, narrowed and turned to Matilda. "Can she be healed?"

The red-haired witch hesitated. "Probably," she said, and Caleb closed his eyes. "If we move fast enough, we may yet glue the pieces together."

"Then yes," Silas said grimly. "Hell, yes, I can operate."

Matilda nodded. "Caleb?"

"I want," he said between gritted teeth, "answers."

"Let's start with this one," Matilda replied, her old chin rising. "They're tracing Juliet through her blood. No matter where she goes, they can find her. Blood magic is far above the level of these hiding wards. I can protect only those whose blood I've added to the magic, and she's not one. We must get her back. We must do so at *all* costs."

"What's the vision mean?" Silas asked. "I don't get it."

Matilda shook her head. "Juliet Carpenter is the key to a plot that has been simmering since long before the earthquake. They've been searching for her for over twenty years."

Caleb jerked his hair out of his face. "When do I leave?"

"Now," Matilda replied. "Before she makes it to wherever they're taking her."

Naomi perched a hip against the porch edge, folding her arms over her chest. "*We* will leave just as soon as we have a plan," she said.

Caleb shook his head. "No time," he said, and straightened. "Give me a working comm. I'll track her now before the trail goes cold. Can you trace the frequency?"

Silas rounded on him, but Naomi cocked her head. "You think you can take on the witches that have her?"

"Watch me."

She studied his gaze, and Caleb met her violet scrutiny head-on. Whatever it was she read in his face—hell, he didn't even know what he was thinking, much less projecting—she nodded. "Here," she said, unclipping her comm from her belt. "It's got Smith's frequency already locked in. Go get her, tiger."

Silas opened his mouth, hesitated. Then, with the faintest edge of a humorless smile, he added, "Go save your girlfriend."

Caleb shot him a narrow look.

"There's a back way in," Matilda said. "Just behind the house. Run your fingers along the cliff edge and you'll all but fall into it. And take this."

Caleb tucked the comm into his pocket, frowning as she extended her open palm. A seven-pointed crystal glittered in her hand, a red gleam buried deep within the carved facets. "What is it?"

"Think about who you want to find," she said simply.

"I can't use magic."

Silas stared at him. "What?"

Caleb ignored him.

"It's not that kind of magic," Matilda said, and pressed it into his hand. Her warm, dry fingers squeezed once. "And you're wrong, you know. You've got a lot more at your disposal than you think."

"What the hell do you mean, you can't use magic?" Silas demanded.

"Smith." Naomi dug her elbow in his back. "Shut up."

"I'll bring her back," Caleb said over them both, his eyes on the old woman's, "and then I swear to God, you're going to tell me everything you know."

Her smile softened. "I promise," she said. "There will be answers."

He spun, fingers clenching over the sharp crystal edges. Jessie was dying in that green house.

Juliet had been kidnapped by a coven desperate to drain her of her life, her magic.

Was that what his vision was? Did they have a ritual? A need for Juliet to act as some kind of caged focus?

As if that wasn't bad enough, an old witch who had taught him how to harvest the lifeblood of the dying now smoked a pipe in what he'd thought was a safe place, casual as if it were a day out in the sunshine, and—Jesus Christ, when had he lost control of things?

It didn't matter.

He had to retrieve Juliet. Before the chains he'd *seen* in the future became reality. Before the shadowy puppets in the background of his visions claimed her.

Before *his* reality turned again to blood and ash.

"Fine. But before you go," Silas said, offering a snub-nosed pistol. "Just in case. Good luck, Caleb. We're hot on your six."

CHAPTER FOURTEEN

The dark closed in around her, held at bay only by the faint path of her captor's powerful penlight. Every step he took was another nail in the already stifling coffin of her fate.

Future. Visions. Fat lot of good any of it did.

The future could be changed on a dime. Caleb had taught her that, hadn't he?

She stumbled over a narrow ribbon of crumbling stone. Pain cinched through her wrists as the plastic ties tightened. The trailing lead in the large man's hands snapped taut, and he stopped, swung the light back around and blinded her with it.

She flinched. "Hey!"

The man said nothing. Juliet bit her tongue before she gave in to the urge to scream at him. It wouldn't help.

He hadn't said a word since she'd woken slung over his shoulder. Kicking and struggling earned her a bone-jarring meeting with the ground as he'd simply rolled her off. The ache in her hip matched the vivid throb of pain pulsing in her elbow, courtesy of the rocks he'd dumped her on.

Asshole.

The light slid away from her face, and Juliet blinked as shards of after-burned spotlights flared in her vision. She didn't get more than a second before the lead pulled tight, all but yanking her off her feet.

Swearing didn't make her feel any better. Slipping and staggering over the uneven ground, she concentrated on staying upright as her kidnapper quickened the pace.

Forced marches through the underground were becoming a bit of a habit. One she desperately wanted to break.

Exhaustion dogged every step, sucking at her. Clawing. Her feet felt like lead. However brief her respite at the cove, it seemed a million miles away.

Despite the fact that she knew it wouldn't help, she spoke anyway. "Where are you taking me?" The fitful silence of the ruined street swallowed her voice. Darkness filled the vacuum left behind.

She gritted her teeth. "Who are you?"

Nothing.

"Are you a coven witch? Do you know Alicia?"

The dim outline of his broad shoulders stiffened.

A reaction. Silent, but something. Juliet pressed on, stepping over a small broken pile of brick and sending grit clattering in her wake. "Don't like her, huh?" she said wryly. "Kind of a bitch. Well, no, more like a bitch to the bone."

Silence.

Blinking sweat from her stinging eyes, Juliet forced herself to keep moving. Keep talking. "I don't like her, either. She's never been what you'd call *nice*."

Her wrists burned fiercely. It was either talk, or cry.

"I think she hated the fact that Curio took me in," she said to his silent back. "Delia always said she was a cat trolling for a fight. I wonder how long she's wanted to kill me and take all my magic? She seems like a plotter."

Not even a whisper of a reply. The shadows pooled all around her, cloaking the treacherous path outlined by the powerful flashlight.

Juliet sucked in a breath as her ankle rolled. Stumbling, she caught the plastic lead in her fingers and barely managed to keep from sprawling face-first over rock and glass and heaven knew what else.

His stride slowed, light weaving back and forth. The ragged edges of forgotten tenements leered out from the surrounding dark. The empty windows yawned, black maws of nothing. Just death. The memory of it.

The taste of it, thick and musty on her tongue. In her nose.

She hated the underground.

"You know," she managed, righting herself as fear painted a slick, icy line down her back, "this would be a lot easier if you'd let me rest a minute."

Wordlessly, he tugged her forward, striding through a narrow corridor between two slanted buildings.

"Or not," she said tightly. "Jesus, you're worse than Caleb. At least he talks. Not all the time, all right," she conceded after a moment. "But enough. At least *he* makes me feel like he's human now and again."

Setting her jaw, Juliet trudged through the narrowing gap, her gaze fixed on the wide line of his shoulders. "He's not even a very good listener. I mean, it doesn't matter what you tell him, he just hears what he wants. But then, I guess everyone does. The only person who ever listened to me is gone."

The raw ache never really went away, but her tired, defenseless heart had nowhere else to focus. Grief welled like a flagging, draining tide in her chest.

Her steps faltered.

The cord snapped taut.

Pain sheared through her legs as Juliet fell to her knees. Sharp rock ground into her shins, forcing a ragged sound from her throat. For a split second, her vision shimmered, white with pain.

Red with anger.

Her temples throbbed.

"It's about time," a sultry feminine voice said behind her. Juliet jerked, half spinning until the pain in her knees forced her to spread more weight on her hands. The ground was cold and damp, sharp with cracked cement.

Alicia knelt beside her, and Juliet noticed she wore boots and jeans this time.

Maybe Juliet wasn't worth seducing.

Laughter bubbled to her lips.

Alicia seized her short hair in one rough fist, yanking her face up. "Where is Caleb?"

Lips peeled back from her teeth, Juliet blinked away painful tears and said tightly, "Fuck you."

Her silent captor's penlight skimmed across Alicia's face, outlining the widened, skeletal grimace of her smile. Her pale blue eyes flashed in the light, so close that Juliet could see herself reflected inside.

"You," she said, "have been quite the handful. I'm half tempted to tell Tobias there he's shit out of luck."

If the giant cared, he didn't say anything. Juliet's nose wrinkled. "Someone yanking your leash, there, Alicia?" The witch's grip hurt, but Juliet forced herself to sound as calm as she could.

To sound like Caleb.

God, where was he?

Alicia leaned down, close enough that her lips brushed across Juliet's temple as she whispered, "No problem. He'll come for you."

"You wish," Juliet spat, wrenching away. The fist in her hair twisted, and she bit back a cry of pain, translating it into one of the many four-letter words she'd heard Caleb mutter under his breath.

Alicia's smile didn't change as she stood, forcing Juliet to her feet. "Let's go. We mustn't be late. Tobias, you know the way?"

The world blurred through her tears, but Juliet couldn't miss the derision shaping the big man's face. Scornfully, he turned away, leaving the lead lying on the ground behind him.

The scarred witch picked it up, but not before she sent him a glare filled with such malice, such hatred, that bile gathered into a burning knot in Juliet's stomach.

What had she been dragged into?

"Let's go, sweetie, before Tobias gets ahead of himself."

Juliet took a step, forced her knees to remain steady by sheer willpower alone, and grabbed the plastic rope once more between her trapped fingers. It was all the leverage she could get.

Alicia walked ahead of her, her stride easy and fluid. Careless.

And why not? It's not as if anything was going wrong in *her* world.

Juliet stared daggers into her back, jaw set.

She didn't know how long Tobias led them into the ruins, or where they were going. Sweat trickled from her temples, gathered underneath her sweatshirt and stuck uncomfortably. A stitch pulled in her side, and still, the darkness never changed, never shifted. Rock, grit, rubble, and muddied glints of glass glittered from the thin path he forged ahead of them, but nothing gave her any idea of where they were. How far in, how close to the trench, how near to the abandoned roads that lead to New Seattle.

Did they even know?

Alicia glanced back at her, the curve of her face a faint, pale crescent in the dark. "I feel sorry for you," she said conversationally.

Juliet concentrated on the rocky ground in front of her feet, step by laborious step. "Oh, yeah?" she said between gasping breaths. "That's a laugh."

"You think so?" Alicia yanked on the lead, sending Juliet staggering for balance over rocks that rolled and cracked beneath her boots. "Oh, God, Juliet. You don't have any idea, do you?"

"Why you want my magic?" Juliet wiped her cheek on her shoulder, but succeeded only in smearing dirt and sweat over her already itchy skin. "I can guess."

"No, you idiot," Alicia said, laughing openly now. Contrary to Juliet's discomfort, the witch didn't sound like she was struggling to keep up with Tobias's pace. "Who you are. Why you're so . . . oh, so *special*."

Juliet squeezed her eyes shut. Popped them open again as her toe collided with a rock and sent her sideways.

Casually, Alicia curled a hand in her sweatshirt until Juliet righted herself. "I don't have anything against you," she continued. "Really, you're a sweet girl."

"Liar," Juliet shot back. "You hated the fact Curio liked me."

The fingers clenched on her shoulder. "You weren't the only bitch he was banging."

It was Juliet's turn to laugh, though it came out tight and choked with the effort to remain standing. To breathe through the knot in her side. "I never slept with him, Alicia. He was old enough to be my grandfather!"

The deformed silhouette of her other hand sliced through the air. "Whatever. If it weren't for your particular magic, you'd be less than nothing. Hell, honey, if it weren't for Caleb, I'd probably have forgotten you existed."

She shook her head wearily. "Lying again. You'd have just locked me away where you could bleed me as you needed it."

The silence that followed her exhausted accusation only confirmed it. Hadn't Caleb said as much?

The hand at her shoulder gentled. Even squeezed affectionately. "Smart girl," Alicia said thoughtfully. "For once. I'm still surprised you contacted us, you know. Why did you?"

Because she was incapable of following through? Because Juliet needed to feel as if she weren't entirely useless to a coven who'd never made her feel anything but?

She shook her head, pressing her lips into a thin line.

"Not that it matters," Alicia said dismissively, coiling the lead's excess length around her scarred hand. "You did, and I'm very grateful. At least, I was."

Juliet's gaze flicked sideways in surprise. The witch glowered at Tobias's back as if her own gaze could be transformed to razors by sheer malevolence.

"And here we are," the once-pretty witch continued after a moment. She removed her fingers from Juliet's shoulder, transferring the coiled lead from hand to hand. "Caleb's probably right. Your powers would be useless to me if I took them from you. I don't really care to make anyone *else* more powerful than me, which means you're about as valuable as any tramp with heart's blood to harvest."

"Nice."

"Nice," Alicia repeated slowly. Amusement laced through the single syllable. "Nice? Have you ever seen the ritual?"

The sound Juliet made could have been a denial. Maybe it was supposed to be, but she couldn't force herself to shape it past the pain in her side.

Alicia didn't seem to notice, or care. "First, a ritual circle is drawn. Cardinal directions, all of that. Then the sacrifice is bound in silk and iron."

Juliet stared at the ground, forcing her leaden feet to move. Saying nothing, she concentrated on the backs of the man's heels.

"Real silk, mind," the witch said, almost cheerfully. "Real iron, which is easier to get. And then the true test of patience comes in. The carving."

Juliet flinched.

"Over every center of power on the body, carved even into the bone. The trick here," Alicia said, sidestepping a slab of cracked cement, "is keeping the sacrifice alive while you bleed her."

Shudders rippled through her, but Juliet fisted her bound hands and said tightly, "Sounds like you already know all about it."

"Oh, no. Not even close." Alicia tucked the lead

over her shoulder, as if out for a casual stroll. Her smile gleamed. "Caleb and Curio are the only ones who've done it all, start to finish. Can you imagine how many times our darling soothsayer had to practice to get it right?"

Something sick knotted in her stomach.

"I wonder how many victims he slaughtered before he got the timing down. A handful? A dozen?"

Juliet's nails bit into her palms. "Shut up," she whispered.

Pale blue eyes flicked back to her, keloid scarring stretched wide around one. "Why, Juliet. Does it bother you? Knowing that he peeled the skin from humans? Humans like your sister?"

"Shut *up*," she growled.

Alicia's laugh trilled like liquid silver. "Oh, you ignorant child. God, I feel so sorry for you. You really fell hard, didn't you?" She tugged on the leash, forcing Juliet to bend awkwardly. "Tell you a secret," she confided, eyes glinting. "I always had a thing for him. Even knowing about the blood on his hands. Or," she drawled, "because of it. I adore a ruthless man, don't you?"

Juliet clenched her jaw hard enough to drill pain through her temples.

"Of course you do," Alicia purred. "You naughty thing. What*ever* would your sister say?"

"You shut up about Delia," Juliet gasped, her side screaming, twisted and cramped. "You shut up, or I swear to God—" The lead loosened, and she sucked in a hard breath. Gasped for it.

"Don't like the truth, huh?" Alicia taunted

softly. "Don't worry, I do understand. Get close to Caleb and you'll be close to your powerless whore of a sister."

Juliet's head snapped up.

Her boots immediately snagged on the craggy ground. She didn't have the strength to right herself, pitching forward suddenly. Only her grip on the shortened lead kept her from breaking her face.

Alicia hauled back on the cord, swinging Juliet around so quickly that her back slammed into packed dirt and rock, leaving her gasping before she knew what happened. Rocks dug into her back, her legs, but all Juliet could see were stars.

"Get up," Alicia snapped.

Juliet squeezed her eyes shut as she breathed through the cramp in her side.

"Get the fuck up!" Then, impatiently, "Tobias, pick her up."

Boots crunched by her ear. Callused fingers poked into her neck. "We rest." His voice was wholly emotionless, matter-of-fact as the rocks digging into her back.

"The hell we do."

"She's no good to us dead."

Footsteps retreated, and Alicia cursed as she threw the rope at Juliet. She felt it strike her chest, slide in plastic coils to the ground beside her, but all she could do was breathe.

Her limbs felt pinned. Too heavy to move.

"Stay put," Alicia said, venom filling her voice. Then, almost as an afterthought, the rope went taut again, plucked hard. "Never mind. You're just stupid enough to go running off."

Juliet heard her footsteps head in the same direction as Tobias's.

Groaning, she pressed her clasped hands to her forehead.

"Let's get this straight," Alicia hissed, far enough away that Juliet struggled to make it out. "Down here, you do as I say."

"Nope."

Despite herself, the man's monosyllabic, matter-of-fact response made Juliet's lips twitch.

"What the hell do you— Don't you *dare* walk away from me!"

Their voices faded to a dull murmur.

Clenching her back teeth as every aching muscle protested, Juliet sat up. Without Tobias's light, the underground pressed inward, an endless sea of black, impervious to her straining eyes. Blind, struggling to remain as quiet as she could as she all but inhaled the choking dark, she pulled her hands in every direction. The rope twanged, cinched tightly into her wrists, and refused to give.

She was well and truly screwed.

Juliet dropped her forehead to her raised knees. "I give up," she whispered. Tears filled her eyes. "I just give up."

"Damn," muttered a voice just over her shoulder. "Does that mean I have to walk back alone?"

Her heart—traitorous, foolish thing that it was—slammed in her chest.

"Caleb!"

"Shhh." Even hampered by inky shadows, he

found her easily. His hands closed over her shoulders, and as she made a sound somewhere between a laugh and a sob, his fingers slid down her arms. Her sides.

Despite every spine-tingling warning to get his ass in gear, his arms closed around her, her back to his chest, his nose in her hair. He inhaled deeply, locking her warm fragrance inside his nose, his lungs, as if he couldn't get enough.

Christ, what was wrong with him?

She shuddered. "They're not far," she whispered.

"Quiet." He knew that. The light that had helped him pinpoint her was powerful enough to cut a lasered swath through the artificial night, and even now shimmered just beyond the crumbling remains of a segmented building ahead.

The glass star pulsed in his pocket.

He fished the switchblade from his boot, flicked it open, and cut the cord from between her hands. Her fingers closed over his wrists. Squeezed. "I knew you'd come after me."

A spike of heat, of anxiety, knotted in his gut. "Let's go."

Juliet struggled to her feet. He caught her elbows, helped her until she tipped her face up to his. Even with excellent vision, he could just barely make out the curve of her cheek. The faint line of her mouth. Her eyes gleamed, a faded slash of awareness in the dark.

Her fingers grazed over his rippled jaw.

The whisper-light touch scorched through his

veins, shot straight to his dick. And fisted like a spike in his heart.

Not the time.

He seized her wrist, jaw tight, and pulled her around him. With his other hand, he fished Naomi's comm from his pocket and pushed it into her fingers. "Straight back the way we— Get down!" he hissed, pulling her to the ground.

She made a sound as she fell into his supporting arm. A beam of light swept around, shattering the darkness over their heads. Caleb's other arm slipped around her shoulder, and he told himself it was to keep her from making any sudden moves. Keep her steady.

It had nothing to do with the fragrance of her skin, sweet and warm and so familiar, it made his body clench. Or the way she huddled into his side as he stared toward the light.

Alicia's voice trilled from the dark. "You be damned glad I'm letting you have her."

His lips twitched, a grim slant. "Shhh," he breathed over Juliet's head.

She said nothing.

"I don't answer to you," a deep male voice replied.

"This is my turf," Alicia shot back. "Mine. One wrong fucking move from you, and you're just another maggot-infested corpse, you hear me?" The flashlight jerked, swung back around and vanished behind the wall, and Caleb breathed out a sigh of relief.

"Very quietly," he murmured, shifting his weight. Rocks ground into his forearm, but he gritted his teeth as she grabbed his free arm and struggled to her knees.

"Where are we?" she whispered.

He ignored that. "Head back the way you came. Slowly, and keep down."

"What about you?" Her voice trembled in the dark.

He knew his smile hid beneath the shroud of black. "I'll be right behind you."

She was a ghostly figure, a splash of black just a shade lighter than the shadows surrounding them as she crossed his field of vision. She hesitated, half crouched, and he could imagine her looking back over her shoulder.

Weighing her options?

"Go," he said, striving for light. "That comm—" He froze.

"Cal—"

"Shhh!" The voices had stopped.

The quiet thickened, too heavy, waiting. Listening.

He threw out a hand. "Run."

Gravel crunched behind him.

Caleb stiffened, spun just as a thin beam of light pierced the dark. It swept over broad shoulders and thick arms, silhouetted a massive body edged in muscle.

He jerked back. It wasn't enough.

Quick as a snake, a meaty hand closed over his throat. "Get the girl," rumbled that deep voice.

"Caleb!"

"Stop." The man's fingers tightened around Caleb's neck, and he choked, grabbing the thick wrist in both hands as it lifted him to his toes. Spots flared in the corner of his vision. "Move, and I snap his neck."

The light jerked. "Tobias!" Alicia's voice, waspish as she strode out from behind the ruined wall. "Don't you dare, I need him."

Juliet hesitated, her face pale in his peripheral.

"Run," he croaked from between the large man's fingers.

Her mouth opened.

The man called Tobias flexed, and pain ratcheted through the fine bones in his neck. His windpipe. Gasping, Caleb hauled back a foot, slammed it into Tobias's knee and heard it crack.

Teeth flashed in the wildly bobbing light, a sideways grimace as Alicia darted around them both.

Caleb raised his arm, stiffened it. Through the crushing weight in his throat, he rasped, "Run!" as Alicia clotheslined herself on his forearm. Screaming in violent rage, she hit the ground on her back; the light spun end over end as it clattered into the shadows, beam flickering wildly.

In the flashing strobe, he saw Juliet raise her hands to her lips. Saw her spin, clenching her eyes shut.

"Run!" he roared, wrenching away from his opponent's grip. He reached for the gun in the back of his waistband and found himself staring into the barrel of an almost identical pistol.

Caleb froze. Juliet's footsteps faded into the black, and as an icy ream of sweat blossomed over his forehead, he breathed out a silent, relieved sigh.

The comm he'd given her would see her safely back to Matilda.

Tobias's aim remained rock steady. "We don't need you," he said flatly. "Just her." It was as simple as that.

Caleb met his eyes. "Why do you want her?"

"Not your business." His finger tightened on the trigger.

"No!" The gun jerked as Alicia slammed into his back, fingers twisted into claws.

Caleb launched himself to the side. The muzzle flare cracked like lightning through the dark.

CHAPTER FIFTEEN

A rapid staccato of gunfire echoed all around her, bouncing eerily in the dark, dogging every step. Juliet choked back a frightened sob.

Caleb was a fighter. He'd always been a fighter. That Tobias guy had nothing on him. Nothing.

Except seventy-five pounds and a gun.

The wayward thought drilled into her temples.

She couldn't think about that. Juliet paused, gasping for breath, hands braced on her knees.

How long had she been running? A few minutes? Ten? She was well and truly lost now. In the encroaching shadows, everything looked the same. Black, gray, more black.

It blurred. Juliet dashed her arm across her eyes and sucked in a trembling breath.

She couldn't stop now.

The comm wasn't a flashlight, but down here, the screen lit the air with incandescent blue. It was the second best thing, and she'd take what she could get.

Swallowing hard, strange echoes skittering from the fringes of the faded blue glow, Juliet pushed on. Every step sent throbbing needles of pain through her feet, and her mind spiraled, over and over. Replaying the final scene. Combing over the details. Tobias's expression, empty but intense.

Alicia's twisted smile, so smug.

The way she'd watched Tobias with such hatred.

You're about as valuable as any tramp with heart's blood to harvest.

Her toes slammed into something hard. It gonged like metal, eerily muffled, and Juliet staggered. Her shins barked into the edge of broken concrete, sending shards of agony up her legs.

Swearing, windmilling, she toppled as her knees gave out. She sprawled back on her ass, sucked in a breath, and let herself go still.

The vestiges of a ruined street ribboned out of the ghostly light, the skeletal remains of its ruined buildings grinning raggedly at her. She fought for breath. For reason. Slammed mental shutters on the worry clawing at her.

Caleb had to be all right.

He'd told her to run. He'd stepped in front of the gun and ordered her to run.

He was fine. He had to be fine.

But the memory of those gunshots echoed in her mind, hollow and cold. Juliet clenched the comm in both hands, staring at it. Willing it to buzz an alert, light up with a caller, anything.

It wasn't until her teeth chattered that she realized how badly she was shaking. There had to be—oh, something. *Anything* that she could do. She had a comm. Whose?

His? He hadn't taken anything from that seedy motel room but his jeans.

Wordless with fear, knowing she was lost and hoping against all reason, Juliet flipped open the unit and cycled through the programmed frequencies.

There were three. Only one had a name. "Oh, thank God," she breathed, and pushed the button. White noise filled her ear. It crackled, spat out fuzzy gibberish as the line clicked over.

"Leigh, where are you?"

"Silas!" Juliet cried, clutching the comm unit to her ear. "Oh, God, it *is* you."

"Juliet? Where are you?"

"I don't know," she said, so fast she was sure the words all ran together. "Caleb rescued me and told me to run, and there was a big guy named Tobias and I heard *gunshots*. I'm so scared—"

"Okay," he interrupted. Tension intensified his voice, fuzzing the speakers. "It's going to be fine. Leave the unit turned on, I'll track it to you."

"But Caleb—"

"He's a big boy," Silas told her firmly. "He can

take care of himself. Stay put. I'll be there as fast as I can."

The line went dead, and Juliet stared at the unit as its screen flickered.

Caleb was a big boy. It was true. God knew he'd taken care of himself for a long time.

But there'd been the gun. And Alicia.

Juliet snapped the unit closed, swallowing back tears. She wasn't just some helpless female to throw her hair and kick her feet, damn it. She'd taken care of herself, too.

Had she? "Shit," she whispered.

She'd mostly had others to take care of her. The prostitutes who had raised two girls off the street. The girls at Waxed. Her sister. Curio.

Bottles of gin.

"Damn it, Jules." She clenched her fists against her thighs. She wasn't helpless.

Scared, yes. Unprepared, definitely.

But *not* helpless.

Wrenching herself to her feet, Juliet flicked the screen back on and illuminated a three-foot square of barren, rock-strewn ground. She wasn't going to sit here and wait to be rescued.

If anything, she told herself as she set off into the dark, she'd haul the comm back to where Caleb was so that Silas could help there.

She wasn't a fighter. She wasn't even a serviceable witch. But she knew how to use what was in front of her.

Juliet stepped over the broken, rotting remains of what looked like an old-fashioned trash can frame. Every ten steps, the comm screen faded, so she clicked it over and over.

Each time, it came back dimmer.

Her heart slammed into her throat as the light winked out again. She clicked the button. Nothing happened.

Freezing in place, her heartbeat suddenly hard and sporadic in the too-thick silence of the underground, she closed the case, opened it again. The blue light flickered once, and faded.

"Oh, no," she groaned.

No, whispered the echoes back at her.

Juliet's skin crawled. Darkness pushed at her. Slammed in tightly around her, too thick to breathe. Too clinging to move in.

She knuckled her eyes. "Get a grip," she said hoarsely.

A whisper slid through the empty ruins. A note, a question? Her imagination? She held her breath, straining to hear.

Nothing. Not a breath of air, not a—

Crack.

Juliet jumped out of her skin, slamming her free hand over her mouth. Her pulse pounded through her temples, her throat, her stomach. So loud, she was sure anyone out there could hear it.

Crack.

The rough sound clattered through the dark. She folded into a crouch, easing to the balls of her feet, fingertips planted to the uneven ground for balance. Her eyes wide, she strained to see through the pitch darkness.

Which direction was it coming from? Which side? Oh, God, what if it was Tobias?

What if Caleb was dead?

She held her breath.

"Juliet?"

Relief short-circuited every nerve she had left. She didn't think. She didn't even hesitate. "Caleb!" As the ruins swallowed her cry, she launched herself into the dark.

Strong arms closed around her. Caleb's voice, thick and gritty in her ear, said something she couldn't make out, but she didn't have to. His mouth came down on hers, one hand cupping the back of her head.

It should have felt wrong and wildly out of place. She kissed a man in the rotting remains of an abandoned city, but Juliet didn't care. It was Caleb. He was safe. He had the devil's own luck, but he was *safe*.

She twined her arms around his neck and threw all her weight into his embrace. She offered her mouth, met his fervor and matched it, opening her lips for his tongue to dart in and taste her. For hers to taste him, richer than anything she'd ever known; spicy and dangerous and so familiar, she shuddered.

His groan echoed from the dark. Echoed in her head.

Her heart.

The heat of his mouth, of his hands and body, warmed her. "Thank God," he murmured against her lips, his voice harsh, raw. "Thank hell. I don't care."

Tears filled her eyes. "Don't ever," she whispered between kisses, "do that again. Don't ever."

His laughter softened, and something wild and sizzling released low in her belly. He cupped her face in his hands, angled her head and slid his lips over her own in a slow, drugging kiss.

For this brief, pulse-pounding, toe-curling moment in time, everything was all right.

His forehead touched hers, hands tight in her hair. She couldn't see anything in the dark, but she heard the tension in every breath. Felt his heart slam against his chest, as fast and hard as hers.

A tear slid over her eyelashes. Trailed a whispered line down her cheek. "Caleb." It trembled.

"We need to—"

"How many people did you kill, Caleb?"

He went still, silent save for the rapid thud of his heart beneath her hands.

She squeezed her eyes shut. "How many?"

The silence stretched. Then, quietly, he said, "Three, by myself."

"When you do it, what happens?"

She felt him withdraw, stepping away until his fingers left her hair and she shivered in the cool, damp air. "Why are you asking?"

"What happened when you killed them?" she persisted. She forced herself to sound calm, to betray no trace of the tears spilling over onto her cheeks.

Get close to Caleb and you'll be close to your sister.

She was, after all, just stupid.

"They die," he said harshly. A light clicked on, a faint glow illuminating his hands. The shadowed planes of his face, callous. Remorseless. "And a part of them belongs to me." *Me.* Not *them.* Not *the witch.*

Me.

The responsibility claimed in that single word knotted her throat. Grief, anger.

Juliet shoved her knuckles into her eyes. How could she be so blind?

Why didn't she know?

The sound that erupted from her chest keened, ragged and wordless. She launched herself at him.

Caleb's eyes gleamed, blue fire deep within shadowed sockets. He batted her hands away, mouth set into a hard line, flung up a forearm to block her wild left hook and seized her shoulders.

Her teeth snapped together on his hard shake. "What is wrong with you?"

"What did you do to my sister?"

Caleb froze, his fingers biting into her upper arms. There'd be bruises later, she knew, but she couldn't summon the energy, the willpower, to care.

Her laugh cracked on a broken sob. "I thought so."

"I don't know what you've been told," he began, but she wrenched at his grip, twisting until he let her go.

She staggered back, rubbing at her arms as if she could wipe away the memory of his touch. Tears thickened her voice, now, and she couldn't stop it. Couldn't calm it. "Nobody told me anything. Not until *right* fucking now."

Caleb was a statue, immobile, his hands fisted by his sides.

"I kept looking," she continued raggedly, staring at his shadowed face, *willing* herself to see through the dark, see his expression. Read him. "Even after everyone else had given up, I kept looking, but she's dead, isn't she?"

His voice was empty. "What makes you think so?"

"Oh, fuck, Caleb!" Juliet scraped her fingers through her hair, shaking. "Alicia said it."

"You believe—"

"I don't know," she said wildly, fists clenching on hanks of her hair. "She said getting close to you meant I could get close to Delia, *you tell me what that means.*" Her head throbbed, throat aching with it. Grief. Betrayal.

Again.

Caleb was silent.

Something raw welled in her chest, razor sharp and desperate. Juliet huddled in on herself, arms cradling her head, hair caught in her fingers. "You can harvest the lifeblood from anyone, can't you?" she whispered. "You can collect power from people. Nonwitches." Her jaw locked so hard, pain shot through her temples as she gritted out, "*Cordelia.*"

The faint blue light picked out the shape of his shoulder, flexing once.

Laughter bubbled up beneath the grief. The fury. "A shrug," she said weakly. She stared at him, helpless. Hopeless. Willing him to deny it.

To say he'd never murdered anyone.

But even as she thought it, even as he opened his mouth, she knew how badly she lied to herself. And how stupid she really was, to have fallen for a killer.

Her sister's killer.

Something fractured in her heart. Through her head. Fury overpowered grief. Dug in with venomous claws. "You used me. You *always* use me, and I am not—I'm not going to sit here and take it anymore!" She swung at him.

He caught her, ready for it, but she didn't let herself be cowed. She lashed out with hands, feet, bared teeth. She wanted to hurt him. She wanted to make him bleed as she bled, make him cry out in answer to the screaming voice pleading in her soul.

"Stop it, Juliet!"

Twisting a hand out from his grip, she cocked back her fist. It collided with his jaw. Pain snapped through her popping knuckles, his head twisted. Mouth set into a thin, furious line, Caleb curled his fingers into her shirt and hauled her to her toes.

"That is enough."

"Never," she swore. "Never, not as long as I live. You can *never* make up for this. I don't ever want to see you again, Caleb Leigh. *Get out of my life.*"

Pain shredded through her temples. The ugly knot of bile in her stomach surged, forcing itself through her chest. Her throat.

Her heart.

"You killed her," she sobbed, wrenching herself away. The words poured out of her, an acidic torrent of grief. "You killed my sister, you killed her, oh, God, why? What did she ever do to deserve it? *What did I ever do to you?*" Her voice broke.

A muscle leaped in Caleb's muscle. Even as he met her eyes directly, a pale glint in the dark, she knew what he meant to do. Heard it, sensed it, *felt* it coming as his features hardened to an icy mask. "You were born," he said, and nothing else.

She was as stupid as they came.

And Delia had paid for it.

"Go away," she said softly, closing her eyes. "Just . . . just go *away*. Leave me here. I'll make my own way out." Or die trying.

"I can't do that, Jules. I need to get you safe."

Safe? After learning that?

She laughed. Shoved her fingers again through her hair, seizing hanks of it in her fists, she laughed until the grief wrenched itself out of her throat, tore itself savagely free. She knew how to make him leave her alone.

She knew how to hurt him.

Screwing her eyes shut, she reached inside herself with her metaphysical nails bared. So much easier than she'd ever expected, she ripped the moorings of her skin loose. Magic welled up in a white-hot tide of sorrow and rage.

She primed it. Focused it.

Let it free.

Caleb's eyes widened. "Shit!"

When he moved, it was all Juliet could do to force herself to raise her arms.

Too late. Stony expression unreadable, he caught her by the collar and raised his free hand.

The world, already dark, spiked on a note of crystal, mind-altering pain, and then slid to nothing.

Caleb bent, sweeping his arm under her knees and catching her before she fell to the broken ground. Her weight curled trustingly into his chest, and though he called himself six kinds of a fool, he savored the weight of her. The shape of her.

It was something he knew he'd never feel again. Not while she was conscious.

His chest burned with everything he wanted to say. Everything he swore he never would.

Tears burned in his eyes.

They weren't his. "She's fine," he muttered, his voice overly loud in the sudden silence. "No thanks to you." His fingers stroked her jaw. "Or me."

Not that it mattered. Talking wouldn't make it any easier. The part inside him that was Cordelia wasn't any less guilty than he.

I could have. . .

"What?" he said to Juliet's pale face. To her lashes, thick and dark against her cheeks. "You could have what? There was never any way this could end well. We've lied to her since day one."

Grief hit him in the chest, hard and sudden and so sharp, his throat closed around a hoarse sound. His arms tightened around Juliet's still body, cradling her gently. God, what a mess. What a fucked-up mess he'd trapped her in.

"I'm so sorry," he said quietly. Roughly. The shadows looming beyond the faint sphere of blue light ate the echoes. Swallowed them whole, stifling and abrupt.

Caleb sank to his knees.

She's just a little rose. . .

In a nasty, killing world. What a fool he was. As much a part of this corrupted city of lies as the coven he tried to destroy.

Juliet slept in his arms, breathing, alive, and all he could do was hold her. Cherish the warmth of her skin, the solid beat of her heart.

Remember her tears, silvered tracks of grief. He'd done that.

It was better for her to think he'd done that.

How could he explain that Cordelia had known she was dying? That she'd sacrificed herself to save the little orphan she'd raised as a sister?

Would Juliet even understand?

No, and he couldn't blame her.

Much better for her to think that Caleb had murdered her sister, give her something to focus on. Someone to bend all of her grief and hatred and revenge on.

She'd understand.

No, she wouldn't. What fool in her right mind would?

Her breath caught in her chest, and Caleb bent his head over hers. His face buried in her hair, he fought back the urges assailing him.

Protect her. Cherish her.

Love her.

Not his to do.

You're a liar.

Caleb always had been. Second only to his own

sister and determined to see it through. He hated this city. These people. He hated the coven, the Mission, the goddamned ruins.

But Jessie loved New Seattle, in her own way.

And the Coven of the Unbinding had threatened that. Had threatened her. Killing them all had seemed the best idea at the time— Damn it, why hadn't it worked? Why hadn't they all died?

Why hadn't *he* died?

Because she needed you.

He squeezed his eyes shut, teeth locking on a low growl. His fingers slid into Juliet's short, tangled hair and he blew out a hard breath, his temple pressed to hers.

As long as Alicia was alive, Juliet was in danger.

He needed to end this, once and for all.

Matilda said she could heal Jessie. Maybe Juliet could live with her and Silas, rebuild a life for herself. Learn to live with her anguish if she had somewhere to direct it. Time cured everything.

Footsteps crunched behind him. A light shimmered, its wide beam focused at the ground by Caleb's knees. "Leigh." Silas's voice rebounded back in a handful of muffled echoes.

Caleb unfolded, rising to his feet. "Take her," he said.

"Is she alive?"

He met the ex-missionary's foggy eyes, a muted shade in the ambient light from his flashlight, and saw suspicion. Concern. Fuck, sympathy.

"Yes," he said flatly. "Take her, get her back to the sanctuary."

The big man shifted his grip on the light as he

approached. "You realize Jessie won't like this, right?" He cupped his arms under Juliet and took her weight easily as Caleb stepped back.

Her black-capped head rested against Silas's shoulder, hands tucked under her chin, and everything in Caleb snarled to rabid attention.

Mine.

He shook his head, deliberately straightened his fingers before they clenched into fists. "By the time Matilda heals her, it won't matter. I'm going to end this, one way or another." A ghost of a smile touched his mouth, tugging at the scarred corner of his lip. "For real, this time."

Silas shifted her weight, but his gaze searched Caleb's face. Intent, and too damned knowing. "You're throwing me to the wolves, man."

"I know."

But they'd get over him. Jessie would know it when he died, and Juliet . . . Hell, she'd be relieved. Vindicated.

He tucked his fingers into his pocket. Delia's ring, warmed from his own body heat, winked as he withdrew it. He held it out. "Give this to Juliet."

Silas took it, eyeing it thoughtfully. Then he grunted. "Fuck me."

Caleb said nothing.

"Fine," he added after a moment. "What do you want me to tell her?"

"That her sister's murderer is dead," Caleb said, turning away.

"Jesus fucking Christ." The man's mouth tightened. "Don't let me go back there and tell Jessie I didn't do anything for you."

"Just tell her you didn't find me."

"No."

Caleb glanced over his shoulder. "Not even to spare her?" He read the truth in the man's features before Silas said anything. Smiling crookedly, he shook his head. "Of course you wouldn't lie." He sighed. "Fine. Tell her the truth. Tell her I went to end this."

"How—"

Caleb looked away. "Take care of them, Silas."

The man hesitated. "I will."

Without looking back—God, without looking at Juliet one more time, memorizing the way her hair fell over her forehead or the way her lighter eyelashes fanned her too pale cheeks—he stepped into the dark.

"Caleb, wait."

Caleb paused mid-stride, foot raised, but he didn't turn around.

The silence lengthened. Stretched taut. Then, Silas rumbled quietly, "There was a body fourteen months ago. A woman, carved to pieces. Blond hair, about—"

"Five-seven, long-limbed." Caleb smiled humorlessly into the dark. "That was Cordelia Carpenter. Her sister, yeah."

"Did you really murder her?"

He closed his eyes. *Promise me.* "Yes," he replied, as simply as if he commented on the darkness, or the rocks beneath his feet. "She died brutally."

He pushed into the smothering gloom before Silas could ask anything else, his heart slamming in his ears. Every step took him farther from Juliet. Farther from the accusation in her eyes, from the touch of her hands or the feel of her mouth under his.

Farther from the insistent ache centered over his heart.

Always a liar.

First, he'd track Alicia.

Then he'd make up for every mistake he'd ever made.

That won't help her.

Ignoring the insistent pressure in his head, the voice at the edges of his mind, he gripped the pointed pendant hanging from a chain beneath his shirt and felt it warm in his palm.

This time, he would kill them all. Every. Last. One.

CHAPTER SIXTEEN

She'd been saving the bottle of pinot noir for decades.

Matilda held the glass tumbler up, admiring the way the firelight scored through its diamond facets. The wine glowed a brilliant jewel red as she swirled it gently.

She adored the old world's wine.

Relaxing into the embrace of the old wooden rocking chair, her aged bones fit into the carved slats in comforting familiarity. It was like leaning into the arms of an old friend, or a lover.

It was like home.

She sipped at the wine and swirled it in her mouth, wincing faintly at the aftertaste. Aside from the unexpectedly sharp finish, she tasted black cherry and plum. Notes of cedar, wild fruit, and fresh herb hovered on her tongue, and as she closed her eyes, she remembered what it was like to travel across a world still innocent and carefree.

What it had been like to link fingers with the man she'd loved while they mingled with others who enjoyed the fruits of the harvest as much as they had.

She remembered, as she often did, the time before the disasters. So different from now.

So much death.

So much to answer for.

Metal clicked. "Don't move."

In abject defiance of the terse, masculine order, Matilda raised her glass to her mouth once more. The wine slipped between her lips, warmed by her hand, and as fresh and plummy as the first taste. She swallowed, opening her eyes, and smiled into the barrel of a gun trained in her direction.

Hazel eyes met hers over the sights. They flickered in the light, dancing and crackling with the fire she'd coaxed to life in front of the house.

Matilda raised her glass in his direction. "I wondered when you'd get here."

"You practically left out a welcome mat," he said. It was a question, for all it didn't end like one. "What the hell are you up to?"

She rested her head back against the rocking chair and sighed. The wine gleamed like blood in her hand. "It's lovely to see you again, Simon."

He stepped around the flame, gun held as easily as if it were an extension of his own hand. His black clothing made him as invisible as a shadow, but she didn't need to see to know when the borders of her sanctuary were crossed.

That's what magic was for.

His eyes narrowed, suspicion etched into every line of a face she'd always considered handsome. And why not? He had the best of her. Carefully, she drew the glass tumbler up between her gnarled palms, watching him over the rim. "I'm alone," she offered. "More or less."

"What game are you playing this time?" he asked sharply.

She only smiled, sipping the rich wine.

"You know why I'm here."

"Humor me, dear boy," she replied, stretching out her overall-clad legs and hooking her ankles together. Her yellow galoshes squeaked loudly.

"What did you steal?" he demanded. "We've got you on camera—"

"What makes you think I stole anything from you?"

Simon approached the porch, but he didn't climb it. His eyes tracked the surroundings, picking out shadows. Shapes.

Sensing.

"You're a good boy," she added, raising a faded red eyebrow, "but too suspicious. There's a sick girl that I suspect interests you greatly, and she's asleep in my bed. Other than that, we're alone."

She knew his senses would confirm what she said. Heedless of the gun he continued to train at her chest, she watched the play of light in her glass instead.

Jessie wouldn't wake up for this. Very little would wake her up now. She was too busy *seeing*, trapped in an endless stream of visions. It overwhelmed her, forcing her consciousness outward to witness God only knew what.

This, perhaps.

To see the present. What could be more terrible? Except, perhaps, seeing the future.

Her poor children. All of them. She had so much to make up for.

Mentally apologizing, Matilda drained half her glass before Simon lowered his gun. "I need your research," he told her.

"As I thought." She laced her bent fingers around the glass, bracing it on her stomach, lazily comfortable. "Is this your game, then, or are you still playing on someone else's board?"

His mouth tightened. "Don't do this. Just give me the codes so this can be done."

Her smile was slow. "Ah, so. Laurence is still pulling your strings."

"I don't answer to him."

She shook her head sadly. "No? He's still got your soul, baby."

Simon's grip tightened on the gun. "Just give me the goddamned research."

"What were your orders?" she asked slowly. The wine moved rapidly through her head, it always did. It polished the world into a pretty, unfocused shine. "Let me guess," she continued as he only stared at her. "Get the data, then kill me. Or, if at all possible, kill me anyway."

His lips compressed, and a wash of longing, of

regret, slid over her. She sighed. "Don't fret, my darling. Consider your duty discharged."

Confusion tightened the skin around his eyes. He studied her, studied the wine she lifted to her lips, and his foot hit the first step. "You took poison, didn't you?" he demanded.

She sipped delicately.

He leaped to the porch, snatched it from her hand. The remaining dregs sloshed over the lip, spattering to the ground like watered-down blood as the glass shattered in the fire pit.

Matilda didn't get up. She wasn't sure she could. Instead, smiling up into Simon's angry eyes, she said thickly, "You can't disobey him."

"God damn it, Mattie."

Mattie. Not many called her that anymore. Not for years.

Mustering every reserve of energy she had, Matilda tucked her hands into her overall pockets and studied the shape of his features. The square line of his jaw, his strong, slightly hawkish nose. He had her cheekbones. Her mouth. Familiar, and so alien all at once.

"You won't be lying now," she said, her tongue struggling to shape the words. "You did your job. But you won't," she added carefully, "you won't get the data. I'm so sorry, baby."

"Fuck the research," he said roughly, his fingers digging into the sides of her throat. Checking for swelling. Trying to figure out what she'd taken.

He'd never stop it now.

Her chuckle was bone dry. "Foolish."

"Parrish will deal," he muttered, tipping her

face up. His eyes swam in her vision. Dimmed. She withdrew her hand, and Simon froze as he found himself staring at a small, old-fashioned revolver. "Mattie."

"You know how he thinks," she said softly. She pulled the trigger. The muzzle flare lit up the porch, gunshot echoing from canyon wall to wall.

The recoil jerked the weapon out of her hand, and Simon spun with the momentum of the impact. He hit the dirt, swearing. Crimson spattered the wall beside the porch steps.

He shoved back to his feet, hand splayed over his side. Blood glistened wetly on his fingers. His teeth clenched. "Motherfucker."

Her hand hit the porch floor beside her chair, fingers trailing limply against the rough wood. Her head lolled, eyes drifting closed as the poison slid like acid and silver through her body. Sweet, painless, but so clear she could all but feel it as it filled her.

Killed her.

"Mattie?"

Strong hands grabbed her shoulder, pulled her upright again as the chair rocked forward. His palm cupped the back of her head, and she smiled. Slow and warm.

Simon seized her chin. "Don't you dare. You don't get out of this that easy. I have questions. You *knew*."

She sucked in a breath through lungs already constricting. "Tell," she began, and choked. Her throat swelled. "Tell him," she managed hoarsely, "I was dead when you got here."

"Mattie!"

Dying, she reflected, wasn't so bad. It was a long time coming. The nearly daily pain of her creaking joints and old bones receded on a comforting swell of golden light.

The feel of his hands at her face, the sound of his furious voice faded.

Everything was in place. Her role in the tale was over.

She had faith in these children. Faith that they would do what was right, faith they could fix the past. Fix the future.

That they could right her wrongs.

Bless them.

Smiling, the old witch let go of her tenuous bond to this world, to this time. Now it was up to them.

CHAPTER SEVENTEEN

There were more ways than one to track a witch. A trail of blood worked as well as any magical crystal.

Caleb's flashlight swept side to side, picking out the grisly signs of someone's torturous passing. Blood speckled the ground, smeared on rocks in lurid red only just fading to brown at the edges.

He knelt, angling the light toward a sharp edge of broken, rusted metal. Frowning, he touched the surface. His fingers came away red.

Even if he weren't standing in the bacteria-filled filth of an abandoned ruin, this much blood was a problem. He didn't know who it belonged to, had no way of knowing without magic to call on, but he knew a mortal wound when it left a trail like this.

One of his quarry was running. But which one? Clearly, there was no love lost between Alicia and Tobias.

Had one of them killed the other?

He could only be so lucky.

Caleb rose, stepping over the pipe, and arrowed the flashlight along a bank of half-buried walls. Nothing moved in the still air. His nostrils flared, senses fighting the mustiness clinging to everything.

Clatter.

There. Turning, the light skated from wall to wall, filling the dark corners of the remains of some sprawling structure. There was no roof, no doors or windows, as if something had sheared it in half and left the waist-high walls to molder in the damp. Rubble filled half the rooms.

Caleb clicked off the light. The tomblike stillness of the underground filled the space like a blanket, packing the darkness into every spare inch and swelling. He turned his head, closed his eyes, and listened.

Somewhere in the shadows, a breath caught.

Caleb's smile was grim. He turned the flashlight back on, dimmed it to a dull golden glow, and picked his way over scattered debris.

The pale line of a dirt-smeared arm gleamed like a beacon as he rounded a wall. "There you are."

Alicia looked back sharply, body jerking, but the pain pinched into her face told him what the trail of blood already had. Time was running out.

His jaw clenched.

"Figures," she said on a half laugh, slumping back. Her long legs sprawled in front of her, jeans nearly black with the blood oozing through her fingers. They pressed against her abdomen, and despite himself, Caleb winced.

Gut shot. Son of a bitch.

"Rough day?"

"Fuck you." Her voice strained, features ashen. "You love this."

"Not really." Caleb tucked the flashlight under his arm and crouched beside her, surveying the wound as best he could. He whistled, low and long. "Have a falling out with your witch?"

She spat out a laugh, blood flecking her lips. "He's not my witch." Every breath gasped, short pants that he suspected were all she could handle. Struggling for air.

He wondered what time it was.

How long she would last.

His fingers flexed. "What do you mean," he asked slowly, "he's not your witch?"

She laughed, choking it off on a painful sound. "Fuck you," she managed between gasps. "You must have seen this coming."

Caleb took the flashlight from under his arm, set it gently on its end by his feet. Then, thoughtfully bracing his elbows on his knees, he studied her face. Her scars were white with the effort she exerted to hang on to life, to consciousness, her permanent grimace strained. Her eyes flickered, so pale in the gloom they looked ghostly. And afraid.

He didn't smile. "What would you say if I said yes?"

Her breath caught in her throat. Wrenched spasms through her body, her heels digging into the rock and grit until it scraped away. Blood flecked her chin as she forced out, "Full of shit."

Caleb pulled up his pant leg. "There you go. Tell me what you meant about Tobias."

Her lashes fluttered wildly. "Hell, no," she croaked.

Fishing the switchblade out of his boot, he thought about the rotting corpse pile. The shadows, the chains.

Shadows in the dark. Rough hands.

Hands like Tobias's.

Her breath, ragged and short, filled the silence. Overflowed it, one desperate inhale into each painful exhale.

He flipped the blade open.

"Fine," he said, and ice slid into his voice. Crystallized every word into a murderous edge. "You'll tell me anyway."

Her eyes settled on the blade. Filled with sudden, brilliant tears. "Oh, God," she whispered. "Please. Please don't kill me. I'll help you, I swear I will."

"Really? After everything you've done?" He reached out and she wrenched away, collapsing like a paper doll as blood oozed from her stomach. Her lips.

She flinched, nearly screaming with it as she hit the ground. "Please! Please let me help you. I'll tell you everything!"

Are you sure about this?

The knife gleamed in his hand, but to his disgust, he found himself lowering it.

She was as good as dead anyway.

One less death on his conscience.

In his soul.

She grabbed his arm. Caleb tensed, but all she did was pull herself up, inch by trembling inch, sobbing against his shoulder. Wracking, wild tears. "Thank you, thank you," she said, over and over.

He pushed her away, sickened. "You can find your own way out," he said flatly, getting to his feet. He unhooked the small medical kit pinned to his belt and dropped it beside her. "Just tell me where he's taking Juliet."

He shouldn't have stooped to pick up the flashlight, he realized, but the thought came too late. Sobs shifted to a sudden, ragged burst of laughter as her bloody fingers skated across the black canvas of the underground. The sigil flared in the naked air, brilliant red, and Caleb threw himself to the ground a nanosecond before a fiery inferno enveloped the very spot where he'd been standing.

His skin prickled, edges of his clothing curling as the vortex seared the air. Alicia screamed, fury and venom, and with adrenaline scorching through his veins, Caleb reared back and slammed a fist into her temple.

She reeled, bowed backward and couldn't balance. Her head crunched into the wall. Loosened rock crumbled to the ground around them as she sprawled.

"Motherfucking son of a—" Caleb leaned over, snagged her shirt collar, and wrenched her back up.

She screamed as the motion tore at her ruined stomach.

In the fire's wild radiance, Alicia's eyes gleamed. Pain, fear. Malice. "I'll tell you!" she shrieked, throwing up her bloody hands. Soot clung to the tips of her fingers. "Please, I'll tell you everything!"

Anger fed anger; determination slid through him like molten steel. *I can handle her.*

So could he. Caleb grabbed his discarded switchblade. "Yes," he said evenly, every breath a harsh rasp. "Yes, you most definitely will."

Fear etched wild lines through her distorted features. "What are you going to do?"

"What you wanted all along, Alicia." Caleb pushed her to the ground, ice and rage and crystal clarity battling beneath his skin.

Whatever it took. He'd have to do it. Better him than anyone else, better him to carry that weight to the grave.

There was only one way to learn what Alicia refused to share.

I'll rip it from her spirit.

His head pounded. That voice echoed, hard and angry and alien. And yet, so damned typical. Was he cracking?

He shook his head, fingers tight on the hilt. "I'm going to teach you the ritual."

All the blood drained from her already pale skin. "You can't. You have no silk or iron."

"They're only focuses," he told her. "Useful, but not necessary. Now pay attention. You're only going to see this once."

"No . . . No!"

He pinned her arm to the ground with his knee. "First," he said grimly, his voice a harsh croak, "the symbols of power."

Alicia threw back her head and screamed, ragged and savage and with such malevolence, it was as if a thousand echoes took it up and spit it back, shattered shards of bloody glass.

The knife gleamed.

She came to fighting.

Large hands circled her wrists, shackling them to her sides even as she fought through the tangled threads of unconsciousness. "Juliet!" The baritone voice rumbled over her head, solid and real in ways every image sliding through her head wasn't. "It's Silas, it's okay. You're safe."

Juliet wrenched away from the dreams, the nightmares; came to awareness, gasping.

A single flashlight painted Silas's face in gold and wicked shadows, but sympathy softened his expression. And worry. "Welcome back," he said, fingers loosening. "You've been out for about an hour."

Her heart slowed its frenetic beat. Swallowing hard, Juliet elbowed herself upright, shoving her hair from her face with a shaking hand.

Everything hurt. Her legs, her feet. Her body.

Her heart.

She swallowed hard. "Where are we?"

He passed her a canteen, steadying it for her as she raised it to her lips. "Almost out of Old Seattle. We're about five minutes away from the barricade."

As she drank, he glowered at the comm unit cradled in one large hand. He stabbed at the buttons, raised it to his ear, and waited.

Juliet washed the grit from her throat.

Had he carried her all this way? What about Caleb?

She fingered her temple, wincing as it spiked a painful note through her head. Had he . . . hit her?

Of course he had. What was hitting *her* compared to murder?

"Right," Silas said darkly, snapping the comm closed impatiently.

She pushed the canteen away. "What?"

He stood, slinging the flask back over his shoulder, and glanced up instead. The light glittered off a maze of rusted, tangled pipes. "I don't suppose you want to know where Caleb—"

She stiffened. "No."

"It's just that he—"

"*No*," she repeated, and clambered to her feet when the word, her voice, trembled. She knuckled her eyes because it was better than looking at him. Seeing the sympathy, the concern, on his face.

She didn't care what Caleb did.

He was a murderer. A user. She wanted nothing to do with him.

He *lied* to her.

"Right," he said again, slowly. "No. Got it." Shifting back on his heels, he fell silent while Juliet struggled to put a cap on the raw edge of her nerves. Struggled to lock the grief behind a wall until she could sort it out.

She wasn't going to just sit here and be helpless, damn it.

She inhaled deeply, opening her eyes. To her surprise and relief, they remained clear.

She could cry later. Much later.

"What's the plan? Where are we going?" she demanded.

"The plan is to keep you safe. They're tracking your blood."

"My blood?" She frowned. "How did they get my blood?"

"I don't know, but we're not safe at the sanctuary. We're headed to the lower city," Silas replied. Forever grateful for it, Juliet read nothing but impassive determination in the man's face.

She could do that, too. "Then?"

"Then we lose them in the rat maze—" He tensed, glancing at the comm as it buzzed softly. "Fuck me for a doorknob."

Her chuckle didn't quite loosen the struggling knot in her chest, but it earned her an apologetic grimace as Silas slid the case open.

"Smith," he said into the unit. "Yeah? Sure." He glanced at her, expression suddenly on edge again. Soldier mode, she thought. Stabbing another button on the unit, he pulled it away from his ear and said, "Go."

The speakers crackled. "Are we all here?"

"Naomi?" Juliet frowned at the box. "Where are you?"

"Topside," Silas rumbled. "Spill it."

"You heard him," Naomi's voice said, and Juliet's eyebrows winged upward as an unfamiliar tenor, clear and even despite the worry infecting it, asked, "Could you remove the gun from my ear, Nai?"

Silas glanced up to the ceiling. "West."

"Better?"

"Ow! Cripes, that's my— All right, all right," he said hastily. "Uh, hi, Silas. I knew you weren't dead."

"*Now*," Naomi said flatly.

"Right," he said, just as Silas murmured, "Jonas." The expression on his face puzzled her. Part pained, part regret. Irritation and something that looked nostalgic. Pleasure?

Juliet's fingers pressed into her temples, focusing her gaze on the comm intently. "I'm so confused," she said uncertainly. "Who are you?"

The man chuckled, as if he didn't have Naomi's frightening shadow looming over him. "You must be the Wayward Rose. Nice to meet you, I'm Jonas Stone."

She raised her eyebrows at Silas, who shrugged evasively.

Naomi's voice crackled. "Missionary, witch. Witch, missionary. Good? Great. Can we please get to the part where the missionary recalls the fucking gun shoved in his spine?"

"Missed you too, honey," Stone muttered, and Juliet slapped a hand over her mouth before hysteria bubbled to the surface. "Fine, fine, here. This is everything I've been able to compile in the day since Director Adams set me on this."

Silas's eyes narrowed, but Naomi beat him to it. "What does little Miss Parker have to do with this?"

"It's a Mission task," Stone replied simply. "Operation Wayward Rose."

"That's me?" Juliet asked, blinking.

"Know any other Juliets?"

Silas only looked blank, and Juliet shook her head. "Just me," she said, and murmured as an aside, "Old story. Not well-known anymore."

"The director has a rarefied sense of humor," Stone said wryly, his grin clear even over the static hazing the line. Keys clattered faintly. "Anyway, long story totally short, she had me dig into the Church mainframe to figure out why you, Madam Rose, suddenly hit the top of the list." He paused. "That's the list that—"

"She knows what it is," Naomi cut in. "Tell her what you told me."

"Impatience only— Hey, jeez! Okay!"

"Naomi," Silas growled.

"Sorry," she said silkily, sounding anything but.

Stone sighed. "God, I miss you, woman. All right, at the same time, Director Adams had me investigating two new boys on the block. I didn't think there'd be any correlation, but lo and behold, that's why I am the master of the wave."

Juliet's eyebrows inched higher. "Is he for real?" she whispered.

A rueful smile tugged at Silas's mouth. "As a bullet," he rumbled back, then asked louder, "What did you find?"

"GeneCorp."

Pressure lanced through her ears, leaving them ringing. Rocks crunched beneath her shoe as Juliet staggered a step, suddenly dizzy. Silas caught her arm, pulled her into a crouch. His thumb stabbed a button. "Are you all right?"

She stared at his face, lips moving soundlessly. *GeneCorp.* Why? Why did that word seem so familiar?

The comm crackled. "Hello? Guys? Did I lose you?"

He raised his eyebrows.

"Fine," she whispered.

Removing his thumb from the mute button, Silas said flatly, "Continue," but his gaze remained on her.

She shook her head, brain turning over and over. GeneCorp? Had she ever heard it?

No. Not that she could recall, not in any sort of relevance that stood out. On the news feed, maybe? In the gossip rags?

She pushed shaking fingers against her forehead.

"It's a laboratory," Stone continued. "Not your everyday experiment on mice, either. This thing was buried so far into the Holy Order mainframe that I'm pretty sure I violated six federal laws getting to it."

Naomi muttered an impatient curse.

Juliet pinched the bridge of her nose, unaware that she held her breath until her lungs clamored for oxygen.

"We're talking airtight security and about a

hundred dead ends," the missionary continued, sounding more than a little pleased with himself. "Someone took a *lot* of time to set up a series of redirects and bypasses. It took me all night and a crate full of energy boosters, but I got in." His tone sobered. "Silas, dude, you aren't going to like this."

"Lay it on me," he said, eyes flicking to Juliet.

She firmed her shoulders, fingertips braced on the ground, and nodded. Not because he needed her to, but because she needed herself to confirm that she could.

A sick knot gathered in her stomach.

"It started as a turn-of-the-century theory, near as I can tell. And I mean *last* turn of the century, folks," he added. "*Over* a hundred years ago. Scientific speculation graduated to some pretty hard-core stuff. From mice to monkeys to . . ." He hesitated. "Humans, man. Not just regular cause and effect, either, we're talking biology on a macro level. Genetic therapy. Cultivating— Jesus, this isn't good stuff."

"Gene therapy." Silas's expression clouded. "They've been experimenting with the witch allele."

The what? Juliet frowned hard.

"Yeah." The speakers clattered. "I'm looking at lists of numbers, man. Thousands of them. Hundreds of thousands. Most are listed as *failed*. Don't quote me, but I think that means dead."

"Numbers?" Juliet whispered.

"Er . . ." Stone's voice trailed off on an uncertain note.

Naomi's rose. "Numbers, kiddo. Bar codes. Each one of these subjects gets stamped, dead or alive. Looks like it's been going on for decades."

Juliet sank to the ground, legs wilting beneath her.

Subjects. She was a . . . subject? An experiment?

Her fingers dug into the pitted cement.

Was she human?

Was she worse?

"What's the status of this thing?" Silas asked grimly. One hand settled over her shoulder, awkward comfort, but she barely noticed.

She was a number.

A freak, even among witches.

"I found a report," Stone told him. "An old one, about two decades old. It talks about moving a lab site from one address to an undisclosed location for security's sake."

"What address?"

"Don't know where it went," Stone said. Something creaked, as if he leaned back in a chair. "But I can tell you where it *was*."

"Shoot."

"I have it here," Naomi said, and read off an address that Juliet didn't recognize. Why should she? She'd never been there.

Had she?

Impossible. The location was somewhere in the lower levels, what used to be the industrial sector before the city got taller and needs changed. Only empty warehouses, forgotten refineries, and the skeletal remains of old buildings were left.

And squatters.

She pressed her lips together to keep them from trembling.

Stone drew in a deep breath, barely audible over the line. "Hey, Silas?"

"What?"

"About your girlfriend." He hesitated. "I nailed a handful of correlations, some commonalities, and I have to tell you that—"

"Let me guess," Silas interrupted, staring at Juliet, his expression inscrutable. "She's numbered, too."

"Yeah. Not all of them are, most don't have names associated with 'em, but I can tell you two things. One, the new boys Director Adams has me scoping out are part of this thing. And two, it's been edited lately."

"How lately?" Juliet asked, her voice thready. She cleared her throat. "How recently?"

"Three months ago."

Silas shot her a questioning glance, but she shook her head helplessly. "I don't know anything."

"Who edited it?" Naomi asked, her voice tinny on the line.

"Can't say," Stone replied, apologetic. "Ow! Come on, Nai, I mean I literally don't know—it's encrypted. Give me another week and maybe I can bypass it. What I can tell you is that it's got Sector Three written all over it."

"Sector Three?" Juliet asked, frowning.

"Sector Three's got the kind of clearance that makes government espionage look like a game of jacks," Silas said. "There were always rumors about plants and secret projects and shit."

"Rumors," Jonas added, his voice crackling as the frequency flickered, "and now fact. We're looking at a genuine conspiracy, guys. Massive cover-up operation."

And was she part of it? Her tattoo, Jessie's . . . they had to mean something. Marked. Numbered. To what end?

Silas stood, taking the comm with him. "Thanks for your help, Jonas. I . . ." His shoulders squared. "I've got no right to ask you for anything, but—"

"Hey, man, this has been one hell of a strange dream," Stone replied easily, laughter sliding through his pleasant tenor. "That's the last time I mix an energy boost with tequila."

Juliet watched Silas run a hand over his face. "Jonas."

"La la la," the man said loudly. "Oh, no, the connection appears to be losing— Ouch, Nai, come on, it's his fault . . ." His voice faded into hurt muttering as the speakers clattered, fuzzing briefly.

Naomi's voice intensified, as if she held the comm to her ear again. "You headed over?"

Silas met Juliet's eyes, his own intent. Thoughtful. Worried, she realized, and dropped her gaze to her hands, tightly clenched in her lap.

"Yeah," he rumbled. "If anything's left over in that place, I want to find it."

"Be careful," she said. "It's smack in the middle of the old refinery district. The place has been shut down for years."

"Which makes it prime squatter ground," Silas finished. "No worries. I remember how to avoid curious eyes."

"Yeah, well, you don't have a badge anymore," she said, "so watch your six."

"Will do. You too. There's a bounty on your head big enough to tempt anyone." The sound she made was scornful. Silas didn't smile. "I'm going back to the sanctuary, first," he added.

"Everything all right?"

"I can't get a hold of Matilda. I've been calling for the better part of an hour."

Naomi blew out a hard sound. "Oh-kay. I'd meant to drop by and check on Phin—"

Silas winced. "Sorry."

"Nope, no problem. I'll go to the sanctuary, check on the princess, and meet you at the lab. Don't do anything stupid." She paused. "Is Juliet coming with you?"

"Yes," she said loudly before Silas could answer.

"Good. Be safe, keep the comm on. Oh, and hey, girl?" Juliet glanced at the comm in Silas's hand. "Stick to his side. There's no one better in a fight."

"Right," she replied, with a hell of a lot more nerve than she felt.

Silas snapped the comm closed. For a long moment, neither moved. The heavy, still silence of Old Seattle pressed around them; loud in its own cotton-thick way.

Silas grunted. "Hey," he said, his voice like sudden thunder. The ruins sucked at it, feeding it back in muted, baritone echoes. "Hang on a second, Rosy."

She blinked, startled. "Me?"

"Listen," he said over her. "I don't know exactly what Caleb did or why—"

She flinched. "I don't care."

He stared at her, mouth a thin, grim line. "Shut up and listen." Her teeth abruptly clicked together. "What I do know is that the kid—the man's never done anything that didn't somehow turn into protecting his sister. Jessie's everything to him, like she is to me. Like fucking sunshine, you get it?"

Juliet stared at him, eyes wide. Emotion rolled off him in waves, anger and resentment. A fierce worry. Intensity like she'd never seen from anyone except. . .

Caleb.

She closed her eyes. "I get it."

"Whatever he did, he's the worst kind of idiot."

Her gaze snapped open. "What?"

"We hated his type in the Mission, too," Silas told her, his gaze inscrutable. "He's the kind of agent who always plays his hand close to the chest, never does anything as a team. He takes it all on his shoulders. Figures, hey, only one of us needs to deal with the shit that comes with the job." He offered his hand, palm up. "Caleb's like that, Rosy. He thinks his secrets will save the rest of us the pain."

She stared at his hand. Shook her head, once. "He killed my sister," she said, struggling to sound as matter of fact as he did. Failing. "I hate him, Silas. I hate him so much, I can't hardly stand to think that I—that we . . ."

"Yeah," he said. "I think that's why he's so god-damned desperate to die." He pocketed his comm, hand still waiting. Ready. "Come on. Let's go."

Juliet slid her fingers into his and gasped as he lifted her easily to her feet, a solid flex of broad muscle and effortless strength. She swallowed the lump in her throat, forcing it down into the chest-tightening ache tearing at the hole that was all that remained of her heart.

Caleb Leigh wasn't her problem. Not right now. Not ever.

"Great," she managed, a reasonable facsimile of calm. "How do we get there?"

"The same way we get anywhere."

She smiled faintly. "Hoof it?"

"Hoof it." A beat. "At least until we get to my truck."

CHAPTER EIGHTEEN

The complex crouched under a ghostly net of emergency and ambient city lights, squat and ugly. Gritty cement walls boasted graffiti too tangled to interpret more than the occasional letter trailing from industriously overlapped ink.

Hammered by incessant rain and squatting silently in the middle of a vast, empty lot, it looked as if it had been abandoned for years.

GeneCorp. He didn't know what it was, or why the word had stood out so prominently in Alicia's consciousness, but this was the place. Juliet was meant to be brought here. Why?

Because the Church is behind the Coven of the Unbinding.

How *obvious* it was. No wonder Curio had managed to be in both factions at once, how he'd known things. He'd held all the cards.

But why?

Alicia's memories were fragmented at best, shredded by the slow, acrid burn of her own insanity. She'd been in so much pain.

He knew that pain. He'd *inflicted* that pain. Been cured of it.

It wasn't an excuse.

She didn't suffer long enough.

"Shut up," Caleb said between clenched teeth. He knelt, working the tips of his fingers into the slatted metal fence. Rust flaked off, ran like blood as rainwater washed it away. Iron groaned, screeching an ear-blasting warning as a segment of the fence peeled away from its moorings.

If it was a coven hideout, they should have maintained it better.

Twisting, he angled his body through the narrow gap and crouched at the edge of the lot. Potholes littered the crumbling asphalt, overgrown with resilient strains of moss and weeds. Here and there, yellow and black stripes outlined speed bumps long since worn through.

He rubbed at his jaw, squinting.

New Seattle loomed high overhead, mazelike streets and tangled levels reaching higher and higher and shedding a permanent, muted glow over the lower layers. He wasn't sure if it was daylight or night. Down this far, only the occasional unbroken streetlight provided anything to see by.

Beneath the drumming rain, he could hear the continued rush and thrum of vehicles, that indefinable snap of constant electricity as it simmered through the grid.

Compared to Old Seattle's tomblike stillness, it screamed.

Eerily warm rain slid past his collar, soaking him to the skin. Rubbing at the back of his neck, he gauged the shadowed doorway a hundred feet away.

No noticeable security cameras. No guards. No signs of life.

What the hell did *that* mean?

He eased to his feet, ducked low, and sprinted across the broken lot. Gravel tumbled and cracked underfoot, but as his back came up hard against the awning wall, he couldn't hear any other sounds. No pursuers. No spotters.

Were they really this stupid?

Caleb slid a hand along the door, testing the release bar as he scrutinized the dark fringes of the visible lot. It creaked under pressure, but gave with a suddenness that swung the door wide.

Whipping around, he caught the edge of the pockmarked metal panel before it collided with the wall behind it. Echoes pinged along the empty corridor, vanishing into the shadows.

Blowing out a silent breath, he eased inside, shutting the door gently behind him.

The air was cooler inside. Even still as it was, his body hummed, crackling, as if he could feel it pushing against his skin. Electrical. Alive.

That was the power talking. The stolen magic.

The rush was always so much more intense when a real witch was—

Pay attention!

Flicking his wet hair from his eyes, Caleb withdrew a flashlight from his inner jacket pocket and clicked it on.

The shadows fled, leaving behind nothing more than dust and silence. Every step he took echoed faintly, rasping between walls as worn and mottled as the façade outside. There was no graffiti here, nothing but the faded impression of paint and nearly illegible lettering.

GeneCorp.

A company. But what kind of company?

Holding the light between two fingers, Caleb traced the letters. Its color had long since leached to a stained impression on the wall. A factory, maybe. A refinery of some sort, long since abandoned when the resources dried up. An old hospital, an orphanage, hell, he didn't know.

He didn't care. He was here to intercept a meeting.

A trade-off.

My Juliet.

He flinched. Turning away from the wall, he strode down the corridor on nearly silent feet, following the hall past moldering piles of refuse and stained rings leaving trails of brown slime in its wake. The dark closed in behind him, stale with neglect, ominous.

The first exit boasted double doors long since fallen off rusted hinges. The narrow beam of light tracked across empty, dusty floors. No footsteps marred the layer of grime, no traces to indicate that anyone other than he had ever been here in years. Possibly decades.

His lip curled. Son of a bitch.

Jerking the light up, he caught glimpses of heavy cabinets, metal structures, and empty storage spaces. Canvas covered bulky platforms, and cobwebs clung to every corner, some industriously spun across the sheer walls, filaments tucked into the narrow cracks between metal panels.

Bolts set iron support beams into the ceiling, and more cobwebs and grime shrouded any hint of lights.

This was a waste of time. If there was anything here, time or looters had long since made away with it. Whatever GeneCorp meant in Alicia's fractured consciousness, he wouldn't find it here.

Anger propelled him across the metal reinforced room. It dug in with razored claws as the light swept over filthy canvas coverings. Gripping the edge of the nearest in one hand, he whipped it off, muffling a sudden coughing fit as a dusty cloud erupted into the air. Batting at the air in front of his face, he surveyed the bulky skeleton of an old-time computer system.

"Shit," he muttered, letting the canvas drop. Three of the five monitors were nothing more than jagged glass teeth in a matte black frame.

There was nothing useful here. Hell.

What did this leave him with? The knowledge that it wasn't the coven's fingers he'd long sensed reaching through the backbone of a city too corrupt to notice.

Why did the Church operate with witches?

Creak.

His thumb moved over the light switch, and the flashlight flicked out. He turned, jaw set, ears straining.

Watch out!

Rubber squeaked behind him. Something rustled, a rasp. Suddenly, he reeled as something bulky and solid slammed into him. The flashlight spun wildly, clattered to the wall, and rebounded in a flurry of ringing echoes as Caleb sprawled.

He leaped to his feet, rotating. Fists ready.

Nothing moved in the darkness. Sniffing the air like a hound, he eased away from the computer table, moving as quickly as he dared. His heart slammed in his chest, his ears.

Squeak.

There. He launched toward the sound.

"Oof!" A masculine grunt. His knuckles cracked on bone, slammed into something fleshy that gave way under another muffled, gritty sound.

Caleb reached for clothing, a shirt, an arm, anything he could grab and use for leverage, but his assailant thrust hard, straight-arming him in the chest and sending him staggering backward.

His back collided with a metal edge. Pain spiked a knot into his spine, gouged deeply by the imprint of the gun he'd tucked there. Glass tinkled as it scattered, and something decompressed under his hip. Somewhere deep in the bowels of the building, a motor revved.

"Oh, shi—" Large hands folded into his lapels, twisted under his chin, and wrenched him around. Power surged through wires long since caked over, thrumming through the metal plates under his feet. Bank by bank, row by row, lights powered on overhead, flooding the giant room in ghostly fluorescent light.

Too powerful for the old connections. Glass cracked, sparks exploded. Embers burst overhead, arced wildly, and Caleb slammed an elbow into Tobias's sneering mouth.

Half the lights abruptly flickered out, but it was more than enough illumination to harry the large man as he stumbled backward, blood streaming from his lip.

Wordless, Tobias scraped his forearm across his mouth. Squaring up, he lowered his head and charged.

Caleb met him head-on, sidled at the last second, and drove his elbow into the bigger man's spine. The witch stopped on a goddamned dime, spun and slammed a jab like four tons of brick into Caleb's nose.

Blood spurted. Cartilage crunched, a sick sound that filled his ears, and he croaked a harsh curse as he blocked the follow-up left cross.

A power current popped overhead, sizzled, and sent sparks streaming to the ground. Tobias sidestepped easily, coming at Caleb with a snarl that—despite the adrenaline, the rage, the pain—twisted his mouth into a smile.

The man bared his teeth, swung hard.

Caleb raised his arm, elbow bent, and caught what felt like a tank in the crook of his arm.

Thank you, Naomi.

He snapped his forehead forward, rebounded off the harsh bridge of Tobias's nose, and sent him staggering.

Caleb held his head, lurching back. Son of a bitch, that hurt.

The man didn't take time to nurse it. He lunged after Caleb, grabbed a fistful of his hair, and spun him around. Caleb braced, pain twisting at his scalp. "You fight," he gritted out, struggling to throw the man off balance, "like a goddamned girl."

Words he ate as Tobias slammed his head against the metal computer frame. His knees buckled.

Taking advantage, Tobias wrenched him around and threw him against the wall. Caleb crashed into it with enough force to make the room gong like a bell, ricocheted, and collapsed in a shapeless tangle of muddled intentions.

The room spun. Gravity flipped over as he struggled to push his hands under him, dumping him onto his left shoulder.

Somewhere in the back of his mind, an insane witch laughed and laughed.

Get up!

Gritting his teeth, Caleb pushed himself to his feet. He spent too many precious moments fumbling for the gun; Tobias closed on him, knocked the gun from his stunned grip, and sent it clattering across the floor.

Caleb lurched as Tobias slammed an uppercut into his stomach. Heaving, flailing for something to grab, to hang on to as his guts surged into his throat, he struggled against the man's chokehold.

The Church couldn't have her.

He'd fucking promised.

"Too bad," Tobias said in his ear, and half pushed, half threw him into the shadows of an empty door frame.

His temple slammed into the edge, sent sparks shooting across his field of vision. As Caleb struggled to right himself, his hands grabbed at bolts of what felt like paper, massive metal wheels. He shook his head clear, spun.

Too late. Something surged into existence as suddenly as a light, whipped up into a burst of magic that knocked him ass over elbows and sent him careening into a glass pane that shuddered with the impact.

What the *hell* was that?

He twitched, shocks arcing through his system. His nerves. Move. He had to move.

Get up, get up!

His body ignored him.

Tobias unfurled a ream of cable and kicked him over to his back. Caleb clenched his teeth, straining to force his limbs to *move*, damn it, but the man only slammed a boot into Caleb's chest and ground hard.

He wheezed. "Fuck!"

As if he didn't feel the pain Caleb knew he'd inflicted, as if the blood dribbling down his chin was nothing, Tobias tied his hands together and dragged him up with one meaty fist in his collar.

Caleb spat blood to the floor. "You can't have her," he croaked. His leaden feet squeaked along the floor, boots screeching. Tobias dragged him down a second hallway, his black eyebrows knotted above a hell of a bruising eye.

He palmed open a door and all but tossed him inside. Caleb wrenched himself around, barely managing to land on his side instead of his face.

Pins and needles swarmed his skin; the nerves struggled to come back to life. He grunted wordlessly. Painfully.

Tobias nodded to the wide screen inset into the far wall. On it, the same room they'd just vacated glowed eerily blue. "Too late."

Caleb stared, transfixed as two figures slipped into the room on the screen. The image flickered, diagonal feedback rippling across it.

"You stay here," Tobias added flatly. He withdrew a small square remote from his pocket. "If we're lucky, it ends with her, and you don't have to worry no more." He depressed the button.

Caleb stared at the screen as small green lights flicked on in every wall.

Juliet glanced up at the security camera, her brow furrowed. Her wet hair clinging to her cheeks. The feed rippled.

His heart lurched into his throat. "No." *You promised.* He wrenched at the cables around his wrists. "You can't have her. You son of a bitch!"

"But we do." Tobias stepped out of the room. The door clicked shut, and tumblers fell into place.

Caleb twisted on the floor, gaze pinned on the screen. As the green lights shimmered—as it spread into a net that meshed across the whole chamber, glided over Juliet's puzzled, upraised hands—Caleb slammed his feet against the wall. Over and over.

"Juliet!" *I'm sorry.* "Run!"

"Juliet?"

She shook her head. The laser lights curved across her skin, shockingly green. "I don't know. What is it?"

Silas's back bumped hers, his shoulders rigid under the strange green net. "I feel like my skin's trying to crawl off and the rest of me wants to go the other way. But it's not the light."

"No." She turned her palms over, studying the play of light. "There's powerful magic keeping this place empty. I can just sort of . . . catch it, on the fringes of my mind." She waved through the green mesh. "I don't know what this is. Is it security? Some kind of—"

"Match, confirmed. Case subject One-Three-One-Zero-Zero-Nine."

The voice seemed to come from everywhere and nowhere. Pleasant, masculine, and precise. Juliet grabbed Silas's arm, her heart slamming. "What is this?"

He grabbed her hand. "Move to the wall."

"What if—"

"Now!"

"Main systems offline. Generator damaged. Video playback malfunctioning," the agreeable voice said. "Audio playback resuming. Case logs, December fiftee— December— Dec— teenth— Lab . . ." *Click!* "Lab assist . . . — Ia Pa— Nadia— Assistant . . ." It fell silent.

Juliet spun as the lights dimmed to a muted white glow. The grid faded away, lasers peeling off into green pinpricks arrayed along each wall. She turned again, met Silas's eyes across the darkened room. "What do we do now?"

"This place looks abandoned," he said quietly, turning to keep an eye on both exits. He backed up, holding out an arm to keep her behind him. "There's no reason the system should still be— The hell?"

Hidden speakers whirred, clicking through several octaves before a high-pitched beep cut through them. Juliet clapped her hands over her ears, hunching as something shrieked stridently, like gears grinding against metal. "—latest batch of subjects have shown remarkable potential, especially given the rapid breakdown of thirty-six fifteen."

A new voice?

Slowly, Juliet lowered her hands. She stared up at the ceiling, gaze flitting across the shadowed rafters as the woman's youthful, level tones continued. "The leaps made in a single generation prove Dr. Lauderdale's theories. There's no chance that the committee will fail to reup the grant this year. We've made so much progress since incorporating stronger genomes from the Holy Order's orphanage program—" *Kzzzt!*

The sound shattered the woman's dialogue, and Juliet dug her fingers into her temples. "I know that voice," she said, half to herself.

But Silas's head cocked. "Where?"

"I don't know." She knew he didn't like that answer, but she could only shake her head as he turned.

"Playback resuming," said the computer voice. "June— June— Lab assist . . ." *Click!*

"—in a matter of *months*," the faceless woman continued. Her voice, exuberantly youthful and polished to an educated gleam, thrummed with excitement.

It wrapped around Juliet's senses, tugged alarmingly. How did she know it?

Why?

"Test case thirty-six forty will blow their minds." The words echoed through the shadowed room. Eager. Confident. "We've already seen these subjects achieve remarkable test scores. The spread of ages falls between six months and five years. Thirty percent of the subjects are routinely scoring at the top of Krakowski's Scale. That's eighteen percent better than only ten years ago. Such a milestone! This latest batch of embryos is promising to be even more efficient. The new incubation racks seem to increase projected success."

Test cases. Subjects.

Embryos.

Her hands fisted. "It's true." Silas slanted her a look caught between wariness and confusion. "It's all true," she said, voice shaking. "I'm just a . . . I'm a—"

"We'll get to the bottom of this," he said grimly. His features set into hard lines as the speakers fuzzed, voices overlapped in a sudden cacophony of recordings.

Suddenly, a man's voice crackled to life over the line. "Dr. Laurence Lauderdale, log entry. October first of the same year," he said, his voice low and soothing, somehow. Quiet.

Every hair on Juliet's neck lifted. Her stomach knotted violently. "My God—"

"Whoa, easy!" Silas caught her as she swayed, lowering her to her knees and steadying her with both hands at her shoulders. Her skin prickled, as if a thousand spiders crawled across it.

"For the purposes of the committee's review, I have included visual documentation." He spoke gruffly, in that familiar halting tone of one who was painfully aware that he spoke into a machine. "Subject One-Three-Zero-Nine-Eight-Four has shown remarkable sensory capabilities that extend well beyond her physical location. Genetic composition includes"—papers ruffled—"an imported subject bearing an active witchcraft allele—for the purposes of this project, we have nicknamed it the Salem genome—and one of the specimens provided by the Holy Order."

The air felt suddenly too . . . full. As if they weren't alone anymore; as if it filled with bodies her eyes couldn't see. Living bodies.

No, not living. Souls. Memories. Hers?

"Turn it off," Juliet whispered.

Silas lunged to his feet, helplessly surveying the canvas-covered structures. "I don't know how."

"The subject in question appears to have an ability that mimics that of—well, in laymen's terms, we shall call the donor her mother—however, extensive testing proves that the subject's *visions*, as it were, are more readily apparent. In short, she is capable of what parapsychologists have termed *remote viewing*, although it lacks finesse or control. It's worth noting at this point that all other subjects bearing the Salem donor's genetic composition have atrophied."

"Turn it off," Juliet repeated, hysteria welling in her throat. Her head. It rode on the back of whispers suddenly clamoring to be heard.

From people she *knew* didn't exist.

See us.

Clapping her hands over her ears, she groaned. "I don't want to hear this, I don't—"

Silas kicked the bank of computers. "Come on," he rumbled, slamming both hands down on the various keys, knobs, buttons comprising the face. "I can't!"

"It seems only by combining the stronger evolutionary composition of a Mission donor will the Salem genome stabilize under duress—"

"What the *fuck*," Silas roared, face tilting to the ceiling.

Remember us.

Juliet shook her head. "No, no, no!"

"—which, until now, has been the obstacle resulting in the loss of eighty-six percent of our trials. That said, case study thirty-six forty-three is our most productive yet—"

Eve!

Silas's fist crashed into the dashboard. Electricity arced in a blue stream, crawling up the metal plates as Juliet screamed.

The voice slowed to a crawling drone, each word stretched across an impossibly deep pitch. The speakers fuzzed loudly, clicked twice, and fell silent.

"Malfunction," said the pleasant computerized voice. "Playback paused. Scanning damaged sectors."

Juliet gasped for breath. Rocking back and forth, she struggled to breathe, to think through the sick knot in her chest.

She felt nauseous. Wrong. Her temples throbbed.

Silas clung to the edge of the computer desk, staring at it in blank disbelief.

For a long moment, neither spoke. Then, slowly, Juliet pulled herself to her feet. "I think . . ." Her voice cracked. She cleared her throat, tried again. "I think we found it." Found them.

His head dropped. "Mission donors," he repeated, almost as if he felt as numb as Juliet. As confused.

Betrayed.

"What does it mean?" she asked.

"I don't know." His gaze hardened. "I'm damn well going to find out. Embryos, incubation racks. How long has this gone on?"

"I wish—" Her eyes widened. "Silas!"

The figure moved out of the shadow, too fast. Too sudden. Silas straightened as a gunshot cracked, deafening in the metal-wrapped chamber. He staggered.

Juliet screamed.

Blood sprayed, a gory flower picked out by the fluorescent lights, spattering the bank of half-shattered computer screens.

"Silas!" Juliet sprinted for him, only to shriek out a ragged curse as Tobias hooked an arm across her chest.

The gun never wavered in his free hand, still pointed at Silas as he collapsed to the grimy floor.

Blood spread like a black stain beneath him.

Juliet squirmed frantically, fingers digging for purchase, for anything she could sink her nails into. Cloth, flesh, his eyes, anything. "No!" she sobbed. "No, Silas, get up . . . *Get up!*"

Tobias hauled her back toward one of the doors. She wrenched at his grip. Her flailing elbow slipped past his guard, slamming into his sternum.

His grip slipped.

Twisting free, she sprinted toward Silas's inert body. He was so pale. Was he breathing?

Was he bleeding to death?

"Fuck, you're a hassle," Tobias bit out, seconds before he tackled her to the ground. She hit the unforgiving floor on her chest, wheezing as the air *whooshed* out of her in one painful squeeze. Briefly stunned, it was all she could do to fight back as he snagged her wrists in one hand, her waistband in the other, and bodily lifted her off the ground.

She watched Silas until tears blurred her vision. "Wake up," she wheezed, panting with the effort. "Get up, oh, God . . ." Jessie. Jessie was going to be devastated.

She'd never forgive them.

A door creaked open. She squirmed hard, her knees slamming against the floor. Pain spiked her kneecaps, lanced through her arms as he forced her past the threshold.

"Stay fucking put," Tobias growled, and shoved her.

She had no balance. No chance to gain any. Feet catching on each other, she sprawled, tripped hard on something, and dropped like a stone.

Her forehead bounced off the floor, and she saw stars.

The door slammed shut behind her.

"Jules."

She shuddered, hot cheek pressed hard to the floor.

Caleb's hands eased around her shoulders. "Juliet, it's me," he said. "Christ, talk to me."

Oh, God, what had she done?

Silas was dead. Because of her?

Because she was a freak. Because she'd been mixed in an *incubation rack*, like some kind of genetic cocktail.

"I'm here," Caleb whispered again, drawing her to his chest.

Shaking manically in his embrace, with her breath harsh in her ears, Juliet fisted her hands into his jacket, and sobbed.

CHAPTER NINETEEN

He loved her.

The knowledge was like a fist to his gut, a sledgehammer to his skull. He loved her; *he*, Caleb Leigh, loved Juliet Carpenter. Just him.

And God *damn* if the memory of Cordelia in his head didn't smile like a goddamned know-it-all at the admission.

Caleb clutched Juliet to his chest, rocked because he didn't know what else to do as she cried. She pressed her face to his chest and he swore to God, to hell—swore to anything listening that he'd avenge everything they'd ever done to her.

GeneCorp. Experiments. He'd heard enough to get the idea.

Missionary DNA sequenced with the composition of known witches. To what end? Some kind of . . . witchy Church soldier? He didn't know a lot about science, but he knew this much: Juliet was far from any kind of soldier.

As he stroked her hair, Caleb's eyes remained fixed on the screen overhead. Narrowed as Tobias dragged Silas to the edge of the chamber, leaving behind a lurid red stain. He left the man—the body—sprawled awkwardly against the wall.

Rage bit deep enough to clench his fingers in her hair.

She sniffed hard, her slim back shaking.

Closing his eyes, Caleb forced himself to gentle his grip. Forced himself to breathe, to slow his heartbeat. His fury.

He had to be calm. He was *always* calm.

Liar.

Juliet straightened, and he looked down into her beautiful face. Her eyes were red-rimmed, swollen from crying, but they glittered with an intensity echoed in the set of her jaw. "Sorry."

"No need."

Her mouth curved down in a heart-wrenching line, and he hesitated. What should he do? Hug her? *Don't be ridiculous.* Caleb had never been soft. That wasn't his language.

Taking a deep breath, she smiled crookedly, disengaging from him as deliberately as if she'd pried him off with a crowbar. Even with her short black hair tangled over her forehead, with her face tear-streaked and set, she was the most beautiful woman he'd ever known.

Inside and out.

"Caleb, I—"

He laid his fingers over her lips, silencing her. They moved, brushing across his fingertips like a kiss. A caress. Despite everything, his crotch tightened. He winced.

She stepped away, turned her back.

It let him adjust his jeans, swearing silently. Not the time.

Was there ever a time?

No. Of course not.

"Okay," she said briskly, her voice roughened by tears. Like velvet and smoke. "We're stuck together. I get it." She didn't look at him. "I don't like it, but this is what we have. So how do we get out?"

This he could focus on. "I didn't get a chance to check everything," he said, mimicking her professional tones. So much better than driving his hands into her hair again.

Under her shirt.

Between her— "God damn it," he muttered.

She hated him, remember?

She doesn't have to.

Yes, she fucking did.

Her hands shook as she pushed her hair back from her face, eyes settling on the screen. She bit her upper lip.

And realization dawned.

Juliet's eyes flicked to him, still too damned wide. Her face closed, shuttered.

He closed the distance between them, seizing her arms. "Don't you dare," he said gruffly. "Yes, I heard everything."

"Then you know I'm a— I'm . . ."

"A what?" he cut in. "A woman named Juliet? Raised by Cordelia Carpenter—no, you don't look away from me." Anger all but scorched the air between them. Her gaze collided with his.

Sparked.

"You were raised by Cordelia Carpenter. It doesn't matter how you were born—" *Created.* "—or where you came from. You're a woman, a witch, a pain in my ass," he continued fiercely, "but you're as human as I am."

More so.

Her eyes filled with tears.

He couldn't stand it. Not knowing what else to do, he jerked her toward him, captured her chin in one hand, and kissed her.

Her surprised sound flattened. Her braced hand at his chest turned into a sudden fist as she seized his jacket and held on.

Groaning, fingers tightening, Caleb dragged her closer. Kissed her harder, refusing to allow her the chance to give up. To give in.

He loved her, damn it. Fucking hell.

His tongue eased over her lower lip. Teased at the corner of her mouth. Her breath caught. Her eyes fluttered closed.

Her lips opened under his and he was lost.

Tentatively, so seductive he thought he'd lose his mind, her tongue slid over his. Velvet and honey; hell, she even *tasted* like something good, something real and achingly vulnerable.

Her body melted into his, hips settling over the bulge throbbing in his jeans. Sucking in a breath, he raised his head, jaw clenched as she wriggled closer. Her lips gleamed in the dim light, damp from his kiss and half parted.

Struggling to keep his breathing even, to ignore the pointed ache of an erection desperate for her, Caleb smoothed his thumb along her lower lip.

Her eyes opened slowly. Hazily. Brilliant green.

"Now," he said quietly.

"Now?"

"We get you the hell out of here."

Her lashes swept over her cheeks, and he let her go as she leaned back. Edged away. Logic would set in just as soon as the shock wore off, he knew.

She'd remember that she hated him. That she needed to.

He had to keep that going. There was no other choice. It was too late for them.

For him, he corrected himself flatly. There had never been a *them*.

"Okay, is there anything we can use to— Oh, my God!" She froze, staring at the screen, her hand at her mouth. "Caleb!"

Her exclamation jerked his attention back to the feed.

All thoughts of logic fled.

"Son of a *bitch*."

A tall, lean man strode into the chamber, angled features settled into a scowl. Blood soaked through the side of his button-up shirt; one hand clenched over it tightly.

The other curved over a lifeless body slung over his shoulder. He knelt, leaned down, and Caleb swore bloody and blue as Jessie rolled to the floor.

Juliet grabbed his arm as he took a step toward the television, fists clenched. "She won't be dead!" she said quickly. "Caleb, she's not dead."

"How the fuck—"

The speakers compressed the man's voice into something tight and canned. "I didn't get the research material," he said to someone out of the camera's view. His eyes were shadowed.

"God damn it, Wells!" Tobias exploded from somewhere off screen. "What the hell were you doing all this time?"

Wells said nothing. He crouched by Jessie, feeling for a pulse.

"She's not dead," Juliet repeated. "They want us alive. God only knows why."

"Fuck," Tobias snarled. "Worthless—"

Another voice slid between them, graveled and worn. "Children, that's enough."

Juliet's fingers clenched on Caleb's arm. He glanced at her, saw the blood drain from her face, and narrowed his eyes at the screen. "Who is it?" he asked. "Jules, what's wrong?"

She shook her head, her teeth suddenly flashing in a grimace. "I feel . . . I feel crowded," she managed.

Crowded?

"Mr. Nelson, go retrieve our guests," the voice said calmly. "We'll meet you in the processing chamber. Mr. Wells?"

"He's coming," Caleb said, turning from the screen.

Juliet stared up at it, eyes huge.

"Juliet? Honey, we've got to—"

"They're angry," she whispered.

"Who?" What was she seeing behind her haunted gaze? Not the screen she watched. Caleb glanced at it again, saw the man named Wells step over Jessie's inert body.

Wells's finger jabbed toward the door he came out of. "What was I supposed to do?" he demanded. "She was dead when I got there!"

"Without that research, Mr. Wells, your life will be very, *very* short."

"I get it," he snarled, the sound creaky through the speakers. His expression screwed into lines so angry that it practically sizzled. "We're all doomed to die young, trust me, I'm *well* aware. But the fucking research wasn't there, and she was a corpse. There is no talking with a corpse."

Caleb spun as the doorknob jiggled. "Jules, get in the corner."

She balked. "But—"

"For God's sake, girl, just do as I tell you!"

The door swung open. Caleb spun, lashed at the panel with a neat back kick, and leaped forward as it swung back on its hinges. Something heavy slammed into the far wall. He dove through the narrow gap, fist hauled back, and came up short as cold, relentless metal pressed into his forehead.

Tobias didn't smile. He only pulled the hammer back on the pistol. Unnecessary for the model, but point loudly made.

Die here or stay alive long enough to figure something else out.

Juliet made it an easy choice.

Caleb backed up slowly. "No sudden movements," he warned quietly.

Juliet froze, a length of cable strung between her hands. Her eyes pinned to the gun jammed against Caleb's head. She licked her lips.

His twitched. "What were you planning to do, Jules? Garrote him with plastic?" Her chin lifted, and a warmth, a wave of radiance slid into his heart and filled it.

That's my girl.

His gaze met Tobias's. "You're not going to shoot me." The man's eyes narrowed over the matte black barrel, and Caleb shrugged ever so faintly. "I won't let you lay a finger on her, and your boss wants us alive, so—"

The cable hit the ground. "We'll come quietly!"

He sighed. "God damn it, Juliet, shut up." He loved her. Stubborn, naïve woman that she was.

"Just don't hurt him," she added. "Or else I swear I'll find some way to make this difficult."

"Move," Tobias ordered. The gun shifted, ever so slightly.

Those light eyes turned to him. Narrowed. "Caleb," she whispered. "Please."

God damn it, Caleb.

He sidled toward the door.

CHAPTER TWENTY

The tall man spun as Tobias led them into a different room. His cheek blazed cherry red, jaw ticking.

His eyes met Caleb's across the room. Narrowed, and flicked back to the petite woman standing in front of him. Her hand lowered, fingers flexing.

"Your failure put everything at risk," she said tightly.

Behind him, Juliet gasped.

He couldn't blame her. The lab—he couldn't call it anything else—wasn't any better lit than the other rooms, with sheets of dust inches thick on every surface. Every three feet, empty holding tanks squatted amid a tangled sea of tubes and wires. Computers mounted to the north wall showed nothing but black screens and grime.

A wide, blank panel of glass segmented this chamber from whatever lay beyond the black interior.

"What was I supposed to do?" the man called Wells was saying, hands tight at his sides. "I don't know if you realize, but ghosts aren't my forte."

"It remains to be seen what is," the woman said thinly, and turned.

Juliet froze, so sudden that Tobias slammed a hand into the small of her back. "Move—"

Patience, what little he had left, snapped. "Hands off," Caleb snarled, rounding on him with murder pounding in his head. His heels dug into the floor, muscles flexed, ready to jump; screw the gun. The pain, the blood.

"Caleb." Juliet's voice was too breathy. Too calm.

He froze. Slowly, hands very cautiously raised, he turned away from Tobias's smirk and met Wells's flat stare over Juliet's head.

It dropped to the knife in his bloodstained hand. To the edge pressed tightly to her throat.

"Now, then," said the woman, stepping out from behind the man's rangy back. Juliet stared at Caleb, her mouth pinched.

Her gaze intent.

"Welcome back, Miss Carpenter," the woman said. She smoothed back her gleaming brown hair, her gnarled hands steady. As if conscious of his scrutiny, she adjusted her frameless spectacles and shot him a narrow, considering stare.

He met it. Matched it. Right up until Tobias

stepped around him, his shoulder clipping Caleb's brutally hard.

Caleb staggered, cursing.

"Mr. Nelson, please," the woman said primly. "A little professional courtesy, if you will. Now, allow me to get to the point."

"Who are you?" Juliet blurted, one hand locked around Wells's wrist at her throat. "Why do I recognize you? Where is this place?"

Caleb righted himself, holding his shoulder. "*What*," he amended, "is this place?"

The woman's thin lips curved into a humorless smile. "You recognize me? Interesting. As I recall, you were little more than an infant."

Juliet blanched.

"My name is Nadia Parrish," the woman continued. "Mrs. Parrish, if you please. Let her go, Mr. Wells."

"Are you sure?"

Mrs. Parrish leveled the kind of glare that made ice look like hot sand on a summer day. "Do as I say."

For a long moment, Wells stared at her. Then, abruptly, he let Juliet go, shoving her hard enough that Caleb lunged to catch her as she cried out.

He pulled her hard against his chest. "Be still," he murmured. *Don't do anything stupid.*

Her shoulders straightened. Deliberately, she pushed out of his arms. "You didn't clear up anything," she said. "Why am I here?"

Mrs. Parrish watched it all with avid interest. At the question, her eyes narrowed. "Because you belong to me." Juliet's head snapped back as if she'd been slapped, and he braced himself in anticipation before she did something stupid. "Mr. Nelson, retrieve the girl. Mr. Wells, if you will."

The tall, rangy man hesitated. Then, expression grim, he strode toward Caleb, unhooking a pair of cuffs from his belt.

Mrs. Parrish folded her arms.

Caleb's fists clenched.

"I suggest you remember that you are only alive by my word," Mrs. Parrish added.

Wells stared at him.

"Caleb," Juliet murmured.

Hell and fuck. Caleb offered his hands, wrists together.

The man's lips twitched. "Nice try," he said, and spun a finger. Gritting his teeth, Caleb turned, biting back a curse as Wells wrenched his hands behind his back.

The cuffs locked around his wrists, cold and solid.

"Now, as to your questions," Mrs. Parrish said. She crossed to a small bank of storage units, cracking open a panel. "This was, many years ago, my place of employment. GeneCorp, the foundation of the future."

Juliet watched her, her jaw tight.

Caleb bared his teeth at Wells. "Pray to God one of you kills me," he growled under his breath.

The man smiled, turned, and walked back toward the door. He leaned by the frame, shoulder braced, one hand splayed over the bloodstain at his side.

It had to hurt. He didn't betray even a hint of it.

"I am surprised you remember me," the woman added thoughtfully, withdrawing a small tray from the confines of the small closet, "but the brain is such a fascinating thing, isn't it? Impressions, translated into hundreds of thousands of signals and chemicals."

Caleb's teeth clenched as Tobias shouldered into the room, cradling Jessie's body in both massive arms. "Don't you dare—"

Mrs. Parrish flicked him a dismissive smile. "Relax, Mr. Leigh. We are attempting to save her life." Deftly, she fit a wickedly long syringe into a vial of clear liquid.

Caleb took one step, froze as Tobias met his eyes over Jessie's inert body.

His grip tightened.

Fists clenching and unclenching behind him, Caleb backed down. Give him time. Give him enough time and he'd have *something* to get them out of here.

Jessie couldn't die here. Not now.

The two most important women in the world. Holy Christ, why hadn't he *seen* this?

Because you didn't want to.

He bit his tongue so hard, blood pooled in his mouth.

"I was Dr. Lauderdale's lab assistant," Mrs. Parrish said. "Together, we developed the Salem Project, and together, we changed the face of science forever." Not a shred of humility colored her statement as she flicked the syringe, then beckoned Tobias over. "Take her into the lab and strap her down. Then Mr. Leigh, if you please."

With a grunt, the large man threaded his way through the empty tube-covered boxes. Jessie's face was a pale, sallow blur in the shadows.

Caleb's gaze flicked to Juliet.

She watched him steadily. Calmly.

But her arms wrapped tightly around her stomach. Fingers clenched. Her light eyes shimmered, so much hurt.

And—*son of a bitch*—apology.

She was sorry? Sorry for what? He thrust out his jaw.

A hand curled around his arm. "Let's go."

"I'm not leaving without—"

"Yeah, yeah," Wells said, pushing him hard enough that he had to walk or fall over. "She's right behind you."

"Follow your nice young man, dear," Mrs. Parrish said as Caleb made his way past the tanks. He turned his head, saw Juliet following behind him. Her shoulders rounded.

"Face forward." Wells shoved him again, forcing him to pay attention to where he put his feet. Cables snaked across the tile floor, bound in places and tangled in others.

Lights flickered on as he stepped into the second room. The glass wall became a mirror, and he hesitated.

Four metal tables, five feet apart and bolted in place, gleamed as if recently cleaned. Over each one, a large maneuverable light fixture radiated light bright enough to pick out the tiny nicks and scratches on each table.

Jessie had already been laid out on one, her eyelids twitching frantically, breath shallow and fast. Tobias snapped restraints around her ankles and wrists, then jerked a head toward the next table. "Lock and load."

Caleb staggered as Wells slammed a hand between his shoulder blades. "Lay down."

He turned.

Juliet's wide eyes met his. Mrs. Parrish pushed past her, seizing her wrist in one bony hand. With surprising strength, she jerked Juliet past the second table. "Let me be clear," she said coolly. "The instant one of you acts up, the other one will feel it. Care for a demonstration?"

Juliet sat on the edge of the table.

Caleb followed suit, mind working furiously. Shit. Double shit. He couldn't do anything without risking either of them. Jessie was still out, Juliet was terrified.

Wells unlocked his cuffs. "Hands at the sides," he ordered. In the unforgiving operating light, the blood at his shirt looked obscene. He moved stiffly, but it didn't show in the easy strength with which he maneuvered Caleb's arms.

The buckles clinked as Wells bolted them in place.

Damn it to hell. Caleb's hands were tied, metaphorically and otherwise.

Visibly shaking, Juliet kicked her feet onto the table and lay down, face turned resolutely to the ceiling. Her eyes looked sunken. Deeply shadowed. Her chin quivered as Mrs. Parrish locked her neatly into place.

She lasted all of a second. Her restraints rattled.

"I can't do this," she said suddenly. "I can't—Please. Don't do this."

"Why, Miss Carpenter," Mrs. Parrish said, brandishing the filled syringe. "I haven't even *begun* to do *anything*."

Juliet squeezed her eyes shut, tears tracking silver down her temples.

Caleb jerked at his restraints. Wells's fingers closed over his wrists, his eyes hard and focused. "Don't test me," he said flatly.

Think. He had to think.

Mrs. Parrish circled the tables, her shoes squeaking faintly. She smiled, a thin little thing, as she paused by Jessie. Leaning over, she peeled open one of Jessie's eyes. Checked her pulse.

Drew two fingers across her chest, as if measuring a line. "Here," she murmured. "Mr. Nelson."

Blank-faced and silent, Tobias peeled Jessie's T-shirt up to her chin, exposing her plain cotton bra.

Caleb lurched. "Don't you touch her!" It echoed viciously, but Wells slammed his hands back against the table edge. Held him as Mrs. Parrish raised the syringe in one steady hand.

The needle winked, arcing through the air. It pierced Jessie's flesh with a sick, sharp pop of sound, sank through her breast bone like it was nothing.

Caleb twisted, wrenching his body hard enough that the restraints creaked. He reeled as Wells slammed a fist into his temple, curving his arm over Caleb's head and forcing him to lie still as the room spun.

Jessie bowed against the restraints, screaming.

It cut off quickly, becoming gasps as Mrs. Parrish wrenched the syringe out. Tobias held her shoulders to the table while the woman examined her.

Caleb bared his teeth. "Jessie!"

"I'm fine!" she gasped. "I'm fine, stop fighting—Jesus, Christ." Too shrill, but alive. Panting.

Less scared, he thought, than she should be. He closed his eyes, all at once giving up the fight. Wells cautiously let him go.

Juliet sobbed, and Caleb turned his head to see her shaking from head to toe. "Jules."

"They're everywhere," she gasped. "Needles and tubes and the beeping—"

"Adrenaline should be enough to keep her lucid," Mrs. Parrish said thoughtfully. "For the moment. Gentlemen, collect the samples."

"Jules!" Caleb repeated insistently.

She turned her head, eyes opening. They glittered. Raw fear filled them. Spilled over in helpless tears. "They're all screaming for me," she whispered. "Begging me to help them— Oh, God, I can't do this."

"Yes, you can," he replied, then cursed as Wells grabbed his arm just over the elbow. A needle slid into his vein, a jabbing pain that only fed his anger. Between his teeth, he said roughly, "Hang in there a while longer, little rose. For me."

Wells withdrew the needle, his features impassive.

Juliet's lips curved into a faint smile, so sad—so fucking brave—that Caleb wanted to . . . to . . . *Damn it*, help her. Heal her.

Make it all go away.

Do something.

Wells unhooked the vial and dropped it into a case. Withdrawing another syringe, he moved to Juliet's side.

Caleb locked gazes with her. Held it.

I love you.

He always had. "Stay strong," he said firmly. "You *can* do this."

Her eyelids flinched as the needle slid beneath her skin. Wells worked quickly, withdrawing a vial full of blood, bracing his thumb against the small puncture. He didn't look at her.

Shaking, Juliet closed her eyes, her skin ashen.

Caleb glanced to his other side, watched as Mrs. Parrish dropped a third vial into a small case. Jessie said nothing, her mouth a thin line, her fists clenched in the restraints.

"Stay comfy," Mrs. Parrish said, and beckoned the men out of the room.

Wells met his gaze as he passed. He held the door for the others, hesitated. Then, his lips quirking at one corner, he eased the door shut.

Caleb's head dropped to the table. The thunk of bone and metal echoed.

Now what? Would they have to wait?

Wait for death, more likely.

To his left, Jessie stirred. "I can think of worse ways to wake up," she said, her voice hoarse. "But not many. Jesus Christ. Juliet? Honey?"

Caleb shook his head as Juliet whimpered wordlessly. "She's terrified," he said. "She's been having . . ." What? "Visions or something."

"Damn it." Her honey brown eyes hazy, Jessie

twisted her shoulders, attempting to get a bead on the room. "We're not totally helpless here. I got a pretty good view of this place while I was out. Cale, listen to me," she continued urgently. "I saw everything that happened—"

His mouth twisted. "Silas—"

"Not now." Jessie sucked in a deep breath, her eyes squeezing shut. "I don't know how long that shot of adrenaline will keep me up, so pay attention. We need out of here. They're testing our blood for something."

Caleb tugged at one wrist. "Yeah, but how—" The strap stretched. He froze.

Jessie did, too, turning her head to stare at his wrist. "Did that . . . ?"

Caleb twisted, clenched his fists and rotated it. It gave. Only slightly, but enough. "Well, son of a bitch."

Jessie stiffened. "Be still."

"Why—"

The look she shot him spoke louder than anything that could have come out of her mouth. He knew that look.

Caleb forced himself to relax, staring at the ceiling. Every sound Juliet made, every muffled whimper tore at his heart. Fueled his rage, locked tight under a seal he could feel fracturing with every second.

He had to get them out of here.

He had to trust them enough to do it.

After what seemed like an eternity, Jessie murmured, "They've tested the blood. Whatever they're looking for, we all register."

He frowned, gaze sliding to the mirror. The warped panels returned a shadowed reflection of them each, laid out like some kind of offering. He couldn't see past the reflection, even worn as it was. If there was anyone there, he couldn't tell.

He kept his voice down just in case. "Register," he repeated. "As what?"

"Correct," Jessie replied, but slowly. Already sluggish. "We all register as *right*. I don't know what it means." She shook her head slightly, her chuckle dry. "This thing . . . it plays like a movie, yanks me all over the place. I was . . . watching, the whole time I was out."

All over the place. His frown deepened. "Your magic has been getting stronger, hasn't it? Out of control."

"Oh, yeah." She flinched as Juliet hiccupped back her distress. "Juliet, please."

Juliet laughed breathlessly. "I'm sorry, I'm sorry. I just . . . I've been here, like—I feel the needles. They're everywhere, they drill through bone and blood and—" Her voice rose, spiky and panicked. "They won't let me go again!"

"Easy," Caleb said, pitching his voice for calm. Soothing. "Easy, Jules. I'm going to get you out of here, I promise."

She smiled. Barely anything more than a clenched jaw and peeled back lips, but even through her teeth, she was trying.

God damn the Church. "Jess, I have to tell you—"

"I know," she said quickly, and dropped her voice. "Wait for it."

The seconds ticked by, interminably slow. Aching with every manic breath Juliet took beside him, Caleb locked every muscle and forced himself to wait. Trust. He had to try.

Jessie had the advantage here. She could *see*.

Electricity hummed through the various cables and wires strung across the ceiling. The lights seared burning holes into his brain, but he counted slowly in his head. Counted each raw sound Juliet made and swore to turn it around on the Church that did this to her.

I see a mountain of corpses . . .

It welled in his head. His chest.

Boiled his blood.

Jessie stirred, lifting her head to stare at the mirror. Then, with a feral little grin, she jerked her head toward him. "Go."

Caleb wrenched at the restraint. It stretched tight, popped free with a sudden clatter of nylon and metal, and fell away. He unbuckled the other one quickly, pulse hammering in his ears as he wrenched the straps free at his ankles.

Quickly, he rolled off, closed the divide, and unbuckled Juliet.

She sprang away from the operating table, rolled away from him so fast that she grabbed the last table for balance. Color filled her cheeks; Caleb hoped to hell it was anger. "Can you—"

"Get Jessie," she said tightly.

There wasn't time to argue. He darted across the room, unbuckled Jessie and slid his arms under her back and knees. She didn't weigh nearly enough for his comfort. "Eat more," he said flatly.

Jessie laughed, muffling it against his shoulder. "Yes, Mom."

He helped her settle to her feet as Juliet carefully rounded the tables, her gaze averted. "How do we get out?"

"Follow me," Caleb began, then frowned down at Jessie's hand as it closed on his arm.

"Follow *me*," she corrected, and tapped her head. "I've got the map."

He hesitated.

Jessie's eyes narrowed. "You just remember who's older here," she said archly, reaching for the door.

"But—"

"I know where they are, Cale."

"God damn it." Feeling as if the world balanced on a needle's point, Caleb stepped aside. Juliet's fingers slid into his, clenched tightly. Her palm was damp. Her pulse erratic.

He glanced down at her in surprise.

Her gaze remained averted. But she was so pale around the spotty color in her cheeks, her lips almost bloodless. So damned scared.

Caleb pulled her arm through his. "I've got you," he murmured, and followed his sister out.

CHAPTER TWENTY-ONE

They'd done things . . . Terrible things.

The ghosts didn't have to move to follow her. She saw them filling every inch of the dark laboratory, the halls. Watching her, crowding her. They called out with soundless voices, staring at her with eyeless sockets empty of life. Of hope.

Juliet clung to Caleb's arm, concentrating on obeying the small signals he gave her. She stopped when he tugged at her grip. Walked when he did, slowed as he pushed her behind him.

But in her head, machines beeped. Babies cried, heartrending wailing that filled her ears until they rang. And the children, the grown children, so silent and reserved. Pale as ghosts, unsmiling. Deathly serious.

Locked away. Like animals.

"Juliet," Jessie hissed.

She jerked her gaze to the blond woman. Blinked rapidly.

"I need you to focus, honey," Jessie whispered. She crouched beside the door that Juliet vaguely remembered led to the main chamber.

The same place they'd shot Silas.

"Oh, God," she muttered, nausea blooming in her stomach.

Caleb eased into place behind her. His fingers settled at the curve of her waist, strong and steady. "Come on, Jules, *focus*. You'll be home free in no time." The warmth of his body soaked into her sweatshirt, her back. She leaned for just a breath, her eyes closing. Absorbed his strength the way she needed to cling to his heat.

His fingers tightened reflexively.

Never going to happen. Juliet swallowed hard and straightened, leaning away. "I'm listening."

Caleb's hand fell away.

Jessie nodded, though her eyes narrowed a fraction. "Silas is in there"—Juliet jerked—"so we'll have to move fast. Run for the door, all right?"

"But he—"

"No buts," Caleb said tightly. She glanced over her shoulder.

Saw the icy set to his features. The twisted line of his mouth. He knew.

He *knew* Silas was dead, and he wasn't saying anything. "You can't," she began, and bit it off as his features hardened. Tightened to a mask of rigid obstinacy.

She sucked in a shuddering breath, shook her head hard enough to dislodge the memories colliding in her brain. The ghosts.

He didn't give her time to argue. "Go."

Jessie beckoned Juliet by, flattening her hand toward the floor in silent signal to stay low.

Juliet crouched, slid through the door frame and eased along the wall. Most of the lights still flickered, but at the far end, the bank of computers glowed vividly. The working screens flashed numbers, graphs, things Juliet couldn't make out as Mrs. Parrish typed into the three-tiered keyboard.

Tobias braced one hand on the back of her chair, his eyes flickering almost white as they reflected the data he studied.

The shadows moved around them. Hungry, restless.

She scraped a hand across her eyes. It didn't help.

"Go," Jessie repeated, a low whisper.

Tearing her gaze away, Juliet followed the wall, staying to the shadows as much as she possibly could, holding her breath. She pulled every footstep, struggling to make no noise to alert them.

In the corner of her eye, she watched Jessie ease out of the doorframe and press herself against the same wall.

Juliet paused as Mrs. Parrish's voice carried. "This makes no sense," she said waspishly. "The Salem genome is present in all three, but only two of them should carry the amalgam."

"He's Jessica Leigh's brother," Tobias pointed out.

Jessie froze, half turning to stare toward the computers. The faintest edges of light cast her silhouette into rigid, shadowed lines.

"Which makes him related, fine," Mrs. Parrish snapped. "That's the Salem genome there. Look, both children and the donor carry it. The samples our agent brought back twelve years ago match exactly. But there's no reason for his blood to be registering with the Lauderdale markers— here and here." She touched several points on the screen. "He was born after the escape. The donor was never exposed— Wait."

Juliet stiffened, fingers rigid against the floor as Caleb stepped into the chamber.

Unlike the women, he didn't crouch. He didn't sidle.

He strode across the goddamned floor like he owned it. His features were set in lines hard enough to cut; fury blazed in his eyes, even shrouded in darkness as they were.

Oh, God. What was he doing?

Juliet opened her mouth, fear thick on her tongue, but Jessie flung out a hand wildly. *Be still.* She didn't have to read minds to know the signal.

Juliet shrank back against the wall and raged silently.

What did he think he was doing? What did he think this was?

A game?

Wasn't it always?

"Here," Mrs. Parrish continued, her tone brightening as she tapped the glass. "It's not a full set of alleles, almost like it's been spliced. Could it be?" She adjusted her spectacles. "Is it adapting— No, impossible. The donor would have to have conceived with someone else carrying the markers, wouldn't she?"

"You killed my mother."

Mrs. Parrish stood so fast, the chair recoiled into Tobias's legs. He didn't flinch, rounding to meet Caleb head on.

The woman raised a hand, halting him midstep. "Wait, Mr. Nelson." She dropped her chin, studying Caleb over her frameless lenses. "If you mean Jessica Leigh's genetic donor—"

"I mean," Caleb growled, fists clenched so tightly even Juliet could see them white-knuckled and shaking, "you killed our *mother*."

Mrs. Parrish sighed. "Fine. Call her what you wish. She wasn't supposed to die, if it's any consolation."

Jessie's face paled in the dark as Caleb's laughter cracked violently. "This." He flung out a hand. "All of this. You can't possibly think you could hide it forever."

So many voices.

"And who would come searching, Mr. Leigh?" she asked, her expression pinched into what Juliet assumed was pleasant. "With the three of you here, the donor—excuse me," she amended as Caleb took a step forward, "your mother dead, all traces of GeneCorp concealed, and the rest of the wayward subjects dying slowly—"

Behind her, Tobias flinched.

"—there is no one left to come looking. Time cures all ills. Including," she added pointedly, "curiosity."

Staying low, Juliet half crawled into the dark. Torn between the formless haunts in her head and the very real dangers in front of her, it was all she could do to keep from throwing her hands out and begging for a reprieve. One problem at a time.

She gritted her teeth, concentrated on Caleb. She couldn't let him take this on his shoulders, too.

Don't leave us.

"You don't give anyone enough credit," Caleb said, his voice low and terse. "You know what I can do. You know what I *see*, and mark my words, this *will* get out. You expect people to just swallow this?"

"I expect people will be happy to know that they are sleeping soundly in their beds." Her glasses winked, reflecting back the computer lights. "I expect they'll discount the rumors in favor of maintaining the strength of the Church that has protected them for decades. Centuries, even."

His lip curled. "You've played them for fools."

"No, Mr. Leigh." Mrs. Parrish braced her hands on the desk, long fingers tense. "We've saved them. We've taken the criminals, the guardians, the worthy and the cursed, and given them all a new meaning. They *matter*."

Tripe. All of it, sick tripe. Juliet shook her head, her hair sliding into her eyes as she mentally forged through the sobbing echoes of her memory.

If she could get to Silas's body . . . The very thought sent chills down her spine. But the man had a gun.

She could shoot Tobias. If she had to.

Jessie waved at her furiously, but froze as Tobias shifted. She withdrew back into the shadows, her face pale. Set.

Caleb laughed, the sound harsh. "Bullshit. You and this doctor were down here playing God. How long?" he demanded, taking a step forward.

Juliet froze, staring at him. At the twisted shape of his mouth, thin and angry.

He was *angry*.

For her? No, it wasn't about her. It couldn't be. It was for this. All of this.

I see a mountain of corpses. Of course. She straightened as the screaming in her head reached a crescendo, tearing at the confines of her skull. Of her own memory. "How many?" she demanded, hoarse with the effort it was taking her not to scream.

Caleb stiffened, but she ignored him. Ignored Jessie, somewhere in the dark.

"How many *case subjects*"—the words tasted bitter on her tongue, grated out like shards of bloody glass—"died?"

Mrs. Parrish folded her arms. "The number of failures is inconsequential. What matters is the data collected from each— Don't come any closer!"

She wasn't aware that she walked forward until Caleb reached out, grabbed her arm as she tried to pass him. "How dare you," she whispered.

His fingers tightened, a painful vise around her forearm, but she didn't shake him off. Didn't look away, her temples bright, vicious points of pain drilling through her head. They reached out to her.

They wouldn't let her go.

Don't leave us!

Mrs. Parrish pushed away from the desk. "The very fundamentals of science precludes such constraints as morality and ethics."

Juliet blanched. "And humanity?" Her voice rose. "What about all the lives you destroyed? All the people you captured? What about the children?"

"Witches," Mrs. Parrish spat.

"And missionaries," Caleb said, drawing Juliet behind him. He was too strong to fight.

She was shaking so badly, she didn't know how to try.

"All missionaries are subject to a yearly physical," Mrs. Parrish explained simply. "During this time, their genetic composition is harvested and stored. The best are then funneled to us. Under no circumstances are active missionaries ever taken." She paused. "Processed agents are, of course, different."

"You *monster*," Juliet cried, fighting Caleb's grip.

Tobias shifted, settling a large, cautionary hand on Mrs. Parrish's thin shoulder.

She shrugged him off. "I won't be spoken down to by this . . . test tube," she spat, pointing a vicious finger at Juliet. "Dr. Lauderdale is a genius. Because of his absolute faith in this world, in this city, he strode through breakthroughs most scientists can only ever dream of. We are safer because of him. We are stronger, and you—no matter how much you look down your nose! You're better than you could have *ever* hoped to be."

Juliet bared her teeth, every muscle in her body tightening as violence filled her senses. Her head. Filled her skin.

They killed us.

Caleb stiffened. "Jules, stop it."

Mutilated us.

"No." The word grated out. Was that her voice, so rough and raw? Was that her body vibrating from within a fracturing shell of control?

Twisted us!

Juliet watched it all from a distance, formless in her own skin. Reaching out with hands that didn't feel like hers; stretching, struggling to be heard in the raging tide of voices calling out for blood.

"You wouldn't even be here if it weren't for him," Mrs. Parrish continued, half snarling. "You and that whole lot of subjects owe him your life. You owe *me* your life."

Eve!

The magic slipped free of shackles she didn't know how to lock down.

Mrs. Parrish didn't seem to notice, but Tobias lifted a hand to his head. His gaze sharpened, pinned on her.

"Jules!" Caleb spun, grabbed her shoulders, and shook her hard enough to clack her teeth together.

It wasn't a pain she felt.

"They're still here," she said, her lips stretched thin over her teeth. She stared up into Caleb's eyes, brilliant blue. White bled into his irises as she watched. White lightning, blue ocean, bright sky.

Her skin crackled.

Power unfurled like a banner. Snapped in the wind of her fury and Caleb staggered. Somewhere in the dark, Jessie cried out, and Mrs. Parrish lurched away as Tobias launched himself at Caleb's back.

Make them suffer!

Ghostly hands grabbed her. Pulled at her, reached inside her chest and seized her heart in icy fingers. Magic coursed through her veins.

It burned. Oh, God, it hurt.

She threw back her head as her vision edged to black.

Choked as long, formless fingers of power pushed past her lips, bored past her tongue, into her throat. Fought for her heart, pushed deeper, drilling through her body and soul until it found that dark place where the power thrashed and leaked and twisted.

Avenge us!

Control shattered.

Her scream vibrated. Split into two voices not her own. Three. More. They wrenched loose from her throat, shrill. Ragged. Desperate. Not her scream; *theirs.* All the faceless, formless, nameless children *cultivated* beside her. The forgotten ones, the hollow ones, the witches and the babies and the sunken-eyed children.

Somewhere in the back of her head, Juliet watched herself break down.

And thousands of voices spilled free.

* * *

Juliet's power erupted.

Her screams didn't ebb, even when Caleb shoved her out of Tobias's lurching path. He staggered around, struggling not to fall on his face. Not to give in to the visions pressing in on his brain, twisting at it. Clawing.

The real world shimmered in and out of focus—*a mountain of corpses, tattooed limbs rotting in the dank air*—and Tobias came at him in fitful starts and stops.

He tried to reach out, to grab Tobias as he lumbered toward him. His fingers spasmed, knees buckling.

She sits at the top like a queen on a throne, her eyes empty—

"Holy Christ," he rasped, sinking to the ground, body bowing, wrenching. "Stop it!"

—and her legs spread wide. The tattoo burns like molten steel, smoke trailing from her blackened skin, and she says nothing as they—

He fought it back, struggled to see past the images assailing his mind. The room blurred, overlaying pictures crashing together. Sweat stung his eyes.

—pull on the chains that bind her flesh to hands in the dark. He watches from the fringes—

"Caleb!" Jessie's scream.

Juliet's scream.

So much screaming.

—and a cross burns bright as day behind him, shadowing his face, but his eyes. Gold then red. Eyes as radiant as the fires of hell—

Long fingers curled around his neck. Caleb choked, managed to grab Tobias's wrists. The man grimaced, his features a snarling rictus of pain, and Caleb's skin crawled. His nerves peeled back, scathing inch by inch, as magic sizzled between them.

Around them.

And still Juliet screamed. It wasn't like anything he'd ever heard before; as if her power hijacked her voice and filled the room with it. His head pounded, a skull-caving rhythm that he saw reflected in Tobias's wild eyes.

He wrenched at the man's hands. Magic flared, a spark to gasoline, and suddenly, there was nothing but hot air and clinging static. Tobias's hands locked into his shirt, eyes wild, mouth distorted.

—*and the mountain moves beneath her*—

"Get down!" roared a masculine voice that fell flat inside the cacophony of Caleb's head.

—*as each leg and finger and rotting limb twitches, an earthquake of human flesh*—

Magic slammed into him like a tank, a bullet; the impact swept him off his feet, sent him careening through the air like so much trash and broken meat. Every muscle in his body twanged, screamed in unison as he collided with a far wall and slid bonelessly to the floor.

—*and she starts to sink into it, swallowed by glistening, grasping hands of the putrid dead*—

"No," he groaned, clawing at his eyes. Struggling to rip the cobwebs of magic from his mind. "Juliet . . . Juliet!"

—until another hand—this one pink and living and warm—seizes the queen's in a living grip. The woman stands atop the shaking mound of death and decay, her blond hair streaming down her back, and strains with all her might to keep the queen from sinking—

Gunshots fractured through the chamber, echoed and reechoed until it became a single, thunderous sound.

—and she glares over her shoulder, green eyes brilliant with unshed tears. "Damn you, Caleb Leigh," Delia says tightly—

Red lights pulsed on, shattering the fitful flicker of half-shattered fluorescent lights.

Save my sister! The whisper was barely a breath of sound, a ghostly murmur in the fringes of his awareness.

And suddenly, the magic was gone. The voices ceased. As if a steel door swung shut behind him, utter silence settled into place.

Caleb found himself splayed against the wall, his shoulders propped awkwardly with his legs twisted out in front of him.

He blinked hard.

Red lights flicked on, flicked off. Again, over and over. An alarm. Something was buzzing; not his head, he realized. A comm.

Silas stared down the barrel of a gun, shoulders hunched around a bloodstain still spreading over his chest. Ashen, but upright.

The barrel smoked faintly.

On the floor beneath it, Mrs. Parrish lay in a pool of blood. Her thin throat worked, eyes wide and surprised, owlish without her spectacles. Her chest shuddered as she reached out a bloody, trembling hand. "The . . ." She sucked in a breath. It rattled. "The doctor . . . is . . . *a hero*," she wheezed.

Mouth set into a grim line, Silas pulled the trigger.

It clicked.

Mrs. Parrish laughed. And fell silent, head sinking back to the ground with a final, heavy thud.

The comm in Silas's other hand buzzed again.

Caleb pushed himself upright, clambering to his knees. Juliet. Where was Juliet?

"What?" Silas rasped into the comm.

The voice filling the red-lit silence was tight and worried. "Get the hell out of there," Naomi ordered. "Alarms are exploding from hell to topside."

Silas spun. "Jessie!"

Caleb dragged himself to his feet, locking his knees. His chest hurt; his throat felt too dry, aching. He couldn't take the time to catalog his bruises. "Juliet?"

Silas jerked around, hesitated.

Swayed. "Over there," he managed, and yelled again. "Sunshine, God damn it!"

"Here!"

His sister was alive. And sounded strong; it was all he needed. Caleb sprinted across the floor, gaze pinned on the sprawled silhouette in the far shadows. As he got closer, he saw Juliet's hands twisted in her hair. Her cheek pressed against the floor.

So still.

Was she breathing?

Caleb sank to his knees beside her. Hands

shaking, he slid his fingers over her sides. Gently rolled her over.

Her head lolled, black lashes shadowing her cheeks.

"Oh, shit," he whispered. "Come on, Jules. Come on, honey, don't do this."

Pressing two fingers to her neck, Caleb prayed harder than he'd ever prayed in his life. For her to be alive. For her to be all right.

He'd promised.

Please, God.

As his chest tightened, a vise of something raw and wordless and so black it hurt to breathe in, Caleb lowered his head. Touched her lips with his. "Please, Jules," he breathed against her mouth. "Don't leave."

Jesus Christ, don't leave him alone. Alive.

Oh, Caleb. Thank you.

A sigh, a murmur, and Caleb closed his eyes as something . . . changed. As if a curtain parted, something heavy lightened.

Juliet's pulse knocked faintly under his fingertips.

Suddenly, he could breathe again.

"Get *out* of there!" Naomi shouted through the comm, her voice tense.

The red light drilled holes through his head as he gathered Juliet's listless body into his arms. "I've got her." The lab flung his voice back at him, overwhelmed only as Silas roared, "Jessie, we need to go!"

"Give me just a second." Jessie's voice, exhausted to the bone, meshed with a clatter of keys. Caleb looked up, found her standing behind the computer. Her fingers flew over the keyboard, lightning quick. "I'm downloading—"

"Now, woman!"

"Almost got it."

"They aren't going to come with sirens," Silas said as he awkwardly refilled the clip in his gun. "They'll come quietly and ready to kill. This shit's way bigger than anything—"

"Debrief later." The comm clipped to his belt crackled as frequencies collided. "Fuck, shit, shitfuck, son of a bitch. They're closing in hard and fast, go!"

"Got it!" Jessie pulled a small black cartridge from somewhere on the computer bank and sprinted toward Silas. She was still so pale, almost yellow with the effort it was taking her to remain standing. Lucid. She slipped an arm around Silas's waist. "We're coming, Nai, and we got injured."

"I'll meet you at the pickup." The comm clicked off.

Caleb made it to the door on legs that were too damned unsteady. He didn't want Juliet to wake up and see the spray of blood and pulpy flesh that was all that remained of Tobias. To see Mrs. Parrish's frail, old corpse.

She'd have enough to worry about without knowing everything he'd only just figured out.

"We'll meet Naomi at the boat," Silas was saying between his teeth, features ashen, and leaning more heavily on Jessie than Caleb knew he'd ever want to.

Caleb nodded tersely.

"She'll get us through— Jesus Christ, where's the back way out?"

"This way," Jessie said, pushing past a half-fallen slab of concrete wall. "Is Juliet—"

"She'll be fine," Caleb replied as he held her close to his chest. He ducked through the hole, sheltering her with his body.

"She'll be awake, anyway," Jessie suggested, her gaze intent on the room they stepped into. "Oh, shit."

Silas grunted. "Fuck me."

The room was only faintly lit, remnants of electricity making it through shredded wiring. More of the storage tanks took up one wall, while a bank of small, six-by-six-by-six containment chambers ran wall to wall. Doors hung open, glass long since shattered.

As Jessie pushed through the darkened room, Silas's pained breath overloud in the tomblike silence, they left smudged footprints in the soot blackening the metal floor.

The carnage, remains of a fire now smudged with dust and time, was impossible to miss.

Caleb cradled Juliet, her head tucked under his chin, and stared at the tanks at the far wall. Incubators, he realized. Tiny little prisons for infants born from a test-tube mash-up of genetics.

Juliet's prison.

"I . . . remember something like this. When I dream." Jessie hesitated, shaking her head. Her eyes so damned haunted, Caleb could hardly stand it. Silas's grip tightened across her shoulders, and they firmed. "We need to get out of here."

Caleb shot her a hard glance. "Jess?"

"Now," she told him. "Hurry."

They strode past the cells, the wide observation windows long since shattered. Left black footprints as they found a hall beyond and followed it hurriedly to a set of double doors. The chain sealing them closed was unbreakable, but the hinges at each side no longer held up.

Caleb slammed a kick to the metal panes, twice, three times, until they gave way with a loud screech and pop.

Blessed air swept over the group, and Caleb inhaled gratefully. City and rain; acid and refuse and thousands of bodies crammed behind protective walls.

Even as much as he hated it, it was better than the stale miasma of death filling the building behind them.

Gripping Silas's side tightly, Jessie scanned the darkness beyond the empty lot. "They're coming in from three quarters." Her mouth quirked. "The fourth team got waylaid by squatters. Go."

Caleb followed her lead. She could *see*, after all.

And as he held Juliet close, he realized wearily that his sister—the second woman he'd do anything to protect—had always been able to see so much more clearly than he ever could.

Too little, too late.

Picture a teacup.

His grip tightened on Juliet's warm body.

They were still going to die.

CHAPTER TWENTY-TWO

Failure. Mission Director Parker Adams didn't like the word. Failure meant someone, somewhere, didn't do their job right. Which came down, simply, to the fact that *she* was the one who failed.

She stalked down the hallway, heels clicking on the scarred floor, shoulders ramrod straight. She knew every eye in the office would be at attention and on her until she was out of sight; expected it, after the reprimand she'd lashed them to the bone with.

If any of them still had skin, they weren't going to give her another reason to strip it.

Two teams. *Two* freaking teams had answered the Church's alarm, and both had come back empty. No clues. No suspects. Nothing but reports of Church operatives they'd never heard of before and a burning building.

The fire brigade had contained the worst of the blaze, but Parker wasn't as concerned about the fire brigade.

Where had she gone wrong?

The report Jonas had sent her had pointed to the very same address the alarms had originated. Evidence of *anything* was scarce enough that Parker suspected either something highly illegal or— as it was the Holy Order of St. Dominic they were talking about—highly political. Which meant top secret.

Which meant something better than Sector Five clearance.

Every motion rigidly leashed to icy control, Parker pushed open the office door.

And froze.

Simon Wells perched on the desk, the defined muscles of his back gleaming in shades of gold and crimson. His dark hair fell over his eyes as he struggled to reach the lurid hole leaking sluggishly down his lower back.

Her eyes narrowed, even as bile rose in the back of her throat.

Don't be sick. Blood was part of the business.

"Why the hell," she asked with deliberate, frozen calm, "aren't you at the infirmary?"

He barely afforded her a glance over his shoulder. His eyes were dark. Empty aside from the pain filling them. Still, he smiled lazily. "Don't like needles."

It came out much too awkwardly for Parker to assume he was all right.

She turned, opening her mouth to call for medical aid.

"Please, Mission Director."

She hesitated.

"Just need . . . to get patched up, that's all."

Parker turned slowly, her palms damp as she braced them at her hips. Her suit was black today, austere and authoritative. And a color that wouldn't show sweat as she surreptitiously wiped her hands on the fabric.

Simon Wells watched her, his rangy body half turned. He held out a clean white square, marred only by a bloody thumbprint on one side. "I could use your help," he said quietly.

Oh, no. Oh, please, not this. Her stomach fluttered with sudden butterflies.

The man looked like hell. A bullet hole decorated the front and back of one side, blood dried to flaky stains where his own sweat hadn't kept it moist and brilliant red. His cheek was split, and the waistband of his jeans was almost black with the amount of blood he'd lost.

He wavered, and Parker shut the door, crossing the small office to grab his shoulder before he fell off the desk.

"Fine," she said, summoning up as much asperity as she could. "But I want a report while I clean this up."

Again, that easy smile shaped his mouth.

It didn't, Parker noticed as she took the bandage from his hand, reach his eyes.

"You're a good woman, boss," he said, turning again so she could reach the torn, gleaming flesh in his lower back.

She stared at it for a long moment before gently, cautiously, she began wiping at the blood surrounding it. More trickled out, slow and thin. "Now," she added, just in case he'd missed the command inherent in the statement.

"Don't have much to say," Wells said. Pain thickened his voice. "Went down on a Holy Order mission with Tobias and got shot. Don't remember much after."

"What mission?"

His broad shoulders rippled with muscle as he shrugged, only, to hunch again. "Shit," he muttered.

"Don't move," she ordered. Gently, she applied the square of woven fabric to the hole and pushed. Hard.

His breath slammed out from between his suddenly clenched teeth.

Hers lodged in her throat as she forced herself to brace her free hand on the warm, solid muscles of his back. "What does the entry wound look like?"

Lucky for her, she sounded normal. And he couldn't see her face.

"Could reach that fine," he replied, gritting it out. "You're a saint."

"Not hardly. Give me another piece." She took the square he handed her and very carefully peeled the blood-soaked one off his back. Quickly, she covered it again, forcing another swiftly indrawn breath from the agent. "Where is Mr. Nelson now?"

"Dead," he told her, so matter-of-factly that she blinked at the back of his head.

He was filthy. Clammy and bloody, stained by dirt and whatever else he'd been up to without her knowledge. Or consent. The ends of his hair dripped rivulets down the skin of his back, and she watched one slide past her hand. Past the wound.

"And your mission?" she asked again.

"Can't say," he replied. "But it's over."

"Over?"

"I'm a free agent, now." His head drooped, and Parker was forced to brace her legs, splaying her free hand at his shoulder before he slid away from her. "Parrish's department is gonna . . . gonna take some time to reboot. Got no one t'answer to."

Silently, Parker reached for the medical tape by his hip. Using her fingernails and teeth, she tore strips long enough to secure the bandage in place. Her clean, soft hands looked almost obscene against the bloody mess of his warrior's body.

But that's why she was the director.

And he the missionary.

"That should hold until you get it stitched," she said, her voice suddenly too loud in the strained silence of the office. She stepped away, but didn't remove her supporting hand until she was sure he wouldn't fall.

He gripped the edge of the desk, his arms bulging as he carefully leveraged himself to the floor. When he turned again, nothing but simple gratitude shaped the angles of his face. Not even pain.

The man was good.

"Thank you," he told her simply. "Sorry 'bout the mess."

He wasn't out of danger yet. The faintly too-thick way he was talking told Parker he was still suffering from blood loss. She reached for the comm clipped at her waist even as she ordered, "Go to the infirmary. I'll have Rosario meet you—"

"Already said," Wells cut in as he turned for the door. He grabbed the bloodied T-shirt he'd slung over one chair and crossed the office on mostly steady legs. At least he wouldn't keel over.

Yet.

"Then," Parker said, annoyed, "go to the mess hall and drink something." The look he shot her over his shoulder as he thrust his arms into the T-shirt sleeves forced her to add, "Something non-alcoholic. That's an order."

"Yes, ma'am." He pulled the T-shirt over his head and Parker forced herself not to flinch as the pattern of blood decorating the stretched fabric became jarringly obvious. The white bandage peeked through the hole left behind.

What the hell had happened?

"Agent Wells."

He stopped in the doorframe, hand on the doorknob, half turning to raise a dark eyebrow at her.

"You are under no means," she said, every syllable etched in glacial emphasis, "a free agent. I expect you fit and ready for duty as soon as possible."

His lips twitched. "Yes, ma'am," he said again, and closed the door behind him.

Parker glanced at the wads of bloody cloth left behind, at the faded imprint of a crimson handprint smudged on the corner of the desk.

And the docket folder left on the chair. Operation Wayward Rose.

Thoughtfully, she picked up the folder and studied the surface. Everything Jonas had been able to find, which wasn't as much as she'd hoped, was in this folder. Everything on Juliet Carpenter.

Everything she'd been able to compile even without Mrs. Parrish's order to do so.

Slowly, she ran her thumb along the flap's neat crease. And the faint trace of blood left behind.

The comm at her waist buzzed. Without looking away from the bloody evidence, she fit the earpiece to her ear. "Mission Director Adams."

"It's Jonas, ma'am."

"What is it?"

The man sighed. "News for you regarding Operation Wayward Rose."

"I'm listening." She didn't sit. She didn't move the discarded bandages from their surreal spot across her desk. She simply studied the folder, and listened as Jonas filled her in.

"I sent in the routine report through the usual channels—"

"Which I have in my hands."

"Yes, ma'am. Well, I got notice back from, uh . . ." He hesitated. "Not you."

Jumped. Again. Parker's grip tightened on the folder. "Who?"

"Classified. The electronic signature's from the mainframe, though."

Damn it. "And?"

"All activity regarding Operation Wayward Rose is to cease immediately," Jonas told her. "All of the Mission's data is to be sealed and passed to Sector Three."

She clenched her teeth before she said something rude in front of her agent.

"I'm under orders to destroy all backups, ma'am," he added apologetically.

Parker scowled, mind working rapidly. "Fine. Do so."

"Yes, ma'am." A beat. "Ah, the folder I sent—"

"I shall have it to you within the hour," Parker said. "You may be assured that you will have *all* currently existing copies, do you understand?"

Another pause. Then, "Yes, ma'am. I'll begin the data demolition immediately."

Parker clicked off the comm, raising her eyes to the window separating her office from the busy cubicles now less manned than before.

Most of the agents had gone out to find something useful to do, she knew. Only those who rarely left their terminals remained, and they studiously avoided looking in her direction.

She sighed.

They heard her coming down the hallway, she was sure of it. All remaining eyes lifted to her as she cleared her throat. "Operation Wayward Rose is now ended," she said. "All data is to be compiled into one drive, sent to Agent Stone, and existing data destroyed. As of this moment, this operation is classified. Am I clear?"

A chorus of "Yes, ma'am!" in various stages of irritation and relief almost made her smile.

Almost.

"Agent Eckhart, I want an updated status on Ghostwatch," she continued. The balding man nodded once and bent over his terminal. "Send Mr. Neely to me as soon as he arrives."

"Ma'am," Eckhart acknowledged.

"I'll be back in the topside offices within the hour," Parker continued, daring anyone to bat even a flicker of a relieved eyelash. "I expect future operations to end with no less than complete success, am I once more clear?"

"Yes, ma'am!" replied the small crowd.

She nodded. And without another word, leaving Wells's mess behind and tucking the docket firmly under her arm, she strode for the elevator. Once inside, she touched the communication button and said, "Bring the car around. We're returning topside."

"Yes, Mission Director," said a tinny, masculine voice.

Parker glanced down at the folder under her arm.

Politics. Not on her watch.

CHApter twenty-three

Silas carried her to the grave site. Juliet wanted to walk, but every limb felt as heavy as cement blocks. Just sitting up had taken everything she had.

Now he set her gently on the ground beside the small, packed mound. One of the obsidian flagstones had been placed at the head, and Juliet stared at the symbol until it blurred beneath a wash of tears.

"Jessie says it means home," Silas rumbled. He loomed over her, over the grave, his arms crossed over a chest miraculously healed from Naomi's efforts.

Juliet nodded. "How?" she asked, and had to clear her throat to add, "How did she die?" She didn't know exactly what happened, or when or why, but she'd been out long enough to make her throat scratchy and rough.

It was Silas who had been sitting beside the bed, staring absently off into space. So he stood beside her now, his expression grim. And sad, she realized.

She hadn't known Matilda at all. But he'd obviously liked her.

Juliet touched the earth as he said over her head, "I don't know. Naomi's witchcraft—" He hesitated. "Her magic doesn't work on the dead. We found blood spatter on the side of the house, so maybe . . ."

He trailed off, and Juliet closed her eyes, her fingers digging into the dirt. Maybe when they'd all come after her, it had left the witch alone. Defenseless.

Hard fingers closed on her shoulder, squeezed gently. "The last thing she told us," he rumbled, "was that you needed to be found and brought back. At all costs, Rosy. She knew what that meant."

She shook her head. "No life is worth mi—"

"I suspect," he said over her, cutting her off with a warning flex of his fingers, "that she always knew more than she let on. If she died this way, it's because she meant to."

"That's a terrible thing to say."

"Is it?" The foliage whispered and rustled around them as Silas crouched, his hand warm and solid on her shoulder still. "I think she went out the way she wanted. That's not so bad. We all should be so lucky to get that choice."

Juliet closed her eyes. But silently, unable to get words past the sudden lump in her throat, she covered his large, callused hand with hers. Gratitude. Comfort.

She didn't know.

Footsteps crunched on the ground behind them. "Hey." Jessie's voice, soft.

Juliet took a deep breath, but any intent she had to stand wouldn't make it through the weakness dogging her every movement. "Hi," she offered.

"How are you feeling?"

Silas shifted away, moving around the fresh grave to stand on the other side. Probably, Juliet thought wryly, to keep an eye on his woman as much as on her.

She tipped her head back enough that she could see Jessie. Her expression was sad, but an edge clung to her features that made a faint, weary smile tug at Juliet's mouth.

It reminded her of Caleb.

Determination, right down to the core.

"Fine," Juliet replied finally, and Jessie's eyes rolled. "All right, mostly exhausted and feeling like none of my body parts are doing what I'm telling them to do," she amended, but with a sigh. "I don't know what happened back there, but I think it . . ." What?

Stole a piece of her?

She shook her head. "Can we settle for *fine*?"

"For now." Jessie raised a small satchel. "While I was out," she said, "I got to *see* a whole hell of a lot more than I ever wanted."

Juliet blinked. "See?"

Silas coughed, once.

She felt her face go up in flames. "You saw us—"

"Aside from that," Jessie said hurriedly. Shooting Silas a look that promised a sharp word later, she circled around Juliet to sink to the dirt beside her. She set the satchel gently on Matilda's grave, smoothing the dirt with a gentle finger.

For a moment, only silence filled the quiet calm that symbolized the sanctuary. Even after the attack, after blood had been spilled in its borders, Juliet still couldn't help but feel safe here.

Maybe it was the people.

Maybe it's just a nice, quiet place to die.

Jessie sighed. "You know I can see the present. You know that our magic has been going haywire." Juliet nodded wordlessly. She knew. "You know where we . . ." Her glance darted to Silas, who shrugged in helpless uncertainty.

Juliet rubbed at her face, even that effort feeling as if she pushed through water to do it. "I'm a test subject," she said, too exhausted to mitigate it. Any of it. The hurt.

The revulsion.

"Case Subject One-Three-One-Zero-Zero-Nine," she repeated bitterly. "A genetic mash-up of missionaries and witches thrown into a test tube and shaken thoroughly. I get it."

"*We,*" Jessie said softly, but with such intensity that Juliet blinked at her. "We are test subjects." Her smile was faint. "Case Subject One-Three-Zero-Nine-Eight-Four. Lydia Leigh was my mother—my donor," she prompted when Juliet looked blank. "Caleb's mother. We're . . ." Her jaw shifted. "Half siblings. Caleb's all natural. Or . . . was supposed to be. I have the same tattoo."

Silas shifted, crouching again to clasp his hands loosely between his knees. He balanced easily on the balls of his feet as he shook his head. "Nothing unnatural about either of you," he told them flatly.

Juliet smiled at him. Still tired.

Still disbelieving.

But he got points for trying. "Nice guy," she murmured to Jessie beside her. "You should totally ask him out on a date."

"Nah." Jessie's smile was opposite of Juliet's in every way. It hurt to look at, so full of love and tenderness that Juliet looked away. "He's a pain in the ass."

Silas snorted. "Point being, so what?"

"Well, nothing," Jessie said, inhaling and exhaling on a long sigh. "Except we're left with the knowledge that the Holy Order is running the Coven of the Unbinding, at least in this city, and we technically aren't supposed to exist. We're products of some kind of genetic experiment, and somehow, we got out."

Juliet looked down at her hands, clasped tightly together.

"Nadia Parrish and her goons are dead," Jessie continued, shaking back her hair from her shoulders, "and we're slowly losing it. Even now, I feel like there's a million things out there all trying to get my attention."

Silas's jaw hardened.

"Some of that is your fault," she added, and Juliet flinched. "Not on purpose, I know. Matilda once said that you're a teacup, and it's cracked, and now all the tea is leaking out. Being near you makes my power go all . . . wobbly."

Juliet straightened, planting her hands beside her as she struggled to her feet. "I'll leave," she said immediately. "Anything I can do to—"

Jessie's fingers settled over her shoulder, same as Silas's had before. "You don't have to, Juliet. Matilda made sure of that."

Juliet frowned. "What?"

Silas reached for the satchel, upending its contents over the grave. Three syringes fell out, making Juliet flinch, and a sheaf of papers. Real papers, yellowed with age and frayed at the edges.

A plastic card sliced through the air, tiny metal links glinting from one edge, and landed at Juliet's feet.

She picked it up with shaking fingers. On one side, a strong-featured woman with long red hair smiled out of a small photograph. Over it, the word *GeneCorp* had been emblazoned in thick orange and black. "Matilda Lauderdale," she read slowly. "And an ID number."

Her eyes narrowed.

"Dr. Laurence Lauderdale was a man," Jessie said, as if reading her thoughts. "Was he her father? Her husband? A brother? I don't know. Is he even still alive?"

"Matilda was old," Silas rumbled.

"Which means maybe not," Jessie allowed, and she picked up the capped syringes. In each, a brownish-colored liquid oozed slowly. "Among everything else I could *see*, I saw this, hidden behind a panel in the house. I saw the ID, and these.

I didn't know exactly what they were, but she explains it here. Listen to this."

Juliet's fingers tightened on the card, its plastic edges biting into her flesh.

She didn't want to listen. She didn't want to hear what the woman who helped GeneCorp had to say.

She didn't *care*.

But, oh, God, she did. And the memory of the tortured voices in that lab needed closure. Peace.

"Okay," she whispered.

Jessie smoothed out the papers. "The genetic composition for each child is destabilized by the very nature of its origins," she read. "Although progress has been recorded, Nadia isn't looking at long-term stability. Why should she? She's too focused on pleasing the doctor, and my concerns are going unheard. Or at least unanswered."

Juliet closed her eyes. "She calls us children. Not subjects."

"It goes on like this," Jessie said after a moment, "talking about how she's positive that our bodies won't be able to sustain the demands that the magic puts on it. She talks about you, too." The witch continued on before Juliet could say anything. "She talks about how she worked on you specifically. How she spliced your—"

"I don't want to know!" Juliet flung out her hands. The ID card slid through her fingers, slapping against the gravestone loudly.

Jessie stilled beside her. Then, slowly, she put down the papers. "Juliet."

Tears filled her eyes. Juliet shook her head hard.

"She talks about how she read at your cradle.

She says that your potent genetic composition could be enough to stabilize all of the children." Jessie paused, then translated softly. "You are the key to saving us. Your DNA or something holds the sequence that will keep us from dying young. She named you Eve."

"Why?" Juliet said, the word breaking on a sob that made Silas's eyes widen. His big body tensed. "Why does it matter? Stabilize them so they could keep torturing them? So they could fill them full of drugs and carve out bits of their brains and—" She jammed her fingers against her mouth as the sobs wrenched through her.

Jessie slid an arm around her shoulders, grip tight. "Shhh," she soothed. "No, honey. You're like . . ." She gestured expansively. "You're made of everything we are. You're the best of us. Matilda made you so she could free us. She tried to unlock the genetic codes of your magic, peel out the bits that made it so the others could live, but she was caught. She only got half the data."

Juliet turned her face into Jessie's shoulder, clenching her eyes shut.

"You were less than a month old when Matilda went on the run. These are the only batches of the serum she could make." Jessie cupped her chin in one hand, raising Juliet's eyes to hers. They were steady, golden brown, and filled with tears. But calm. Reassuring. "She wanted us to use it."

"More testing," Juliet said, but it lacked heat.

"I think," Silas said carefully, in the cautious tones of a man surrounded by weeping women, "that she wanted to fix everything."

Juliet eyed the syringes in Jessie's hand. A shudder slid down her spine. "I hate needles," she muttered.

"I know." Jessie's mouth quirked. "Funnily enough, so do I."

Juliet swallowed hard. Swallowed the fear, the tension. The deep, raging fury that couldn't all be hers. Squaring her shoulders, she said, "This will fix us?"

"No," Jessie said, cupping Juliet's hand in hers. "But it'll make sure that our magic doesn't kill us anymore. We can't be *fixed*. Just . . . stabilized."

Juliet nodded slowly. "It's a start."

"Silas?"

He took the syringes Jessie offered, taking a deep, long breath. "I hope she knew what she was doing," he said.

"Reassuring," Jessie replied wryly, and tipped her face up for his kiss.

To Juliet's surprise, as he turned to her, his eyes were kind, and he touched her cheek. "You're a good kid, Rosy. A good *person*. Don't let anyone tell you different."

Her smile was wan. "Just . . . stick me before I have a total freak-out."

"Close your eyes," Jessie encouraged, and held Juliet's arm for the needle.

Her mind screamed. Her body stiffened, and Silas's hand closed over her other arm to hold her as a sound strangled in her throat. They were going to shove a needle in her skin. In her body.

They were going to—

She sucked in a breath. "Where's Caleb?" The needle punctured through her arm, and Juliet all but climbed out of her skin. "Is he here?" she demanded.

"Easy," Jessie said softly. "He's not here."

"Where?" she gasped. Her arm burned, like liquid fire being pumped into her vein. "Does he know?"

"And done," Silas rumbled, smoothing a thumb over the tiny hole.

Juliet opened her eyes, her breath coming too fast, too hard.

Jessie's expression was torn. Hesitant.

The liquid, whatever it was, traveled up her arm, burning everything in its wake. Her skin throbbed, her muscles contracted hard enough to make her grit her teeth. Juliet clamped her hand over her arm and closed her eyes. "He's gone," she said tightly. "Isn't he?"

"Yeah." Jessie's fingers, smooth and cool, cupped her cheek. "Breathe, honey. He left while you were recovering."

She nodded. Once. "I . . . thought so," she managed, just as darkness came crashing down around her.

"It's okay, this is expected!" she heard Jessie say, and then nothing.

The computer screens glowed, luridly bright as Caleb sat back in the chair. He watched the feed play, tinny voices and a cacophony of constant, rhythmic beeps undercutting the silence of the forgotten chamber.

It had been two days since they'd escaped from this building.

Two decades, he thought grimly, since his sister and Juliet and God only knew how many others had escaped the first time.

There should have been more activity here. Missionaries, Church people, hell, he didn't know. Someone. There'd been four teams—whatever a team was made of—arrowing in on this spot just two days ago.

But nothing had moved in the twenty-four hours since he'd begun his vigil. Everything was empty, quiet.

Including his head.

Cordelia was gone.

Babies cried through the tinny speakers, but he tuned it out. He'd already watched it play through twice. Now he let it unfold again, background because anything was better than the echoing thoughts within his own head.

The ring glittered warmly in the monitors' cold light.

He twisted it, turned it over and over; a delicate thing, wildly incongruous against his larger, callused fingers. Silas had given it back without a word, but Caleb understood the message loud and clear.

Do your own dirty work.

The gold winked at him, warm from his pocket. Warm like the woman who had worn it; the woman who had loved her sister so much that she'd given up everything for her. Her life. Her secrets.

Her magic.

Screaming and yelling poured through the tiny speakers, and his glance flicked to the monitors again. A woman with short blond hair plastered herself against a wall as orderlies hurried by, smoke billowing from somewhere out of the security feed's view.

As it had each time, Caleb's chest squeezed at the image of his mother. So much younger than he remembered, but there. Right in front of him.

And still so out of reach.

His fingers clenched on the ring.

"She was pretty."

Adrenaline slammed into his body, but Caleb forced himself to tamp it down. Willed himself not to move even one muscle as the voice licked out from the dark.

He curled the ring into the center of one, white-knuckled fist, his eyes steady on the monitor.

"Get out," he said curtly.

It hadn't worked the first time. Caleb didn't expect it to work this time, either.

Juliet stepped out from the shadows and into the pale light afforded by the screens, her hands in the pockets of an oversized sweatshirt. She ignored him, her gaze fixed on the feed.

Even in his peripheral, even drowning in clothes too big for her, she was beautiful.

Caleb's heart pounded. Adrenaline. The scare she'd given him by sneaking up, that was all.

God, what a liar.

He didn't need Delia's voice to tell him that.

"Was that her?" Juliet asked, her voice soft. Oh, fuck, gentle. "Was that your mom?"

He didn't trust himself to speak. He nodded once.

"You look like her," she observed. "You and Jessie both have her fine structure. And her hair." She glanced at him. "You have her eyes, though."

He flinched. "What do you *want*, Juliet?"

She went still beside him. Then, slowly, she took one hand out of her pocket and rested her fingertips on the desk beside him. Lightly.

Cautiously.

"You left."

Guilt kicked him between the eyes. Again. "The data Jessie tried to take was corrupted," he said, his tone even. Calm. Everything he fucking well wasn't. "I thought I'd come back here and see if there was anything left."

Alarms rang out, causing Juliet to visibly jump, but they only echoed from the feed as it played. She shook back her hair from her eyes, and he hated the fact that he wanted her closer.

That he wanted to search her gaze, to soothe the hurt he knew she must be feeling.

Would only feel stronger.

The silence stretched between them, thick enough to choke on. Too heavy with everything he knew he should say, and couldn't.

She'd find out.

Right . . . about . . . He closed his eyes.

"Oh, my God." Three words, edged on a strangled sob.

Caleb didn't have to look to know what she saw. He opened his eyes anyway; forced himself to turn his head and study Juliet's shocked profile.

She was pale, but thank God, not as pale as she'd been when he'd left her in that bed. Not as fragile.

But hurting, still.

She raised a shaking hand to touch the closest of the screens. Between her fingers, a young child crept between six-by-six-by-six-foot cells. Her closely buzzed hair was blond, lighter than the color it had turned when she got older. A bar code blackened the skin at the back of her head, lightly dusted with golden fuzz.

She glanced up, around. For a brief, shattered second, her dark green eyes met the camera's.

Met Juliet's.

Her knees buckled.

Caleb reached for her, unable to keep himself from trying, but she stiffened, bracing her hands on the desk. Her jaw tightened. "I don't understand," she said raggedly.

"She was there." Every nerve screaming to take her in his arms, to soothe her, Caleb forced himself to drop his hand. It fisted with the other against his thighs. "Delia was one of the children in that lock-up."

Visibly trembling, Juliet watched as smoke hovered near the ceiling. As children of all ages clambered out of cells suddenly unlocked, some grabbing infants, others sobbing for help.

And the little girl eased between two incubators, reaching down into the open top to gather a tiny bundle into her arms.

Tears slid over Juliet's lashes.

Caleb's jaw clenched so hard, pain shredded

through his temples. She had to see this. She had to know.

But God, it killed him to see her cry.

Chaos filled the screen; alarms and screams, crying and shouting and orders. He assumed the rushing noise he heard behind it all was the fire that had scarred the interior corridors they'd passed through earlier.

It would take this room, too.

Without warning, Juliet sank to the floor. She landed on her ass, lips parted on a sob, tears tracking silver down her cheeks. "She was there," she repeated brokenly. "She was a witch, like me? Why? Why didn't she—Oh, God, why didn't she tell me?"

Caleb dropped to the floor beside her, reaching out.

She flinched, and he froze.

Then, slowly, he lowered his fists to the floor. He couldn't touch her. Not again. But maybe he could give her the closure she needed. "She didn't tell anyone," he said quietly. "Believe me, she didn't let on in any way. Nobody knew, Jules. Not Curio, not me, not . . ."

"Not me," she whispered. Juliet fisted her hands against her mouth, struggling to hold back the keening sound he knew was building inside.

He knew, and he felt it, too.

He kept talking, faster now. Intent. She had to understand, before she broke. Before it shattered her forever. "When she came to me, I thought she was just some ho . . ." He hesitated.

"Prostitute," Juliet said around her white knuckles. "She was never . . . She didn't care."

"She was your sister," Caleb said fiercely. "She was just some powerless sister to a witch I knew"—she flinched—"and I didn't have any time for her until she offered me a deal."

The remaining blood drained from Juliet's face. "Did you . . . ?"

It took him a moment. "Oh, Christ, no," he growled. "Fuck. What do you think I—" *Am?*

Her sister's murderer, obviously.

He dragged a hand down his face as the feed speakers crackled. "I never slept with her," he said from between gritted teeth. "She was dying, Jules. She knew it, and I think it was the same thing killing you and Jess now."

"Before," she whispered.

Caleb slashed a hand through the air. "She made me promise," he said over her. Get it out. He had to get it out.

The whole story.

Her pain.

"If I harvested her heart's blood, then I had to promise to get you out of the coven."

Her eyes jerked to him, wide. Shimmering pale and green with her tears. "What?"

"She made me promise," Caleb repeated, and sat back on his heels. "I already had a plan for the coven. I'd made connections, set the timetable. All I had to do was get you away from that damned gathering, and then it'd be done. I wouldn't have to worry about the rest of it."

Her eyes narrowed, even as a tear trickled down the smooth line of her cheek. "What rest of it?"

He took a deep breath.

"Caleb, what else did you promise?"

And let it out on a hard, angry sound. "I was never to tell you."

Her fists clenched. "I don't care if—" She stopped. "Wait, what? That was it? She made you promise never to tell me? Tell me what? That she was a witch?"

"None of it," he said quietly. "I couldn't tell you about the ritual, about her deal to secure your freedom, about her voice in my goddamned head—" He lurched to his feet, swiping a hand through the air. "Nothing. Ever."

"But why?" she demanded, and in the question, he heard every wound, every hurt. Every empty, aching, sleepless night.

He shuddered. "I don't know."

In the feed beside him, fire licked at the edges of the room. The girl with the wide green eyes carried the baby, almost too big for her little arms. She picked her way over tangled wires and melting cords.

Juliet covered her mouth with one hand, muffling her tears.

"I never realized she was a witch until now," Caleb said quietly. "I didn't know how unusual it was to have a remnant of that person stay in your head until—" He caught himself, bit off his words with a vicious, angry curse. She didn't need to know how much of Cordelia he'd carried around.

How often he'd heard her voice when Juliet had nothing.

He stalked away from the computers. Away

from Juliet, hunched over the hole he knew filled her chest. How could it not?

She'd spent her life being lied to.

And he hadn't helped her. Ever.

But someone had. Since the beginning, Cordelia had guided things. Manipulated things. Just as bad as that red-haired witch in the trench. As bad as he did. Connivers, the lot of them.

Cursing savagely, silently, he spun again and closed the distance between them. She was damn well going to see this.

He wrapped a hand around her arm, jerking her to her feet. "Look at this," he said, every word a growl.

She shook her head, hair sticking to her damp cheeks in lines of faded black ink.

He shook her hard enough that her eyes widened. Hoisted her closer to the monitors, until they all but filled her vision. Until she had no choice but to see.

The child they knew as Cordelia held the bundle close to her chest, coughing as she scurried away from the flames. She cradled the baby's head in one hand. "There, there," she said lightly, even as the world turned to flame and chaos around her. "It's okay, baby. We'll be safe soon."

The screen fuzzed as fire ate at the camera, but Caleb wordlessly jerked Juliet closer to his side as the second monitor showed the six-year-old carrying the infant down the hallway. Orderlies fled. Screams filled the speakers; trapped subjects, injured technicians, he didn't know.

Juliet trembled in his grip, shook violently as

the child passed under a camera. "I'll take care of you," whispered the tiny voice, all but drowned out by the madness around her. "It's just you and me, now."

Familiar emerald eyes glanced up at the camera as they passed under it. Protectively, the little girl's skinny arms tightened around the white blanket.

Caleb caught a glimpse of a tiny, round head, capped with a fine tuft of light brown hair, and they were gone.

Slowly, he let go of Juliet's arm.

Her head lowered, shoulders shaking. "I never—" Her voice broke, and Caleb's heart shattered with it.

"Here."

She didn't look up, so he picked up Juliet's slack hand and pressed Cordelia's ring into her palm. Her fingers closed over it. Fisted.

"I'm sorry," Caleb said, so quietly even he wasn't sure he'd said it aloud.

Juliet didn't move.

He didn't expect her to. She needed to say goodbye. He understood that.

More than she even knew.

Silently, he withdrew from the flickering light. Left her there in the crackling silence of the ended feeds.

His footsteps echoed down the empty hall, clattered back at him in a thousand recriminating words. He pushed open the double doors, turned up his collar against the summer rain, and strode into the dark.

CHAPTER TWENTY-FOUR

"Caleb!"

He froze at the edge of the empty lot, rain already soaked through his clothing and sliding down his collar.

"Wait!"

Footsteps pounded the broken, pitted ground behind him, and his heart echoed the frenetic rhythm. Barely even daring to breathe, he turned.

Juliet sprinted across the dark lot, her pale skin gleaming beneath the faint lights the city always cast. Her eyes were shadowed, and within moments, she was as soaked as he was.

"Go back inside," he told her sharply, "it's— God damn it!"

It was all he could say as she threw herself at

him. He caught her, but it wasn't to fight her this time. She didn't flail at him; she didn't try to hit him. Trembling, gasping for air, she threw her full weight against his chest, and he staggered.

He meant to peel her off. To pry her away from him and send her back inside, but his traitorous hands splayed over her wet back. Crushed her to him. "Don't," he said, even as his fingers slid beneath the wet sweatshirt. Found warm skin and that damned bra.

She grabbed fistfuls of his coat. Tipped her face to his, eyes flashing. "You don't break promises," she said fiercely.

"I don't—"

"I know you," she said over him, even as her hair dripped into her eyes. Her fingers tightened. "You never break a promise."

"You're wrong." But oh, God, her skin felt good against his palms. She sucked in a breath, her breasts flush against his chest, and he groaned. "Don't," he said again. "You're wrong about me."

"I'm not," she shot back, as if reading it in his eyes. In his thoughts; fuck, his heart. "You promised her and you kept it, even when you knew how badly I needed to know. I understand, Caleb."

God damn it. "You don't understand anything!"

She flinched at his shout, but she pulled herself to her toes. Pressed her lips against his wet jaw, and murmured, "Everything you've ever done was to protect." He shuddered. "You love your sister, you want to help, you *see* things—God, such terrible things—and you want to stop them. I know."

Groaning, one hand left her back to fist into the wet tendrils of her dark hair. He wrenched her head back, her mouth away from his skin. Her eyes met his, haunting and sweet and filled with—oh, fuck, with *trust*.

With understanding.

Sympathy.

He meant to yell at her. To push her away with words and action and any weapon he could, but she met his eyes, licked the rain away from her top lip; he was lost.

A savage curse wrenched from his chest as he hauled her mouth to his. She met his kiss eagerly, opened her lips to slide her tongue between his, and made a sound that may as well have grabbed his erection and squeezed.

Spinning, he pushed her back against the chain-link fence; grabbed the wire at either side of her head, and crowded her. His mouth never left hers, feasting. Devouring. God, her lips were soft, warm. So giving.

She was so damned giving.

She understood?

Could she? Really?

His fingers tunneled under her sweatshirt again. Found warm flesh and soft curve; she arched into his palm. He nipped at her lower lip. She gasped, and the sound became his name.

Something wild filled his head. His heart. Something sweet and sharp and bloody and soul-deep.

Say it.

"I love you," he said against her mouth.

Rain slid over her face, sluiced over them both, and she laughed. He swallowed the sound, pressed his hips firmly against hers to lock her in place and leaned back to capture her head in both hands. To frame her face, wet and flushed.

Her eyes blinked into his, hazed with lust. But was that all?

Smoothing back her wet hair, he said again, "I love you. I wish I didn't," he added, frowning, "but I have since the first time I ever saw you watching me."

Her breath shuddered in her lungs. Again, her tongue slid over her rain-slick mouth and the muscles of his arms clenched as he fought the urge to lean in, to taste the same top-heavy curve her tongue just had.

She said nothing. For a long moment, only the wild rush of rain and his own heartbeat filled the silence, until he thought his veins might explode from the wild beat.

"Say something," he said hoarsely. "Anything. Tell me you hate me—fuck, Jules, I don't care, just say—"

"You're the worst type of idiot."

He froze, every muscle locked as the words kicked him squarely in the gut. "What?" He shook his head, bewildered. "With the who?"

Her eyes held his, so goddamned steady, he felt like the one falling apart. The one who needed comfort.

Damn it, he just needed her. Didn't she see that?

"I can't imagine," she said, her body trembling against him. "I can't even begin to think what you must have gone through." Her fingers touched the scars at the side of his mouth. Traced the ridged edges along his neck, and he flinched.

Her smile turned crooked.

"You try all the time to do everything your-self, to carry the crap so no one has to. You make promises and do these things and you just go wandering off hoping that the rest of us will just let you."

That hand dipped into his collar. Curled in, fist-ed so hard that it dug into his neck as she hauled his face close to hers. He was forced to let her go, to grip the chain link around her for balance as light green eyes filled his vision.

"Don't," she said, voice taut with strain. "Don't ever make that mistake with me, Caleb Leigh. I'm not your sister. I'm not your coven mate, I'm not anyone you knew before."

A tiny seed of hope germinated in his heart. A flicker, a faint glimmer of light.

She raised her hand, and gold glinted between her fingers. "You both used me. You *and* Cordelia."

"I'm sorry," he said hoarsely.

She shook her head. "Don't *handle* me," she told him. "Don't *maneuver* me. I can't—" Her voice shook, and she blinked. Hard enough to wipe the rain from her eyes. Or tears. "I love you, Caleb, but I can't do it. I can't be used again. I can't just be some kind of—"

He plucked the ring from her hand. "Shut up."

Her lashes flared. "What?"

She loved him. She *said* so.

It was enough. Caleb shrugged out of her grip,

stepped away from the warm, soft heat of her body and pulled her upright. The fence clanged, water spraying from the wire as it swayed.

He sank to his knees in front of her, ignored the broken cement digging into his flesh. Ignored the rain, warm and insistent as it soaked through every layer to the skin. He captured her hand in his, met her wide gaze, and demanded, "Marry me."

Her mouth opened. Rain slid along her lip, but she only stared at him. As if he'd lost his mind.

Maybe he had.

"You aren't like anyone I've ever known," he said, knowing his voice came out too rough and unable to control it. To control himself. "You're everything. You're sweetness and light and softness in a world I never expected to have those things."

She bit her top lip.

"I never *saw* this. I couldn't have ever seen anything like you. Marry me, Juliet. Stay with me forever. Be my light." With hands that trembled, he slid the warmed gold ring onto Juliet's finger.

It fit. Glinted warmly against her skin.

Her fingers shook. "I didn't say yes," she whispered, but she made no move to take it off.

With his heart in his throat, Caleb laced his fingers through hers and said, "You didn't say no."

"You conceited—!"

He tugged her hand so hard, she folded, colliding into his chest, knees straddling his waist and her words smothered against his mouth. He tangled his hands into her hair, held her still for a kiss that tried to put into words everything rioting through him. His heart. His soul.

He loved her. He wanted her, he *needed* her in every aspect of his life. Every day. Every night.

He had no world without her.

When he lifted his head, she was flushed and gasping. His thumbs stroked along her temples. "Say yes, little rose. I swear to you, we'll find a cure."

She blinked rapidly. Her smile, slow to start, filled her eyes with sunshine. Flowers and spring rain and all those things he never expected to think about. "You idiot," she said, laughing. "Yes. And I'm already fixed."

He reeled.

Juliet threw back her head, her laughter wild and husky and free as the rain beat down on them both. Before he could ask how, when, she pressed her mouth to his. No unruly kiss, she slid her lips slowly, tantalizingly along his. Like a drug his body craved, every sensor slammed into over-drive; from dick to heart to brain and back again.

When she leaned back, it was his turn to blink hard. To shake away the fog of lust, of love, hazing his mind.

"Come home," she whispered, tunneling rain-cool hands into his coat. "We'll explain it all."

Home. How long had it been?

For either of them?

Caleb wrapped his arms around her, pulled her close enough that her heart slammed against his. His cheek rested against her hair, and he didn't care that they were soaked through. That the gravel was cutting into his knees or that her hand was resting on the corrugated scars of his side.

She said yes. Yes to him, yes to his past. Yes to the scars of his body and his heart.

Yes to marrying him, even.

He pressed his mouth to her temple. Her cheek. "I'll love you forever," he said.

Juliet's eyes shimmered. "And you always keep your promises."

All except one. But as he helped Juliet to her feet, linking his fingers with hers, as the metal band on her ring finger settled against his skin, he knew Cordelia—wherever her soul was now— would understand.

Love her.

He promised.